The Singularity series:

Redshift
The Observer Effect
Uncertainty Principle
Quantum Entanglement
Event Horizon
Point Singularity

Prequel
Ani, or, the care and feeding of your great tree-
dwelling venomous tentacled land-devil

POINT SINGULARITY

R.M. OLSON

ISBN-13: 978-1-990142-30-7

Cover by MiblArt

To dad. Thanks for always believing in me.

"In a non-rotating black hole, the singularity, rather than existing in a ring or a circular line, exists at one specific point, the point singularity."

-From an introductory astrophysics textbook, University of Sao Martim, Vila Nova do Sol, Colorida

1

Aran

Aran winced as something shattered on the wall behind him. He hit his communicator. "Dessi!" he shouted through it, then ducked behind the fallen table as another object came flying through the air towards his head.

"You can't hide there forever." The raider man's voice was smooth and cold with menace, and made even more menacing by the fact that this was someone Aran knew by name. The two of them had been discussing logistics calmly, if not with outright cordiality, a few minutes before.

Circumstances considered, Aran couldn't particularly blame the raider for his lack of friendliness. But still …

"I will drag you out, Aran, and then I will kill you." There was an unpleasant, sibilant hiss to the raider's voice, and Aran bit back a yelp as a shock of electricity jolted up his arm from the worn bracelet on his wrist.

If it hadn't been abundantly clear that the raider in front of him had succumbed to the charak that had infested the minds of most of the raider crew, that would have been a very good hint.

He peeked out from where he'd taken refuge behind a table. Ani was hissing angrily from inside his cabin, one door away, but she hadn't tried to melt her way through it yet, thank the Holy damn Mystery. Aran had taken to leaving her in the cabin. The bracelets that he and Istvay had made to prevent the charaks from taking over their victims' minds and bodies were failing on an unfortunately regular basis, and Ani had unfortunately black-and-white views on anything that attacked Aran, whatever the reason. And despite the raiders' current hostility, Aran couldn't exactly let his crewmates— former crewmates, a small, uncomfortable voice in the back of his mind reminded him—be murdered by an irate Ani.

On the bright side, the charaks didn't seem to have realized yet that it was the bracelets that were keeping them from taking over their hosts' minds as easily as usual. That wouldn't last forever, probably, but in the meantime, it meant that all Aran had to do to stop this was—

The raider grabbed the table, the material splintering under his claws, and yanked it away, leaving Aran exposed in the centre of the floor. "I found you," the raider crooned, his sharp canine teeth gleaming white in the corridor lights.

Aran yanked out the vial of acid wash he'd shoved into his supplies pouch earlier and upended it over the raider's wrist where corrosion had all but eaten away the thin metal bracelet he wore.

The raider snarled in pain, grabbing Aran's shoulder with his free hand, claws cutting through fabric and into flesh. "How dare you …" he began.

Then he winced as the acid, which had been chewing steadily through the corrosion, cut through it at last, and an electric spark buzzed up his arm.

He let go of Aran, cursing, and Aran tumbled to the floor, gasping for breath. Blood soaked through his shirt where the raider's claws had bitten through his skin and into the muscle, but in the breathtaking relief he could hardly register the pain.

"I am—I'm sorry, human." The raider's words were a mix of embarrassment and hostility.

Aran drew in a shuddery breath and pushed himself to his feet, shaking his head. "It's fine."

"Do you—do you need me to get you a bandage?"

Aran sighed.

The war with the yibos, started by Krevai and Sharda, had been, as far as he could tell, popular among the raiders. And after he had essentially blackmailed them into suing for peace, rather than wreaking absolute destruction across the entire system, he couldn't exactly blame them for not feeling friendly towards him. He still felt an uncomfortable surge of guilt every time he remembered the betrayed look on Krevai's face when he'd told the captain that he'd burned the cure Istvay had found for the charak infestation, and that the only way of getting it back was to stop the war with the yibos, sue for peace, and find a cure for Istvay so that they'd be able to rewrite it.

He couldn't feel entirely sorry for what he'd done, not really. He'd disappointed his friends, angered possibly the most dangerous species in the system, and given everyone a very solid reason to murder him as soon as Istvay had given them the cure, but he had stopped the war. And when he remembered the sight of the screaming, terrified yibos as they fled from the raiders, blood and viscera strewn across the streets as the raiders tore into their prey—if he'd had a way to stop it, and chosen not to, that would be on his head.

"Aran?"

He sighed again. "Let's—let's just get this done, I'll take care of it when I'm back in my cabin. Not like I don't have practice."

The raider looked, if possible, more guilty than he had before. "I'm—I am sorry, human, truly. I didn't mean—I'll call Dessi. She'll be angry if her human gets injured, and I don't want her taking it out on me."

Aran managed a tight smile. The pain in his shoulder was soaking into his consciousness now, and he couldn't help but wince every time he tried to move his arm. "Just scrub your bracelet with acid, please, and don't take it off while you're doing it. It'll sting, but—"

"I understand," said the raider gruffly. He was looking more guilty by the moment. "Listen, why don't you let me—"

"I told you, I'll be fine," snapped Aran through his teeth.

The raider looked at him in mild shock, and he drew in a deep breath. "I'll be fine. You can call Dessi if you want, but in the meantime, you said Krevai wanted some information. So let's damn well give him the information so you can go take care of your damn bracelet and I can go back to my cabin and deal with this before I pass out. This is the third time in the last two days yours has failed."

The raider looked unmistakably shamefaced now. "Yes, yes, of course," he muttered. He pulled up his data pad and handed it to Aran.

Aran peered over it quickly, then squeezed his hand to pull up his palmscreen, trying to hide his wince, and copied the figures onto the data pad. "There," he said, handing the data pad back to the raider. "Those are the atmospheric gas concentrations on Colorida. They're very similar to most of your planets, but with a slightly less oxygen-rich composition. You shouldn't need breathing apparatuses, though."

The raider nodded and took back the pad. "I will let Krevai know, then," he said. He paused a moment. "If you're sure you're—"

Aran's shoulder was throbbing in earnest now, and he was trying very hard to hold onto his temper. "Just go. Please. If I—"

The door to the small room where the two of them were standing slammed open, and Dessi stepped in.

The other raider's shoulders drooped in relief, and he picked up the data pad and ducked out the door past her.

"Aran."

Aran's stomach sunk at the tone in Dessi's voice. He glared down at the ground, not actually wanting to meet her eyes.

"I've told you a hundred times not to hold your little meetings—" she stopped, sucking in a breath, and crossed over to him quickly. "Are you alright?"

He sighed and looked up, trying to smile. "I'm—I'm fine, Zoran just—his bracelet failed, but I was able to get it back under control pretty quickly, so—"

Dessi, who'd clearly decided to ignore him, was examining the claw marks on his shoulder, a hint of concern showing through the sharp irritation in her expression.

He jerked his shirt back up over the injuries and stepped back sharply. Something about the way his heart was pounding, and the sick feeling in his stomach at seeing the anger in the face of the raider scientist he'd once considered a friend, was too much to bear at the moment. "I was trying to keep anyone who's bracelet failed from either attacking the crew, or being killed by Ani," he snapped. "That's why I've been holding my 'little meetings' in here, and if you really want me to change that, then tell Krevai to make it a damn order." His voice was shaking, and he knew it, but Dessi knew him well enough by now that there was really no point in trying to hide it.

Dessi sighed, and her voice was a little more gentle when she spoke again. "At least let me take care of that," she said, gesturing to his shoulder. "If you bleed out, you won't be any help to us on our way back to Colorida."

The flood of adrenaline was draining from Aran's system, leaving every muscle in his body shaky, and his shoulder throbbed, and he was pretty sure that if he took the time to actually examine the injury, he might throw up. "Fine," he said shortly. "I was—I was just going back to check on Istvay anyways."

Dessi followed him out the door and down the corridor of the raider ship without speaking. She hadn't seemed to have much inclination to speak to him, except on the most urgent matters, since —well, since he'd given Krevai his ultimatum to stop the war, and then had returned to his cabin to find that Ani had, through some form of parthenogenesis that the part of his mind that wasn't completely drowned in guilt was absolutely fascinated with, produced offspring. Seventeen of them.

The horrified raiders had insisted that a portal be opened to Joias immediately to return himself, Istvay, Ani, and her offspring posthaste, along with everyone else from Joias, and since then, everything had been a blur of trying to keep Istvay alive, trying to keep Ani from killing the raider crew to avenge his honour, trying to keep the raiders from killing each other and himself, and trying to figure out if he was going to have to stop the raiders from destroying the whole of the Joias system as soon as they arrived.

Thankfully, it seemed the last point wouldn't be a problem—Ani's offspring had terrified even the raiders enough that their sole motivation appeared to be getting Ani and all of her babies back through the portal, getting the cure for the charak infestation that Istvay had come up with but was currently far, far too weak to replicate, and then getting back home as quickly as possible.

Probably after exacting some unspecified revenge on Aran for his part in all this.

It had been enough of a whirlwind that Dessi had been just as busy as he had. But somehow, he doubted her coolness towards him was based on how busy she'd been.

"Wait just a minute—" he said over his shoulder when they reached the door. He pushed it open and ducked through the thick webbing that Ani had begun to spread with reckless abandon across their cabin. Why she needed to build a nest once her offspring were hatched, he wasn't sure, but she seemed inordinately proud of it, and he didn't have the heart to ask her to take it down. If she would even listen to him anyways, which was unlikely. But it did mean that there was always the possibility that you would bump into a hanging strand that contained one of the seventeen infant land devils, and then you would either be stung by the baby, or hissed at by a protective Ani. For Aran, it was less of an issue—in his three-years' association with Ani, he'd long since developed a partial immunity to land devil poison, and Ani might hiss at him, but she'd never actually try to hurt him. Warning noises aside, she seemed relatively unconcerned when he interacted with the newborns. This indulgence did not, however, carry over to the raiders. And with the newfound tension between the raiders and Aran, her attitude had not improved.

"Hey, sweetheart," he called softly, pushing aside a strand of webbing. "Dessi's coming in, okay? No need to kill anyone, she's a … a friend." His voice choked a little on the last word, but he cleared his throat and ignored it.

A moment later, there was a suspicious chirp from Ani, and then she dropped down onto his uninjured shoulder, grumbling. He reached up and stroked her, and he could feel her alert posture relaxing a little. "She just wants to make sure I'm not hurt too badly, I guess," he whispered, scratching Ani under the chin.

She must have sensed his distress, because she clamped her suckers down harder across his shoulder and shoved her bulbous head under his chin. He laughed a little, despite himself, and she chirruped questioningly.

"Yes," he whispered. "It'll be alright. We'll—we'll get back to Colorida, and we'll get Istvay fixed up and—" he trailed off.

No use thinking past that. At this point, even reaching Colorida was beginning to look impossibly far away.

He looked over the hanging web strands between himself and the door once more, checking carefully for any sign of a land-devil hatchling that he'd missed on his way in, then called, "You should be okay to come in."

Then he turned to the complicated machine next to Istvay's bed that the yibo medics had instructed him and Dessi how to set up. The line that indicated Istvay's heart rate was a steady pattern of uniform spikes, and his friend's breathing, though shallow, was steady. Aran laid his hand on their chest anyway to reassure himself, and closed his eyes wearily.

Istvay had regained consciousness once or twice since the yibo medical team had taken over their care via holoscreen—no one would agree to come onto the ship, not with Ani nesting on it—but never for more than a few minutes at a time.

Aran closed his eyes and swallowed hard, the slow rise and fall of Istvay's chest under his hand equal parts reassuring and terrifying.

The ship was on its way back to Colorida. He and Dessi had the technology and the information to cure them, and between that and the genetic research files they had in the labs in the Sao Martim University, Istvay just had to hold on for a few more days.

"Aran." Dessi had ducked through the hanging webbing, and now she was standing behind him. There was a mixture of exasperation and something else that he couldn't quite read on her face. "You may as well let me get you bandaged up," she grumbled. "I doubt your Istvay will agree to help us if we cure them, and you keel over two minutes later."

Aran managed a small smile and stood, and she sliced through his ragged shirt with a medical knife, peeling the blood-soaked cloth gently back from the injury. He gritted his teeth at the sharp sting of spray-on disinfectant, and then she fitted a bandage carefully over the wound and stepped back, examining her handiwork. "There," she said. "That should at least keep you from losing too much blood —I'm not going to overwork my replicator just because you refuse to be careful."

Aran nodded, not meeting her eyes. "Thanks, Dessi," he mumbled.

He could feel her watching him, but he didn't look up, and at last, she sighed. "Well, if that's the only place you were hurt, I'd best get back to my lab. I've got plenty to do. I'll send through some information for you to work on, since I know it's next to impossible to get you to leave your Istvay for five minutes."

He nodded again, still without looking at her, and after a moment, she turned away. He could hear her footsteps leaving, and the click of the door behind her, and he felt the way Ani relaxed on his shoulders when they were finally alone.

He sank into the chair he'd pulled up beside Istvay's cot, pinching the bridge of his nose between his thumb and forefinger.

He wanted to cry. He wanted to curl up under a blanket and not come out again until everything had blown over. But that wasn't an option—he'd known it wouldn't be an option, from the moment he'd decided to infuriate the raiders, and turn all his friends against him, to stop the war and save Istvay.

It had been the right decision. It was worth it. At least, intellectually, he knew it was worth it. But he wasn't sure how much longer he would survive this.

Ani gave him a comforting little chirrup and wrapped her tentacles around his upper arm, and he reached up to rub her head, trying to smile.

"Hey, Pishti," he whispered, laying his hand on his friend's chest again.

Istvay's face was turned away, their shoulder-length black hair spread across the pillow. Their skin was stretched so tightly over their skull that they looked almost like a corpse already, and their restless movements beneath the blankets had subsided over the past couple of days, as if even that was too much effort.

"It's going to be alright," he whispered, even though he knew they couldn't hear him. "We're already back through the portal. We should have you to the university in less than twenty-four hours, and getting the cure finalized and ready to administer should only take another twenty-four hours or so after that, according to Dessi. You're going to be alright."

Istvay moaned softly, the sound almost too quiet to hear, and Aran squeezed his eyes closed and dropped his head back against the wall.

The fact that Krevai hadn't deigned to speak to him in days, Dessi's icy silence, the attacks of the charak-infested raider crew that were growing all too frequent—none of that mattered, ultimately. None of that compared, even the slightest, to this.

He would get Istvay back in time. He'd do it if it killed him.

And he was increasingly coming to think it might.

2

Alba

Alba took a deep breath, fighting the panic tightening her throat, forcing her hands to unclench from her tunic as if it was a lifeline and she a drowning swimmer.

This was ridiculous.

She knew it, but it still took an almost impossible force of will to make herself turn her gaze out the porthole in the small, cramped cabin on the yibo transport ship.

It was a testament to her newfound importance that she had been given a cabin with a porthole, and she wasn't about to complain about anything the yibos decided to do that showed the smallest measure of respect for humankind. But she would have much preferred an interior cabin, with no view out into the blackness of space.

She was still shaking after their passage through the portal, twelve hours previous.

It had gone off without a hitch—of course it had. The yibos were the ones who'd created the portal technology to begin with, and a yibo captain was piloting the ship. Of course there hadn't been a mishap.

And yet, none of those facts made the slightest bit of difference to the icy, horrifying flashbacks—the portal closing, the jags of bright electricity, the way the diplomatic ship had looked from the plex windows of the tiny escape pod as it split itself apart, disgorging its cargo of human lives in an icy wash of death.

Now, though, the stars she saw when she looked through the porthole were the ones she recognized from her childhood, almost unsettling in their familiarity.

And far away … Yes. She could see it, even from here—the small, blue-green dot shining in the reflected light of the sun.

Colorida.

Home.

She stared at it for a long moment, and then had to close her eyes against the blur of tears.

They were going home.

There was a tap on her door, and she blinked hard and cleared her throat. "Just a moment," she managed, and fumbled for the control that would open the door.

When it slid soundlessly open, she was unsurprised to see Yosip standing there. His usual good humour shone in his eyes, and there was concern written across his features that she knew was for her— but even that couldn't disguise the pallor of his brown face, the shocked relief still half-hidden behind his expression.

She knew him well enough to guess that for him, as much as her, the thought of going home was something so viscerally, unutterably relieving that it was almost frightening.

"Alba," he said. "May I come in? It turns out we have an old acquaintance aboard." He glanced over his shoulder with his usual friendly smile. "Feliu ran into her last night—she was looking for you. But she said it wasn't urgent, and we both thought that you needed your rest after everything we've been through the past few days."

Alba almost laughed at that. If only Yosip had any idea of how entirely ineffective her trying to sleep was, under the circumstances—going home, yes. But going home when their home system could well be under control of a dictator who had every reason to want her and everyone else in the diplomatic party dead, and she in the company of aliens who, although aboard a civilian ship currently, had the military power, only a message through the portal away, to destroy their entire system.

The yibo had destroyed the Labarinto System, settled five hundred years earlier by their sister colony-ship. Their transport ship was bringing some of the survivors of that destruction back through the portal with them, seeking refuge in another human system.

And Alba knew very well that if she could not ensure that the yibos' brief presence in their system was met with peace, rather than hostility—which would almost certainly be Cavaco's preferred method—that could be the story of the Joias System next.

"You may as will bring her in," said Alba.

Yosip stepped through the door and nodded over his shoulder, and a moment later, a tall, familiar figure ducked through the door after him.

Alba raised her eyebrows in surprise. "Reka?"

The government agent's face was drawn in exhaustion, her torso heavily bandaged, and Alba could see even through the stoic expression on her face the pain she must be in. Her uniform was torn and stained with blood, her sleek half-shave partially grown out. There was a look to her face that was neither exhaustion nor pain, although it contained both, but a sort of haunted sense of loss. But she still exuded the same cool, smooth self-assurance that she'd been known for back on Colorida.

"Chief Justice," she said curtly, nodding her head.

Alba frowned. "Reka. I was under the impression you were travelling with Savina and Joska."

She caught the small, almost involuntary reaction at that, the way Reka's face tensed and her shoulders drew in. But she just shrugged. "I was. I joined the transport ship at the meeting point."

She didn't elaborate, and Alba didn't press her. It was hardly her business. "Please, have a seat," she said instead.

Reka nodded, a flicker of gratitude in her expression, and sank into the seat that Alba beckoned her to with a barely concealed sigh of relief. "I appreciate you making the time to see me, Chief Justice."

Alba shook her head. "Please. The usual formalities are hardly necessary, I think, after what we've been through."

Reka studied her, and Alba almost found herself stepping back from the intensity of the woman's gaze. At last, though, Reka nodded. "You're right. We don't have the time for formality." She leaned forward. "There is a good chance that when we come back, Cavaco will have taken power. What is your plan to deal with that?"

Alba sighed. "I'm not entirely sure. I'm hoping that there will be enough sane voices left in the Council that I will be able to convince them of Cavaco's duplicity. But until I understand what's happening on the ground—" she shrugged helplessly.

Reka's dark eyes bored into hers with an uncomfortable intensity. "You think that will be enough?"

Alba snorted. "If you have a better suggestion—"

Reka huffed out an amused breath. "I'm no politician, Madam Chief Justice. I thought that would be very apparent, considering my history."

Alba watched her. "I—am aware of your history," she said at last. "I hardly think I need to tell you that as far as I'm concerned, your record will be wiped entirely clear when we return."

Again, that sharp flash of something that felt almost like pain in Reka's expression. "I didn't fulfil the warrant on Savina," she said quietly.

Alba raised her eyebrow. "Perhaps not. But you have saved hundreds of civilian lives. I'm not going to begrudge you a warrant."

Reka flashed her a small, wry smile. "Maybe. But the next person she kills might feel differently." She sobered. "That's not why I'm here, though. Madam Chief Justice, I know you worked across from Cavaco. But I doubt you know him like I do." Alba was silent, watching her, and again she saw that flash of a sardonic smile on the woman's face. "He's very respectable in public. And you all, you politicians—you believe that. Because you don't want to believe the kind of thing that lurks underneath the pleasant smiles. You want to believe that someone who knows the correct protocols, and calls you by the correct names, follows the silly little rules of your Council meetings, would never stoop to brute violence."

Alba had to pull in a steadying breath.

Reka was right, of course. Back on Joias, the violence inflicted by politics had always been something far away and removed, something that happened to someone else, carried out by other, less civilized people than those who sat in the halls of law.

Her time in the yibo system had disabuse her of that notion forever.

It was funny how the moment one experienced such violence oneself, it became that much more difficult to ignore, even when happening to someone else.

And she still could see Karri's face, the yibo politician who'd put her reputation on the line to protect human lives, and who'd been killed for it. In the horror of the raider attack, and then the chaos of trying to get Aran and his pet monstrosity back through the portal, Alba had hardly had time to think of it. But she knew when she did, the thought would make her ill.

"He's not going to try to win people over by arguments." There was still that sardonic note in Reka's voice. "Oh, he will as long as he thinks that will gain him what he wants. But make no mistake, Alba. He will not hesitate to kill every last person on this ship, if he thinks that's in his best interest. He will not hesitate to plunge the system into war—yibos, raiders, it doesn't matter. He believes he has the power to deal with any alien threat. I know him. So I came to warn you—don't make the mistake, in your calculations, of thinking that Cavaco will play by any of the rules you 'civilized people' put on yourselves. He's far more like me or Savina than he is like you."

For a long moment, there was silence in the small cabin. At last, Alba nodded slowly. "Thank you, Reka. I appreciate your insight. If you have any suggestions on a course of action—I would welcome them."

A spark of surprise flickered across Reka's face, instantly concealed, and for an unsettling moment, Alba was forced to consider how very shocking her willingness to listen would be to someone who hadn't spent the last few weeks or months in crowded refugee quarters with her and the others.

At some point, she would have to confront the reputation she'd earned on Colorida, and she was quite sure it would not be a pleasant experience.

But there would be time to worry about that later. At the moment, what mattered was getting the humans back through the system without sparking a human-alien war, and then, somehow, finding a way to draw Cavaco's fangs for long enough to warn the rest of the Council about him.

At last, Reka stood. Her sardonic smile was gone, her eyes once more respectfully on the ground. "I'm sorry, Madam. I don't have suggestions, just cautions."

"Thank you," said Alba at last. "I appreciate your candour."

Reka nodded and slipped from the cabin, leaving Alba and Yosip alone.

Yosip sighed and sank into the chair that Reka had vacated. "I wish I could say I disagreed with her, Alba," he said quietly. "But those of us who have worked farther away from the centre of politics —" he shook his head. "I've seen what his policies in the Rim Mountains have done. Anyone who would be willing to inflict that sort of brutality somewhere far away, where it can't be seen—that person will not hesitate to inflict it closer to home, if he thinks he can get away with it. Violence begets violence, and those who thrive on it know that."

Alba nodded, and closed her eyes wearily. "Cavaco has always been a threat. I suppose Reka is right. I was simply never prepared to accept the extent of it."

For a moment, the two of them were silent.

"Well, Alba, if you feel up to it, I think perhaps we should call Feliu in," said Yosip at last. "Even putting aside the danger Cavaco poses, I doubt anyone on Joias has any idea of the extent of the danger that a combined yibo and raider aggression could cause. We should strategize our next move to ensure this encounter remains peaceful."

Alba sighed. "You're right."

Yosip gave her a weary smile, but there was that ever-present twinkle in his eye despite the seriousness in his face. "Best not to borrow trouble when we have plenty that's rightfully ours." He paused. "And our yibo hosts—are they, too, preparing for war?"

Alba shook her head uneasily. "I believe I've made them understand that their ships appearing in our airspace without warning will look like a threat, and they must not act the part of aggressor unless absolutely necessary to defend themselves."

"It's reassuring that this is clearly a transport, not a military ship," Yosip murmured. "At least, it is if the democratic government is still in control. I'm afraid that if Cavaco has seized power, however, the perception of weakness may be more a liability than an asset."

Alba nodded grimly. "We shall have to hope, then—"

She was cut off abruptly by shouts from the hallway, and the harsh buzz of the yibo communicator attached to her wrist. She swore under her breath. "Just a moment," she said grimly to Yosip.

"Alba." The yibo voice came over her communicator, translated by the program Ines, the diplomatic interpreter, had placed in her wavelink. "There are armed ships approaching our position. Please report to the bridge."

Alba glanced at Yosip. "Armed ships. There's no way they would have reached our position already if they hadn't been expecting us."

Yosip's face had gone grave. "And there's no way anyone should be expecting us."

For a moment, the two of them stared at each other, and she could see her own sharp fear reflected in Yosip's face.

"I shall join you on the bridge," said Alba tersely through the communicator. "Do not take any action until we open communication with the ships."

She shot another worried glance at Yosip. "Ask Feliu to meet me on the bridge, if you would." She hardly waited for his nod in response before she made her way out of the cabin.

The halls of the transport ship, always busy, were twice as crowded now, and she had to fight the unexpected claustrophobia that she'd never had before this trip, the horrifying memory of pushing her way through the crowded hallways of a dying ship, a bloodied Feliu propped against her shoulder, unsure of whether they'd get out or be crushed in the press of bodies.

She gritted her teeth and forced herself forward.

When she arrived, the yibo soldiers who'd been sent to accompany them through the portal were clustered around the communication dock. They stepped back to make room for her.

"We've opened a line through to the ships and requested communication," one of them said in passable Common Dialect.

Alba nodded, grim faced, and peered down at the holoscreen in front of her, grateful once again for the assistance of the diplomatic ship's engineers, who'd managed to modify the yibo ship's transmission lines to allow them to communicate with Joias ships.

She recognized the ships at once—sleek Joias military design. There were five of them—enough to easily overpower and shoot down their yibo transport ship. But it was also possible that, as large as the transport was, the Joias ships wouldn't be certain of its military capabilities, or lack thereof.

Alba took a deep breath and hit the communication button. "This is Chief Justice Alba Espina, paging the Joias military ships."

For a long moment, there was no answer.

When a voice came back through the communications system at last, sharp with incredulity, it carried a homey do Sol accent that, despite the circumstances, made Alba have to swallow back tears.

"Madam Chief Justice?"

"Yes," said Alba. She managed to add the tinge of icy disdain to her voice that would have been expected, back on Colorida—a tone she had, quite frankly, not dared to take for so long that it felt unfamiliar on her tongue.

"Chief Justice Alba Espina?" the speaker's voice still sounded disbelieving. "We assumed you'd been killed."

"I am happy to inform you, then, that I am very much alive, thank you," Alba snapped. "Please turn on your visuals, if you'd like to ascertain my identity."

A moment later, the holoscreen flickered to life.

Alba found herself looking into the faces of two ships captains, their grim expressions cut with what could only be described as shock.

She waited patiently as the identity scans were run. At last, one of the captains met her eye. "It's really you."

Alba sighed. "As I said."

"Madam Chief Justice." The automatic respect in their voices was enough to make something odd catch in her throat.

It had been so long.

"Madam. We have been instructed to ask if you will please accompany us back to Colorida."

"I appreciate the gesture," said Alba dryly. "However, as you can see, we are a civilian ship on a peaceful mission. We are not in need of a military escort."

"I'm sorry, Madam Chief Justice," said the captain. "We've been instructed to bring your ship back to Colorida. Those were our orders."

Alba glanced at Feliu, who'd come up behind her.

He looked as worried at this new development as she felt, but when she caught his eye, he gave a quick shake of his head.

He was right—no point in antagonizing these captains until she was certain what they wanted.

If it was Cavaco who'd sent the ships, they wouldn't hesitate to use force, and the yibo ship was a civilian transport, not fitted out with military-grade weapons, and loaded with civilians—both the remnants of the diplomatic ship, and refugees from Labarinto looking for a new home.

So at last, she turned to the yibo, muting the ship-to-ship communication.

"Alba." The yibo captain's voice was grim. "Are these ships peaceful?"

Alba sighed. Her breath was tight in her chest. "For the moment, it appears they are," she said. "I hope they will remain that way. But I am afraid that any attempt at hostility will lose us whatever tentative goodwill they may be willing to grant. I suggest we go with them."

There was a long moment of silence. At last, the yibo commander gave a brusque nod. "Very well. But I'm sending word back through the portal first, so they can be prepared should something untoward happen."

Alba hesitated.

But this was likely the best she could expect, honestly.

She tapped the communicator back on. "We'll follow you," she said to the two captains. "As long as you can assure us of your peaceful intent."

"Of course, Madam Chief Justice. We simply want to ensure that your return to Colorida will be uneventful." But there was a tone under the captain's words that made Alba cast a quick glance back at Feliu, and she saw on his face the same unease she felt on hers.

3

Savina

"Savina?"

Savina looked up quickly at Joska's voice.

The others had been tiptoeing around her for the last three days, as if they were afraid she might break.

Which was stupid. She didn't break. She was perfectly capable of brushing off Reka's betrayal this time, just as easily as she had every other time. The fact that Reka had thought she was worth loving only as long as they were trapped behind the portal with no way out, and the moment she discovered they were coming back, learned Savina had grown up in an Old Believer compound and realized she'd have to reckon with that, she'd simply walked away without looking back, was irrelevant. Savina wasn't stupid enough to actually have believed that Reka could look past who she was and love her anyways, and ... well, if she had been that stupid, she damn well deserved every bit of the hurt.

Joska, at least, still treated her normally, and if there was that hint of concern in her voice when she spoke, and if her mouth tightened when someone mentioned Reka, Savina could ignore that, at least.

She stood and made her way over to the captain, her legs still trying to remember how to use the mag boots after weeks of yibo ships with their artificial gravity.

"Do you recognize these ships?" There was a worried note to Joska's tone that made Savina frown and peer closer at the screen.

She tried to avoid letting her attention wander to the familiar Joias stars. Something about coming back through the portal had started a lump of ice in the pit of her stomach that had spread, creeping through the core of her and out into her limbs until she couldn't seem to get warm no matter how she tried.

She hadn't realized, until the *Dolphin* had made it back through the portal, how much she'd come to accept that she'd never make it home. That she'd live out her life in a place where she could forget who she'd been and where she'd come from, and be ... someone new, maybe.

And then Reka had reminded her of how impossible that was. That, at least, was one good thing that had come of all that.

But when she peered at the ship's screens, it wasn't the familiar stars of the Joias System that caught her eye—instead, her attention was pulled to five blips surrounding the yibo transport.

"Those are Joias military ships," said Savina slowly, unease starting in her chest.

Joska nodded grimly. "Can you think of any reason why they'd have military ships waiting by the portal? Aside from the obvious one?" The tone of Joska's voice told Savina that the woman had already gone over all the possibilities, and that what she'd come up with wasn't any more optimistic than any of the ideas currently swirling half-formed in Savina's brain.

"Rafel," called Savina over her shoulder, her voice sharper than usual.

Rafel stood, grumbling, but came over without any retort, and Savina had to consciously avoid looking at him so as not to see the pity in his gaze.

He caught sight of the ships the moment he was close enough, and his customary scowl grew tight with sudden concern. He turned to Joska. "The only way they'd have those type of ships up here is that the top military brass had political permission to send them. I think we all know what that means. I don't know why they're here, but as far as I'm concerned, we don't want to wait around to find out."

Savina and Joska exchanged glances.

Savina had never worried too much about politics, other than what she needed to know to do her job. But even she knew that this was not a good sign.

As they watched, the ships moved in closer around the transport.

"I don't like this." Rafel's voice was tight with worry. "Captain, I don't like this at all."

"Neither do I." Joska glanced over her shoulder "Beni? Chart us a course, please. I'm inclined to agree with Rafel—I don't think we want to be here when those ships come looking."

Beni appeared a moment later, their face a scowl of concentration. They felt their way into the chair, then sat quickly, running their fingers over the controls to orient themself. "Give me a minute." Their tone was clipped and businesslike, and Savina was struck with how much Beni had changed in the last few weeks.

"There," they said at last. "I've sent you coordinates. This will take us behind some space debris that should keep us off their scanners."

Joska nodded grimly, bending over the controls.

"Captain." Rafel's voice was grim. "I think we may be too late."

Savina glanced back out the window, and swore under her breath.

A handful of smaller ships had peeled off one of the larger destroyers, and were starting towards them.

"Not if I can help it," Joska muttered, and the old cargo ship turned ponderously, and started off towards the cloud of space junk that Beni had pointed them to.

"What's happening?"

Savina didn't have to look over her shoulder to recognize the worried voice of her little brother, Nicolau. And, if the past was any indication, his girlfriend Ines, the former diplomatic interpreter, would be with him, considering they'd been all but joined at the hip since they met weeks back.

"Joias military," Rafel snapped. From Ines's sharp gasp, she'd caught the implications as quickly as any of them.

"We're not going to try to outrun them," said Joska tightly. "I doubt we could if we wanted to. But the *Dolphin* is just a cargo ship. They weren't here when we came through the portal, and they have no reason to suspect that we're doing anything but running cargo." Despite her wards, there was a note in her voice that told Savina she was as worried as any of them. "We'll get behind the space debris, and we'll watch and see how things go from there."

The *Dolphin* was moving at a steady pace towards the new destination, and Savina's eyes were glued to the control screen. The military ships were still following, but they'd pulled back a little, seemingly willing to wait and see what the *Dolphin* was planning.

Even at their new, sedate pace, however, the ships were approaching much too quickly for Savina's comfort.

"Can't this piece of space junk move any faster?" she snapped.

Joska glanced up with a look of mild reproach, but there was a touch of humour in her voice. "Savina. That's no way to talk about your ship."

Savina stared at her for a moment before she remembered.

Of course. The ship hijacking. When she'd stolen the *Dolphin* from Joska, and sent them all through the portal in the first place.

The thought did absolutely nothing to make her feel better.

She glowered at the captain, and despite the tension of the situation, she could see the way the corners of Joska's mouth twitched.

"To answer your question," Joska continued, "It takes time to warm up the *Dolphin's* auxiliary systems, and I have a feeling if we start doing that, those ships behind us will start to wonder if there's a reason we're running away. I don't know if they'll shoot down civilians, and I don't particularly want to find out."

Savina gave a tight nod.

"Rafel and I have some experience dealing with pirates," said Joska. "This isn't entirely unprecedented."

"A lot of good that did you," Savina muttered. "You got your ship hijacked just a few months back."

Rafel turned to glare at her, and Joska's mouth twitched again with that hint of amusement.

They were coming up behind the edges of the cloud of debris clustered around a large asteroid, big enough to easily block the ship from any sensors.

"We'll watch and see what they do," said Joska quietly. "It's possible that this is just scouting mission, or that they want to make sure that we're not posing a threat." She glanced at Rafel.

"It's possible." He didn't sound convincing.

The *Dolphin* had almost made shelter.

Savina's entire body was tight, her teeth clenched hard enough that she was giving herself a headache. She unclenched them with an effort.

The military had no reason to suspect the *Dolphin* was anything other than a cargo ship, and Joska was right—the fact that the portal had reopened and a ship had come through, even a ship that was clearly nonmilitary, would mean a cautious government would almost have to send out a force to investigate. But she couldn't keep her shoulders from slumping in relief when Beni said, "There. We should be off their sensors now."

The release of tension in the cabin was almost tangible.

Joska pulled back on the controls, pulling the ship around to nestle behind the asteroid. "We won't be able to get a clear view of what's going on through our sensors, not with the space junk in the way," she said. "But the yibo ship is big enough that we'll get a general idea of its movements. We should be able to make an educated guess as to—"

Her words broke off as the *Dolphin* shuddered violently, like a rat shaken by a dog.

"What the hell—" Rafel began, his voice rough.

Savina managed to catch her balance, turning hastily to the control screen—but there was no need. As her eyes brushed past the plex window, the scene outside caught and held them.

The asteroid they'd sheltered behind had been vaporized.

"I think that answers your question about whether they'll shoot down civilians," said Rafel through his teeth. "Captain, should I go on the missiles? We don't have anything that will make a difference against ships like that, but—"

"No!" Savina snapped. "Joska, power down the ship, everything but the life-support systems."

Joska glanced at her, eyebrows raised, but did as Savina asked.

The *Dolphin* was spinning gently, and Savina, watching through the plex, could see the other ship rotating dizzyingly in their field of view.

"What the hell does that assassin think she's doing?" Rafel hissed, but Joska shook her head.

"It's a good idea—with all the debris from the asteroid, we'll be hard to pick up on the sensors with most of our power shut down. This might be enough."

Rafel glanced out the window again, his expression tense, but he gave a short nod.

They drifted for what seemed like hours, although it couldn't have been more than fifteen or twenty minutes. The military ships were flying in slow, sweeping motions, obviously searching for them. Savina gritted her teeth, her heart pounding in her chest hard enough to make her feel nauseous. But the ships passed by them, just far enough distant that they must not have picked up on the trick.

Savina felt herself slump in relief.

"So," Rafel said into the quiet. "What now?"

Joska turned to them, her face grave. "They know we were here. If they were willing to shoot down a civilian ship, they really don't want anyone to know what they're doing out here. They won't give up on us quite as easily as all that."

Savina swallowed back the tight sickness in her stomach.

Joska was right.

"So what, then? We just give up and let them shoot us?" she asked, her voice unintentionally sharp.

Joska was quiet a moment. "As far as I know," she said slowly, "the *Dolphin* is still registered to land on Colorida."

Savina turned to stare at her. "You want to go back to Colorida? Where those ships came from?"

Joska shrugged wryly. "Unless you can think of a better idea." She paused. "They're looking for us, Savina, and they'll keep coming until they find us. From my point of view, best if we're not in the ship when they find it."

"And how do you know that they won't be waiting for us when we come in? How do you know they haven't tracked down our ship's registration number, and the moment we register to come down, they'll send us a welcoming party?" Savina snapped.

Joska shrugged again. "I don't. But I can't think of a better idea. So unless you can—"

Savina swore.

"Your ship, Savina," said Joska still, somehow, with that touch of humour to her tone. "You make the call."

"Until we get down to Colorida," said Savina, making no attempt to hide the sarcasm in her tone. "And then it'll be your ship."

Joska smiled, just a little. "So it will," she said.

Savina closed her eyes. "Fine," she said. "We'll go back. And we'd better hope like hell Cavaco doesn't have a surprise waiting for us when we get there."

$$4$$

Alba

Alba and the others stood in tense silence on the bridge as their ship followed the Joias military ship, escorted by four other armed warships on all sides.

They'd already spoken about all the possibilities. She'd briefed the yibo captain on correct protocol to ensure they were broadcasting nothing aggressive, and she, Feliu, and Yosip had, between them, gone over every possible response they could give to whatever Cavaco had planned.

Now, there was nothing left to do but wait.

"Madam?"

She turned to Feliu, who stood beside her. His expression, when he caught her eye, was in no way reassuring. "Madam, they've cut us off from the other ships. I don't see the raider ship or the *Dolphin* on the screens."

Alba glanced over at the display.

He was right—the military ships had split them off neatly, and the blocking technology they were running distorted the signals enough that it was impossible to make out either of the two ships that had traveled through the portal with the yibo transport. Whether the interference was accidental or on purpose, there was no way of knowing. But Alba had her grim suspicions, and from the look on Feliu's face, so did he.

"Can you get ahold of them over wavelink?" she asked in a low voice.

He shook his head. "I've been trying for the last twenty minutes. And I don't dare suggest using the inter-ship communication system, as the military ships will almost certainly intercept the transmissions."

She paused, irresolute. It was possible that one or both of the ships accompanying the transport ship had made a run for it when they saw the Joias military ships. They'd been flying in a loose enough formation that it was possible that they'd made their escape without either the yibo ship or the military ships noticing. It was even possible the *Dolphin* would have made it clear, although she was quite certain that Cavaco would track it down sooner or later. But the raider ship was impossible to mistake for a ship from this system. Besides, from what Alba had seen of the raiders, it was much more likely that they'd attempt to take out the Joias System singlehandedly than that they'd run at the first sign of trouble.

That, of course, had always been the greatest danger of this entire enterprise. And it was very possible that Cavaco had just unwittingly triggered the doomsday option.

She would do her best to avoid betraying Joska to the military ships, but if they'd lost track of the raiders, that was something everyone present should be aware of.

"This is Alba Espina, paging Starfleet Ship 117," she said at last, speaking into her wavelink line. "Please explain why we are cut off from those accompanying us."

There was a long pause before anyone answered. "I apologize, Chief Justice," said a voice she recognized as one of the captains. "But considering the circumstances, we thought it best that we not broadcast your arrival too widely until you have had a chance to be debriefed. This necessitated a communication shutdown that, unfortunately, had the side effect of cutting off communications between ships. You can contact us, but you will not be able to contact your friends via wavelink until you've landed."

She paused, biting down hard on her teeth.

A total communication blackout, orchestrated by the military ships that Cavaco had almost certainly authorized. The same man who'd tried to have her murdered on the diplomatic ship months earlier.

"Captain," she said at last, managing to make her voice icy and imperious, rather than sick with dread. "I demand—"

"I am sorry for the inconvenience. You are welcome to express your displeasure once we've docked."

The line clicked off, and Alba was left staring straight ahead, fists clenching and unclenching unconsciously.

The yibo captain glanced at her, a question in his eyes, but she gave a short shake of her head. "We can't be certain their intent is hostile, not yet. Even if we could, as they are armed, and we are not —" she shrugged helplessly.

The yibo captain tipped his head to one side in reluctant acquiescence, but even as difficult as she found yibo expressions to read, Alba could see the grimness around his mouth.

She hoped, desperately, she wasn't leading all of them into a deathtrap.

She very well could be.

She was still on the bridge when the ships broke through the atmosphere several hours later. The familiar lights of Vila Nova do Sol spread out beneath her—the yellow-white of the houses and streetlights, the rich purple glow of the Cathedral of the Holy Relics in the centre of the city, the outline of the Old Quarter clear from the softer, warmer glow of lights designed to keep the atmosphere of the place as close as possible to what it had been five hundred years ago.

She had to fight back the sharp ache of nostalgia in her chest.

Her life had been so much simpler, the last time she'd seen this city.

She closed her eyes and drew in a long breath.

No. That wasn't true. She'd just been blind—unable to see the problems lurking beneath the surface, unable to admit her own complicity in them. It had never been simple at all; she'd just been insulated enough that she could pretend it was. And if part of her still ached, irrationally, to be that insulated again, at least now she understood that it never would have solved any problems, not really.

The ships brought them down towards the site of a military base an hour's or so transport ride from the city. Alba could feel the tension building in her muscles the closer they came to landing.

If she recalled correctly, when she'd left, this base had been stripped down to the bare minimum personnel, on the point of being deactivated. Now it was buzzing with activity—ships swarming around it like flies around a bit of rotting meat, the lights flickering across the base easily visible at their approach.

When they were close enough, the massive bay doors of a hangar slid open for them, looking unaccountably like a gaping maw.

When they finally touched down inside the massive hangar, Alba could see people in Joias military gear swarming around the base of the ship like ants.

She tapped through her wavelink to the military ship's line. "Captain," she said, forcing her voice calm. "I wish to remind you that everyone on the ship is a civilian. And please be aware that my diplomatic privilege extends to all of them—harming anyone on board the ship will be tantamount to an act of war."

"Of course, Madam Chief Justice." The man's voice held exactly the right notes of courtesy and gravity, and yet, she couldn't hold back a shiver. "Once your ship has finished docking procedures, we ask that you please come out alone. We'd like to ensure that you are safe and unharmed. After that, of course, accommodations will be provided for the rest of the crew, but we would like to speak with you first. I'm sure you understand the caution—especially considering we had heard reports of your death, we would like to be sure that you are here of your own free will."

Alba glanced around her uneasily. She couldn't exactly argue with the captain's words—even had she been inclined to, she doubted, at this point, that it would do any good. She and every person on this ship was entirely at their mercy.

She drew in a steadying breath. "Very well," she said. "I will be unarmed. Please show me the same courtesy."

"Of course."

"Madam?" Feliu was frowning at her in concern. "I'll come with you."

She shook her head grimly. "They said alone. I have a feeling they mean to enforce that."

There was sharp worry on Feliu's face. "Madam, if they intend to murder you—"

She managed a small smile. "If they intended to murder me, they could have shot our ship down in deep space with no one the wiser.

And in the position in which we currently find ourselves, I hardly think we have much choice in the matter."

Feliu nodded uneasily, and Alba pushed herself up from her chair.

Her body ached, down to her bones, with exhaustion. Even putting aside the strain of their return trip through the portal, she wasn't sure she'd slept more than a few hours in a stretch since news had come through of the yibos' and raiders' sudden renewed interest in depositing their human visitors, and their accompanying land-devils, back through to the Joias System.

But then, she could hardly remember what it felt like anymore not to be exhausted.

"I'm certain I shall be fine, Feliu," she said, glancing over at him. "I'll keep my wavelink on an open channel. I doubt very much that the room they take me to will allow open communications, but you should be able to hear if my wavelink clicks off, at least. If it does not, then you may assume that I am alive, and you have no cause for alarm."

Feliu muttered something about how those two things did not necessarily correlate with each other.

She ignored him.

He was right. But so was she—they didn't exactly have another choice.

"Your escorts will await you at the base of your loading ramp."

"Thank you," said Alba through her wavelink.

She turned to the yibo captain. "They wish to talk with me privately," she said. "I shall inform them of the purpose of our mission, and of the fact that you have helpfully volunteered to transport myself and the remainder of the diplomatic ship, as well as other human refugees from Labarinto, back into our system. My hope is that will be enough to convince them of our peaceful intent."

The yibo man tipped his head to one side in grudging acknowledgement. "I hope you're successful," he said quietly. "I sent word back through the portal before we left to follow your military ships, and the Synod will be uneasy at their lack of communication with us if this goes on for too long."

"And I told them back in the Advisory Chambers that the people in our system would be cautious of anyone coming through the portal, until they were able to reassure themselves of your peaceful intent," Alba snapped. "Please inform the Synod, the moment you are able, not to take any action until at the very least I have been able to speak with my colleagues in government."

The captain nodded. "I passed on the message that you gave me. But you know how politics are. And you know how many of the Advisors are suspicious of humans."

Alba sighed heavily.

She knew both of those things far too well.

"With luck, it will not be long until you are on your way back to reassure them in person," she said briskly. "And now, if you would be so kind as to ask one of your people to open the hatch door?"

"I'll do so when you're in position." His voice was terse with worry, and Alba could hardly blame him.

When at last she'd made her way through the airlock, and the outer door hissed open, Alba looked out into a broad, whitewashed hangar bay, the style and function of it familiar in a way that made her chest tighten oddly. Even the sight of the soldiers—there was something about the familiarity of stepping down into a building designed by her own species, surrounded by people with whom she could speak without the need for a wavelink translation, that tightened her throat with a mixture of terror and relief.

She braced herself, then stepped out onto the loading ramp, and into full view of the soldiers below her.

She made a perfect target, and she was very well aware of it.

But she was a politician. She knew how to maintain appearances.

The shot she'd been half-expecting didn't come, not while she was standing on the top of the ramp, and not during her slow, cautious descent. Her legs shook, and even the short walk down the ramp, which should have been simple, was a greater effort than she really wanted anyone to know.

When she reached the base of the ramp, two of the Joias soldier stepped forward. She held herself back with effort from flinching, but they dipped their heads deferentially. One held out his arm.

"Madam Chief Justice. I'm sure you had a long flight. Allow me to assist you?"

She hesitated, pride stinging at the implication—but truth be told, she was weary enough that she might simply collapse where she stood. So she took the man's proffered arm and leaned on him heavily as they made their way across the gleaming, echoing floor of the hangar bay, the brilliant white lights bright enough to hurt her eyes.

Two or three other soldiers stepped fell into position in front of and behind her—an honour guard, or execution committee, she wasn't sure which—and they led her through a small human-size door and into a hallway.

Alba had grown accustomed, among the yibo, to being the tallest person in a room. Now, she was once more reminded of the discomfort of someone towering over her, someone who had the ability to hurt her, if he wished.

They escorted her down a long hallway, and into a small, bare room. The two captains from the military ships were seated inside, surrounded by their aides.

"Please, have a seat, Madam Chief Justice," said the most senior of the captains, standing in respect and gesturing her to her chair. The other captain stood as well, and Alba crossed to the seat, sinking into it gratefully.

She never would have believed how badly her body would crave the feeling of a cushioned chair, with a hard back to lean against.

"Captains," she said once she was seated. "I appreciate your escort. However, as you can see, I am entirely unharmed, and here of my own free well. And so you may believe me when I assure you once again that this ship is civilian. Our diplomatic ship was destroyed when the portal closed inadvertently, stranding us in the alien system. But due to—a series of events, the contents of which I shall be happy to present in my official report to the Council, we were rescued by these aliens, the yibo, who agreed to bring us back through to our system."

The captains were watching her appraisingly. Alba tried not to let her crawling discomfort show. "I assume, then, that I am free to go?"

Even to her own ears, the sharpness in her voice was underlaid with fear more than with irritation.

The captain smiled. "Of course. As I told you, this was only a formality to ensure you were safe and not being coerced." He rose. "Now, if you'll follow me, my colleague is calling ahead to prepare your quarters. My soldiers are waiting outside to escort you there."

"My …"

"I assume you'll want to rest and refresh yourself before you speak with the assistant to the Acting President."

Alba's stomach dropped. "Acting President? Surely you mean President Seguir." Again, her voice was sharper than she'd meant it to be.

This time, the captain did smile, but his smile was not entirely pleasant. "I'm afraid, Madam Chief Justice, that the system has changed somewhat since you left. With your disappearance and the threat of alien aggression, combined with the recent internal disturbances—Cavaco is now Acting President." He held out his hand to help her to her feet. "But I'm certain he will be very interested to hear your report, Madam. In the meantime, you will be taken to a secure place where you can refresh yourself, and your companions will be attended to."

She tried not to let her horror show on her face, but she could feel it, a weakness spread through every muscle of her body.

Reka's warning echoed in her ears.

"Very well," she said, ignoring the captain's hand and pushing herself upright.

If she was to be a lamb brought to slaughter, at least she'd go with her head held high.

5

Aran

"Aran."

Aran's head jerked up at the tone in Dessi's voice. He'd been so caught up in his thoughts that he hadn't noticed her come in.

She looked worried.

"I think you'd best get into the cockpit."

He sighed and pushed himself to his feet, casting a worried glance at Istvay as he did so.

Ani tightened her tentacles down his shoulder, grumbling, and he gave her a quick pat as he tucked the blanket up around Istvay. "Hold on, Pishti," he whispered. "I'll be back as soon as I can." He turned to Dessi.

"I'll keep an eye on them," she huffed. "I don't want them to die any more than you do."

He nodded, not quite trusting himself to speak, then turned and ducked out through the hanging webbing and into the corridors of the raider ship.

One or two of the raiders greeted him as he passed, but most of them seemed to have taken their cues from the captain, ignoring him in icy silence.

Which, he reminded himself, was better than them actively trying to kill him.

Still, the guilt that had become an ever-present weight on his chest grew just a little heavier with every grim-faced raider he passed.

"Come in," snapped Krevai, at Aran's hesitant tap on the cockpit door. The captain's voice was rough, and Aran swallowed down a lump in his throat.

This would be the first time he'd spoken to Krevai since he had, in Krevai's eyes, at least, offered up the most craven betrayal possible.

He braced himself, then pushed the door open and stepped through.

Krevai was seated in his usual place in the cockpit, scowling at the controls in front of him. Zondra, Sharda's second-in-command who'd come along to monitor, was standing next to the captain, watching through the plex window.

Krevai glanced up as Aran came in, and there was a look on his face—a sort of miserable hurt under the anger—that took Aran aback.

He hadn't considered that Krevai might be as upset at the loss of their friendship as Aran was.

Krevai gestured him to a seat without speaking, and Aran sat carefully. He wasn't entirely sure whether Krevai wanted to talk to him, or slit his throat—no, he amended, he knew perfectly well that Krevai wanted to slit his throat, he just wasn't sure if that was the express purpose of this particular meeting. But Krevai didn't snarl or lunge at him, teeth bared, just glared down at the control panel as if it held the answer to all of his problems.

"Your human military ships have instructed us to follow them," he said at last, irritation and disdain equally mixed in his voice. "Landru hasn't shot them down yet, but they're certainly not acting friendly. The yibo captain has agreed to go with them, but I see no reason why we should do the same." He gave a bleak smile that showed his canines to full advantage. "I suggest we take their military ships, kill everyone on board, and get your Istvay to your medical facility in the hopes that they will be able to get us a solution to the charak infestation before my crew rips out each other's throats in front of me."

Aran almost winced at the stinging sarcasm in the captain's words. And then his brain belatedly picked up what Krevai had just suggested. "No!" he said quickly, half standing. "No, we can't—" he cleared his throat and took a deep breath. "Captain. I … suggest that we wait and find out what they want. If we kill them, the military will take it as a declaration of war, and we can't take on the entire Joias military with one ship."

Krevai glanced at him, a trace of a familiar interest on his face. "You are right, it will be much more difficult for the humans to send in additional ships to shoot us down if we're inside their base." He smiled, but the expression was less than reassuring. "You may be right. Probably best that we get onto their base. We can figure out our next actions from there."

Zondra just smiled, a thin, vicious smile.

Aran squeezed his eyes closed and clenched his teeth.

It was a damn good thing he'd asked Dessi to keep an eye on Istvay, because it looked like he wasn't about to go back to his cabin anytime soon.

Landru brought the raider ship into the military base after the yibo ship, and landed it, steaming and hissing, in one of the smaller docking bays, following the instructions of the Joias military ships.

Half the raider crew had assembled in the cockpit by now, and despite Aran's fall from grace, it seemed the prohibition on talking loudly around the human was still in place—the raiders kept their tones at a whisper, casting quick glances towards him that he wasn't sure whether were meant to be affectionate or threatening. Either way, he didn't exactly have time to worry about it—from the excited tension in the raiders' postures, the way they watched the human troops through the plex windows of the cockpit, the hungry expressions on their faces as a small cohort of humans started towards the raider ship, he was going to have his damn hands full if he wanted to prevent a bloodbath.

He wasn't sure how long they were left to wait—long enough, at least, that the raiders in the cockpit had come and gone several times, and at one point he found himself almost nodding off in his seat, despite the stress. But he jerked awake, at last, to the crew's excited whispers.

"Look! The humans are coming over to our ship! Look at them! No sign of fear at all!" "Do you remember Labarinto? This is just like that—it's like they've never heard of us!" "They'll taste so much better, the meat's always tougher if they're stressed before we slaughter them. This is wonderful!"

Aran fought back a groan.

He was not equipped to deal with this, not right now. Probably not ever, if he was being honest with himself. Istvay was the one who knew how to deal with this sort of thing, but of course Istvay happened to be unconscious in their cabin right now.

"Paging the ship." The voice came through the communicator. "Paging the ship. We are asking for permission to board and search your ship. We do not mean you any harm."

Krevai grinned, reaching out to hit the communicator.

"No, wait!" Aran gasped. "We had an agreement! We weren't going to start a war, you promised we would just come through, get the cure for Istvay, get you the solution for the charaks, drop off Ani and her babies, and then you'd go back."

Krevai hesitated. "I don't mean to start a war," he said reasonably. "But even you have to agree that if the humans are the aggressors —"

"Let me talk to them!" Aran snapped in desperation.

Even as he said the words, he realized, with a sinking feeling, exactly what they meant. With his luck, these people would have heard of him. And this time, there would be no Istvay to stand between him and ... everyone else.

Krevai sighed heavily. "Fine," he grumbled. He turned, and called irritably over his shoulder, "Let the human out, he's going to go talk with his human friends."

Aran stood, and the raiders stood back to let him pass towards the airlock.

By the time he reached it, his hands were already sweating, and sick nausea was twisting in his stomach. But he swallowed hard, and forced himself to hit the inner airlock door, and then the outer, closing them carefully behind him, and step out on the short loading ramp, face-to-face with at least two dozen human soldiers.

For a long moment, they all stared at each other.

Then one of the soldiers near the back said, a tone of horrifically familiar admiration in her voice, "Aran? Aran Romeu?"

Aran closed his eyes and tried not to swear.

"Yes, it is! That's him! It's Aran Romeu!" He could hear the whispers spreading through the soldiers like a breeze through tall grasses.

The captain stepped forward, a hint more respect in his posture than there had been a moment before. "Aran!" he said, holding out his hand. "We didn't realize you were on the ship." He grabbed Aran's hand in a tight grip, and Aran fought back a flinch.

Ani growled, and he could hear the murmur of discontent through the open communicator line.

"They're touching our human without asking his permission." There was a low menace in Landru's voice that told Aran, clearer than words, that while he might be a persona non grata on the raider ship at the moment, they still considered him their personal property and were prepared to defend his honour at all costs.

He hit his communicator line and muttered weakly, "No, no, it's alright, they just—they're just—"

The captain was frowning at him. "Who are you talking to?"

Aran managed a sickly smile. "It's just the … my—my crewmates are in there. They're not human, exactly, and—"

the military captain's scowl was deepening. "Are they holding you prisoner? That—that friend of yours, that research assistant—they're not holding them hostage or something, are they?"

Aran knew his smile was coming out as more of a grimace than a smile at this point. "No! No, they're not—they're actually helping me, we're just … We need to get into do Sol, it's kind of an emergency. Istvay's sick, but if we can get into the city, I'm pretty sure I can—"

"I'm sorry, we have to check the ship. I don't mean to question your judgement, but this is a matter of national security. So if you'll just stand aside, please …" He put a hand on Aran shoulder, and Aran fought back another flinch at the unwanted touch.

"If that man damages my specimen, after everything I've gone through these last past few months—" Dessi's voice was as close to homicidal as Aran had ever heard it.

"Yes, Aran, let them come in," came Landru's voice over top of Dessi's, silky with menace. "I'm sure they'll be more than happy with what they find in here, especially after they disrespected our human."

Aran stepped back quickly, holding out his arms to bar the way. "No!"

The captain frowned, then reached out to push his arm out of the way.

Aran stepped back again, before the man could touch him and further infuriate the raiders. "No!" He tried for another weak smile. "No, please don't—"

"Aran. I think I can speak for all of us here that we admire your work, but this is a military matter. I must insist you get out of the way and let us inspect the ship. None of us wants to cause trouble for you."

"Yes, move out of the way, Aran," said Landru, the silky menace in her tone growing heavier. "I can hardly see how we could be considered the aggressors when they're threatening one of our crew, and I haven't had human flesh in longer than I'd like to think about."

"No!" Aran snapped, not entirely sure if he was talking to the raiders or the humans. "No, please, let's just—why don't we—"

"What the hell—" the human captain began, seeming to notice Ani for the first time.

Aran swore hopelessly under his breath as Ani hissed, her eye-pouches bulging out. "Just—just give me a sec," he snapped at the captain, stepping back again smartly to keep the man from touching him.

His back was pressed to the airlock door now.

"He asked to come on the ship. We can hardly be here peacefully if we won't allow him to do his job." There was undisguised delight in Krevai's tone.

"Aran, I hate to do this, but if you don't stand back—"

"Quiet!" Aran snapped. "Shut the hell up, all of you!"

There was a moment of stunned silence.

Aran drew in a deep breath, one hand still stroking Ani, who'd startled at his raised tone. "Stop. Please, all of you." He turned to the captain. "I—I can't let you on the ship. If you want to come on, you'll have to do it over my dead body."

Now the captain was staring at him in frank astonishment, and he could hear the click of rifles being moved into position.

They wouldn't have to actually kill him, stunning him would do, but either way, if the raiders wanted an excuse for war—

"And over the body of my land devil," he continued quickly. "You remember Ani. She won't be very happy if someone tries to hurt me. She's very protective."

His pulse was racing far too quickly, and he felt sick to his stomach. But he resisted the urge to shrink from either the military captain's cold glare, or the angry grumbling of the raiders through his communicator.

He was bloody well used to cold glares after the last few days.

At last, the captain stepped back and conferred with a couple of the other soldiers, then appeared to be talking to someone over his wavelink. When at last he turned back to Aran, his expression had gone menacing. "If I understand correctly, you are threatening bodily harm to our duly appointed military officers to prevent them from their duty to inspect your ship."

Hell, it wasn't like he had anything to lose at this point. "I am," he said through his teeth, before Krevai could say anything.

"You understand that this opens you to charges of treason?" The captain's voice was even colder than before.

"Oh, for the Holy damn Mystery's sake!" he exploded. "I don't actually care about that right now!"

The captain gave a sharp shake of his head. "Very well. I have received instructions that, considering the nature of your threat, we are to close off this portion of the docking bay. No one will be allowed in or out of the ship. You are to come with me. And your actions, threatening legitimate military authority, will be brought before the Council, I can assure you."

"No one will be allowed on or off the ship while I'm gone?" Aran's voice was almost shaking with relief.

"That's correct." A hint of uncertainty was creeping into the belligerence in the captain's tone.

Aran sagged, grabbing at the wall of the airlock in sick relief. "Good," he gasped. "Good, yes, of course, that's your prerogative. We will—we'll have to—"

Ani hissed louder, and he cursed, grabbing for her before she could jump at anyone. "For God's sake let's go! I'm sure your commander wants to talk to me."

"This is all well and good, human." Aran could hear the disdain in Krevai's tone through the communicator. "But if we're locked in here, it will be difficult to get medical attention to your Istvay, and I can't get rid of the charak infestation in my crew. If the charaks take over, I think you know as well as I do how little ability I will have to stop them doing whatever they see fit to do. And in a human system like this ..."

"I know," Aran muttered into his communicator. "I know. I'm doing the best I can, okay? Just ... you promised to let me talk with them."

The human captain seemed, finally, to have recovered from his shock. "Follow me, then," he said gruffly. "And I'm warning you, any attempt to escape and we'll be forced to shoot you."

"I know," Aran muttered bitterly. "At this point, though, you may have to damn well get in line."

6

Savina

Savina's body was tight with strain, every muscle on edge as the *Dolphin* entered Colorida airspace.

"Rafel," she said tersely. "You and Beni get the ship's weapons online."

Joska looked over at her, expression severe.

"We're not going to be firing on innocent civilians, for the Mystery's sake," Savina snapped. "But if our registration is expired and they call in the military to arrest us as we step off, I'd just as soon be able to shoot back."

A glance over her shoulder told her that, for once, Rafel was on her side.

Joska let out a short sigh, and Savina could hear in it that the captain was just as tense as she was.

"I have the weapons online," said Beni from the corner where they were sitting. Their face was a scowl of concentration as they listened to the audio instructions over their wavelink.

"We're getting within hailing range." Joska's voice was brusque, but she managed to sound at least mostly calm. "Beni, keep a scan out for any ships they might send after us. We won't know until we're down there if our registration is still current unless they decide to tell us. And if they have any idea who we are and why we're here, I suspect they won't do that. But at least we can try to avoid being shot down before we dock."

Beni grunted their agreement, their focus still fixed on their wavelink.

Savina glanced around the small, familiar cabin, the closest thing to a home she'd had in a very long time, and tried to remind herself to breathe.

Half an hour at most before they'd know if this ridiculous plan was going to work.

"Paging Savina Moya." The voice through the ship's communicator made Savina jump, her hands going unconsciously to where she'd tucked her throwing knives.

"The ship's registered to your name," whispered Joska from behind her, her voice amused.

Savina scowled. "This is Savina Moya," she said through the ship's com, sweetly enough that everyone in the cockpit cast a suspicious glance in her direction.

There was a short pause. "Savina Moya. Your docking bay assigned is number two seventy-three. We will instruct you when you're cleared to proceed."

"Thank you!" The breathy sincerity in her voice earned her more suspicious glances, but she ignored them, her hand tightly around the hilt of her knife.

For the briefest moment, her body remembered how it felt, at a time like this, to be able to lean back into the steadiness of Reka's arms, feel the woman's warm breath ghosting over her skin and know that there was at least one person here she could trust to be just as deadly as she was.

The thought shot a jolt of pain through her so sharp that she almost gasped at it.

Stupid. It was a ridiculous thing to worry about when they were all about to be killed.

But knowing it was ridiculous didn't stop the way it sat in the pit of her stomach.

The cabin was quiet enough that Savina could hear Nicolau's quick breaths, the rustle of cloth when Beni shifted position.

And then, at last, the voice came through the ship's com again. "You're cleared to proceed."

Savina's ears were straining for a hint of anything suspicious in the speaker's tone, but over the com, it was impossible to tell.

She took a deep breath, and tapped the com to reply. "Thank you! Proceeding to dock two seventy-four."

"Acknowledged."

Savina glanced over at Joska.

The woman shot her a wry smile, then turned the ship and began their descent through the atmosphere.

Almost as soon as the *Dolphin* was settled into the docking bay, Savina's wavelink buzzed. When she blinked to open the notification, the script in her retinal screen read, "Ownership transfer successful."

She glanced up, startled, to see Joska watching her in mild amusement.

She narrowed her eyes. "There, Joska," she said. "The *Dolphin's* officially yours again."

Joska glanced around, a twitch of humour still tugging at the corners of her lips. "Who would've guessed? You kept your word after all. Though I must say, you brought her back a little worse for the wear."

Savina glared at her reflexively, and Joska chuckled. Then the captain turned back to the others, her face going businesslike once more. "If they're expecting us, we'll know the moment we step out the door. And even if they're not, I think it's safest to assume we won't be returning to the ship. You've all got everything you need?"

Savina glanced quickly around the cockpit. Ines and Nicolau were holding hands despite the light cast on Nicolau's arm, a remnant of the injuries he'd suffered back in the yibo system, and both of them had knapsacks on their backs—the remainder of their earthly possessions tucked in among the survival packs, battered and worse for the wear, that had made it through the portal and back. Rafel and Beni, too, had their small knapsacks, and Joska's was tucked beside the pilot's chair.

Savina didn't have anything to speak of, except her weapons. But then, she hadn't had anything to speak of when she'd arrived on the ship months ago—just a small suitcase, the contents of which were long since destroyed or scattered.

"Well," said Joska, shouldering her own knapsack. "Let's go, then."

Savina found she was holding her breath as the hatch opened.

Beni reached out, their hand fumbling until it found Savina's, and they gave her a wordless squeeze.

Then the door opened, and the loading ramp lowered, and, swallowing back the bitter taste of fear, Savina stepped out with the others.

She was braced for a shot, but no shot came, not when they appeared in the doorway, and not as they descended the loading ramp. Savina looked around quickly again as her feet touched the ground, but again—there was no sound from the corners of the docking bay, no hiss of rifle fire. She glanced over at Joska, and saw the same sick relief on the woman's face that she felt.

And then, from the corridors ahead of them, there was the tread of boots ringing off the floor, a sharp, commanding voice. "We're to investigate anything suspicious, Cavaco's orders. It looks like the ship that just landed has a docking code that's over a month old."

Savina and Joska exchanged glances. Then Savina gestured at the opposite door with a jerk of her head and hissed, "Go!"

No one argued. They turned, and slipped out into the back corridor as quickly as they could, the door swinging close behind Rafel just as the door on the other side of the *Dolphin's* docking bay was shoved open.

"Where to now, Savina?" Rafel muttered as they jogged down the empty back corridors of the docking bay. "You're the one that suggested this port, back when you hijacked our ship."

Savina swore. "I suggested this place because it was within a couple hours transport ride of the Rim Mountains. I've never been to the damn port in my life."

They rounded a corner, and came face-to-face with a startled dockworker. "What are you—" he began, but Savina shoved past him before he could finish the sentence.

It was only when they were halfway down the next corridor that she realized, with an uncomfortable start, that a month ago she would have simply slit his throat without thinking twice.

She gritted her teeth. Whatever Joska said about turning over new leaves, the Savina of a few months ago would have stood a much better chance of survival than she did now.

"This way," hissed Beni, turning down another corridor. They must have found the station map in their wavelink, because the corridor they led the others down ended after a few steps in an emergency exit.

"Give me just a second, I should be able to disarm this—" Beni muttered, stepping forward to run their fingers down the door until they found the control panel. "I still have all the standard lock codes stored in my wavelink from before."

A moment later, the door clicked and swung ajar, and Beni shoved it open.

Stepping outside into the brisk, early autumn air of the evening was almost enough to bring Savina staggering to a halt, the weight of memories, the fondness, relief, regret, the ache of finally coming home almost a physical blow.

The others looked almost as stunned as she felt.

She recovered herself somehow and grabbed Nicolau by the arm as he stood gaping, tears forming in his eyes. "We can cry about this later," she snapped. "We need to get out of sight, now! They're going to be after us."

Nicolau swallowed hard and nodded, and then they were running down the back alleys behind the docking bay, and towards the centre of the small Belt city.

When they were far enough in that Savina judged they'd be safe from immediate pursuit, she slowed, wincing and digging her elbow into her side to ease the running cramp.

It seemed that even without Reka, she was fated to have to run every damn place she went for the rest of her damn life.

The others came to a stop around her, panting, and she leaned up against the wall, gasping for breath and scowling at the world in general.

"We can't stay here long," said Rafel uneasily, glancing around. His pale pinkish face shone with sweat in the streetlights, and the agonized expression on his face, and the way he kept leaning to rub the place his prosthetic met his flesh, told her he hadn't enjoyed the run any more than she had. "They're going to come after us. They'll assume if we ran, it was because we had something to hide."

"They wouldn't exactly be wrong," Joska said wryly.

"Be that as it may," Rafel grumbled, "the fact that they're investigating an unusual docking, and acting on Cavaco's orders to do it, isn't reassuring. We'll have to find a place to lie low."

Nicolau cleared his throat and stepped forward. "This—this city isn't too far away from my parents' village," he said. Savina could see the tension in his muscles, the way his fingers toyed with the edge of his shirt, his other hand clasping Ines's. "They'll take us in. They'll hide us, if we need it. If I—if I tell them what you've done for me all this time—" His voice choked a little.

Savina closed her eyes, feeling sick.

She could still picture the farmer's face that night so many years ago, when Savina had told her that members of the compound were coming to kill her and her husband because of the child they'd taken in. She could still see the strained, terrified look in the woman's eyes, still hear the gentleness in her voice when she asked Savina if she wanted to come with them.

She could still feel the ache of loss when she'd shaken her head *no*.

"Won't that put them in danger?" She asked the question before she had time to think it through.

Nicolau turned to her with a fierce look on his face. "Savina," he said in a low voice. "After all this time, and everything you've done, I thought you'd finally realize—it's not just you who's willing to die to keep people you love safe. My parents would be heartbroken to know that one of us was hurt because we didn't want to put them in danger, just as much as you would be."

Savina stared at him.

He turned to the others. "Come on, let's go." His voice was suspiciously rough. "If we don't get out of here in a hurry, were not going to be able to."

7

Aran

The sanitizing shower the soldiers escorted Aran to was cold and uncomfortable, and Ani didn't like it any more than he did. When they emerged, she was wet and bedraggled and hissing angrily at the world in general, and he chuckled a little despite himself. "Come on, sweetheart," he whispered. "Let's get this over with. The faster we figure this out, the faster we get Pishti—" He broke off the thought quickly, because he couldn't afford that right now.

Right now, it was going to take all of his mental focus to keep from actually losing his crap for long enough to figure out a way out of this.

He shrugged into the clean clothes the soldiers had provided, the feel of them stiff and uncomfortable against his skin after the worn, comfortable mix of human, raider, and yibo clothing he'd become accustomed to, then stepped outside to where the soldiers were waiting for him.

They gestured him ahead of them down a long corridor and into a small, white-walled interrogation room, empty except for a metal table and two uncomfortable-looking chairs. He glanced around helplessly, then took a seat as the soldiers stepped out, the door closing behind them.

The room was cold, and the hiss of the ventilation whined on the edge of his consciousness. Aran's skin prickled in goose pimples, and the dryness of the air made his eyes itch and water.

He clenched his teeth grimly and tried to force his body to relax.

At last, the door swung open again, and a woman who must be a commanding officer strode through the door, flanked by half a dozen guards. The *clang* of the door closing behind them was loud enough to make Aran jump, and the look on the officer's face sent a shot of dread through his stomach.

She came to a stop across the table from him and dropped her hands down on it without bothering to take a seat, studying him with cold eyes. "Aran Romeu," she said at last. "I've heard of you. You think you're famous enough that you can defy military orders?"

He closed his eyes and took a steadying breath. "No. No, that's not what—"

"Shut up!" She slammed her hand down on the table, and Aran jumped. "You will speak when I tell you to speak." She leaned forward, until her face was much too close to his for his comfort. "You thought you could get away with breaking the law, putting our system in danger, just because you're a celebrity? Did you think that you could dictate to me what my soldiers' orders should be? What's safe procedure and what's not?"

Aran's teeth were gritted tightly, and he could feel the shakiness through his muscles.

"Answer me!" She screamed the words in his face. He jerked back involuntarily, and she grabbed the front of his shirt and yanked him forward. "Answer me, damn you! Do you think you're too important to follow my orders?"

"No, I—I'm just trying to—"

"Shut up!" She shoved him back into his seat.

Ani was hissing like a teakettle, and he grabbed for her before she could do anything rash. "Would you please just listen to me!" he said frantically. "I'm bloody well trying to keep you and your soldiers alive! I need to get to do Sol. It may be our only damn chance of stopping a war."

The woman's face darkened in outrage. "How dare you—" she began, reaching out to grab him again.

He leaned back out of her reach, holding onto Ani with both hands. "For the Holy Mystery's damn sake, please just listen for one minute! The aliens on that ship need medical attention, and I've promised to get it for them, and in return, they aren't going to damn well start a war with the entire Joias System. I can get it for them if we can get to do Sol. You can escort us, I don't care, just please let us go before—"

"You filthy traitor!" she was shouting, spittle flying from her lips. "I'll show you what we do to traitors, no matter how famous they are. See how much use you are to your alien friends when we line you up and shoot you. While you were stalling, I heard from a scientist friend of yours, Emeric Furtado. You're happy to sell out the entire Joias System for your own fame. Well, you won't under my watch. You'll be locked up, right now, and you can make your case to General Cavaco." She grabbed his arm, her fingers digging into his flesh, and he flinched, his grip on Ani's tentacle loosening for just a moment.

The woman's words cut off midsentence, her hand going limp on Aran's shirt as Ani swarmed up her body, leaving rapidly swelling spots of bright green in her wake where her tentacles had stung. Her face was stricken, eyes wide, foam starting at the corners of her mouth.

Aran jumped to his feet as she collapsed. "Stand back, please don't—"

The guards had already started forward. "It's an alien creature!" someone shouted. "The alien is trying to kill us all!"

"No," Aran began helplessly as Ani leapt for her next victim. "No, no she's not an alien, she's a land-devil, she's from here!"

Ani hadn't waited for the results of the discussion. Two soldiers were lying on the ground now, and the third was bringing her weapon to bear on the place the land-devil was crouched to pounce.

"No don't shoot, she's not—"

The woman shot.

The pulse fire rippled through Ani's body like an impact through gelatin, and she turned, fixing her protuberant eyes on the woman with a gun.

"Damn it—" Aran gasped, grabbing for her.

It was too late. The soldier was dead before she had time to do more than utter a startled exclamation.

"She's not an alien, she's—she's from here—" Aran mumbled, grabbing for Ani again. Another soldier raised their weapon at Aran, and was dead before their finger had time to twitch on the trigger. "Just—just everyone please calm down for one minute—"

The last soldier grabbed Aran by the upper arm, then screamed and went limp.

Everything was quiet.

Aran closed his eyes and dropped his head wearily into his hands, leaning against the table.

Ani, from her perch on the body of the last soldier, foam still gathering on his lips, gave a self-satisfied little chirp, and he reached down and snatched her up before she had time to start feeding. "No, Ani," he whispered, swallowing back the vomit rising in his throat. "I can't let you eat humans if I'm not going to let the raiders do it. Dessi would be furious."

Reluctantly, he forced himself to glance around at the carnage.

Seven dead soldiers, the scars from pulse pistol blasts marring the clean white walls.

And from outside, screams and shouts of alarm.

He sighed heavily.

Ani gave a questioning little chirp, and he managed a weak smile, scratching her under the chin. "It—it wasn't exactly your fault," he muttered. "I did try to tell them."

This wasn't good. This wasn't good at all.

And … well, he hadn't been paying as much attention to the commander's words as maybe he should have been, but he was pretty sure she'd said something about hearing from Emeric.

Which, if it were true and he hadn't misheard, meant Emeric was still alive, somehow, and had somehow found a way to get a message through the portal.

He swore quietly, and tried, very hard, not to think about the other option—that Emeric had managed to get himself through the portal.

It wasn't exactly like he could do anything about it now, anyways.

He paused a moment, then bent beside the commanding officer's body, pulling out the command chip from her inner pocket. "Sorry," he muttered under his breath.

Ani hissed in disdain.

He took a breath and crossed quickly to the door. At his command, Ani spat, and he shoved the door open as the lock dissolved, glanced around quickly, and started off back towards the hangar bay at a run.

It was only moments before he heard the shouts of soldiers behind him, who must have discovered the interrogation room. He swore, glancing back, and picked up his pace, turning the corner to the docking bay.

"Dessi!" he shouted into his communicator as he ran. "I need you and Landru out here, now. If we don't get the ship out in the next ten standard minutes, we're not going to without a full-on war."

8

Savina

In the end they decided that Nicolau was the least likely to attract suspicion. And so Savina sat crouched in one of the small alleys with the others, her entire body aching with impatience and worry, as Nicolau stepped out into the streets. By the time he returned half an hour later, she'd been almost ready to burn the city to the ground and go out searching for him.

"Here," he whispered, dropping a bag of clothing on the ground of the alley. "Thank the Mystery the credits on my wavelink were still there." He laughed, and Savina could hear the shellshock underneath it the sound. "I mean, I guess there's no reason they wouldn't be, it's just—" He trailed off.

Savina knew what he meant. It was still difficult for her brain to grasp the fact that the world had continued to function, just the same as it always had, despite everything that had happened to them over the past few months. That while the tiny group of them had been running and fighting for their very lives, people here on Colorida had simply … gone about their days, exactly the same as they always had.

"Anyway, this should be enough that we can blend in."

That, of course, had been the whole reason for the delay—with their mismatched, stained, and tattered clothing, most of it some combination of yibo tunics and whatever human accessories had survived their trip, there was no way they wouldn't attract notice. And if they were going to show up on the doorstep of Nicolau's home, Savina was damn well not taking that chance.

They changed quickly.

It was odd, changing into sturdy clothing that would have fit in on any Rim Mountain village. The fact that it felt so natural—that all of the memories and sensations returned so quickly and easily—was maybe the strangest part of it.

Nicolau had guessed sizes surprisingly accurately, although the sundress Savina wore was a little tight, and Rafel had to roll up the sleeves of his jacket. It was good enough, at least, that no one should look at them twice.

"We'd best get out while we still can," said Joska. Savina nodded, and they stepped out of the alley.

The worn cobblestone of the streets was still warm from the day's heat, and Savina could feel it through the thin soles of her boots, the surface uneven and cracked from age and the way the ground had settled. The buildings in the centre of town were old stone, worn and not as nicely kept up as the Old Quarter in do Sol, but with the weight of age and time giving them a presence nonetheless. There were evergreen trees planted down the centre of the wide boulevard, and the familiar spicy-sweet scent of them in the evening air caught in Savina's chest in an odd way that she couldn't decide whether was fondness, or fear.

Ever since she was old enough to leave the compound, she'd

stayed away from the Rim Mountains as much as she could—tried to ensure that her jobs kept her out for days or weeks at a time.

And yet, she'd always come back. Because as much as she might hate it, that was where home was.

This place, here, wasn't quite the Rim Mountains, but the familiar scent of evergreens was enough to tighten her chest and turn her stomach.

They reached the transport hub in the centre of town without incident. Ines purchased tickets, as her name wouldn't show up in the *Dolphin's* documents, and they sat on the bench waiting for the small transport to arrive.

Savina tried to disguise her impatience, watching idly as other passengers came and went.

And then, outside, she heard the sound she'd been dreading—the heavy tread of soldiers' boots, the harsh barked commands.

She swallowed hard, and forced her hands to unclench, forced a friendly, unconcerned smile to her face.

"No killing, Savina," came Joska's low voice in her ear. "They don't know who they're looking for, likely. As long as they don't notice us—"

Savina turned to the captain, her smile bright. "Joska," she said. "I respect you. There are a lot of people in this city who are still alive right now because I respect you. But I promise you—if for one second there is a threat to my brother, I will kill every soldier and every civilian in this transport station, and I will not feel bad about it for one second."

She turned away before Joska could respond, and touched the comforting weight of the throwing knives in her belt.

The soldiers stepped into the station, and began stopping passengers on the far edge of the platform.

"If they ask for IDs, we don't have them with us," hissed Savina. "We're from the Rim Mountains, just travelling into the city to pick up a few things, and we didn't bring our IDs, except for Ines, because she bought the tickets."

"We'd need IDs to get on the transports—" Rafel began, but Savina shook her head sharply.

"Here in the smaller settlements, they never enforce it. I traveled without an ID most of my life, and so has everyone who lives out here. They may lecture us, and we may have to pay a fine—but they're not going to be surprised."

The transport hissed into the station, and the voice announced, in garbled tones, a local transport to Campo.

"Come on," Nicolau whispered, standing quickly. Savina could see the mixture of tension and eagerness in his posture as he helped Ines to her feet.

Again, her chest ached in an odd way that she didn't really know what to do with.

Nicolau was going home. Nicolau was going back to the family who'd raised him, far away from the lies and fear and violence that had formed Savina's childhood.

He was going home in a way she could never go home.

She stood. "Beni, that's us," she whispered to her sibling.

They turned their face towards her, and she could see in their expression the same odd mix of emotions that she felt.

The group of them made their way towards the local transport.

The soldiers were working their way down the station, but it appeared that they were focused on the passengers waiting for transport to Vila Nova do Sol—they apparently hadn't considered that whoever had run from the station authorities would take one of the slow local transports to a Belt city just as small as this one.

Savina dropped into her assigned seat. She was sitting beside Rafel, who didn't look any happier with the arrangement than she felt, with Joska and Beni on the seats behind them.

Other passengers were making their way onto the transport as well, casting uneasy glances over their shoulders at the soldiers.

The soldiers were getting closer.

Savina bit the inside of her cheek and closed her eyes, trying to keep her expression calm and friendly.

The soldiers wouldn't be suspicious because of their lack of ID. But if the soldiers wanted to be sticklers, their lack of ID might be enough to get them pulled into the station for questioning. And then …

She'd been telling Joska nothing but the Mystery's own truth— she'd kill every person in this damn city if that was what it took to keep Nicolau safe. But with nothing but her throwing knives and pulse pistol, she wasn't stupid enough to think that she'd be able to make a difference against the Joias military.

The soldiers were coming closer.

The transport's AI hummed and coughed in a voice that sounded cracked and electronic, "Passengers, please take your seats. Service to Campo, through Agua Fria and Dos Coelhos."

Savina glanced around the crowded transport, trying to keep her breathing steady.

A woman sat in one corner, four or five chickens cooing and grumbling to themselves in a wire basket on the floor beside her feet. A small boy beside her clutched her hand, his head drooping wearily against her sleeve. Two men sat in another corner, a holodisc pulled up between them with some game open on it, and beside them sat a man with one child draped across his lap sleeping, and two others huddled on either side of him.

The soldiers were almost across the open space of the station, and she saw one of them look up, seeming to notice the transport was about to depart.

She raised her hand, opening her mouth as if to call something.

Savina tightened her hands on her knives.

The transport doors hissed shut, and the transport jolted off the station in a series of small jerks that made the chickens cluck in irritation, and woke the child in the man's lap.

And then they were moving forward, the whine and groan of the rickety machinery loud enough to cover Savina's long breath of relief.

She glanced over her shoulder and noticed that Joska's posture had relaxed as well.

Nicolau, who was sitting across from Joska, was clutching Ines's hand, a bright, almost painful anticipation in his eyes.

Savina shoved back the ache in her chest, and leaned back against the worn padding of the transport seat and pretended to sleep.

It was an agonizing four hours to their destination. The transport stopped at every small town to let people on and off, and at one point, Savina was crowded between Rafel and an old woman with elbows as sharp as Savina's throwing knives, talking loudly through her wavelink in Mountain Dialect. Every time she shifted in her seat, she managed to jab Savina with one of her bony elbows, and by the time she got off an hour later, Savina had been on the point of murdering her out of sheer irritation. But at last, when the moon was high in the sky, the AI's cracked voice called their destination.

Savina blinked and stood, stretching the kinks from her muscles, as around her, other passengers did the same. Nicolau nudged Ines awake—the girl must have been tired to be able to sleep through this, Savina thought sourly—and Beni stood, almost tripping over a piece of luggage a fellow passenger had left under their feet. The echolocator in their wavelink had always struggled with items that were low to the ground and hadn't moved position recently. Joska caught Beni's elbow, and the small group made their stiff way off the transport and out into the cool of the night air.

This village was much smaller than the city they'd come from. Nicolau glanced around and started forward without hesitation, up the narrow cobblestone streets winding through the tall stone buildings, built out so they almost reached over the streets. Even in the cool of the autumn, the scent of late summer roses and clematis climbing the walls of the buildings and spilling out of the window boxes hung sweet and heavy in the night air.

The streets were steep, and Savina was out of breath long before they reached the smaller cottages on the edge of town. And then Nicolau paused in front of a cottage with a neat yard and climbing roses. There was a tension in his posture that was almost tangible.

A small black dog exploded out of the door, barking frantically, its tail wagging so hard that its entire body wriggled back and forth. It jumped up on its back legs at the gate, whining, and Nicolau gave a choked little laugh and started forward, letting go of Ines's hand to rub the dog's head. "Hey Anjina," he whispered, his voice choking. "Hey girl, it's me. I'm—I'm home."

The cottage door creaked open, and a woman in a housecoat stepped out, a dim torch in her hands. "Anjina," she said, her voice cracked with sleep. "What's—" She stopped abruptly, the torch falling from her hand and clattering to the ground.

Nicolau didn't bother with the gate, just vaulted the low stone fence and was across the yard to her in a few steps. "Mother!" his voice was choking with emotion. "Ama, it's me, I'm home." He wrapped the woman in his arms, and she collapsed against him, letting out a little choked sob of her own.

"Son? Son, your aba and I thought you were dead—" And then she buried her face in his chest and sobbed, and he buried his in her hair, for a few moments the two of them rocked back and forth, clinging to each other as if they'd forgotten there was anyone else in the world.

At last, the woman drew back, wiping her eyes. "Nikki, come inside right now, it's cold out. I'm going to go get your father—" Her voice faltered as she glanced over the gate at the rest of them.

Nicolau put his hand through her arm and drew her towards the gate. "Ama." His voice was choked, but there was a note of pride in it. "Ama, this is—these are my—" He faltered, as if suddenly realizing he wasn't entirely sure how to introduce them.

He cleared his throat. "Ines, this is my mother," he said, drawing her forward. Even in the dark, Savina could see the shy smile on Ines's face. "Ama, this is Ines." There was a tenderness to his voice that, Savina assumed, precluded him from having to explain his relationship to Ines any further. "And this is Joska and Rafel," he continued, gesturing to them.

Joska stepped forward, a small, genuine smile on her face. "Hello," she said. "It's good to meet you. Nicolau has spoken of you often."

"And … and this is—" Nicolau broke off.

The woman was staring at Savina, and her brown face had gone very pale.

"You're that girl, aren't you?" she said quietly, stepping forward and reaching out a hand to touch Savina's face, as if she wasn't sure whether Savina was real. "You're the little girl who saved us. Aren't you?"

This close, staring into the woman's eyes, Savina could see the cheerful, round-cheeked farmer woman she'd trusted Nicolau's life to, so many years ago. The sparkle in her eyes had dulled a little, her face lined with age and strain that hadn't been there when Savina had known her. But there was still that kindness in her expression that had made Savina know, instinctively, as a seven-year-old child with a filthy, crying bundle in her arms, that she could trust her.

"You've grown up." The woman's voice was soft. "I always wondered what had happened to you. I felt guilty over it my whole life, that we couldn't talk you into coming with us." There were tears gathering in her eyes again, and suddenly Savina found she was blinking back tears of her own.

Nicolau was looking between the two of them, and he cleared his throat softly. "Mother, this is—this is Savina and Beni. My ... my siblings." His voice choked on the words.

The woman was still watching Savina, and now she looked up so her glance took in Beni as well. Emotions flitted across her face, too fast for Savina to read, but at last, slowly, she nodded. "Thank you," she said, her look now taking in all of them. "Thank you for bringing me my son back."

Nicolau shifted uncomfortably. "Mother. I—I'm sorry. But—there are people looking for us. I thought you might—"

The woman's expression turned businesslike in an instant. "Of course, what am I thinking having you all stand out here in the cold? Come in, come in, I'll wake up my husband and we'll get you something to eat. You must be exhausted, and I know they don't serve food fit to eat on the transports that come through here."

It wasn't long before they were all gathered around a worn, homey kitchen table, the rich scent of arroz caldoso bubbling and spluttering on the stove behind them filling the small cabin. The woman's husband, Markel—Nicolau's adopted father, Savina reminded herself—had joined them, a grey-haired man with a tired face and friendly eyes. Nicolau's mother, Edite, had made the introductions, and now they sat in silence.

Savina took a mouthful of the soup Edite had set in front of her, trying to avoid the woman's eyes.

Trying to avoid the inevitable explanations, which she knew at some point she'd have to give.

"Nicolau," Edite said at last. She'd been wiping her eyes the entire time, and she couldn't seem to take her gaze off Nicolau. "Son, your father and I—we were sure you were dead ..."

Nicolau wasn't even trying to pretend. Tears were dripping down his cheeks, and he brushed them away ineffectually. "Ama—Ama, I'm so sorry. I would've sent word if I could have, I was—Ama, I didn't think I'd see you again ..." He dropped his head into his arms and sobbed. Markel reached over and put his arm around Nicolau's shoulders, rubbing his back in small circles that reminded Savina, somehow, of Joska.

"It's alright, son." His voice was suspiciously thick. "It's alright, we're not angry we're just—we're just so happy you made it home."

At last Nicolau drew in a long, deep breath and straightened. "Mother, father." He glanced at them both. "I—I'll tell you everything that happened. But first—what have you heard?"

The two of them exchanged glances. At last, Edite turned back to Nicolau, a frown pinching her brows. "We heard that your ship went through the portal, and that the portal closed behind it. The government was saying that it was a hostile action on the aliens' part, and that we needed to prepare for war. That if they'd killed one of the Joint Heads of Government, the rest of the system was in peril as well. They were stationing more and more soldiers in the Rim Mountains, and when people protested, more soldiers came in to put the conflicts down. But with the alien threat, no one except those of us out here paid attention. And now the portal's reopened, and we've been told to be on standby in case something comes through."

Savina's stomach tightened at the woman's words. "You haven't heard word from Alba? The Chief Justice?"

Edite turned to her, still frowning. "The Chief Justice? She went through the portal on Nicolau's ship. She's presumed dead."

Savina glanced at Joska, and the grim look on the captain's face told her everything she needed to know.

She leaned forward. "Alba's not dead. We were all on the other side of the portal, all of us. We came back through, and Alba came through with us, on another ship," she said quietly. "The last we saw, Joias military ships were surrounding the ship she came in on."

Edite fell suddenly silent. From the look that passed between her and her husband, Savina guessed they were coming to the same conclusion Savina and Joska had.

"This is Cavaco's doing," Edite said quietly. Her hands were twisting the hem of her shirt between her fingers. "It must be." She turned back to Savina. "What happened, then, really? What's Cavaco trying so hard to hide?"

Nicolau told the story. It was stumbling, and he had to go back and correct himself a few times, but by the end, Edite and her husband were staring at the group of them around the table with a mixture of awe and horror.

"I don't know what Cavaco is planning," said Rafel, leaning forward slightly on the table. "But if the rest of the system has any idea what happened behind that portal, he's not going to get it. I'd be willing to bet that's why he's keeping the Chief Justice hidden— probably waiting to make sure he doesn't need her for anything, and then kill her."

"If he hasn't killed her already," Savina muttered, almost under her breath.

The grim look on Joska's face told Savina that she wasn't the only one thinking it.

"So," said Edite last. There was a note of shaky determination to her voice. "What do we do now?"

Nicolau turned to look at Savina.

She realized, belatedly, that everyone had turned to look at her.

She closed her eyes and drew in a steadying breath.

That was the question, really—what could they do?

"We have to stop this," she said at last, quietly. "We have to stop Cavaco. Because whatever the hell he wants, it's not going to end well for any of us." She turned to Rafel. "If he provokes an uprising in the Rim Mountains…"

Rafel shook his head and cursed under his breath. "Of course that's what he's going to do next." He turned back to Edite and her husband. "I'm ex-military. I was—I was there. At Swan River. Back then, everyone was horrified at what had happened. That's what stopped it, public pressure. Without the public and the politicians screaming about it, it would have gotten worse. Much worse." He shook his head grimly. "If he starts an uprising again, while everyone else is watching for an alien threat? It will be a massacre. He'll finally get the Rim Mountains under his thumb for good, and I don't want to think about what that means for anyone living up there."

For a few moments, there was silence around the table. Edite's face was pale, her eyes glassy with shock, and Markel didn't look any better.

At last, though, the woman shook herself from her reverie and turned to Savina. There was a hard determination under her tone that made Savina realize, suddenly, where Nicolau had gotten his stubbornness. "Savina," she said quietly. "You're right. We can't let this happen. So what do you need from us?

Savina closed her eyes.

A few months ago, the thought of anyone asking her how to fix something like this would have been laughable.

But then, she'd been trying to fix things she had no idea how to fix, been out of her damn depth for so long that by now it felt almost familiar.

She opened her eyes and smiled, that bright, innocent smile that always made Joska tense in suspicion. "You heard what Nicolau said. We just got back from stopping a bully trying to kill off a bunch of defenceless human settlements." She pushed herself to her feet. "Cavaco may have already killed Alba. I don't know. But he sure as hell can't worry about starting a war with the yibos if he's so busy in the mountains that he doesn't have the troops to spare. So we're going to make sure he regrets the moment he damn well heard of the Rim Mountains."

Edite and Markel were watching Savina, a desperate, aching hope in their faces that made her want to look away.

"Savina?" Edite asked. She paused. "I apologize, but—you're from that compound, aren't you? You're an Old Believer."

There was a sudden silence around the table, and beside her, Savina could feel Joska tense.

Savina met the woman's gaze. "I am," she said quietly.

Edite nodded. "It makes no difference to my husband and me," she said. "But you know how they feel about Old Believers up in some of those villages."

Savina drew in a breath.

She could still feel the disdain dripping from Reka's voice, the coldness in it. The feel of her hand slipping from Savina's as she stood and turned away.

It hurt, so badly that if she ever got a chance to slow down and think about what had happened, it might tear her open from the inside.

"I know," she said, her voice so low she could hardly hear it. "I know. But it doesn't matter, does it? I can't change who I am. So they can either accept help from an Old Believer, or they can let Cavaco kill them all."

"And you'd help them, after all that?" The woman said.

Savina swallowed down the lump in her throat and scowled. "Well, it doesn't look like they have anyone else."

9

Alba

It was an odd feeling, waking up in a soft, comfortable bed with sheets that smelled like clean laundry. The breeze that drifted in through an open window was scented with sweet jasmine, and she could hear the familiar sound of the morning songbirds from the courtyard outside.

For a few moments, Alba simply lay in bed, eyes closed, trying to figure out if this was a dream—like so many times in the yibo system when she'd woken to the half-remembered scent of jasmine and feel of a silk pillowcase against her head, and opened her eyes in a drab, hard cot in an alien world that wanted her dead.

But this time, when she blinked her eyes open, the scent on the breeze, the softness of the pillows against her head and the mattress against her back, the sound of birds from outside, didn't disappear.

Light was streaming in through the tall bay windows, cracked open to let in the fresh air, and she could hear footsteps outside, the brisk, quiet footsteps of serving staff.

For a moment, her entire body drooped with relief, tears pricking at the corners of her eyes.

She'd dreamed of this so many times. And she'd always had to push it to the back of her mind, because she'd known she'd never be able to come back. She'd never wake up in a sun-soaked room, on a comfortable mattress and soft pillows to birdsong through an open window.

And yet … here she was.

She blinked hard, trying to shove back the overwhelming wash of emotion, and leaned her head back against the pillow, trying to piece together the previous day's events through the fog of exhaustion overlaying her memories.

The ship being brought into the military hangar bay. The captains sitting at the table in front of her, telling her that Cavaco was Acting President. The numb dread that had filtered through her body, soaking through her so that the ride on the military transport to a secure location on the outskirts of the city was a blur.

Stumbling off the transport, almost too weary to hold herself upright. Someone guiding her through darkened hallways and into a bedroom—this bedroom, apparently.

Barely having the presence of mind to change out of her stained, travel-worn clothing and into the night clothes that had been provided.

And then … waking to this.

She closed her eyes and drew in a long breath.

Whatever this was, whatever Cavaco intended, at least she was alive, for now.

With a grimace, she pushed herself up into a sitting position, her muscles aching residually from the strain and exhaustion of the last several weeks.

She sat on the edge of the bed for a few moments, gathering her wits. Her brain felt foggy, still thick with exhaustion, and her body, now that she'd had what may have been her first actual sleep in days, was making known its long catalogue of indignities.

She sighed, and pushed herself to her feet. She'd seen a door to the side of the well-appointed room that likely led to a steam cleanser. Even the thought was almost enough to make her weak. After weeks of the harsh, lukewarm water showers in the yibo system, the thought of a steam cleanser felt like unimaginable luxury.

There were clothes in her size in the closet, and she'd cleaned herself and finished dressing by the time there was a soft tap on the door. "Madam?" came a polite voice. "Are you awake?"

She cleared her throat. "Yes, thank you."

"Good." The voice paused. "I'm meant to tell you that the advisor to the Acting President has arrived. He would like to speak with you, but he has asked me to convey that he is happy to wait while you make yourself presentable. I'm to bring you to him when you're ready."

Alba finished fastening the last of the clasps on her jacket with fingers that were suddenly trembling. "Of course," she said. "I shall be ready momentarily."

When she opened the door, a soldier in uniform stood outside her door. He saluted stiffly as she came out.

"Thank you," she said, trying to keep her voice steady. "Now, if you please?"

"Of course, Madam," he said, turning sharply and starting off down the hallway at a pace that was clearly meant to match her own. He paused at the door to what must be a dining room and stepped back, gesturing her in ahead of him.

Alba forced her back ramrod straight, her head up, as if she was stepping back into the halls of the Council Chamber, rather than into an audience with a man who may well hold her life in his hands.

The man sitting in front of her was one she recognized—General Samso. Unelected, but Cavaco's right-hand man, and he'd been present at Council meetings frequently enough that Alba knew him by name.

"Madam Chief Justice," he said smoothly, standing as she entered. "It's a pleasure to see you again, despite the circumstances."

He looked similar to how he had when she'd left, months earlier—his iron-grey hair now had no trace of black in it, and the creases around his eyes and mouth were deeper than they had been, but his eyes were sharp and calculating, his smile predatory.

He stepped around the table and pulled back her chair. "Please, Madam. Sit."

She took the proffered chair with a brief nod of gratitude. "General. I hear your employer has done well for himself while I've been away." She made no attempt to hide the irony in her voice.

She could see his irritation in the slight tightening around his eyes, but his tone in response was perfectly pleasant. "If you're speaking of Cavaco's position as Acting President, I'm afraid that was less of a personal benefit, and more of a role he was forced to take on in order to keep our system secure." The man resumed his seat, and leaned forward. "I'm certain you're not aware of what has been happening here since you left, so I shall enlighten you. There was mass panic after the portal closed—riots in the cities, uprisings in the Rim Mountains. People were frightened, and things were falling apart. Whatever your view on the military, I can assure you, Cavaco's use of the emergency measures was the only thing that held the system together."

"Panic Cavaco enflamed," Alba snapped, meeting his eyes. "Cavaco and I have known each other long enough, I think, that you may drop the pretences. He didn't expect me to come back alive—that much I'm perfectly aware of. So tell me: now that I'm back, what does he intend to do next?"

Samso sat back in his chair, studying her. At last, he leaned forward again, resting his forearms on the table. "I've heard enough about what you've been through in your ordeal behind the portal that I suppose I can hardly blame you for your unwarranted suspicions. But you must see that the state of the Joias System is exactly as I've explained to you. I can show you proof, if that is required, but think, Madam. A portal mysteriously opened, and then closed, swallowing the diplomatic ship carrying one of our three Joint Heads of Government without a trace left behind? Any creature or civilization powerful enough to do that must be dangerous. You know what that would have done to the morale of the people left behind."

"With Cavaco stirring them into a panic? Yes, I can well imagine." Her voice was cold.

Samso shook his head, still smiling. "Accusations for which you have no evidence. You truly think him a villain, do you not?"

She half-rose, pushing herself back from the table. "If Cavaco expects me to play along with his games—"

"Madam, please. Sit." He sighed. "I've worked with you long enough to know you. You are a politician. You, of all people, understand the importance of calm heads and rational decisions, and of politically expedient bargains. That is exactly what Cavaco is proposing to you—a bargain."

"And what would this bargain entail?" Alba asked warily, not returning to her seat.

Samso's gaze was sharp. "Cavaco is willing to bring you in front of the Council to testify," he said at last. "He asks that you commit to limit your public testimony to the actions of the aliens behind the portal, but under those conditions, he is willing to let you make your case."

Alba frowned.

It sounded too good to be true. Yes, Cavaco was attempting to hamstring her ability to bring treason charges against him, but even she knew that, as things stood, he could ensure that they would be accusations without concrete proof.

"And what does he want in return?" she asked at last.

Samso shook his head wearily. "In return, we ask for your support in returning the system to order. That's all—use your influence to help Cavaco return things to balance."

Alba closed her eyes for a moment, sinking, at last, back into the chair. "So," she said at last, in a flat voice. "The kitten you caught turned out to be a mountain cat, and you need my help to tame it."

Again, there was that small tightening around Samso's eyes that told her she'd hit the mark.

"And if I refuse Cavaco's bargain?"

His eyes narrowed, just a little, but the menace in his glance was unmistakable. "Then you will be less canny of a politician than I remembered," he said. "I understand that, despite your ordeals in the alien system, you still wish for peace. I hear from my soldiers that there was another ship accompanying you that carried aliens that could pose a significant threat indeed to our system. I would hope your cooperation would ensure that such a situation need not arise."

He didn't make threats against her, personally. But then, he hardly needed to. She was entirely in his power, and both of them knew it.

"When is the Council meeting at which Cavaco proposes for me to speak?" she asked at last.

Samso smiled. "In five days' time. You have until then to make a decision." He pushed back his chair and rose. "And now, Madam, I have duties I must attend to. Please inform me should any matter of your comfort be neglected."

"Samso," she snapped, rising quickly enough that her chair teetered on its legs. "What have you done with Feliu and Yosip? With the remainder of the civilian population on the ship, to whom I promised shelter?"

He paused a moment.

At last, he turned back. "They are being well taken care of," he said. "They've requested to remain on their ship, and we've allowed them their preference. As long as they do not attempt to threaten us, we will offer them the same courtesy. And as proof of Cavaco's good intentions, I shall ask my people to bring Feliu and Yosip here, as I understand they are the last remaining members of your diplomatic corps. The last still alive, after your encounter with these peaceful aliens." His smile held all the warmth of a Rim Mountain winter as he turned away.

Alba could barely bring herself to eat the meal the serving staff brought—hot, freshly brewed coffee, pastries still warm and flaky from the oven, fresh fruit cut into elegant shapes.

She felt as if the world had suddenly shifted, leaving her disoriented and unsure of her footing. There was a surreal feeling to lifting the coffee cup to her lips and tasting the strong, earthy bitterness of it, the smell of the pastries, the birdsong from outside, a familiarity that felt wrong, after everything she'd been through.

She jumped at the polite tap on the door to the dining room, and it took her a moment to regain her composure enough to answer.

"Madam? Madam, are you alright?" She recognized the familiar voice, cracked with strain and fear, and then the door swung open, and Feliu stepped through, followed by Yosip.

Both men looked exhausted, their faces drawn with worry, but their expressions relaxed when they saw her.

"What happened to you?" she snapped, pushing back her chair. "What did Cavaco do?"

"Nothing," said Yosip with a small smile, despite the concern clear on his face. "We were taken to a safe house similar to this one, and given a place to rest and refresh ourselves, and then left to twiddle our thumbs until a military escort showed up an hour or so ago." He sighed, shaking his head. "We were both convinced that Cavaco had simply had you murdered."

The pinched look in Feliu's face told Alba more than words the truth of Yosip's statement.

She sighed. "I had feared the same for you," she said at last. "And the yibos?"

Feliu shook his head. "I don't know any more than what Yosip's already told you. What happened to you?"

She filled them in, briefly, on her meeting with Samso that morning.

When she'd finished, Feliu was already shaking his head. "I don't like this, Madam," he said tersely.

"I don't like it either," she said. "Cavaco is smart enough to know the danger we pose to him, even if I agree to hamstring my testimony."

"I agree." Yosip's voice was quiet, but she could hear the worry in it. "As much as I hate to say it, Alba, his offer is far more generous than what I'd expected. Things must be going badly indeed if he's willing to allow you to speak to the Council, even with the stipulations he's put you under."

"Or," she said slowly, "do we know that all the ships that came through with us were taken? If the *Dolphin* or the raider ship escaped, there will be people in the system who know that we were alive when Cavaco's ships arrived to escort us to do Sol. He may fear what would happen if word got out he'd had me murdered."

"He still didn't need to agree to allow you to appear before the Council," Feliu muttered. "He has something else in mind that he's not telling any of us."

Yosip nodded. "The question is, what is he after?"

"And," Alba added wearily, "considering communication through our wavelinks is still fully cut off, how in the Mystery's holy name are we going to find out?"

10

By the time Dessi and Landru appeared on the loading ramp, the pounding of the soldiers' boots had almost reached the docking bay.

Landru was grinning, the first time Aran had seen her smile since the raiders had called off the war. She pulled a butcher's knife from her belt. "Well, human. Since Dessi is nonviolent, it's a good thing you invited me along."

Aran swore. "That's not why brought you! I need your help to get the ship codes to let us off this place."

Landru looked disappointed.

"Let's go," he snapped. "No one's attacking us yet, so if you kill anyone, that's a declaration of war."

Landru's smile broadened. "I'm pretty sure that if we wait a moment—"

"Let's go!" Aran's whole body was shaking as he turned and started down the hallway indicated on the holodisc he'd taken from the commander's lifeless body.

Guilt rose uncomfortably in his throat at the memory. But—well, he had asked them not to provoke Ani. Anyways, he'd have to feel guilty about that later. Right now, he had to get them off the base before the raiders killed everyone here and started a war that would burn the Joias System to the ground.

He sprinted down the hallways through the base, the raiders behind him. Word must have spread—he could hear the shouts and calls of soldiers, the noise of troops mobilizing all around him, but so far, they didn't seem to know where he'd gone.

They'd probably start by searching at the docking bay. Which would be a problem when he and Landru and Dessi tried to get back to the ship, but he could deal with that when it came up.

When they reached the door to the room that, according to the holodisc in his hand, held the unlock codes, he skidded to a halt, heart pounding. Half a dozen soldiers stood in front of it, and they sprang to attention as he skidded around the corner.

"What are you—" one of them began.

Then Landru and Dessi rounded the corner after him, and sudden terror spread across the soldiers' faces.

"Get out of the way. Please," he panted.

They were staring past him at the raiders, and he remembered, abruptly, his own first encounter with raiders—the horrifying sight of them, a good head and a half taller than a tall human, their ice-pale skin and blood red eyes set in an almost human face, the snarl that showed their elongated canines, the thick black sheet of hair that hung down, in Landru's case, well past her waist—they could start growing it out when they'd made their first kill, he'd learned over the past few weeks, but even without knowing that, the sight of it painted a picture that was utterly terrifying.

"S-stand back." The soldier's voice was shaking, the gun trembling in her hands.

Aran held out his empty hands in a placating gesture. "Please." His voice shook. "Please just get out of the way. I'm really, really trying to keep anyone from being hurt."

She didn't move her aim from his chest, and he could see her blinking to activate her wavelink.

"No!" he began, "No, don't—"

Thunk.

The sound of the butcher knife slamming into the wall next to the soldier's head was loud enough that everyone froze.

"Your people have illegally detained our ship." Landru was speaking in Common Dialect, which was close enough to Mountain Dialect that at least some of the soldiers should be able to understand it. "Our human has asked you, very politely, to step out of the way, because our human wants to avoid a war." She smiled, and every centimetre of her smile was a threat. "I, on the other hand, don't. We promised our human we would be peaceful, but if you attack us—" she shrugged expansively. "That wouldn't be breaking our word, would it? It would be self-defence." She leaned in closer, and Aran could see the raw terror in the soldier's face. "So please," Landru whispered. "Call in your friends. It's been far too long since I've hunted humans."

The soldier caught herself on the wall, her body shaking.

Cautiously, Aran stepped closer. "Listen," he said in a low voice. "Just stand to one side, I'll take care of the lock. I just—I don't want anyone to get hurt, and there's only so much I can do."

She must have seen the desperation in his face, or else her conversation with Landru had done the trick. She stepped back, her legs almost collapsing under her, and Aran brought Ani down from his shoulder.

"Don't worry, she's from our system, she's just a land-devil," he said over his shoulder as Ani's acid ate through the heavy steel door. "She's my pet, she's—she's very friendly, usually—"

He trailed off.

Everyone, raiders and soldiers alike, were looking at him, and none of them looked convinced.

He cleared his throat. "Anyways. Thanks." He shoved the door, and it swung open.

Landru surveyed the soldiers, still smiling the vicious smile that showed her fangs to best effect. "Please, humans," she purred. "Do call your friends in to attack us. I'm very, very hungry."

The soldiers stood where they were, frozen in fear.

"Come on!" Aran snapped, and with one final leer at the soldiers, Landru strolled after him and Dessi.

Dessi had slowed almost involuntarily as they went, staring around her in fascination. "This is your human military technology centre?" Her voice was shot with wonder. "Landru! You'll have to be there when I tell this to Krevai, he's never going to believe it."

Landru grinned back, interest in her own expression. "Pity the captain's not with us. He'd have enjoyed this, I think. Look at this, the humans have their own little technology!" The indulgent surprise in her voice would probably have been a little insulting if Aran had stopped to think about it.

"Dessi!" he hissed. "Come on! We have to get moving!"

She was still looking around an absolute wonder.

Aran sighed. "Listen, Dessi. If we can get down to do Sol, I'll take you through our research facilities there."

Her face lit up, and she turned away from the technology to follow him.

He could already hear the pounding of soldiers' boots outside. Someone must have lost their nerve and called in their location, and he was trying very hard not to think about what that was going to entail.

They reached another door, and he tapped the security screen, glancing over the commander's holodisc for any sort of activation code.

Dammit. He'd never actually been good with technology, Istvay had always dealt with the technology.

Sweat was forming under his hairline, and his palms were damp with it.

He cursed under his breath. The frantic pounding of boots outside had resolved into something much more orderly and much more menacing than the chaos of a few minutes ago. If there were enough soldiers out there, he wasn't sure that he, Ani, and the two raiders would survive it. But he was very sure that if any one of them didn't, Krevai would waste no time in sending for reinforcements through the portal.

"Dessi," he hissed. "Find a way to bar the door somehow! Landru, do you have any idea how the hell to make this work?"

Dessi frowned, glancing around quickly, and then Landru stepped forward, slammed the door shut, and swung her butcher knife through the melted latch. The splinters of metal and fabricant were enough to jam it tightly in place.

She smiled at Aran, that same vicious smile she'd given to the soldiers moments earlier. "Never let it be said, human, that we raiders don't honour our bargains. Now. Let me see."

Aran gasped out a desperate breath of relief.

Even with Landru's terse instructions, it took him several minutes to get through the system. By the time he did, he could feel the pulse blasts humming through the walls.

This wasn't going to last for much longer.

"I need you to enter the ship's ID," he hissed at her.

She'd turned to watch the door with the sort of hungry interest with which a cat might watch a bird's nest, but at his words, she glanced down at the screen and keyed in a sequence of numbers.

An authorization code appeared on the screen. Aran held up his palmscreen to record it.

And then the soldiers burst through the door, and Landru drew her weapons, grinning.

"Stop!" Aran threw himself forward between the raider and the soldiers, who'd pulled up short at the sight. "There's no need to start a fight, we just—"

The captain, who seemed to have finally recovered from his shock, gestured at Aran with his rifle. "Get out of the way. We received a report of hostile aliens—"

"For the Mystery's damn sake!" Aran exploded. "Landru was doing her absolute damn best to avoid being hostile! And I don't know about you, but I would very much like to keep it that way, so if you could please just stand the hell back—"

The man raised his rifle.

A moment later, he was twitching on the floor, Ani perched happily on his chest.

Aran swore through his teeth as the rest of the soldiers backed away. "It's a damn land-devil," he gritted out. "It's from our own damn system."

Ani was clearly searching for her next target. He scooped her up. "Come on, sweetheart, it's time to—"

Another soldier moved. Ani slipped from Aran's grasp, swarming across the floor with a speed and a grace that, in any other circumstances, Aran would have stopped to admire. Now, he just felt faintly sick as a soldier dropped, foaming at the mouth.

"I told you, she's a damn land-devil!" he shouted over the panicked noise. "Your weapons won't work on her, and if you try to touch me, she'll kill every damn person in this room. I'm trying really hard to prevent that, and I feel like at this point I'm the only one!"

Half the soldiers were shouting into their wavelinks, the other half had brought up their weapons. There was the hiss of weapons fire, and Aran flung himself to the ground, although honestly, most of it was probably aimed at Ani.

"Ani—" he began hopelessly.

Someone grabbed him by the back of his jacket and yanked him bodily to his feet, and when he looked up, Dessi was standing over him with a grim expression on her face. "If you get hurt, there's no avoiding a war," she snapped. "I think you and I might be the only people who care about that right now, so let's get out of here before you get shot!"

He swallowed hard and called, "Ani!"

She looked up at him from where she was gnawing on the shoulder of a fallen soldier as he shrieked and convulsed, her eyes wide and innocent.

"Ani, get over here, right now! I'm leaving, and I don't want to leave you behind!" He turned to the soldiers. "I told you, it's a damn land-devil! Shooting her isn't going to do you any damn good!" He glanced over his shoulder. "Landru! You can't eat them, Ani poisoned everyone here. They'll probably make you sick. Come on!"

Ani launched herself sulkily from the chest of her victim, who'd finally stilled, and landed on Aran's shoulder, her entire posture broadcasting offended dignity. The soldiers stumbled back from Aran at the sight of Ani on his shoulder, and he started forward at a dead run, Dessi and Landru pounding after him.

Landru appeared as disappointed as Ani was that their disagreement with the soldiers had been cut short, but she had at least refrained from bringing any of the bodies back with her. Which, Aran thought desperately as he ran, was probably a good thing, if it ever came to convincing anyone this hadn't been the raiders' fault.

By the time they got to the first turnoff, their way was completely blocked by soldiers.

"Put up your hands," shouted the soldier in front, pulling out her weapon.

Aran shoved past her, gritting his teeth. "Please get the hell out of the way," he snapped.

He heard the click of a rifle, then the unmistakable wet squelch of a blade through flesh.

He flinched.

"She was going to shoot you." Landru's voice was far too cheerful. "That was self-defence."

The other soldiers stepped back, taking aim, but in the confusion, Aran and the two raiders shoved past them and were running again.

Aran swore as pulse-fire rippled around them.

"Please, just get the hell out of the way and let us through," he gasped as they came up short at another blockade. "Please, I really, really don't want to hurt you."

This soldier, at least, seem to hear the sincerity in Aran's tone. He glanced between Aran, Ani, and the two raiders following him, and stepped smartly back.

"Thank you," Aran gasped as they pounded past.

Aran squeezed his palm to activate his wavelink, and then cursed. Of course the military would have shut off their communications.

He tapped through to Alba's line on his yibo communicator.

There was a moment of startled silence, then Alba's cautious voice. "Aran?"

"Alba, listen to me. I don't have much time. I'm getting the raiders off the damn military base before they find an excuse to eat everyone. I thought I should let you know."

There was another pause. "*Have* they eaten anyone yet? If Cavaco is looking for proof that the aliens are hostile …"

Aran sighed. "Um. The raiders haven't eaten anyone, technically, and the only people they killed were in self-defence, and they killed a hell of a lot fewer than they might have, honestly. Ani … I mean, the military captain was going to lock me up, and she grabbed me, and Ani might have … look, but technically, land-devils are from our system, so I don't think they can blame the raiders for that."

The silence on the other end of the comm gave him absolutely no indication of how Alba was taking this news.

"But, um, anyways, I ended up with the commander's holodisc, and we used it to generate the code to get the ship off the base. I think our best bet is to break out."

"I suspect you're right," Alba's voice was grim. "I also suspect that Cavaco has not informed the Council that we've returned. May I send you the code to link my communicator through your wavelink? It may be my only option to contact anyone."

The footsteps behind him were growing louder. Aran swore quietly. "Yes, that's fine, go ahead. If it stops working, it probably means I'm dead, but I'll … I'll try to not let that happen."

His wavelink buzzed, sending a quick tingle up his arm from his wrist where it was implanted. "It should be on your palmscreen," said Alba tersely. "Now, I would advise you to get out while you still can."

Aran swore again, glancing behind him. The soldiers were close on his heels.

"I've got to go," he snapped.

"Good luck."

He squeezed his hand to shut off the communication, and pounded around the corner to the docking bay.

And then they were into the open area of the docking bay, and Landru had hit the control for the ship's hatch.

The entire place was swarming with soldiers, and they turned as Aran and the two raiders burst in. Aran didn't give them time to react, just shoved his way through to the loading ramp and pulled himself up, Dessi and Landru at his heels. Soldiers started up the ramp after them, and Dessi hit the controls. Aran winced at the shrill scream, abruptly cut off, as the door slammed shut.

"Don't worry, it will still seal." Dessi's voice was grim. "They're designed to cut through whatever might be trying to hold them open."

Landru was already striding down the corridor, calling out, "Captain, I've got us the codes, but I have a feeling they're going to lock it down in a minute. We've got to go."

The ship shuddered as it started up. Aran caught his balance on the corridor wall, then sprinted after Dessi towards the cockpit.

By the time he arrived, Landru had already dropped into the pilot seat, and the ship lifted off the floor of the docking bay.

"Stand back." Landru's voice echoed in the open space of the docking bay through the ship's communicator. "Or, don't, either way. But we're leaving." She tapped the communicator off and hit something on the control system.

On the far side of the docking bay, an alarm began to sound, loud and insistent, and soldiers scattered as the bay doors swung open. Landru hit the controls, and the raider ship shot forward through the opening.

Aran could feel his whole body go slack with relief as the ship burst through the open doors. The military ships would be after them in a moment, but they had a head start, and he doubted they'd guess that the raider ship would head for the centre of do Sol.

"Aran!"

He jumped at Dessi's voice through his wavelink. She sounded worried.

"I think you'd better come back to your cabin."

He started down the hallway towards his cabin at a dead run.

When he ducked inside, Dessi was crouched beside Istvay's bed. He paused in the doorway, his stomach tight with dread.

"They must have a blocker on the military base that's affecting the communication between ships," Dessi said, looking up at him. Her expression was tight with concern. "Our ship lost contact with the yibo medical team as soon as we got out, and with the technology they've been sending through to us. And I'm afraid without it—"

Aran pushed past her, swallowing back his terror, and dropped down beside Istvay's cot.

His friend was deathly pale, their breathing coming harsh and laboured, and he cursed under his breath, his voice coming out choked.

Without the yibo medical tech, Istvay would be dead in a matter of hours, days at the most.

He had to keep them alive until he and Dessi could administer the cure.

He closed his eyes, trying to remember the standard Joias medical protocols for people suffering from the final stages of the defect.

"Oxygen," he snapped. "We need to get them on oxygen, and if you have any artificial adrenalin, that should help their heart keep beating."

It could also come with serious side effects, but at this point Aran was more worried about making sure they lived for long enough for side effects to be a concern.

Dessi nodded and slipped away, ducking under the tangle of Ani's webs, and Aran sank down beside his friend. His whole body was shaking, the residual adrenaline from the last couple of hours combined with a thick, chest-clenching dread. "Istvay," he whispered. "Istvay, just hold on. Please hold on, we're almost there."

There was no response. Aran hadn't really expected there to be.

He choked back a quiet sob of desperation.

Dessi returned a few minutes later with a portable oxygen tank and some vials of adrenalin. Aran prepared the injection as she set up the oxygen, but he had to tie a tight compression around Istvay's bicep for longer than he wanted before the vein stood out enough that he could find it.

Istvay stirred weakly at the injection, a touch of colour coming back to their face, and Aran gasped with relief, almost too lightheaded to stand up.

But it wouldn't last. This was the treatment they gave in do Sol, but in do Sol, people with the defect usually died before thirty.

"How long until we get there?" he whispered through his communicator.

"At the rate were going? Not long, according to your map." Landru paused. "Why?"

"Because if we don't hurry, I don't think Istvay is going to be alive to save," he said grimly.

11

Savina

When the small transport doors opened onto the dirt streets of the tiny Rim Mountain village where Edite's sister lived, Savina almost couldn't make herself step off the transport.

She'd grown up in the compound. Villages like this one had been as much a foreign country to her as the city of do Sol. But the warm smell of the sun on the evergreens, the hot, dusty scent of the end of summer overlayed with the cool sharpness of autumn, the dirt streets and the colourful clapboard houses …

She'd grown up in the compound. But the compound had been in the Rim Mountains, and there was something about the Rim Mountains that got into your blood, seeped through your marrow, made itself part of you.

The others disembarked behind her, and Edite cast a quick, concerned glance at Savina before she stepped around her and started off towards the centre of the village. "I called my sister, she said she spoke to the majordomo," she whispered as she passed. "They'll be waiting for us."

Savina swallowed hard, and forced herself to start forward after the woman.

When they reached the municipal building in the centre of town, a woman whose features proclaimed her immediately as Edite's sister hurried forward, embracing Edite then turning to grab Nicolau into a hug.

"Auntie Llora," he said in a choked voice. "Auntie, I missed you!"

When they both finally stepped back, Llora looked quickly over Savina and the others, then turned to Edite, her face pinched in a frown. "Come inside, quickly," she said, her voice low. "The majordomo's waiting, and some of the rebels. They're willing to listen, because my brother-in-law is one of the leaders." She shook her head uneasily. "It's been bad up here, Eedie. It's like the soldiers are provoking us on purpose. Everyone is angry, and everyone is scared."

Edite sighed, her voice tight. "I suppose we do what we can, and pray to the Holy Mystery for the rest." She cast a glance over her shoulder at Savina. "Savina? Are you ready?"

Savina nodded.

She wasn't ready. She'd never be ready for something like this.

But … well, it had been a very long time since not being ready had been an option.

They stepped inside the old stone structure that served as a village hall, and Savina had to blink to adjust her eyes to the dimness.

She could make out the people they'd been brought there to meet —a ragged group of hard-faced men and women, their postures tense, hands on weapons as if they thought perhaps this was a trap.

They relaxed a little at the sight of Edite and Llora, and at Savina the others in a close huddle behind the two women, looking, Savina knew, more pitiful than threatening. But they didn't take their hands off their weapons.

"Llora," said one of the men, turning to the woman. "It's good to see you. Ramir told us you'd contacted him. What is this about? Who are these people?"

"Eedie will explain better than I can," Llora said, stepping back a little.

Edite nodded at the men. "Ignasi. It's been a long time." Her smile was genuine, if weak. "And as to who these people are—I think you need to hear what they have to say."

Ignasi's eyes scanned over Savina and the others, and she could feel the wariness in his gaze.

"My son, Nicolau, was on the diplomatic ship that was sent through the portal," Edite continued. "I assumed he was dead. But last night he arrived on my doorstep to tell me that the Chief Justice survived the trip and had come back through the portal on another ship. And that the last view he'd had of it was the ship surrounded by Joias military vessels, before those same military vessels attempted to shoot down the ship he and these others had come through on."

The quick intakes of breath around them told Savina that everyone here realized the implications of the news.

"So Cavaco's been lying." Ignasi's voice was grim. "We'll have a war whether the aliens start one or not." He shook his head. "I don't know how this changes anything, though—he's going to kill us first, before he starts in on the aliens, and we all know it."

"No," said Savina, stepping forward. "He won't kill you." Her teeth were clenched, her voice tight with anger. "I was behind the portal with Nicolau. So were the rest of my friends. We've spent the last few weeks fighting a guerrilla war from settlements no more well defended than this village against aliens with the technology to break through force-fields and vaporize entire cities. Cavaco isn't going to win here."

The man looked at her in surprise. Then he gave her a small, bitter smile. "I applaud your courage. But what exactly do you think you can do?" He gestured at them. "A handful of people who, no offence intended, look like they're nearer dead than alive from exhaustion. Do you really think you can make a difference here?"

Savina smiled. "You forget. We came in from an alien system." She turned to Joska. "We still have yibo tech on the *Dolphin*, don't we?"

"We do," said Joska slowly. "But by now the military have likely taken the *Dolphin* and locked it up with the rest of the ships that came through the portal. So I don't see—"

Savina had already turned back to Ignasi. "If we could give you weapons the military won't know what to do with, and ..." she paused, calculating. "Maybe ... a couple hundred people who were veterans of another guerrilla war? Would that change things?"

Ignasi frowned. "It could."

Savina closed her eyes. "Joska," she said quietly. "Do ... do you happen to have a line through to Reka still?"

There was a long moment of silence. When Joska spoke again, her voice was harder than Savina had heard it in a long time. "I believe I do," she said. "Why?"

"Because she was on the yibo ship. If you're right, they've taken the *Dolphin* back there. We need someone on the inside, someone who could get everyone ready to get out when we get there. Reka's the best one to do that."

There was another long silence.

At last, Joska nodded. "I'll call her, then. Best figure out if we can even get through to her, before we make our plan based off it."

From the corner of her eye, Savina saw Joska squeeze her hand to activate her wavelink, wait, and then shake her head in disgust. "I'm going to have to try the yibo communicator," she said.

Savina stared straight ahead, and tried to ignore Joska's and Nicolau's eyes on her.

"Yes?" Reka's voice through the communicator was sharp and strained, and Savina's muscles tensed at the familiar sound.

"Reka. It's Joska. Are you still on the yibo ship?"

"Yes," said Reka after a moment. "They took Alba and the rest of the diplomatic corps off, but the rest of us are still here. They haven't killed us yet." She paused. "Is … are the rest of you safe?"

"We're safe, for the moment." There was no noticeable thawing in Joska's tone. "We're going to try to keep Cavaco from burning the Rim Mountains to the ground, but we need more people with combat experience. If we make it to where you are and cause a distraction, do you think you can get the people we worked with back in the yibo system off the ship?"

Another pause. "I … believe I could."

Joska glanced at Savina, raising her eyebrow.

Savina closed her eyes. "Your call, Joska. Can we do this?"

"If Reka is working with us on the inside, it's possible."

Ignasi sighed. "If you can, we'll have a chance, at least. That's more than what we have now, Mystery knows," he added under his breath. "And you'll bring everyone back here?"

"No." Reka's tone through the communicator was flat and uncompromising. "I won't be coming with you."

Ignasi frowned, but Savina stepped forward, jaw tight. "I know Reka. She won't come, because she's a government agent, and starting a rebellion in the Rim Mountains that might get people killed isn't in the government agent code of conduct. Nor is …" Her voice faltered a moment. "Nor is working beside Old Believers. I'm from an Old Believer compound." She managed a ghost of her usual innocent smile. "And I guess you'd all better know that too, so we can figure out right now who feels the same."

She'd thought, once, back behind the portal, that this wouldn't matter. It hadn't, to Joska, or Rafel, or Nicolau or Ines, and she'd finally allowed them to convince her that it *didn't* matter. That people would judge her for who she was, not where she'd come from.

Reka had shown her how naive that was.

And then meeting Nicolau's adoptive family, watching her baby brother and his girlfriend, seeing Joska's uncompromising, selfless stubbornness in the face of injustice, had shown her she couldn't just run away and leave these people to their fate, even so.

Reka made a sound through the communicator, quickly bitten off, and Savina wasn't sure if it would have been agreement, or argument.

It didn't matter. She'd made her position clear enough back on the *Dolphin*.

There was a long silence.

At last, Ignasi gave a small, bitter smile. "I won't say we don't have our disagreements with the Old Believers. But in a famine, you may find it easier to dip your bread in the stew alongside a heretic than to starve, isn't that the saying?" He shook his head. "If you'll fight alongside us, I won't ask questions about how you pray."

Savina kept the smile fixed on her face, and tried to ignore how much it hurt that this man could say that, and think he was being gracious.

How much it hurt that Reka couldn't do even that.

How much it hurt that Savina was going to fight for them anyways.

She felt the pressure of Joska's hand on her shoulder, the small squeeze that told her that Joska, at least, had heard the words the man had said, and the ones he hadn't. "Let's go, then," the captain whispered. "The sooner we can get this over with, the better."

12

Alba

When the line clicked off with Aran, Alba, Feliu, and Yosip stared at each other for a few moments.

"The yibo communicators," she said at last. "I can't believe we didn't think of that. The military technology to block communications wouldn't be set to work on frequencies the yibo communicators are set to."

She was trying not to think too hard about the implications of what Aran had told her.

She couldn't do anything about it right now anyways. She'd simply have to trust he'd figure it out.

Feliu nodded, his expression going businesslike. "Very well. We don't have time to waste, then, since we have no idea if or when Cavaco's people will see the loophole. Madam, you try to get through to Ander. In the meantime, I'll attempt to contact the yibo ship, to be sure that what Cavaco told us is true and everyone's alive and unhurt."

Alba nodded, and turned quickly to her communicator.

By the time she had the line set through to Ander's wavelink, the signal bounced through Aran's connection, Feliu was speaking quietly into his own yibo communicator, face grave.

Alba and Yosip shared a glance, then waited. Better to find out what was happening before they attempted to call out.

At last, Feliu tapped the communicator off.

"Are they still alive?" Alba asked, her voice sharp with strain.

Feliu hesitated, then nodded. "They're alive and safe, it appears. They have not been allowed to disembark, but the ship was supplied with an extra week's worth of provisions, so they are currently in no danger of starving. The military has, at least, made no attempt to board them and given no overtly hostile signals, so the captain is content to wait, for the moment. But I don't know how long it will last. I was unable to reassure him that the situation here is stable, and at some point they'll start to run low on provisions."

Alba closed her eyes in relief. "They're still alive, at least, and we are not yet at war," she said at last. "We'll simply have to ensure we work through the diplomatic roadblock before that becomes a problem."

Feliu nodded grimly. "The captain is content to wait for now. But if the situation does not improve, I would anticipate yibo warships appearing in the portal long before running out of supplies becomes a danger."

"Well then," said Alba. "We shall have to do our best to prevent it."

She tapped through her communicator and waited as the line buzzed.

When Ander answered, a few moments later, there was stunned disbelief in his tone. "Aran? Aran Romeu?"

"No, Ander," she said. "This is Alba Espina. My communication is currently routed through Aran's wavelink, for reasons we can discuss later. But first, I should like to know what exactly is happening in do Sol."

There was a long moment of silence over the communicator. When the president spoke again, his voice was just as shocked as it had been, but distinctly more uncomfortable. "Alba? We all got word they were dead! What the hell … what are you doing here? Where are you?"

"I'm sorry to disappoint, but I am currently very much alive—although I'm uncertain how long that will last."

"How did you—the portal closed! We all saw it. We were told you were dead. That's why Cavaco—" he broke off, and Alba could almost hear him shaking his head.

She sighed. "Yes. We were trapped behind the portal for a time. But we were able to make contact with the sapient lifeforms on the other side, and after some negotiation, they agreed to reopen the portal to send us, along with various refugees from our sister system of Labarinto, back through to Joias." It was a gross abbreviation, perhaps, but she hardly had time to detail the history at the moment.

"Refugees from Labarinto?" Ander still sounded shellshocked. "What do you … Where are you, Alba? Things have been—" he broke off. "Wherever you are, I suggest you stay there until this blows over. Things have gone badly in your absence." There was a grimness to his tone that confirmed every worry that Alba had.

"What happened?" she asked sharply. "When we came through the portal, we were met by a fleet of military ships and escorted to a military compound outside of do Sol, and Feliu, my diplomatic aide Yosip, and myself were taken to what Cavaco terms a 'safe house,' which I believe to be here in the city. Since then, I've had no contact with anyone not under Cavaco's direct control."

Ander paused, as if trying to organize his thoughts. "When we last spoke, you remember that Cavaco was already raising the temperature on planet with his warmongering even as the diplomatic ship went towards the portal. That would have been bad enough, even if his guess about the likely fate of the diplomatic ship hadn't been proved quite so prescient—"

"There was no guessing involved," said Alba grimly. "The actions of the aliens were irrelevant to what he had planned. He staged a mutiny on the ship, with the soldiers you warned me he'd smuggled on board. The captain of the ship, Mattin, was part of it. Aran, it turns out, discovered something in the particles that had been broadcast into our system through the opened portal that urged caution, but the captain refused to turn the ship around when so ordered. The mutiny was staged shortly before we went through the portal." She paused, swallowing hard. She still couldn't think of that train of events without her throat tightening and her mind going momentarily blank with remembered panic. "I don't think even Cavaco foresaw what would happen next. The portal closing was, it seems, an event that even the aliens who opened it did not foresee. But Cavaco's people certainly wasted no time in taking advantage of the situation. If I'm still alive, it is no thanks to anyone sent through the portal by Cavaco."

"A mutiny on the ship." Ander's voice was horrified. "Alba—I didn't foresee it going that far. I foresaw him trying to undermine you, but a mutiny? A murder attempt, if I'm understanding you right?"

Alba almost laughed. "A murder attempt is rather underselling it."

Ander was quiet a moment. When he spoke, his voice was grave. "We all saw when the portal disappeared. Cavaco was in front of the Council the next day, requesting an immediate grant of full war powers. He cited the closing of the portal, and the presumed deaths of everyone on board the diplomatic ship, as conclusive proof of the aliens' intentions, and with the panic he'd already stirred up, among the Council members as much as the citizens, there weren't many willing to speak against it. Your replacement had not yet been appointed, and as I told you, Alba, my voice doesn't carry the weight yours did." He cleared his throat. "Does, I mean." He paused again. "Even so, there were voices on the People's Committee and the Judicial Committee who mistrusted Cavaco's motives, especially considering the political situation immediately before the portal opened—your proposal to remove the Military Committee from power was a clear threat to Cavaco's interests, and there were still those who were uneasy with the speed of his request for war powers. But Alba—you must understand the public sentiment. Cavaco had whipped the people into a frenzy. Everyone was going home at nights convinced that their children would be murdered and their towns destroyed by alien weapons before they saw the morning."

Alba let out a quick breath, her stomach tight with dread.

It was exactly as she'd feared. Ander wasn't a bad man. But he was a spineless one, and if Cavaco had managed to convince the populace, Ander would never have had the moral fortitude to stand up to him. Perhaps her replacement on the Judicial Committee might have, but Cavaco had been canny enough to call the meeting before her replacement was appointed.

"At any rate," Ander continued, "he didn't get full military powers at the time. But he got enough that by the time your replacement was appointed, she was already hamstrung. And you know Cavaco— he knows every protocol, every procedure. He managed to amass more power than any of us anticipated through the War Act. You're the only one who knew the Council protocols and procedures as well as he did, and with you out of the way…" He trailed off helplessly.

Alba stared blankly at her communicator, her mind churning through the implications of Ander's words.

"Even if he used every protocol he could find, even if he'd been granted full powers under the War Act, we have safeguards in place —" she began.

Ander gave a small, humourless chuckle. "We did. But then the uprisings began in the Rim Mountains. I suspect that those were provoked by Cavaco as well, somehow, but there was no proof. And once enough people had been injured, and there were casualties, stories of burning homes and crying children on every news packet —again, it wasn't hard for him to convince the Council to grant him the additional police powers to manage internal unrest. And with both of those powers together—"

Alba closed her eyes and leaned back in her seat.

Of course. How had she not foreseen this? If Cavaco had managed to gain the powers granted him via declaration of war, plus the powers to quell an internal threat—powers that, if she remembered correctly, had hardly been changed since the end of the Cleansing a hundred years back—

She could understand the horror in Ander's voice.

Cavaco would have almost unlimited power. Ability to act without putting matters before the Council, ability to sway the vote in his favour by adding additional members to the Military Committee, ability to govern by fiat on more matters than she really wanted to consider.

And on top of that, the power to control what information was passed on to the rest of the populace.

She felt sick to her stomach.

"And what has he done with his powers so far?"

Ander sighed again. "Nothing too drastic yet—increased military presence in the Rim Mountains, increased the military budget, called up all the reserve troops to active duty. But now that the portal's reopened? This may be exactly the chance he's looking for. If he drags us into a war, he cements his power until it's over. That will give him plenty of time to rework the government in his image. And he'll do it, you know that as well as I do."

"And you think he will declare war on the civilization through the portal?" She tried to keep the dread from her voice.

"From the rumours I'm hearing from the Council staff, it's almost inevitable."

"He cannot be allowed to declare war," she said, her voice sharp. "He cannot. I told you that I was travelling with refugees from Labarinto? They are refugees because their system was destroyed. Completely. The survivors are scraping out a living in an alien system because their planets were reduced to bombed-out husks."

"And you brought these—these creatures back through the portal with you?" Ander's voice was now sharp with panic.

"They had the technology to come through at any time," Alba replied. "At the least, they're coming through at the moment with a negotiated commitment to peace." She paused, bracing herself for Ander's reaction. "And we do have one thing in our favour. If you recall, Aran was a member of our diplomatic party."

"Yes?" said Ander cautiously.

"You—you recall his pet. The land-devil."

There was a moment of silence.

"The creature, apparently, made as much of an impression in the alien system as it has in ours. And it—it has somehow managed to reproduce."

Again, there was silence from the other end of the line, but there was a distinctly horrified air to it this time.

She took a deep breath, and soldiered on. "The aliens are frightened enough of land-devils that they intend to close the portal permanently after depositing us through it. The land-devil and her offspring were enough to tip the scales in our direction, barely, and there is just enough sympathetic public sentiment on their end to allow us to negotiate this highly fraught situation without suffering the same fate as befell Labarinto. But that took a great deal of negotiation on my part, and promises of mutual non-hostility. If instead they are met with aggression—" She let her words trail off.

"Then they won't hesitate to call in their warships, will they?" Ander finished. He sounded stricken. "What do we do? There's no way Cavaco is going to listen to me, you know that, and without proof—"

"You, Ander, are going to grow a damn backbone and help me fix this," Alba snapped, finally out of patience. "Cavaco has told me there will be a Council session convened in five days' time on this topic. We shall have to—"

"Five days' time?" Ander's voice still held a note of barely repressed panic. "He's called a meeting for tomorrow. He says he has a witness who can testify as to what happened behind the portal. When I first heard you, I thought perhaps it was you he was referring to."

Alba sucked in a breath, closing her eyes.

That was why Cavaco had been willing to let her speak—he'd pre-empt her testimony with testimony of his own. Which meant their ships must not have been the only ones to come back through the portal.

"Ander. Listen. Get me through to the rest of the Council—the ones who aren't entirely in Cavaco's pocket, at least. If he has a witness, it will be someone whose testimony he can completely control, and we both know it. I must be permitted to speak at that meeting. Which means one of you will have to call me as your witness."

"Alba. I can't—"

"If you don't want our system to suffer the same fate as Labarinto, you're going to have to," she said through her teeth. "I'll talk to whichever members of the Council you think will be open to reason, so that you can have supporters for your witness request should Cavaco try to overrule you. But I am warning you, Ander—this is a life and death matter for the entirety of the Joias System."

There was a long moment of silence from the other end of the line. "Very well," Ander said at last. "I'll speak to the councillors who will be open to listening, and if they require confirmation, I'll ask them to call through to you." He paused. "I suggest Tais to sponsor you as witness. She will be less likely to receive pushback from Cavaco, as she's fairly new to the Council."

Alba heard the words under the words he was saying—and that way, it wouldn't be his neck if things went sideways.

She sighed.

It was better than nothing. It hardly mattered who sponsored her, as long as she was able to speak.

"I doubt I shall be able to be there in person," she said at last. "She'll have to request her witness appear via wavelink. And you will not be able to call through to me, so I shall have to call in beforehand to set up the link."

"Of course." Ander's voice was grim. "Call me back at the end of the day, Alba. I should have news for you by then."

The line clicked off, leaving Alba and the others in silence.

Alba drew in a calming breath through her nose, trying to slow her racing heart.

If what Ander had told her was correct, Cavaco was on the brink of plunging the Joias system into a war that would destroy it so completely that within a generation, no one would remember the warm sun off the ancient stones of the buildings in Old Quarter, do Sol.

Cavaco wasn't stupid. She knew—or at least, she still hoped—that faced with the prospect of the entire destruction of the system, he'd back down. But if he was getting his information from any of the people who'd taken Kachik's side rather than her own, she doubted he was getting accurate information. Kachik, if he was still alive, had a vested interest in humans coming back through the portal, and if that was by way of a declaration of war on the Synod, so much the better. Either Kachik would have threatened whoever it was to keep them from disclosing the danger posed by the Raiders, or he would have downplayed the enormity of the threat to the humans. She knew Kachik well enough to know that once he had the bodies he needed in his war, he had no use for humanity in general. He would happily watch the raiders hunt the humans in Joias to extinction, and not raise a hand to stop it.

Unless she could somehow convince the Council to listen, their system would go the way of Labarinto.

13

Aran

It couldn't have been more than an hour later that Aran felt the hiss and deceleration of the raider ship preparing for landing. It spoke to how stressed he was that it hardly registered in his brain.

Istvay was alive—barely. But they were alive, and that meant that he still had time.

"Aran! Your docking bay is denying us entrance, I think." Landru's voice through his communicator made him jump.

"Tell them it's an emergency landing, and you didn't have time to get the codes," he snapped, hitting the button on his communicator.

"That will work?" Landru sounded amused.

"It'd damn well better," Aran muttered under his breath.

A sharp beep from one of the sensors monitoring Istvay yanked his attention back to his friend.

Blood oxygen desaturation. The third time in an hour. He readjusted the oxygen mask on Istvay's face with shaking hands—it had been built for raiders, and the seal kept coming loose—and slowly dialled up the oxygen until the alarm stopped sounding. Then he closed his eyes for a moment, his hands shaking.

"It worked!" Landru sounded delighted. "It's a pity that the captains promised they wouldn't hunt in this system. This is truly an unspoiled hunting ground."

He ignored her, hitting the communicator line through to Dessi. "I need help getting Istvay ready to transport," he said grimly. "We'll be about a twenty-minute transport ride to the University medical facilities, and Istvay's not going to last that long without oxygen."

Dessi appeared in the doorway a few moments later and ducked through the hanging strands of web to join him at Istvay's bedside. She was dragging a narrow hoverboard stretcher. "Landru is a going through landing procedures," she said. "We'll be able to disembark shortly. Let's get Istvay onto this. There's a place to attach the oxygen, and power cells to keep it functional. Pack any medication you think we might need from a ship into the storage compartment."

He nodded wordlessly and set to work.

By the time the ship had hissed to a halt, they'd managed to transfer Istvay to the stretcher. Istvay had stopped breathing twice during the procedure, but both times Aran had managed to get their breathing started again by readjusting the oxygen mask.

His entire body was shaky with panic, his heart stuttering in an odd, dizzying way.

"Aran! They're asking to come on board and see our credentials." Landru sounded even more cheerful this time. "What would you like us to do?"

Aran cast a helpless look at Dessi.

"I'll help you get your Istvay up there," she said, sounding as grim as he felt. "Landru and Krevai will start a war otherwise, whether they mean to or not."

Aran nodded gratefully, and between them, they moved the

stretcher through the corridors of the raider ship and over to the airlock doors, Ani suckered down on Aran's shoulder. "Tell them they can come aboard," he called through his teeth when he was in position. "I'll talk to them."

The door hissed open, and a small group of cautious looking dockworkers and officials started up.

Aran stepped forward quickly. "I'm—I'm sorry for the emergency landing, um, it's just, my friend is sick, and—"

They were all staring, gazes slipping between him, Ani, who was perched protectively on his shoulder, and Dessi, standing behind him in the entrance to the ship.

Dessi smiled, her fangs gleaming in the low light.

"What the hell—" one of the dockworkers began.

Aran closed his eyes. "Yes, I'm Aran Romeu. Yes, I'm still alive. Yes, this is my land devil, Ani. She's very friendly. Dessi's helping me, she's also very friendly. Istvay is sick, and we've got to get to the Sao Martim University research facilities as soon as possible."

Everyone's jaws had dropped by ten centimetres.

"That—that thing behind you?" The dockworker in the lead gestured at Dessi with a trembling finger.

"She's—she's from another system, but she's a pacifist. And she's a scientist, and she … well, she studies us, so I doubt she'll—"

"What the hell is she?" The man's voice was sharp with panic.

"She's my damn friend, and she's helping me get Istvay somewhere I can save their damn life," Aran snapped. "And the rest of the raiders on this ship aren't pacifists, and won't take nearly as kindly to being delayed by stupid questions."

The dockworkers were backing away slowly. "I'm—I'm going to have to call the authorities—" one of them began.

Aran gritted his teeth.

It probably couldn't be helped. The military was almost certainly already after them, and at this point, his best bet was to keep the raiders from eating anyone for long enough to get Istvay stabilized.

"Do whatever the hell you need to do, just please stand the hell back and let us through," he said.

They looked at each other uncertainly, then up at Dessi.

She smiled, showing her fangs. "Please?"

The dockworkers scattered.

"Landru, we're going to need a transport," he called through the communicator.

"Don't worry, I'll find you something," said Landru, appearing in the door beside him. There was a smile on her face that was far from reassuring.

"Um, Dessi, maybe you'd better go with her," Aran muttered.

Dessi glanced up at Landru and nodded grimly.

"Ani," he whispered, taking her gently from his shoulders. "I'd … I'd love to have you with me, sweetheart. But are you going to need to stay here with your babies?"

The hatchlings didn't need her to keep them alive, technically, not anymore. He'd been watching—they'd been validating his hypothesis that land-devils hatched through parthenogenesis would mature differently than regular hatchlings. Already they were eating solid foods, and he'd been careful to always leave enough food and fresh water in his cabin to keep them satisfied for a few days without him, and he'd instructed the wary raiders on how to care for them should it be necessary. They didn't technically need their mother for survival, and hadn't for several days now. But he wasn't going to keep her from her babies, even if the thought of leaving her behind made his whole chest ache with a panicked loneliness.

Ani gave a small, irritated growl, and tightened her tentacles down on his shoulder.

"Sweetheart," he said, trying again to lift her free. "I'm going to be gone for a while. I don't want—"

She growled a little more loudly, and refused to budge.

He closed his eyes, not entirely sure whether the sick feeling in his stomach was relief, or guilt.

But he honestly wasn't sure he'd survive the next few hours without Ani's familiar, comforting presence, and besides, he didn't have time to argue with her right now.

By the time Aran reached the door of the hangar bay, careful not to jostle Istvay's stretcher, Krevai and Zondra had joined him.

They hadn't been bothered by anyone since the small crew of dockworkers earlier, although he had heard muffled gasps and running footsteps ahead of them as the small group of them strode through the hangar.

And, glancing over his shoulder at Krevai and Zondra, their fangs gleaming in the low light, red eyes glistening with anticipation, Aran couldn't exactly blame them.

"Dessi?" he muttered into the communicator. "Get here with a transport as fast as you can. I'd hate for anyone to get too hungry while we wait."

"We'll be there in a minute." The short, clipped tone in Dessi's voice did nothing to reassure Aran, but a few minutes later she and Landru arrived in the doorway. Dessi looked harried, but Landru was grinning broadly, her hand on the arm of a horrified transport driver, who looked on the verge of fainting from fright.

"Aran!" Landru said. "This human has volunteered to take us and your Istvay wherever you need to go."

"Good," said Krevai. "Zondra and I will come with them. Landru, I'm leaving you in charge."

Aran didn't bother to ask why Krevai had decided to come. Whether he was scouting out the new hunting territory, or it was yet another indication of how little he trusted Aran now, it hardly mattered. Istvay had almost died multiple times in the last hour, and he really actually didn't have the energy to pay attention to anything else right now.

"Remember, eating a human will be considered an act of war," Aran called after Landru. She turned and shot him a toothy grin over her shoulder.

The transport driver, who Dessi had taken control of, swayed as if on the verge of passing out.

"Come on, we don't have time to waste," Aran snapped, grabbing the edge of the stretcher.

Once inside the transport, Aran left Istvay with Dessi, with instructions that if anything should happen, she was to call him immediately, and then climbed into the seat beside the transport driver.

The man looked so relieved to see another human that Aran worried he might actually pass out this time.

"Get us to the Sao Martim University," said Aran, through gritted teeth. "We have about twenty minutes."

The man stared. "This is rush-hour. It'll take—"

"It will take less than twenty minutes, because you're damn well going to make sure it does," Aran snapped. His voice was probably shaking, but he didn't even care enough to try to modulate it. "My friend on the stretcher is dying, and the moment they're dead, the raiders will have no incentive not to hunt their way down the streets of do Sol. And I've seen them hunt. Believe me, there would be nothing left."

The man's eyes widened. "Less than twenty minutes," he

managed.

Normally in a transport going at this speed, weaving in and out of air traffic, Aran would have been hunched over, his head between his knees, trying not to vomit. Now he just stared sightlessly out the window, jaw clenched.

Istvay couldn't die. They couldn't. The thought beat in his chest like a heartbeat. They couldn't, that was all.

When the transport reached the university gates, Aran gestured with a jerk of his thumb for the driver to keep going. The man didn't protest. Students dived out of the way as the transport hummed down the broad walkways between the ancient buildings, and behind them, Aran could hear the whine of the peacekeeper vehicles, who must have been called at some point in their wild journey.

The transport screeched to a halt, and Aran yanked out his credit chip, tossing it to the driver.

He wasn't sure how much was still on it, but it should be more than enough to cover the ride and whatever fine the peacekeepers were going to impose. After all, he and Istvay had been about to start a research trip to the northern Rim Mountains before all this began …

He couldn't think about that, he couldn't, because he didn't have time to break down right now.

He ducked back towards where Dessi was standing beside Istvay, readjusting the oxygen mask. Istvay's face was an almost greyish colour, and Aran's chest tightened painfully to see it. There was no time to worry about it, though, because they needed to get out before the peacekeepers got here—Krevai and Zondra carving a path through the middle of them would be the opposite of helpful.

Together, Dessi and Aran pushed the stretcher down the transport exit to where Krevai and Zondra waited impatiently outside.

"This way," Aran said shortly. He set off towards the research building at the fastest pace he could manage without jostling Istvay. Once inside, he pushed past terrified students and shocked faculty and staff to the large cargo lift. He shoved the stretcher inside, and Krevai and Dessi crowded in after him, and then he hit the button and waited in an agony of impatience as the lift creaked and groaned its way up to the third-floor research station where the genetic laboratory was located.

He knew the way by heart—every time he'd been in do Sol over the past three years, he'd spent every spare moment there, trying to see if anything he and Istvay had found on their most recent adventure would give him a clue to somehow fix the thing that was killing his best friend.

The lift doors creaked open, and he grabbed the edge of the stretcher and started down the hall at a pace that was almost a sprint, Dessi beside him and Krevai and Zondra striding after them.

This floor wasn't as busy as the main floor had been, and the benefit of being in a research laboratory at the university was that people were accustomed to the unaccustomed. Honestly, he might have been able to play the raiders off as some student prank, if he'd had the time to worry about that.

They reached the end of the hall, and Aran keyed in the code to the laboratory. He shoved open the door and stepped inside, and four or five graduate students turned to stare at him, their eyes going wide and horrified.

He tried to smile. "I'm—look, I'm sorry, this is—I'm going to have to ask you to leave, I'm doing an urgent test." From the corner of his eye, he caught sight of Ami, still hunkered down in his shoulder, and sucked in a deep breath. "Genetic analysis on my land-devil. I need to use the lab, and I don't want to put anyone at risk, so—"

The students had already dropped their equipment, and were backing towards the door.

"I'm sorry for the disturbance," Aran called after them. "Just—just tell them to lock down this lab for the next few days until I give the all-clear, probably safer for everyone!"

As soon as they were gone, he slammed the door, keyed in the lock code, then barred the entrance. He hardly had time to feel a sick surge of relief before the alarm on Istvay's monitors began to sound again.

"Aran—" Dessi began frantically.

He grabbed for the adrenalin vial, measuring out the dosage with shaking hands, and injected it by guesswork into the sunken vein on the inside of Istvay's elbow.

For a moment, it seemed to do nothing. And then, slowly, the pallor of their face lessened slightly, the greyish-purple tinge around their mouth and eyes fading.

Aran let himself sag against the edge of the stretcher for a moment. He was so lightheaded that the world seemed to be floating strangely around him, but he managed to push himself upright again, catching his balance on the edge of the stretcher. Some clinical, dispassionate part of his brain told him it was the effects of too much adrenaline over too long a period of time, combined with lack of sleep, and the fact that he hadn't eaten in—actually, he couldn't remember the last time he'd eaten. It had seemed somewhat irrelevant, with matters as they were.

"This way," he said shortly, and Dessi followed him towards a small cot in a curtained-off corner of the lab, pulling the stretcher along with her.

Transferring Istvay to the cot was a bit of a nightmare, but they managed, and he hooked his friend up to the built-in monitors with shaking fingers. Their blood oxygen was desaturated, the heartbeat weak and irregular—but then, it was nothing he hadn't expected.

"Hold this," he said, shoving the oxygen apparatus at Krevai. "Make sure the mask over their nose and mouth seals, and keep turning it up little by little until their blood oxygen stabilizes. Call me if anything happens." He grabbed Dessi's arm. "This way, I'll show you where our genetic templates are stored." He strode across the laboratory, and flipped on the machine, his entire body aching with impatience as it grumbled and moaned and beeped its way to life, and then, finally, the display blinked blue. "Our genetic readouts look different than yours, but I'll put the key through to your data pad again, you should be able to use it to translate this," he said over his shoulder. "The data pads won't hook in, but I'll run the information through my wavelink to your pad."

"Aran!" Krevai's voice was frantic.

Aran swore and shoved the data pad at Dessi. "Call me if you have any questions. I'm going to need to stay with Istvay."

"Don't worry," said Dessi brusquely. "I've worked with yibo technology, I'm used to working with unfamiliar tech."

He was already halfway across the floor to Istvay. When he reached them and peered desperately at the monitors, he almost choked in horror. Their heartrate had flatlined.

"Get back!" he snapped at Krevai, yanking a set of defibrillators from the emergency box over the cot.

Istvay's body jerked as the electricity jolted through their chest, and Aran almost lost whatever was left in his stomach in the sheer horror of it. But then the monitor started up its steady, reassuring beep once more, the flat line on the monitor going back to a jagged rise and fall.

Aran closed his eyes and caught himself, barely, against the wall as his knees gave out under him.

"Sit." Krevai's voice was gruff. He shoved a chair under Aran, and Aran sank into it. His own breath was coming erratically, but he couldn't afford to pass out.

"I'll—I'll keep an eye on them," he mumbled, not looking up at Krevai. "I know enough about the way we treat the defect in do Sol that I'll be the best person to keep them alive while Dessi does her work."

Krevai nodded, but there was a sharp concern in his face. "Dessi?" he called across the lab.

She looked up.

"How long will this take? I'm not sure our Aran's Istvay has that much longer."

Dessi sighed, a short, sharp sound the told Aran she was as worried about this as he was. "I'm doing the best I can," she snapped. "But the program will take at least twenty-four hours to run once I get it set up."

Krevai glanced over at Aran, almost involuntarily, and Aran sucked in a long breath, held it for a moment, then blew it out.

He'd known this. He'd worked this into his calculations.

But he hadn't anticipated Istvay getting thrown off the yibo medical tech that was keeping them alive before they even reached the university.

Dessi glanced over at him, then turned back to Krevai. "Go find some food. Our Aran looks like he's about to faint."

Aran jerked upright in panic. "No, don't unlock the doors! I—I don't want anyone getting in here until we've dealt with this."

"So we should just let you starve to death? Krevai and I are going to start getting hungry too—"

Aran shook his head, trying to force his brain back into a

functional state. "No, there's food in here, it's in the vending machines—"

Krevai's eyebrows rose in interest. "A vending machine?" he asked.

"It … it sells you food." He could hardly keep the words straight in his head.

"Ah. That seems like a practical mechanism, if your culture has made it taboo to eat the flesh of your enemies."

"It's—it's very taboo to eat the flesh of your enemies," said Aran weakly. "They're—the vending machines are right out that back door there, it just leads to an emergency stairwell. They look like—like a box, and you have to put currency in—" He broke off, and swore as he realized he no longer had any credits to his name.

"Don't worry, I'm sure I'll find a way to get the food out," said Krevai cheerily, starting away.

Aran closed his eyes and leaned back against the wall for a moment, gasping in a quick breath.

And then another alarm sounded from one of the monitors, and he jerked back upright.

Krevai returned a few minutes later with food of some sort—Aran couldn't possibly have told anyone what it was. He shoved it into his mouth because the captain insisted, chewed and swallowed mechanically, but he didn't taste any of it.

The rest of the day passed in a blur. He was aware, dimly, of Krevai pacing back and forth irritably, Zondra hovering over Istvay's cot like an oversized bat, Dessi huddled in the corner over her data pad, but most of his attention was held by Istvay, and the monitors that told him whether or not their heart was still beating. He had to use the defibrillators twice more before the lab grew dark, and Krevai figured out how to turn on the artificial lights. At some point,

Krevai pulled a spare blanket and pillow from a corner that Aran directed him to with the jerk of his chin, comically small for his massive frame, and curled up by the door like a cat. Zondra followed his example a few minutes later.

Dessi was blinking and yawning, and at last she stood, laying the data pad on the table. "It's running," she said, coming over to him. "I can't do anything else right now, and it'll be a few hours still. Do you want me to trade you off?"

Aran shook his head numbly.

There was no way he'd be able to sleep anyways, no matter how tired he was.

Dessi watched him with concern for a moment. At last she sighed. "Alright. I'm going to get some sleep myself, then—wake me if you need anything." She pulled out a blanket and pillow from the cupboard as well, and leaned back against the corner, close to the table where the data pad hummed away.

Every part of Aran's body felt strange and insubstantial, like if he closed his eyes, he might float up to the ceiling, or dissolve into a puddle. But he couldn't close his eyes, not even for a moment, because he couldn't afford to look away from Istvay. And every time he did doze off, for a few seconds or a few minutes, some alarm from the monitors would jerk him back awake, and he'd scramble for a moment, completely disoriented, as he tried to figure out what he could do to save his friend.

He didn't notice the room growing lighter, or hear the raiders waking up, but it all must have happened. The first thing he realized, Dessi was crouched in front of him. "I said," she said, speaking loudly and slowly, as if he were a small child, "The program is finished running."

He stared at her for a moment, as his brain tried to decode her words. Then he swore and jerked upright, and Dessi caught him as he almost keeled over.

"I'm sorry, human," she said apologetically. "But Krevai said we don't need to ask permission to touch you if you're about to die, and with the way you look—"

"It's—it's fine," Aran mumbled. "I don't care. Where's—what have you got?"

Dessi held up the data pad. "I've got the data we need to feed into your genetic splicing mechanism, but I don't know how your technology works."

"It's—we can program it in to a nanovirus." Aran shoved Dessi's hand off his arm and started towards the corner where the nanotech was stored. "We inject a copy of the repaired DNA strand in, and it floods through the body and changes the cell's mechanism to replicate the altered DNA strand. It'll take a little while to take effect, but hopefully—" He swayed, and Dessi caught him.

"Be careful, Aran! I'm not going to do this on my own because you passed out."

He tried for a shaky smile, but he couldn't quite manage it.

They reached the nanotech storage somehow, and he pulled open the freezer, the hiss of liquid nitrogen smoke from the inside enough to make him cough. He shoved on some protective gloves and extracted a vial, then carefully closed the freezer door behind him. He slid the vial into the programming machine on the low table beside it, then activated his palmscreen with a quick squeeze of his hand and tapped it against the machine. "Dessi, feed the information through to the palmscreen," he said in a hoarse voice. He turned over his shoulder. "Krevai. Keep an eye on Istvay. You know what to do if they stop breathing, and if their heart stops again, call me."

Krevai nodded and strode over to Istvay's cot, and Aran turn back to the machine, glancing down at his palmscreen and the data from Dessi's data pad scrawled across it. He checked it quickly, typed in a few commands, then fed it into the machine.

He and Dessi stood there breathlessly as the machine buzzed and whirred. At last, the light blinked blue, and Aran snatched the vial out.

"Get me a needle," he snapped at Dessi, and strode back across the floor to Istvay, rubbing the tube between his hands to warm it.

He knelt beside the cot, and Dessi handed him a needle. He fixed it to the end of the vial with shaking fingers, and straightened Istvay's arm carefully. Their forearm was bruised and purple from the multiple injections in the last few endless hours, but he found the vein and slipped the needle in, the motion by now almost automatic.

He found he was holding his breath as he depressed the back of the vial, the liquid disappearing under Istvay's skin.

He pulled the empty vial free, and it fell from his nerveless fingers and clattered to the floor.

For a long, long moment, the three of them stood there, staring at Istvay.

"How long—" Krevai began.

An alarm on a monitor wailed, and Aran swore and jumped for the defibrillators.

"It will take a few hours, at least," said Dessi grimly, when Istvay's heart rate had returned. "But all Aran's and my calculations say it should work. We'll just have to wait and see."

Aran sank back down in the chair, grateful for the silence. He couldn't have formulated a sentence if he'd wanted to, his mind still flailing in panic, going over and over and over the imagined scenario, Istvay dying even as the cure worked in their veins.

When he looked up again, it was dark.

Krevai had already gone to lie down on his nest of blankets by the door, and Zondra was curled up on the other side of the room, snoring softly. Even Ani had crept under the jacket Aran had dropped on the floor, pulling it over herself with one tentacle, another tentacle reaching out to wrap comfortingly around Aran's ankle. Dessi rose, stretching. "I'd offer to take watch tonight, but I know you'll say no," she said. "Call me if you need me to switch you off."

Aran nodded wearily—he didn't have the energy to do more than that.

Another alarm beeped, and he leaned forward quickly to readjust the oxygen mask over Istvay's mouth and nose. He hesitated, then brushed a strand of sweat-damp hair from their forehead, blinking back tears of exhaustion and strain. "Pishti," he whispered. "Pishti, please. You've got to be okay. You've got to hold on, just a few more hours. You're the most stubborn damn person I know, I know you can hold on for just a few more hours—"

His eyes were falling closed, and he let them for a moment, too tired to fight back the tears any longer.

He blinked awake to sun streaming in through the windows.

It took him a moment to realize what had happened.

And then his mind went blank with panic.

How had he fallen asleep? How had he not woken to the alarms? He should have taken Dessi up on her offer, he should have told her to take watch, he must have slept through an alarm, and Istvay was dead, and it was his fault.

He couldn't bring himself to turn and look. That picture had haunted his nightmares since he was ten years old, and Istvay's mother had gone to sleep one night and had never woken up. Ever since that moment, there had always been that haunting fear in the back of his head that one day, that might be Istvay. That one day, his best friend, the person he loved, the person he didn't know how to live without, would be lying there, still and cold and pale, and there would be nothing at all that Aran could do to change it.

Tears were burning in the corners of his eyes, and he didn't have the energy to wipe them away.

He'd been so damn close. They'd found the cure, they'd gone through hell and back to get Istvay here, and then—and then he'd been too bloody stupid, and he'd slept through the alarms.

He turned his head at last, despair sitting thick and heavy in his stomach.

Istvay lay where he'd left them, very, very still.

For a moment, he thought his heart would actually stop.

And then, with a gasp of relief so strong that it was almost a sob, he realized that the monitors were still running. The alarms hadn't woken him, because Istvay's blood oxygen levels were normal, their heart rate weak, but steady.

He stared for a few moments, not sure if he could actually trust what he was seeing.

And then he dropped his head into his hands and sobbed, thick, choking sobs that racked his whole body.

In the back of his mind he could feel Ani pulling herself up to her usual position on his shoulder, her movements broadcasting alarm, feel her trying to push her bulbous body under his chin to get his attention, hear noises in the background that were probably raider voices and then, at last, feel a hand on his shoulder. But it all seemed very, very far away, like something happening to someone else.

"Aran. Aran!"

Someone was speaking to him, but he couldn't understand the

words they were saying. His body felt oddly distant, and his brain couldn't really make sense of anything that was happening around him.

Something cold splashed across his face, and he jerked his eyes open to see Dessi crouched in front of him, a look of sharp concern on her face. "Krevai, you'd better come. I think we might have killed our human." Her voice was tight with worry.

Aran blinked at her, trying to make sense of her words. Then Krevai was beside her, his face, too, tight with concern, and Aran couldn't entirely understand why.

"Well, he certainly is stressed," Krevai muttered. "Dessi, how long is it been since he slept?"

Dessi shrugged. "I woke up in the middle of the night to come check on his Istvay, and he'd fallen asleep, but before that—" she shrugged helplessly.

Aran was still trying to make the words make sense.

Krevai sighed. "Aran, can I touch you?"

He just blinked at the captain.

Krevai shook his head. "I'm sorry, Dessi, I'm just not sure that I can actually stress him out any more than he already is at this point."

"I think it's probably fine," said Dessi.

Aran felt arms lifting him, and he suddenly realized what was happening, and gasped, "Istvay! Dessi, check on Istvay, I—I think —"

He was deposited in a second cot, and a pillow was shoved under his head. He struggled weakly to sit up, but Dessi's hand on his shoulder pushed him back down.

"Aran," she snapped. "Your Istvay is fine. The treatment worked, and now we just have to give their body time to recover. In the meantime, can you imagine how they'll react if they wake up and you're dead from the stress?"

"I'm not—" he tried, struggling again to sit up. Again, Dessi shoved him back.

"You can sleep, Aran, or I'll give you something that will put you to sleep."

"You've—you've got to take care of Istvay—"

Dessi sighed heavily. "I know how to take care of your Istvay. At this point, I think I have almost as much experience as you do."

"You … you have to—" He was still struggling weakly against her grip.

"Aran." Krevai crouched beside him, face cut with concern. "I swear to you, Aran—you can cut my heart out and eat it in front of my crew if I let your Istvay die while you sleep. Alright?"

Somehow, the captain's words loosened the tension in Aran's body.

He collapsed back on the pillow, and Dessi sighed in relief and pulled the blanket up over him as Ani shoved herself in beside him. "Let me know if you need any—"

Her voice faded into darkness, and he was asleep.

He wasn't sure how long he slept. When at last he blinked his eyes open, looking around in complete disorientation, the morning sun was streaming in through the narrow lab windows.

He must have slept for the rest of the day and through the night. He couldn't remember, for a moment, why he'd been so tired.

Then memories flooded back, and he jerked upright so fast that he almost fell over, staring around wildly as Ani grumbled at the disturbance.

His eyes caught on a familiar form on the cot across from him, hooked up to far too many monitors, but chest rising and falling in a slow, steady pattern. He gasped in a breath, his shoulders drooping with the released tension.

Istvay was sleeping peacefully, the monitors showing a steady heartbeat that was stronger than it had been in days. Some of the colour had returned to their cheeks, the grey cast finally gone from their skin, and they looked better than they had since they'd collapsed in the cabin on Krevai's ship.

Aran sagged back against the wall, so lightheaded with relief he wasn't sure he wouldn't simply fall over.

He heard a crackle of something, and blinked his eyes open to see Dessi beside him. She shoved a package of biscuits into his hands. "Here," she said. "Your blood sugar is low enough that it's going to affect your functioning."

At her words, Aran's stomach rumbled loudly, and he realized, for the first time since Istvay had collapsed, that he was famished. He took the biscuit package from her with shaking fingers. It took him a few tries to get it open, but when he did, he shoved them into his mouth as fast as he could chew them.

He went through three more packets of biscuits, two packets of crisps, and a bottle of fruit juice before Dessi let him get to his feet. Just as well, really. Even after the food he felt shaky, but much less delirious than he had the night before.

He couldn't take his eyes off Istvay.

They'd actually done it. Istvay was getting better. Istvay was going to live. And for the first time in his life, Aran let himself actually believe it.

He had to blink hard to push back the sudden tears.

"Aran?" he could hear the worry in Dessi's voice. "Aran, are you going to go into shock again? Because if you are—"

He shook his head, wiping his hand across his face. "No." His voice came out shaky, but at least he was able to form words. Which was a definite step up from the night before. "No, I'm—it's just—"

he gestured helplessly towards his friend.

Dessi followed his gaze and smiled, a soft, genuine smile, and Aran swallowed hard against a lump in his throat and found that he couldn't speak after all.

He spent the rest of the day hovering by Istvay's cot, and for a wonder, none of the raiders disturbed him, except to force some more food at him. He ate it without tasting it. He knew very well that Istvay wouldn't wake for a while yet. Honestly, he was happy they were sleeping—even with the defect gone, it would take time for their body to repair the damage the defect had inflicted, and the more sleep they could get, especially in the early stages, the better.

But he couldn't seem to take his eyes off them, couldn't seem to keep from running his hands over their face in a sort of awe, resting his hand on their chest to feel the rise and fall of it.

He could hear Krevai and Zondra grumbling to each other in the background, and Dessi answering, her tone as sharp as ever, but he wasn't paying attention to any of it.

At last, as night fell again, there was a sharp *ting* of Krevai's communicator.

"It's Landru," the raider captain said, glancing at Dessi. "I'll let her know we're just waiting for the human to wake up, and we can bring back the solution." He hit the button on his communicator. "Landru?"

"Captain!" Landru's voice was frantic. "The bracelets are failing, faster than we can deal with them! I've done everything our Aran usually does, but it doesn't seem to be working anymore. I doubt I have much time myself." There was a grim tone to her words. "I've instructed everyone to lock themselves in the rooms, and I've hit the control from the outside. I've locked myself in as well, and destroyed the controller. But—but if the charaks take us over, I don't know how long we can—" She broke off. "I'm sorry, Captain. I have to go."

Dessi, Aran, Krevai, and Zondra stared at each other in horror.

Aran's stomach felt like ice.

For a few moments, the only sound in the room was Krevai's cursing.

At last, though, the raider captain turned to Aran. His expression wasn't angry anymore, like it had been almost since Aran had given his ultimatum. It was set and grim, and even paler than usual.

"Well, human," he said quietly. "Let's hope your Istvay feels up to writing their charak solution soon. Because if my crew gets off that ship while they're being controlled—"

He didn't finish. He didn't have to. Aran had seen the attack on the city of Chrr, and he knew exactly what would happen next.

14

The sharp tap of the Speaker's ceremonial staff on the floor of the Council Chambers was such a familiar sound that Alba hardly noticed it. Her nerves were keyed up tightly enough she wasn't sure she was in a position to notice anything but the loudness of her own breathing.

She was outside. They'd decided this would be safest. Feliu and Yosip were standing nearby, within easy earshot, but far enough to intercept any overcurious guard or house staff.

"This Council session is called to order." The speaker's voice through the amplifiers was loud enough even through the earpiece on her wavelink that Alba could hear her perfectly.

The view on her retinal screen told her that the Speaker was the same mousy woman as when Alba had left, and for some reason, that hint of familiarity seemed almost more strange than anything else about this scene.

From the screen Tias had linked through to Alba's retinal screen, she could only see a portion of the room. But she studied it carefully nonetheless, trying to read what in the composition of it had changed since she'd been gone.

She recognized most of the faces in the Judicial Committee, and the majority of those in the People's Committee. But from what she could see of the Military Committee …

She shook her head, her stomach tight.

She'd never gotten along with Cavaco, and she'd always mistrusted the Military Committee in general. But there had been people there she could work with, people whose sense of honour and integrity she trusted, even if their positions had not entirely aligned with hers.

Now, that side of the Council Chambers was filled with hard-faced men and women who she didn't recognize, but whose posture and attitude she recognize perfectly well. Were this the yibo Advisory Chambers, she would've pinned those people immediately as the antihuman faction.

Which, she thought in an odd, half hysterical way, was not that far from the truth, if their politics were as she suspected they were.

"Council in attendance, Acting President and Head of the Council, General Eniko Cavaco. Also in attendance, President Ander Seguir, Head of the People's Committee, and Benadita Oliveira, Acting Chief Justice, and Acting Head of the Judicial Committee."

Alba breathed a small sigh of relief. Acting Chief Justice. They hadn't officially replaced her yet, then. That would make things easier.

"Madam Speaker." Cavaco's voice was the same as it had always been, cold, stern, with just a touch of arrogance to it that had always rubbed Alba the wrong way. "I would like to present a proposal before the Council."

The woman tapped her staff again, and the holoscreens around the room and at the desks flickered to show Cavaco's face.

"Esteemed councillors." There was a grave note to his voice now, a man delivering bad news. "As many of you know, we have been preparing for the last several months—since our Chief Justice and former Head of the Judicial Committee, and the diplomatic party that went with her, disappeared, presumably trapped or killed by aliens—for the time that these aliens would return. And recent events have demonstrated that our concerns were not unfounded. The portal, as you all know, has reopened." He glanced around the room, taking stock of the reactions, and Alba bit back a scoff.

Always one for theatrics, Cavaco.

"Our diplomatic ship was destroyed. That has now been confirmed. But there were survivors, and one of them has made it back through the portal in order to warn us of what awaits on the other side." Cavaco turned to the speaker. "Permission to bring forth my witness?"

"Permission granted," said the woman.

All eyes were on Cavaco, and he knew it, judging from the slow, measured way he turned. "Guards, bring forth the witness."

The guards at the doors to the rotunda pulled them open, and a man stepped through.

Alba had to bite back a gasp.

Mattin, the mutinous former captain of the diplomatic ship, looked much worse for the wear—although he was clean and dressed in fresh clothing, there were dark circles of exhaustion and strain under his eyes, and a haunted, hunted cast to his posture.

He would have been in Chrr, most likely, when the raiders attacked.

Alba fought back a small shiver.

As much as she despised the man, she couldn't wish the brutality and horror of that event on anyone.

"You may approach the stand," said the Speaker.

Mattin strode across the floor of the Council Chambers, and the sound of his boots clicking off the hard floor echoed in the silence.

He paused in front of the podium, as if gathering himself. Then he leaned forward, and the amplifiers picked up his voice, hoarse and exhausted. "Councillors," he said. "I—I hardly know how to address you. This is not how I had hoped to bring you back news. But—" He drew in a deep breath, as if fighting back emotion. "But I feel duty-bound to tell you what I know." He paused, as if searching for words. "As you know, I was the captain of the Firedawn, which was sent out as a diplomatic ship through the portal. En route, the diplomatic scientist, Aran Romeu, made a disturbing discovery that signified that these aliens on the other side of the portal may not be as peaceful as the Chief Justice wished us to believe. However, Chief Justice Espina was completely committed to the mission as she'd set it out before this Council. Despite Aran's advice and my pleading, she refused to give orders to turn the ship around."

Alba narrowed her eyes, and behind her, she could hear Feliu's quiet curse.

She shouldn't have expected anything less, of course, but the memory of the frantic councils in her small cabin, of the terror of stepping into the communications room to warn the crew with the full knowledge that she might be killed for it, the icy, mind-numbing horror of watching a man raise his pistol, the first time she'd ever been threatened like that, the memory of Feliu's eyes widening, his grunt of pain as the shot meant for her hit him, made it difficult for her to retain her equanimity.

"As captain of the ship, I was bound to follow the orders issued by the Chief Justice. Once through the portal, however, every misgiving I'd had was borne out. The portal closed behind us, and the resulting energy bursts were enough to completely break up the diplomatic ship, killing most of those on board. Some few of us managed to escape, but thousands more died in the breakup."

His words brought back the sight that had been seared into Alba's memory—the massive ship exploding into nothingness, its dead pouring out across the empty expanse of space.

"Those of us who survived made it to the nearest planet, which, fortunately, was suited to sustain human life. However, the jungle where we landed was—extremely hostile." He shuddered, and again, Alba bit back a grim smile.

She had survived, and the others with her, because of Aran and Istvay.

Mattin hadn't been nearly so lucky.

"Before we were able to escape the jungle, we lost perhaps half of the people who'd made it onto our escape pod. Vicious animals, even the vegetation itself—everything seemed designed to murder us. And it was only when at last we were rescued and brought before the alien government that I discovered we were not the only survivors. There had been others, led by our Chief Justice. And they had made no attempt whatsoever to find and rescue us.

"At first, I was relieved to hear that she had survived. But as I attempted to communicate with these aliens, I learned that the Chief Justice, in fear of her own life, had sold us out. And not only us, but the entire Joias System. I don't know if it was intentional, or if the strain and the physical toll of her escape had dimmed her cognitive abilities, but she was refusing to enter into any sort of negotiations with these aliens that would lead to peace.

"I knew my duty was to the Chief Justice. But more than that, my duty was to the Joias System. The Chief Justice had not inquired about our survival and had not been informed of it. And so, reluctantly, I took the only course I saw open to me: I began my own negotiations with these aliens, in the hopes of brokering a peace the Chief Justice would not.

"It wasn't too long after this that the Chief Justice and a few of her closest allies fled. I had no idea where she'd gone until much later, but I assumed it was because the aliens, sensing, perhaps, that she was not dealing with them in good faith, began to negotiate with me in earnest, rather than with her. I managed to broker an agreement that would allow the aliens to reopen a portal, this time with the promise of peace. However, before the agreement could be put into effect, the Chief Justice and her people contrived to sabotage and destroy the mechanism that the aliens used to create the portal. I don't know if it was because the strain of her experience had finally driven her mad, or because she simply couldn't bear that her failures become known."

"Captain Mattin." The speaker, Benadita, was the woman who'd replaced Alba as acting Chief Justice. And from the sharp note to her tone, she, at least, had not yet rolled over and showed her belly at Cavaco's threats. "You expect us to believe that the Chief Justice sold out the Joias system, and intentionally stranded you on the other side of the portal, for nothing more than her pride?"

Mattin frowned. "I—as I said, I don't know that this was intentional. She may well have thought she was doing what was best for the system. Mystery knows we'd all been through enough, at that point, to break even the strongest of minds." He paused, shaking his head. "At any rate, I discovered in the course of my negotiations that there was another group of these aliens. These were aliens who'd rebelled against the legitimate government, and whose intent was to use the portal technology to destroy humans as a species. They saw the Joias System as an easy target, and my negotiations with their government was the only thing standing in the way of them obtaining their goals. Because there are …" He paused again, and this time, Alba could hear the tremble in his voice. "There are other aliens in that system, raiders, they call themselves. Aliens who hunt humans as food. These are the aliens that hostile rebels set loose on their own capital city, an attack from which I barely escaped with my life. The rebels intended to allow these creatures through to our system. When I realized their plan, the survivors of the legitimate government helped me and a few others get to a ship to come back and warn you. They've still offered their help, if we will ally with them. But I'm told that already, a raider scouting ship has been sent through the portal. Our time is almost out. If we don't act quickly …" He broke off. The choke of horror in his voice was entirely genuine, and again, Alba squeezed her eyes closed against memories that were enough to bring the acid taste of vomit to the back of her throat.

"And where was the Chief Justice in all of this?" asked another councillor. "Are you accusing her of working with these rebels to destroy our system? Why has she not returned with you?"

Mattin shook his head. "As far as I am aware, the Chief Justice is dead. Perhaps she honestly believed she was doing the right thing— we'll never know. But she had allied herself with the aliens who set these raiders loose on our city. She assisted them in reopening a portal through to our system, once she believed the rest of us were dead and she would be able to control the narrative of what had happened. And after that—they had no further need of her. None of us have heard from her since that time."

There was a long moment of silence. Even in this quiet, Alba could hear the rustle and muttering of the councillors.

At least some of them seemed suspicious of the details of Mattin's story, or of the fact that it was clear there would be no one capable of proving or disproving it.

But—the portal was open. The diplomatic ship had disappeared. Mattin was clearly a man who had been through an experience so traumatic that his hands were still trembling from it. And as far as any of these councillors knew, Alba herself had entirely disappeared.

"I move that, on the strength of Mattin's testimony, the Council grant me the powers to ally with the alien government in order to prosecute a war against those rebels who would see us destroyed." Cavaco's voice rang out over the whispers. "We must not be the easy target they expect us to be. I must be permitted to take whatever action necessary to protect us from destruction by these raiders, and to do so, I must request that the Council grant me all necessary powers."

The room was still buzzing with shock and confusion, and finally the Speaker stepped forward, rapping her ceremonial staff on the ground for order. "Councillors—" she began.

Tais stood. "Madam Speaker. We've heard from Cavaco's witness. But if you recall, I had asked to place another witness on the roster before any motions are passed."

There was a pause, and Alba saw the faint shadow of worry chase itself across Cavaco's face.

The Speaker peered down at her holoscreen, then nodded. "Bring forth your witness." Her voice shook a little.

"My witness was unable to be present physically, but I've asked that they be allowed to present via wavelink."

The Speaker nodded, and tapped her holoscreen.

Alba saw her own face broadcasted across the holoscreens on the walls and in the desks of the councillors.

For a moment, there was silence. And then what could only be described as chaos broke out—councillors shouting, chairs being shoved back.

The Speaker rapped her staff against the floor for a few moments before finally giving up and shouting, "Order!" through the amplifiers, loud enough that it made Alba's ears ring.

At last, grudgingly, the noise dimmed and stilled.

"I call as my witness Chief Justice Alba Espina, Head of the Judicial Committee, and one of the Three Joint Heads of Government," said Tais into the silence.

"The witness may present her testimony." The Speaker sounded half-stunned herself.

Alba stood and cleared her throat. "Councillors," she said, pitching her voice just loud enough to carry. "I apologize for speaking to you like this, rather than in person. I am only able to be with you as I am because a friend was able to escape, and my wavelink is routed through his."

"Escape?" said one of the councillors.

Alba held up a hand to forestall the question. "Mattin's story was more falsehood than truth. After the diplomatic mission had begun, we discovered that the ship records had been tampered with. Additional passengers had been placed on board without our knowledge—soldiers. As Mattin admitted, in the course of the voyage, our diplomatic scientist, Aran Romeu, made some disturbing findings that reopened the question of the wisdom of going through the portal without further studies. We presented his findings to Mattin, but he defied my orders, refusing to turn back. When we tried to alert the crew of the danger, the soldiers executed what I believe to have been a pre-planned mutiny, and forced us through the portal. Once through the portal, the ship broke up—that part, at least, is true—and I and a few members of my diplomatic corps escaped in the confusion.

"Mattin is correct—we made contact with aliens who purported to want an alliance. But what he did not tell you is, the faction of the aliens he was negotiating with wanted an alliance with our system to provide humans as cannon fodder in an internal political struggle they hoped to turn into a war. When I refused to commit our system to such a destructive course of action, Mattin, who stands before you, colluded with the aliens to have me and the surviving members of my diplomatic team murdered."

There was utter silence throughout the Council room. Alba didn't bother to look at Cavaco's face.

"That we survived at all is a testament to the courage and ingenuity of the surviving members of the diplomatic team," she continued. "But one thing which Mattin is not exaggerating is the danger to our system. We were, after an effort that almost killed us and perhaps should have, able to broker a truce that did not involve committing ourselves to die in an alien war. The alien faction with whom we negotiated, which currently holds political power, agreed to return us home and close the portal after us. Their intentions, at the moment, are peaceful. However, if Cavaco insists on allying with their political enemies and thrusting us into war ... I fear very much, my friends and colleagues, that our system will not survive it."

She made the remainder of her account as brief as she could, although there were moments she had to pause to collect herself, the horror and exhaustion and terror of the past few weeks trying to flood into her words. When at last she'd finished speaking, the room was so quiet she could hear every creak of a chair, every rustle of fabric as someone shifted in their seat.

"And when you say the only reason you can speak to us now is that one of your colleagues made an escape," asked one of the councillors at last. "You're speaking of escaping from the aliens?"

"No." Alba's voice was grim. "Because I have no wish to make allegations which I cannot prove, I will not speculate on who might have ordered this. However, I am currently being held at a location somewhere near the city. To the best of my knowledge, the human civilians who came with me, seeking refuge in our system, and the yibos who agreed to bring us back through this portal at considerable risk to themselves, are being held at a military base. There was, indeed, a raider ship that came through the portal, also with a sworn intent of peace, but I have currently no information on where that ship might be, or what might have happened to it. I am certain that none of us here wishes to be the aggressor who, unprovoked, opens a war with an alien society capable of destroying us. Therefore, I can only hope that this was due to some misunderstanding or miscommunication."

The chamber dissolved once more into a flurry of questions and outraged shouts, until the Speaker was forced to shout into the amplifiers to restore order.

"Councillors! I expect the dignity of this chamber to be respected!" she snapped.

"Permission to address the Council, Madam Speaker?" said Benadita, standing quickly. When the woman nodded, she turned to Cavaco. "General." She was speaking through her teeth. "Would you please explain to this Council why you are holding one of the Joint Heads of Government captive?"

"This was not my doing." Cavaco had risen as well, spreading his hands. "I am as surprised as you to learn that the Chief Justice is alive. And as to why my military officers thought it prudent to hold her in a safehouse, I can only speculate that—"

"You are the head of the Military Court, correct?" snapped Benadita. "If your generals are acting outside the scope of your orders, surely you have the power to reign them in? If not, perhaps we should, as a Council, reconsider our confidence in you remaining the Head of the Military Committee."

"If Mattin was lying about this, how are we to believe anything else he's told you?" asked another councillor, once the Speaker had granted them the floor. "It seems to me that our best course would be to call a halt to all military activity in any sector until we are certain the information we are receiving is correct."

"Are you insinuating that Cavaco is intentionally deceiving you?" snapped a member of the Military Committee, standing quickly. "That he is committing treason? If you believe the General would go so far as to—"

"At the moment, it's hardly relevant whether he's intentionally deceiving us, although I should certainly hope that in the future we will investigate that more thoroughly," the other councillor replied. "Regardless of intent, it's clear we cannot trust the information that we have been provided."

In a matter of minutes, the chamber had devolved once more into a shouting match. The Speaker was forced to call for order at least three separate times before it was finally restored.

She glanced around the Council Chambers. "Councillors. I understand that this has been an eventful and unexpected Council session. However, our Council has lived through such events in the past, and I must insist on the decorum due to this chamber!"

When the noise finally died down, she turned to Cavaco. "Councillor Cavaco. There have been a number of questions asked of you in regard to the current apparent captivity of the Chief

Justice. What response do you wish to make?"

Cavaco rose. There was something cold and furious in his gaze, but when he spoke, his voice was as measured as always. "Councillors," he said, looking deliberately around the room. "I am as surprised as any of you by this development. I shall have to speak more in depth with Mattin, but from what I understand of his story, he, too, is shocked by this. I am overjoyed to hear that the Chief Justice has returned to us, alive and apparently unharmed. However, considering the serious nature of the allegations Mattin has made against her, I think it prudent to ask for more witnesses."

"Which, as you know, Cavaco, will be difficult to do if the Chief Justice is being held hostage by your military troops," snapped Benadita, over the noise of the speaker tapping her staff on the floor.

Cavaco held up a hand. "Of course," he said smoothly. "I will look into who gave the orders to hold her, although I'm certain that it was an innocent misunderstanding on the part of one of my soldiers. But, as you say, as head of the military Council, it is my full responsibility to ensure that those under my command are doing their duty to the system. Therefore, I will happily instruct that the Chief Justice be brought back, and when she is ready and willing to stand in front of the Council, we may reconvene." The fury in Cavaco's eyes undermined the smooth neutrality of his tone, but Alba was grudgingly impressed at his delivery.

"Very good," said Benadita, at a nod from the Speaker. "However, considering the number and nature of the ... miscommunications that have plagued this mission—" the sarcasm in her voice was impressive— "I suggest that a committee be formed to observe and oversee the details of returning the Chief Justice to Vila Nova do Sol, and ensuring that she receives the appropriate medical aid, should that be necessary."

Cavaco's shoulders had stiffened at the suggestion. But, Alba knew with grim satisfaction, there was no way he could protest without proving the allegations true.

"Furthermore," continued Benadita, "I suggest that any and all war powers be returned to the Council Body until such time as we can thoroughly investigate this threat. We cannot afford to enter into a war without full understanding of what we are agreeing to." She turned to the speaker. "Madam Speaker, as we have heard all listed witnesses, I propose a vote."

Alba closed her eyes for a moment as the results scrolled over the screen, and she wasn't sure whether it was relief, or anticipation.

But Benadita had made her argument well. The vote returned, split neatly down party lines—eighty-seven percent of the Military Committee voting in favour of granting Cavaco full war powers, eighty-three percent of the remainder of the Council voting to strip them away. Even with the extra Members of Council Cavaco had been granted, the vote passed at well over the fifty percent necessary.

Alba sank back into her seat, almost dizzy with relief, as the councillors discussed the makeup of the committee that would oversee her and the others being returned to the city. And then, at last, the meeting ended and her wavelink went blank.

Alba dropped her head against the back of her chair and closed her eyes in relief.

They hadn't beaten Cavaco, perhaps—they still had to refute Mattin's story, and Alba was certain even now, he and Cavaco were holed up in Cavaco's office, attempting to find a way to damage her credibility.

But the Council hadn't started a war. He hadn't been granted war powers. Going forward, he would have to convince the majority of the Council to agree with any redeployment of troops or weapons.

It wasn't a total victory. But it was more than she'd dared hope.

It wasn't long after that that the first communication from outside, not routed through Aran's wavelink, came through. It was a member of the committee, who let them know, politely, that the military captains had been ordered to reopen the communications through to the safehouse. And not long after that, the military captains themselves appeared, apologizing profusely for the misunderstanding, and asked if they would be so kind as to ready themselves to be transported into do Sol.

It wasn't as if any of them had many personal belongings to pack. It only took Alba a few minutes to ready herself, and then she sat with Yosip and Feliu on the sun-soaked patio, drenched in the hot, lazy scent of autumn blossoms, and waited for their escort to arrive to bring them to the military transport.

There were a few moments, en route, that Alba wondered if the soldiers might simply shoot them down, and pretend there had been an accident—but it seemed Cavaco had been too thoroughly discredited to trust his luck to such strategies.

And then they were inside the city proper, and the transport came to a smooth halt.

Two military escorts were waiting for her outside as the three of them disembarked from the military transport.

"Madam Chief Justice," one of them said, nodding to her.

Alba frowned, glancing around. "I was under the impression that the members of the committee would be on hand when we disembarked."

The man nodded. "I was asked to bring you to them. If you'll please follow me …"

Something uneasy stirred in Alba's stomach. "I think it best that we wait for them here," she said sharply. "Considering that Cavaco's witness has accused me of treason, I hardly think it prudent to take any further action without at least checking in with them."

She could see, from the corner of her eye, Yosip's and Feliu's postures tensing as well. The hatch of the military transport was already swinging shut behind her, and two more soldiers had drifted idly around, standing behind the group.

Alba saw the way their hands were tucked into their jackets.

Perhaps before, she would have been too naïve, or at least, too blindly confident in her own importance, to believe in a potential physical threat.

But she'd seen, now, what it looked like when someone was hiding a weapon.

"I'm sorry, Chief Justice," said the soldier stolidly. "I'm afraid these are my orders."

"I shall contact them myself, then," said Alba, blinking to activate her wavelink.

The council members didn't answer their lines. And when she refocused her gaze on the soldier in front of her, he was wearing a small, thin smirk that did nothing to reassure her.

"As I said, Madam Chief Justice," he said, his tone soft, but with a sharp edge of menace under it. "I think, for your safety, you'd best come with me."

"I think perhaps he's right," Yosip whispered, coming up to stand beside her.

She closed her eyes and drew in a deep breath. At last, she nodded, trying to ignore the way her heart was pounding in her chest.

The other councillors knew where she was. They'd been tracking the military transport. Whatever this was, whatever final gamble Cavaco was making, she would simply have to trust that the committee would see through it.

"Very well," she said. "Lead the way."

The soldiers stepped up around her small group, and led them out of the hangar a back way. Alba caught a glimpse, through one of the side alleys, of commotion from the street outside. But before she had time to figure out what was going on, she had been bundled into another small military transport, the windows blacked out.

Even from inside the transport she could hear the chaos in the streets, but she had no way of knowing what it portended.

"Feliu," she whispered as they rode. "Do you have any idea what's going on?"

He shook his head tightly. "Our wavelinks have been jammed again."

She blinked her wavelink open, then swore under her breath.

Feliu was right.

The building they pulled up to this time was small and drab and grey, a military building at the base on the northeast side of the city, most likely. They were bundled inside, and taken down to a suite of bare, sterile rooms.

"You will find cleansing facilities and beds, and we will bring you dinner as soon as possible. We want to ensure your comfort," said her escort, his voice showing not a hint of irony.

"I—" Alba began, but soldiers herded her and the others inside before she could finish. The steel door clicked shut behind them, and she heard a lock fastening.

"Madam. I'm certain the committee will immediately call Cavaco to account the moment they realize that he's not been dealing honestly with them," said Feliu.

Alba shook her head. "This is far too easy a ruse to see through. He couldn't possibly expect them to accept that we've simply disappeared. So what is he after?"

Feliu shook his head, and didn't answer.

They'd been sitting in the small, cramped room for almost two hours when the communication lines of the prison, set into the ceiling, crackled.

And then she heard a voice that she recognized immediately.

"Citizens of do Sol," said Cavaco. "Please do not be alarmed. At this time of grave danger to our civilization, and indeed to our species as a whole, I have taken the unprecedented step of placing my military in command of the government. This is a temporary measure, and will last only until this threat can be dealt with. I have no intention of harming any of our citizens, only protecting you, so that the internal disagreements of the Council will not prevent me from taking the defensive actions you have trusted me to take. As soon as the threat is dealt with, I will once again hand the reins of government over to our democratically elected officials. But in the meantime, I consider it my highest duty to the Joias system to keep you safe from threats both internal and external."

There was a long moment of silence after the message had faded away.

Alba, Feliu, and Yosip stared at each other. Feliu had gone very pale, and Yosip sank down on one of the cots.

"A coup," he said, his voice soft and horrified. "That was what he was after."

Alba nodded heavily, her tongue thick with dread. "So it would appear."

15

Savina

Savina sat in the back of the farmer's transport, shoved up beside Nicolau and Joska on one side, and a towering stack of smoked hams on the other. The overpowering tang of salt and spices from the meat roiled in her stomach as the transport bumped along above the rough dirt track that led down the side of the mountain.

Beni had stretched out on a pile of boxes and closed their eyes, and seemed to have fallen asleep, and Savina scowled at her sibling.

Beni had always been able to sleep anywhere.

"We're getting close to the city," the farmer called back over her shoulder, her voice muffled through the stacks of produce and meat. "I'll have to drop you at the edge, but you should be able to take public transport from there to where you're going."

"Thank you!" Joska called up, shifting in her seat to turn enough that her reply would be audible.

"At least they're not going to assume anyone in their right mind would travel in one of these things," Savina muttered sourly.

On the other side of the transport bed, Nicolau leaned up against the back with Ines, pointing out the view through a small crack in the hull of the transport. He was whispering to her, the words inaudible over the grinding and shifting of the transport, but the enthusiasm in his voice unmistakable.

Once again, Savina felt a stabbing ache through the centre of her chest at the sight of them.

They hadn't known each other at all before they were thrust together by circumstance. They, too, had come back to a world they'd never thought they'd return to. And now that they were back, Nicolau was clearly overjoyed to show Ines every part of his world, and learn about every part of hers, and Ines was clearly more than happy to reciprocate.

And Reka ...

She had to suck in a quick breath, the sharp pain almost too much to bear.

Joska followed her gaze. Her expression, when she glanced back at Savina, was kind and understanding, and made everything so much worse.

Savina turned her face away and squeezed her eyes closed angrily against the sting of tears.

It didn't matter. Reka wasn't worth being hurt over—just a stupid, bigoted, self-important government agent, who only cared about power and her own position.

But even as she thought it, her mind pulled up the sight of Reka standing in the mouth of an alley in Clirr, her posture tight and face set, telling Savina to leave, go somewhere safe—but she was going to stay and try to save the desperate band of captive humans, even though she knew she wouldn't survive it. Reka's expression after they'd crashed on the small moon, Kachik's soldiers after them, and Savina had asked, in despair, why they couldn't just give up. *"Because*

I can't just let them kill you," she'd said, the words sharp with desperation. The gentleness in Reka's hands as she'd bound Savina's wounds, held her as she cried, stroked her hair and kissed her and told her it would be alright.

The tears were blurring Savina's vision despite her best efforts, and she clenched her teeth.

Reka could damn well burn.

She felt Joska's hand, warm on her shoulder. "Savina," she said quietly. "Do you want to talk about anything?"

Savina shook her hand off and wiped her eyes on her sleeve, then turned and gave Joska a bright smile. "I don't know what there is to talk about."

Joska sighed, but didn't say anything more. Her eyes, though, were dark with sympathy.

Savina swore under her breath.

This would teach her to open up to people again.

She still wasn't sure which was worse—the fact that Reka had betrayed her, or the fact that Joska hadn't.

When at last the transport shuddered to a halt and the farmer's husband came around back to open the hatch, Savina had managed to shove thoughts of Reka to the back of her mind. The place where she kept the memories of her parents, and of the compound, and everything else that had the power to cut her open.

They climbed out of the transport, and Savina drew in a long breath of the evening air, finally away from the thick miasma of salted smoked ham.

"Thank you," Joska was saying to the man, pressing his hand gratefully.

"Yes, we appreciate it so much!" Savina gave him a wide-eyed smile that made Nicolau give a quick, involuntary glance in her direction, his expression so panicked that she almost laughed despite herself.

The man nodded. "Best of luck to you," he said quietly. Then he climbed back into the transport, and it rose back into the air and jolted forward, leaving the five of them alone at the outskirts of do Sol.

They made their way to a public transport, and Ines purchased tickets. There were soldiers, their weapons held loose in their hands, standing outside the entrance and planted throughout the terminal, and soldiers striding by in the streets.

Savina kept the pleasant, innocent smile on her face, and a look of wide-eyed wonder, a Rim Mountain village girl who'd never been to the big city, like she'd done so many times before when it was just her and Beni. But the fact that it wasn't just her and Beni—that Nicolau and Joska and Rafel were with her, too, and that these soldiers wouldn't hesitate to kill them if for one moment they guessed who they were—made it hard to keep from glancing over her shoulder, and her hands, tucked into her jacket pockets as if against the cold, were clutched tight on the handles of her throwing knives.

The transport that made a stop near the ports arrived an interminable twenty minutes later, and by the time it did, Savina's grin felt painted on her face, strained and uncomfortable. But no one gave them a second glance as they stepped onto the crowded transport and found places to sit or stand, and no one gave them a second glance when they finally disembarked on the dirty, narrow streets of the ports district.

Once they were all off and the transport had pulled away, Rafel jerked his chin towards a small, narrow street that ended at a fence, garbage blown and caught in its stones, and on the other side of it, a dirty open-air park, dimly lit in the rapidly darkening evening.

They climbed the fence, Rafel with some difficulty, and followed him into the shadows under the trees. There were tents near some of the thicker stands of brush, and Savina could smell the scent of campfire smoke or burning charcoal. "Peacekeepers come through here once a month or so and throw everyone out, but it's the best shelter on this side of the city, so people always come back," Rafel whispered as they moved towards an unoccupied clearing. "I stayed here once or twice myself, back before I signed on with the captain." He turned his head and spat on the ground. "Damn the peacekeepers, is what I say."

Savina could hardly argue with that.

When they reached a stopping place, they shrugged into the long farmer's jackets they'd borrowed from the villagers, pulling up the hoods to hide their features.

"I don't know for certain where they'll be holding the ships," Rafel whispered. "But they'll almost certainly be down here by the ports. I haven't been in the army in ten years, but I have friends, and there are only so many places big enough to hold yibo transport ship. I'm sure that's where they'll have taken the *Dolphin* as well. Follow me. They're all within walking distance from here, but we'll have to be careful with the soldiers around."

'Within walking distance' was a relative term, Savina thought sourly hours later. The uneven cobblestones under her boots had tripped her more than once, and her feet ached, her lungs protesting at the thinner atmosphere here than on the planets she'd spent her time on in the yibo system.

They'd been to three of the sites Rafel had guessed might hold the ships and the prisoners, but none of them had had the military presence outside to make it likely that anyone or anything important was being held within. There were soldiers patrolling the streets in the port sector, more than should have been necessary, but it was all but impossible to tell what exactly they were guarding. More than once the small group of them had been forced to shove themselves into the mouth of an alley or the doorway of an abandoned building, holding their breaths.

They were approaching the fourth possibility now. Rafel, who was in the lead, gestured behind him for silence, then stepped forward around the corner of a street.

As the minutes stretched on and he didn't return, Savina felt a spike of worry. She turned to Joska, opening her mouth to whisper something—then Rafel stepped back around the corner and beckoned them forward, his movements sharp and excited.

When the rest of them reached him, he whispered, "I think we've found it. There's a military docking facility ahead of us, and it's crawling with soldiers."

When Savina peered around the corner, she could see what he meant—there were at least three dozen soldiers patrolling the streets, and more stationed outside the doors.

She drew back. "How in the hell do you want us to get in there?" she hissed.

Rafel gave her a grim smile. "Believe me, assassin, you aren't the only one who knows how to playact. I'll keep their attention; you and the captain are going to have to figure out the rest."

Savina scowled at him as he pulled a flask from his pocket, trying not to let the worry show in her face. She could smell the contents of the flask when he uncorked it—cheap liquor, the kind you drank when you didn't have money or the prospect of getting more, and you wanted to forget about all your problems in the quickest and most efficient way. He took a mouthful, swished it around in his mouth, and spat, then dribbled liberal amounts down the front of his shirt. Finally, he tipped some into his hands and slapped it onto his cheeks like cologne.

Savina had to stop herself from stepping back involuntarily. He smelled like he'd been on a twenty-four-hour bender.

He shoved the flask back into his pocket, pulled off the dark farmer's coat and balled it into the corner of a boarded-up doorframe, and gave them a small smile. "Don't take too long to get in. I don't know how long they'll put up with me before they get tired of it."

He didn't say what they'd do to him if they got tired of his act. He didn't really need to.

"Be careful." Joska's voice was tight with concern. "If you get in trouble—"

"Worry about yourself, Captain," he said, his own voice gruff. "I've told you a hundred times, if you stopped worrying about everyone else for long enough to take care of your own self, you'd be better off."

"Wealthier, maybe," Joska said quietly. "Not better off." It sounded like an argument they'd had plenty of times in the past. "And if you want me to take care of myself, start by taking care of my crew." She squeezed his shoulder affectionately, and he turned quickly away.

Savina watched after him as he stepped out onto the street, weaving unsteadily on his feet, and tried to ignore the twist of worry in her stomach.

"He'll be alright, Savina."

She jumped and cursed, turning to glare at Joska. "I'm not worried about him," she hissed in a whisper.

Joska's mouth twitched at the corners, but she just turned to beckon to Nicolau and Ines. "Come on, no use in wasting the distraction he's giving us," she whispered. "I'll call Reka, let her know we're on our way."

They made their way quickly and carefully down a street and towards the back of the building. Every so often they'd cross a side-street that connected to the street Rafel had taken, and every time, Savina found herself glancing down it, trying to catch a glimpse of him.

She did, once or twice—he was standing in front of a small knot of soldiers, arguing belligerently. More soldiers were drifting over, drawn by the spectacle, and she could make out, faintly, some of his words: "Bloody disgrace, not to let an old soldier in here. Heard about the aliens, don't think you can trick me. I served my time, you can look up my record. Honourable discharge, and I lost m' damn leg for it, and you lot won't even let me take a look inside."

Then they were around the back.

There were still soldiers here, but they seemed distracted by the commotion out front.

Joska turned to Savina, a stern expression on her face, and Savina gave her an innocent look. "I know," she mouthed. "No killing unless I have to."

She pulled her hood back and stepped forward towards one of the guards, eyes wide, steps faltering. When he turned to scowl at her, she smiled brightly, pulled out one of her knives, and slid it quickly up the inside of his arm. Blood spurted out in a red spray, and as he opened his mouth to shout, Savina stepped up beside him, throwing her arm around his neck and clapping a hand over his mouth.

There was a moment of stifled shouting, muffled by the commotion at the front of the building, and then he went limp, and Savina lowered him to the ground.

"Savina!" Joska stepped forward quickly, and Savina could hear the anger in her tone. "I thought you said—"

She looked up from where she was crouched beside the soldier, and yanked the tourniquet tight. "I didn't kill him," she said brightly. "A blood transfusion, a few weeks in the hospital, and he should be good as new." She paused. "He'll lose his arm, with how tight I had to tie the tourniquet, but ..." she shrugged. "You didn't say anything about limbs."

Joska stared at her for a moment, then shook her head, the expression on her face a mixture of horror and amusement. "Well," she said at last, "you did keep him alive, I suppose. And that will teach me to be more specific." She sighed, and beckoned Nicolau and Ines forward. "Let's get going, before they discover him."

Savina pulled out the soldier's ID chip, rolled him over, pulled open his eyelids to reveal his sightless eyes, and blinked twice to activate her wavelink's recording device. When it had finished reading, she stood. "There," she whispered. "Let's go."

She paused at the lock to the door, and waited for Beni to sign her in, like the two of them had done so many times in the past. Her wavelink replicated the man's key, retina scan and biometrics, and the door lock whirred and clicked open. Then the two of them stepped through, and Joska, Nicolau, and Ines followed.

Once inside, they started off down the hallways, keeping to the sides of the walls. The place was crowded with soldiers, but then, all of them had plenty of experience in the recent past with getting places undetected.

And then, at last, they reached the entrance to what must be the hangar bay.

Again, Beni bent over the lock control, and Savina stepped close, allowing her wavelink to copy over the soldier's credentials.

The lock clicked, and the door slid open.

And there, in front of them, was the massive yibo transport ship, soldiers standing guard on all corners.

They turned as Savina and the others stepped through, and Savina hissed to Joska, "Permission?"

She didn't actually need Joska's permission anymore, but somehow, it had become a habit.

She was pulling out her knives even as Joska sighed, and she sent them through the throats of two of the soldiers guarding the *Dolphin*. "Get in there!" she hissed. "Once they open fire, we're done. Beni, get on the yibo weapons."

The others were already sprinting towards the *Dolphin* as shots hissed around them. Savina stepped behind the shelter of the doorway and yanked out the yibo gun she'd been carrying. She aimed and fired, and the entire knot of soldiers who were running towards her evaporated. She turned the weapon on the soldiers lining up shots on Joska and Nicolau, and a moment later, they were nothing but a fine dusting of ash.

The other soldiers had stopped, horrified, and Savina called out in a cheerful voice, "Sorry! We're just coming for our ship, don't mind us. We don't want any trouble. But if one of you puts one damn finger on the trigger of your weapons, or so much as thinks about putting a call in—" she raised her weapon suggestively.

The others were inside the *Dolphin* now, and she breathed in a quick sigh of relief.

"Stand down and drop your weapons," came Nicolau's voice over the *Dolphin's* amplifier. "We've got larger versions of the weapon you just saw on this ship. Put down your weapons and surrender, or there won't be anything left of you."

The soldiers looked at each other. Then, one by one, they slowly began laying down their weapons.

It would give them time, but Savina wasn't stupid enough to believe they hadn't already put a call out. They had minutes, at best, before they were all dead.

"Get the ship started up, and get ready to blast your way out," she hissed through her teeth. "Joska, it's your damn ship now, so don't give me any bloody lip. I'm going to get as many of the people on the yibo ship out as I can."

She was already running across the floor as the *Dolphin* hummed to life. The soldiers stepped back out of her way, and she pushed her elbow into her side to hold back the sharp stitch, cursing under her breath.

She pointed her weapon at the hatch of the yibo ship and fired as she got close enough, but the material held.

Of course. It was yibo technology, it would be designed to resist yibo weapons.

"Open the damn hatch!" she shouted through the yibo communicator she still carried from her time in the system. "It's me, Savina. And I'm about to bloody get shot if you don't!"

There was a moment where nothing happened. Savina was cursing steadily.

If this didn't work ...

And then the hatch creaked and began to lower, and she sucked in a quick breath of relief.

Already from outside the room she could hear boots pounding down the corridors towards them. They had maybe seconds at this point.

"Savina ..." Beni's voice over her communicator was sharp with worry.

"I'm fine," she snapped. "Get the ship up, and be ready to fire on the soldiers coming through the door. If Joska doesn't want to do it, you take the controls, but tell that woman that these are damn soldiers, not civilians, and we've just started our own Mystery-damned war, so she'd damn better not start exercising her scruples now."

The hatch was half-way down now, its movement slow and ponderous.

"Come on!" she snapped over her communicator. "We're not going to get your ship out. Send out everyone who's willing to come with Joska and me, and get yourselves into the *Dolphin*. But don't come unless you're willing to do what we did back in the yibo system. This is a war."

Again, there was a moment where she wasn't certain they'd heard her, or if they had, if they'd reply.

And then a woman she recognized from one of the human villages swung herself off the side of the still-lowering ramp.

"Go!" Savina snapped, gesturing to the *Dolphin*, and the woman nodded and ran.

A handful of others, some who she recognized, some who she didn't, followed the woman, and then more. She was sure she caught a glimpse of at least a couple of the violent criminals she'd trained for their attack on Chrr, and others who'd worked with Reka.

The footsteps outside were growing louder, and when she glanced over her shoulder, the first handful of soldiers rounded the corner.

"Shoot them, damn you!" Savina shouted into her communicator, and then there was a blast of blinding light from the ship. When it cleared, what was left of the soldiers painted the walls and floor.

"There's no more time," she shouted through to the yibo ship. "Shut the hatch, that's all we've got time for, and damn well lock down. We'll come back for the rest of you if we can, but it's not likely."

Then Savina turned and ran after the last group of humans, heading for the *Dolphin*.

She pounded across the floor, and reached the ship along with the last of the stragglers. The hatch was already closing as she scrambled inside, and whoever was on the guns had shot twice more, turning the soldiers into bloody fragments. But it wouldn't last forever, and unless they got the *Dolphin* out soon, Savina was certain the military would cut its losses and bomb the whole place, killing not only them, but every yibo and human civilian in the transport ship.

"Go!" she shouted as the door clicked shut, and sprinted down the now-crowded corridors towards the cockpit. "Go, now! We're going to have to blow our way out of here." She paused. "Is Rafel …"

"He's fine. He got out as soon as they started to realize there was something going on inside the building. He's going to meet us in the park," said Joska shortly as Savina stepped into the cockpit. Her face was set and grim, and Savina knew, abruptly, who'd been on the guns. "Strap in, we're getting out of here before anyone else gets hurt."

The *Dolphin* rose gently, spun in the air, and hovered for a moment. Then a white-hot blast seared through the air towards the massive bay doors. Before the echoes had time to die down, Joska fired twice more, and at last, the doors crumpled.

The *Dolphin* shot forward, bursting out of the hangar and into the evening air, skimming low over the buildings of do Sol and away.

16

Aran

Aran closed his eyes, focusing hard to try to block out the shouting. It wasn't aimed at him, but somehow the sound of raised voices always yanked his mind back to a time when it usually had been, and opened something small and shaky in his chest.

He drew in a steadying breath, and readjusted his hands over his ears.

Currently, the shouting was between Krevai and Zondra.

"Our Istvay is Sharda's crew, and I'm here representing Sharda. And if I say we wake them up—" Zondra was yelling.

"Sharda clearly has no idea how to deal with humans!" Krevai was shouting back. "Did you see what the lot of you did to our Aran's Istvay? They were in perfectly good health when they left my crew. And then our Aran gets them back, and they look like they've lost about half their body weight! I even saw your Sharda grabbing them without asking permission, and shouting at them, while they were in the room! Anyone who treats humans like that shouldn't be allowed to keep them!"

There was a momentary pause, as all three raiders glanced guiltily to the corner where Aran was crouched by Istvay's cot, his hands clasped over his ears.

Aran studiously avoided their gazes.

The argument resumed, but this time in awkward shout-whispers. "The Istvay may be your Sharda's crew, but they're my Aran's mate. And they're the only chance we have at this point of getting rid of the charak infestation, so believe me when I say I will cut your heart from your chest if you try to touch them right now!" Somehow, Krevai managed to make his whisper loud enough that Aran could probably have heard it from outside the door and down the hall.

He took a deep breath, and tried to force back his pounding headache.

Ani, who'd clearly picked up on his mood, was huddled on his shoulder, growling uneasily.

"Pishti," he whispered, reaching out towards his friend. Their vital signs had improved significantly in the past few hours, but Aran wasn't certain how many more hours he'd survive the shouting. And … well, he'd heard Landru. The charaks must have taken over Krevai's entire raider crew. She'd been smart enough to take precautions, but he'd seen raiders fight, and he was damn sure the precautions, whatever they were, wouldn't last long. Charaks fed on decaying flesh, and since they didn't have a physical form that was capable of hunting, they used their hosts to hunt for them.

And he'd seen how very efficiently raiders could provide dead bodies, especially in an unsuspecting city like do Sol.

He gritted his teeth, hand hovering over Istvay's shoulder.

At last, gently, he grasped their shoulder. "Pishti? Can you hear me?"

Istvay sucked in a sharp gasp, and their eyes flew open. "Aran!"

their tone was panicked, their voice hoarse from disuse. "Aran? Where's—" Their gaze flicked frantically around the room. When it finally rested on Aran, Istvay's entire body sagged with the sudden release of tension. "You're alright. Thank the damn Mystery! I had the most horrible dream—" They broke off. "Aran? What's wrong? For hell's sake—"

Aran shook his head, grabbing their hands in his and blinking tears from his eyes. He couldn't speak at all, and he was pretty sure it would be a moment before he'd be able to.

"Oh hell, Aran, don't cry, please don't cry. What's wrong? What happened?" Istvay pushed themself up on their elbows, wincing, and glanced around the room.

Aran wanted to reassure them, wanted to say ... something, anything, but he couldn't manage it.

Istvay was alive. They were alive, and they were getting better, and the cure they'd both spent so much pain and blood and anguish to find had worked, and here he was, crying like an idiot and unable to form a sentence.

Istvay noticed the shouting raiders across the room, and their expression went dark. "Would you please shut the hell up?" they snapped.

All three raiders turned at the sound of Istvay's voice, startled into silence.

"If you need to scream about something, go do it in another room, for hell's sake! Aran doesn't like loud noises."

There was another moment of silence.

Then Krevai was striding across the room towards them, Zondra and Dessi close behind.

"Istvay! You're awake! That's fantastic news. Now, let's get you hooked up to some sensors, try to analyse how the cure worked—"

Dessi was bending over Istvay with a handful of medical paraphernalia.

"Istvay! Captain Sharda demands that you replicate your solution for the charaks immediately—" Zondra snapped at the same time, while Krevai, speaking over her, bellowed, "Istvay! It's good to have you back!" He seemed to remember, suddenly, that he and the human members of his crew were not on good terms at the moment, and his expression turned from one of delight to a scowl. "Our Aran caused quite the stir trying to save you," he grumbled. "And no one can say I didn't keep my part of the bargain. But considering there's a very good chance that the raiders on my ship are going to get off my ship and destroy your entire system, I suggest you get to work getting that solution for the charaks you were developing."

Istvay grimaced, putting their hands over their ears. "Good hell, Aran, I think I understand how you feel," they muttered. They still looked disheveled and exhausted, and like it had been at least three months since they'd had a good night's sleep. But there was a glint in their eyes and an energy to their movements that hadn't been there for—well, Aran wasn't quite sure. He wasn't sure he'd noticed exactly when it had stopped, but now that it was back, it was so achingly familiar that it was about to make him cry again.

Istvay looked at him, a small, soft smile on their face, and ran a hand along Aran's cheek, and Aran had to squeeze his eyes shut against the tears.

Then they sighed, turning back to the raiders. "Listen. I'm more than happy to help you solve whatever the hell problem we're all in the middle of right now. But would you please give me five minutes to talk to Aran alone?"

The raiders looked at each other for a moment. Then Dessi glanced down at Aran and yelped. "Go! Go on, both of you! To the other side of the room, now! Look at our Aran, he's clearly stressed. You really want one of them to keel over and die right now? I have told you and told you and told you about loud noise around humans ..." She shoved Krevai and Zondra back, and they went with surprisingly few protests.

And finally, Aran and Istvay were alone—or, as alone as they could be, in a wide-open research laboratory in a university with three raiders who measured in at well over two metres on the other side of the room watching them with intense interest.

Istvay closed their eyes in relief, then ran their hands down Aran's shoulders, squeezing his arms. "Alright," they whispered. "It's alright. Take your time, Aran, I'm right here. Take as long as you need."

Aran drew in a few deep breaths, and finally managed to force himself to form words. "Pishti," he whispered, swallowing hard. "Pishti, I—I thought you were going to die. You almost died so many times, and ... and now you're here, and—"

"Shhh, I'm right here, you don't have to cry." Istvay reached up, sliding their fingers into his hair and stroking his cheek with their thumb. "I'm alright, I'm ..."

And then, for the first time, they seemed to actually realize where they were, and why.

Their face went very, very pale.

They glanced up at the monitors, then over at Aran. "Aran," they whispered. And then they seemed completely unable to continue.

Aran managed a weak smile. "Yeah," he whispered. "We—we got you through the portal and down to do Sol. And ... and the cure worked. Or at least, it seems to have. How are you feeling?"

There was another long, long moment of silence. Istvay was so pale Aran was almost worried that they would pass out.

Then, at last, they closed their eyes, reached up, and pulled Aran down into a kiss.

Aran was laughing and crying, and there were tears running down Istvay's cheeks as well, and their lips were salty with tears, and somehow the kiss was better than Aran could have possibly imagined.

When at last the two of them broke apart, Istvay shook their head in disbelief. "I can't believe …" They trailed off, their voice stunned.

"I know," Aran whispered. "Me neither." He blinked back the tears that wouldn't seem to stop forming in his eyes. "I told you we'd get you a cure. I told you."

Istvay managed a weak chuckle, wiping at their own eyes. "I guess I should have listened to you earlier." Their voice was suspiciously thick. They cleared their throat and glanced over at the corner where the raiders were still gathered, watching the two of them with sharp eyes. "While we're on the topic—what exactly was everyone shouting about?"

Aran groaned internally. "Um. So here's the thing—we got you down here, but, um, there were a few complications …"

By the time Aran had finished explaining, Istvay was already scrambling out of bed, yanking the medical sensors from their arms and chest with blatant disregard. "Damn it to hell, those idiot raiders could have woken me up sooner," they muttered, and Aran had to jump to his feet to grab them as they swayed.

"Easy there," he managed, catching Istvay before they toppled over. "You're doing a lot better, but you literally almost died just a couple days ago. More than once. I think I had to hit you with the defibrillator something like six times. You probably have burn marks."

"Istvay!" Dessi was hurrying over. "You can't just pull those out, we need to take some measurements—"

Istvay groaned in frustration. "Listen," they said through their teeth. "I appreciate the concern, Dessi, but either the cure worked, and I'm going to be alright, or it didn't, and I'm going to die anyways, and either way, I should probably start working on the damn solution to the charak problem before everyone in the system is killed!"

"That's not exactly true, your body has been severely weakened by the genetic defect, and even if we've cured the underlying problem —"

Istvay closed their eyes. "Please," they said, their voice taking on the tone that Aran recognized as Istvay trying very hard not to swear. "I understand that I am incredibly lucky to be alive right now. I also understand there are a lot of people who won't be alive in a few hours if we don't figure something out, and that our good friend Emeric Furtado is probably on this side of the portal and, as we speak, actively working to sabotage us. So. Can someone please bring me to a table and give me something to write on?"

Krevai and Zondra jumped into action, and a moment later, one of the small research tables had been forcibly uprooted from its position in the floor, the legs snapped off to appropriate lengths, and then the whole thing dumped in front of Istvay, along with a handful of writing instruments.

Istvay was swaying on their feet by this point, Aran's arm around their waist the only thing holding them upright.

"Pishti, please at least sit down," said Aran, and Istvay glanced over at him, irritation clear on their face. When they saw his expression, theirs softened.

"Alright," they said. "I'll sit, and you can help me. But we've got to get this figured out."

"I know," said Aran, his own voice grim.

Istvay dropped down into the chair Dessi shoved at them and pulled up the data pad she thrust into their hands. They glowered down at it for a few moments, a tight frown pinching between their eyebrows.

"Aran," they said quietly. "What do we have? I—" They ran a hand across their face in a weary gesture. "I'm going to be honest, everything that's happened in the last little while is a bit of a blur. Do we have any of our old notes?"

Aran fumbled around in his jacket and pulled out a handful of paper scraps. "I've got these—that's the last thing the two of us were working on together. And we have the sensor data we were working with, and some of the other analyses." He squeezed his hand to activate his palmscreen, and held it out to Istvay. Istvay glanced over it, paging through the screens, and shook their head slowly. "I have no damn idea where I was going with this." Aran could hear the frustration in their tone. "I know it had something to do with bioelectric signatures, but I have no idea how we got around the fact that the initial charak infestation would short out what we did with the bracelets."

"Sorry, Pishti," Aran mumbled, a thick knot of guilt in his stomach.

Istvay looked over at him, their expression immediately contrite. "No, Aran, I didn't mean—" They sighed. "Burning the notes was your best option. Honestly, it was a stroke of genius—that was the only possible way you could have ensured the raiders couldn't threaten you into revealing it. The only flaw in the plan was that apparently, my damn brain hasn't decided to start working yet." They squeezed their eyes shut. "I guess we start from the beginning." There was a forced cheerfulness in their voice.

From over their shoulder, Zondra growled, a soft, menacing sound. Istvay turned to glare at her. "If you want to do this yourself, be my guest," they snapped. "But if you want me to do it, you're just going to damn well have to be patient. Aran and I will get it done as fast as we can."

Zondra's smile was smooth with menace. "I see you haven't lost your sharp tongue," she purred.

Istvay narrowed their eyes. "And I'm sure Sharda will have plenty to say about it when I get back. But until then, kindly let us do our work."

Zondra opened her mouth as if to speak again, but Krevai grabbed her and hauled her bodily across the room, and Aran could hear their furious whispered argument from the corner.

Istvay turned back to Aran, a grim smile on their face, exhaustion showing through every line of their posture. "Well," they muttered. "I guess we should get started."

17

Alba

Alba closed her eyes, sucking in a deep breath.

A coup. A military coup. In retrospect, it was obvious that was what Cavaco had been planning all along. She'd been naïve, just like Reka had said. Assuming he'd abide by the rules of polite decorum, when he'd shown, over and over and over again, who he really was.

Feliu was pacing the room, his pale face pink with a helpless rage. "Everything we've done to get here, and we're too damn late!" His voice was sharp with anger and despair.

Yosip rested a hand on Feliu's shoulder. He didn't say anything, but Alba knew from experience the calm inherent in Yosip's touch.

She drew in another deep breath, and straightened. "We did not escape a dying ship, make our way through a hostile jungle, flee a yibo execution squad, and survive more assassination attempts then I can count at the moment, to simply roll over and admit defeat. So. What are we going to do about this?"

"He's already taken over the government." She could tell that Feliu was stunned, by the lack of decorum in his words. "It's all very well to escape a yibo execution squad, but—" he spread his hands helplessly. "Cavaco has control of the government infrastructure, weapons, lines of communication—no doubt any councillor powerful enough to oppose him is already on house arrest, or worse. What, exactly, do you want us to do?"

Alba pushed herself from her seat. "He has the military, yes, and he's built up a military culture of intense personal loyalty to himself. But you saw the Council yesterday. They didn't believe his lies in the face of my testimony, despite all the months he's had to prepare for this. If everyone in the system had been as convinced of an alien attack as he wants them to be, do you think the councillors representing them would have listened to us?"

Feliu was silent, frowning at her.

She bit the inside of her cheek, going over the political calculations in her mind. "We'll have to get somewhere Cavaco can't touch us, that's the first step. And then we will concentrate on getting the word out that we're still alive. I'm certain that's the only reason we are still alive—it appears that Aran and his crew of raiders, at least, have evaded capture." She shivered. "Although only time will tell if they're more dangerous free than they'd be in Cavaco's grip. But be that as it may, there are people who know I am alive, and until he is able to control them as I'm certain he is controlling the councillors who saw me, he can't risk killing me. You must remember, we are not only witnesses, but proof that Cavaco is lying. He has not made himself universally popular over the years. Perhaps the citizens of do Sol are not yet protesting the coup, if they think it's peaceful, temporary, and necessary. But the knowledge that Cavaco tried to assassinate a fellow Joint Head of Government, and thereby endanger the entire system? That may be enough to drive people to act. Perhaps his military commanders are loyal to him, but how long will their soldiers stay loyal to them when they are being asked to fire on civilians in the street? When obeying Cavaco means turning their guns on the populace—their own families and friends? He doesn't have that kind of sway, not yet. He'll need more than wild stories of an alien invasion to convince the population that the murder of civilians—their own neighbours and friends and family—is justified." She shook her head. "I doubt he allowed our testimony to spread past the Council yesterday. Therefore, if we want to give the people something to fight for, we get out. And then, we do what we did back in the yibo system—we fight until we haven't got any strength left in our bodies to fight with."

Feliu was looking at her in slack-jawed astonishment. But Yosip was smiling, the corners of his eyes wrinkling with it. "Alba," he said. "I think our friend Istvay would be proud of you."

She stared at him. His smile broadened, and she cleared her throat quickly and turned away. "Be that as it may, the fact remains that we are currently locked inside a guarded military safehouse. I believe that's the first obstacle we will have to confront."

Feliu snorted gruffly. "We are not action heroes, Madam. And we don't have Aran and his ... murder-creature, or Savina and Reka, to fight our battles for us this time."

"Perhaps not." Yosip's eyes were twinkling. "However, I do know a thing or two about picking locks."

Alba turned to look at him in complete astonishment.

He chuckled. "I was a bit of a troublemaker as a child. Some skills never leave you."

"Well then," said Alba at last. "I suppose we'd best make a plan."

"Let's give it until nightfall," said Yosip. "Fewer people about once we get outside—although," he added grimly, "if the occupation of the city is anything like the military occupations in the Rim

Mountain villages, they'll have curfew patrols."

The wait seemed endless. They ate the bland dinner that had been provided, though Alba didn't taste any of it, waited until the tray had been taken away. And then they simply ... waited.

Yosip's soft hand on her shoulder, hours later, was enough to make her jump.

"Shhhh," he whispered, and when she looked up, Feliu was already beside him.

"Are we ready?" she asked softly.

"I hope so." Feliu's expression was grim.

"We'll see if I remember how to pick a lock as well as I think I do," said Yosip, but she could hear the good humour under the tension in his tone.

He stepped over to the door and crouched beside it for a moment, running his fingers gently over the latch.

Alba could practically hear her heart pounding.

Then he looked up, the customary twinkle sparkling in his eyes. "Apparently, they don't think we're much of a flight risk. I think the front door of my house back in the Rim Mountains was harder to pick than this." He inserted a thin spike that he must have bent off one of the forks from their dinner into the lock, and a few moments later, the lock clicked open.

Alba bit down on the inside of her cheek, bracing herself. And then she and Feliu followed Yosip out the door.

Yosip hadn't been exaggerating when he said that they apparently weren't considered a flight risk—there were no guards directly outside the door, and it wasn't until they'd crept down the hallway and turned into another that they heard voices ahead of them.

Yosip beckoned them quickly back into a smaller side corridor, and a few moments later Alba stood, trying to control the volume of her breathing, crammed against the wall with her clerk and her diplomatic aide. Despite the gravity of the matter, she had to bite back a snort of incongruous laughter at the utter absurdity of the entire situation.

The voices passed, the footsteps clicking off the corridor in a leisurely fashion. When they'd faded around the corner, Yosip beckoned, and the three of them slipped out the door again.

"We want to get out on a back alley," Yosip whispered as they walked. "But they brought us in through a back alley, if I remember correctly, so all we need to do is go back the way we came."

"And do you remember which way we came?" Feliu's whisper did nothing to hide the irritation in his tone.

"I'm afraid my mind was on other things at the time," Yosip whispered back, his voice still good-humored. "Unless Alba recalls, I suppose we will have to play it by ear."

Alba shook her head mutely.

"Exploring it is, then," Yosip whispered, sounding entirely too cheerful about the whole situation.

They tracked down, and then backtracked up, at least five different hallways.

At least, Alba thought sourly, they now knew where the kitchen, the lavatory, and the pantry were located, should that knowledge ever be necessary.

At last, they found a corridor that looked familiar—long and narrow, with a steel door at the end.

"I think that's it," she whispered.

They were half-way down it when they heard, from outside, the click of the door unlocking.

They stared around them frantically.

"In here!" Feliu hissed, yanking open a broom cupboard. They tumbled inside, landing practically on top of each other, as Feliu pulled it shut with the toe of his boot.

The click of the cupboard door closing was muffled by the click of the outside door swinging open.

"Wait until she hears what I've got planned for our anniversary tomorrow," one of the soldiers was saying.

Her companion laughed. "You got married just last year, didn't you? You'd better make it nice. You don't get to start forgetting anniversaries for at least five years after the wedding."

The two of them chuckled, their footsteps fading around one of the corners.

When they were certain the soldiers were gone, Feliu nudged the closet door open, and they stumbled out. Alba's heart was pounding, and her right hip ached where it had been jammed up against the wall of the cupboard, and her kneecap that had been broken in the flight from the yibo city of Chrr so many weeks previous twinged like it always did when she overexerted herself.

"Quickly, before anyone else comes in," Feliu whispered, and they made their way as stealthily as they could down the corridor.

It took Yosip more time to pick the outer lock, and Alba tried to contain her impatience as they stood in the hallway, in full view of anyone who might walk by, for endless minutes.

"Well?" she asked at last, unable to contain her nerves. "Can you do it?"

Yosip was frowning at the lock. "I've almost got it," he said. "But there's an alarm. The moment we open it, they'll know we've escaped."

Alba blew out a quick breath. "Well, I don't see that there's any help for it."

Yosip nodded, his jaw tight, and twisted the lock pick.

There was a click as the lock released. And then the loud, jangling wail of an alarm rattled through the empty corridors, making Alba wince.

"Come on!" Yosip whispered over the noise, shoving the door open, and three of them stumbled out into the night air.

It was early autumn, which, in Vila Nova do Sol, meant the sticky, muggy heat of summer had transformed into a tepid evening air that promised cooler days ahead, but didn't yet deliver.

Alba could already feel the humidity sticking her clothes to her back, even before the three of them took off at a stumbling run.

Alba was gasping in pain after only a few steps—her injured knee was not up for this kind of effort, and she could see the red splotches forming on Feliu's cheeks at the unaccustomed running. He'd never walked as much as she had, back in the days when he clerked for her here in the city, and she knew well enough how his injuries in the alien system had left him weakened.

But at least, she thought grimly, if the past few months had taught them anything, it was how to push through pain.

They reached the turnoff to an alley just as Alba felt her knee give out. Yosip caught her as she stumbled, preventing her from landing on her face, but his expression was grave. "We've got to keep moving," he whispered. "They're not going to let us go this easily."

Alba nodded, her breath coming too short to allow her to answer, but she leaned on him and kept moving. Her chest burned, and fire shot up her knee through her hip every time she put pressure on her injured leg, but Yosip was right—they either got farther away, or they died.

Already, she could hear shouts behind her in the direction they'd come. By now, their guards must have gone to check on the prisoners and found the room empty.

They had minutes, maybe, before the streets were swarming with soldiers.

Yosip was looking around quickly as they went. "I know where we are," he whispered. "We're in the south district of the city, near the prison. I lived here for a while when my son was first locked up, so I could be closer to him." Then his face relaxed in relief. "This way," he said, and pulled them forward.

Ahead of them, a small café's lights flickered in the twilight. They reached the door at a stumbling half-run, and Yosip pushed it open and gestured them inside.

The man behind the counter glanced up, frowning. "It's closing time," he began.

His eyes rested on Alba, and widened in shock.

"Cayo, my friend!"

The man tore his gaze off Alba, his eyes finding Yosip.

The look of shock on his face turned to one of surprised delight. "Yosip? Yosip, it is you! What are you doing here?" The man came out around the counter, drying his hands off on his apron as he came.

"I'm sorry to show up at your doorstep like this," said Yosip after they'd exchanged greetings. His voice was grave. "But ... I came to ask for your help. We need to get away from here, and we need to do it without the soldiers outside knowing."

The man's face creased with worry. "I'd tell you you're welcome here, but soldiers stop by here regularly, and I'm not sure it would be safe." He hesitated, thinking. "We have half an hour to curfew," he said at last. "My daughter can get you out in the transport. If anyone comes asking, I'll say she was picking up supplies for tomorrow morning—I need more coffee beans anyways, if the soldiers want their morning coffee."

"Thank you," said Yosip quietly, clasping the man's hand. "We're all in your debt."

The man clasped Yosip's hand in return. "If you owe me a debt, pay it by coming in here for a chat over coffee when this blows over." He turned towards the stairs. "Miciela! I need you downstairs."

They waited behind the counter, where they wouldn't be visible from outside, as Cayo tapped the sign in his window from "open" to "closed."

He and Yosip chatted quietly while he worked. Once he'd gotten over his tongue-tied awe at having one of the three Joint Heads of Government in his home, Cayo proved to be a kind, open-hearted man with a quiet sense of humour that Alba found surprisingly enjoyable.

At last, a young woman came down the stairs, pulling on a jacket as she came. She looked no older than eighteen, but she had her father's friendly face and a brisk energy about her. She, too, paused a moment on the stairs when her eyes fell on Alba, but she recovered herself more quickly than her father had. And when she saw Yosip, her face split in a broad smile.

They exchanged quiet, hurried greetings, and then Cayo explained the situation. The girl nodded. "I'll take them out the back way, and we'll head out to the south-east district," she said. "I'll pick up coffee beans from Cascata's on the way back—I meant to remind you earlier, we're running low."

She led Alba and the others out to the back, and they ducked into the rear seat of the transport parked behind the cafe. It was designed for carrying cargo, and the girl directed them to a small, dipped compartment in the back, then threw a blanket over the top of them. "If people are looking for you, best not to make it easy for them," she said. Then she climbed into the front, and Alba could feel the transport hum to life and lift gently off the floor.

She had no idea the direction they were headed, and under the blanket it was impossible to see anything anyway. So Alba closed her eyes, and tried to focus on fighting back the nausea that threatened to rise in her throat at the bumping and jolting of the small vehicle.

At last, she could feel the transport come to a shuddering halt. The blanket was pulled off, and the girl beckoned them out. "Go quickly," she whispered. "The soldiers are definitely searching for someone. You don't want to be caught out in the streets." She paused, turning to Yosip. "Do you have a place to stay?"

He nodded. "I have some friends on this side of the city. Thank you."

They clambered out of the transport, and Alba brushed herself off. "Thank you," she whispered.

The girl's eyebrows shot up in surprise. At last, though, she smiled. "Good luck to you," she whispered. She turned to Yosip. "And don't forget—you promised Aba you'd come for coffee."

"I won't forget." His smile was warm in the darkness.

The girl climbed back into the transport, and a moment later, they were alone on the darkened street.

18

Savina

Joska brought the *Dolphin* to hover low over the wooded park, and Rafel scrambled on board, cursing, before the hatch had time to fully lower. "Get going! Go, now!" he snapped, as Savina and one of the Labarinto refugees grabbed his arms to pull him up. "They're going to be after you, if they're not already!"

"They know we have alien weapons," said Savina as Rafel limped up towards the cockpit, the people crowding back against the walls of the corridors to let him through. "They might leave us alone."

He turned to her, scowling. "You're just as naive as you damn well pretend to be if you think that," he snapped. "Do you have any idea the kinds of weapons the military has? Ours are new and novel, sure. But one cargo ship with a few modded weapons isn't going to stand up to the Joias System military."

They reached the cockpit, and he dropped into the copilot seat beside Joska. Joska's face was grim as she bent over the controls, and Savina could feel the speed at which they were moving in a way that you couldn't do in space.

"Beni, what do we have?" Joska asked, without looking up.

"The ships sensors are saying we have about seven military ships following us," said Beni after a moment. "They seem to be hanging back for now, probably because they don't know what we can do yet. But I don't know how long that will last."

Joska swore under her breath. "Alright. Beni, take a crew and get them to start stripping out the weaponry. Nicolau and Ines, get everyone else ready to move as soon as we touch down. We can't risk taking the ship back to the Rim Mountains without bringing the military on our tail. I've already called ahead, and they're going to have people waiting with transports, but we're going to have to get the weapons and people out as quickly as possible if we want to get them out at all."

"Alright," said Beni, turning. "I'll get them started."

"We'll have forty minutes at most," Joska called after them.

Savina dropped into a seat and strapped in before she could get knocked on her butt by the ship's acceleration. "What now?"

"I've been in contact with our friends in the Rim Mountains," said Joska quietly. "They believe the weapons will be helpful enough that they're worth the risk. We'll be doing the mirror image of what we did with the yibo—we'll use strategies and weapons from the yibo and from Labarinto, and hopefully be able to hit the military where they're not expecting it."

Rafel grunted. "Probably the best option we have at the moment. Let's just hope the military doesn't shoot us out of the sky before we get there."

By the time the *Dolphin* neared the rendezvous point, everyone on the ship had been divided into teams—one to haul out weapons and anything else that might be useful, and one to hold off the military until the others were safe.

Rafel, to Savina's intense disgust, was in charge of the group holding off the military. Still, she couldn't exactly argue—he had more experience with the military than she did, and he'd be better positioned to predict what the soldiers might try to do.

"I'd just better not hear any lectures about killing people," Savina snapped at him.

He glared back. "I'm not the captain, more's the pity," he snapped back. "And you can be damn sure I'm not going to let Cavaco get away with this."

Savina nodded, and Rafel turned to the small group of assembled people. They were grim-faced and tense, but these were people who'd had plenty of experience with defending themselves in life-or-death situations.

"When we get out, you're going to get as far away from the *Dolphin* and the people transporting out the weapons as you can. You'll have about five minutes, if that." He held up a large hand-held reflector. "Once I call in, you're going to point your brightest torches and light-tubes onto one of these, and you're going to reflect the light back up at the ship sensors. If we spread out, they won't be able to get readings, and they won't know where to shoot. There's a good chance that they'll try to take us out, but if we're far enough apart they won't be able to hit everyone, and it'll stop them from targeting the people hauling weapons. That's the important thing. If you're afraid of dying, speak up now, because there's a good chance at least some of us aren't going to walk out of this, and I can't afford anyone who is going to run away when the bombs start falling."

He glanced over the group quickly, then nodded in satisfaction. "Alright, then. As soon as we land, you three go east, you three west, the four of you can head north, and the three of us will go south. Run straight until you hear my signal, then your groups will split up, get as far away from each other as you can. Then, on my second mark, turn on your reflectors and point them at the ships."

Savina glanced at the two people she'd be fighting beside. One of them was one of the criminals she'd trained back in the yibo system —a murderer, if she remembered correctly—the other, the majordomo of one of the human villages.

There was the shudder of the ship touching down, and as the hatch cracked open, Rafel barked, "Go!"

They slid out the hatch as soon as there was space, dropped to the ground, and ran.

Savina glanced at the two women running beside her, cursing steadily under her breath. They were both looking to her for cues, as if she was the one in charge, but she didn't have the attention or the energy to scowl at them.

"Now! Spread out!" Rafel hissed through the wavelink.

The three of them stumbled to a halt and glanced at each other. Then, without speaking, they each picked a direction and ran.

The forest at night was a minefield of tangled brush and chances to roll an ankle, but she stumbled on until Rafel called through the line, "Light up! Now, we're out of time! Now!"

Savina caught herself against a tree, gasping for breath, and fumbled with the awkward reflector, hands slippery with panic. She managed, at last, to balance it on one arm, then she yanked out the industrial-strength light-tube that Rafel had handed her, flicked it on, and pointed it at the reflector, tilting the beam up towards the approaching military ships.

She could tell when she'd hit her target—the ship veered away sharply, rising higher.

More lights were flickering on around her, and in the distance, Savina could hear the grunts of effort and muffled clanking of metal as the rest of their party hauled the heavy weaponry and equipment towards the waiting transports.

And then came the bombs.

There was a searing flash of light, a roar of sound that was almost a physical blow, the whine and scream of rocks and tree branches splitting and popping in the searing heat, and then the shock of the explosion, an ear-popping pressure that made Savina stagger back.

She blinked the water from her eyes and steadied herself against a tree, reaching up to brush away a trickle of blood from her nose.

She felt battered—dazed, blinded, disoriented.

She hadn't been afraid before—she hadn't had time to be afraid. But there was something about the raw destructive power of the blast that started a hot, animal terror inside her, and for a moment, she just stood where she was, eyes closed, trembling.

She sucked in a shaky breath, cool Rim Mountain air mixed with the harsh burnt-chemical scent of the explosive.

Nicolau was with the group hauling the weapons, Nicolau and Beni.

She pulled in another breath and forced her arm up, forced herself to refocus the beam of light, hands shaking.

When the next blast hit, she was more prepared, at least. But the roiling wave of sound and pressure still made her freeze momentarily in panic, like a rabbit freezing under a diving hawk.

"Hold on," Rafel's voice came through her wavelink, sharp and harsh. "We still need to hold them for another fifteen minutes."

Savina swallowed hard, closing her eyes.

Fifteen minutes.

Fifteen minutes of standing still, holding up a beacon like a target, while overhead the military ships brought their guns to bear.

There was another roar of sound, close, too close. Savina was caught up in the wave of noise and heat, thrown backwards into the trees, shrapnel stinging and burning her cheeks and her hands, cutting through the rough fabric of her jacket. She didn't realize, until it was over, that she was screaming, the sound high and thin in the night.

It hadn't been her. The shot hadn't been aimed to hit her, she'd be dead.

It had been aimed to her right, the direction the woman she'd trained back in the yibo system had taken.

She swallowed against the vomit rising in her throat, and forced herself to climb back to her feet.

Her legs were shaking almost too much to hold her, and she hurt, every part of her hurt, but she didn't have time to be hurt. Nicolau was down there. Nicolau, and Beni, and Joska.

She forced herself to pick up the light tube, forced her shaking fingers to focus the beam. She tilted the reflected ray into the sky and closed her eyes, her mouth coated with the coppery taste of fear.

Fifteen minutes, Rafel had said. Fifteen more minutes.

And then it was over.

"Shut it off, get back here, now!" Rafel's voice through the wavelink made her jerk, losing her grip on the light tube.

"Come on!" he snapped. "There's a transport waiting in the forest just north of the *Dolphin*. Call in if you can, so we know who to wait for. But we won't have much time."

A handful of voices answered, but not many. Not nearly as many as had gone out.

It took Savina two tries before she could make her own voice work, but she could hear the relief in Rafel's tone when he called back on her private line. "Thank the Holy Mystery you're alive. Nicolau would have skinned me. Now, get back here."

She ran as fast as her shaking legs would let her, but still, by the time she arrived, she was one of the last. Two people were climbing up into the small rural transport as she came up to them, and someone else was limping in through the trees. There was something odd about their gait, and it took Savina a moment to realize it was because their left leg was a mangled, bloody mess, their foot blown off at the ankle, and they were leaning heavily on a stick, hobbling as fast as their uninjured leg would let them.

She swallowed back bile, and looked away.

When the last of them were in, the woman driving the transport hit the controls, and they rose into the air and lurched forward up the winding mountain track through the trees.

Savina sat back, still gasping for breath, and closed her eyes, trying to shut out the moans of pain, the thick, iron scent of blood, the choked cursing and crying from around her.

She hadn't counted how many were left. There hadn't been time, and she didn't want to know. But there was a part of her brain that wouldn't shut off, that reminded her that she'd been the only one running in from the direction she'd taken.

The criminal and the majordomo, both dead. And Savina still alive, somehow.

Once, that thought would have felt smug and well-deserved. Now it sat in her stomach like a stone, cold and nauseating.

She could hear Rafel moving through the back of the transport, muffled sounds of gratitude—probably handing out painkillers or strong alcohol or both. At last, she heard him crouch beside her.

"Savina?" he whispered.

She blinked her eyes open. He was holding something in his hand, and she realized it was a flask, and a roll of bandages.

She had to bite down hard on her teeth to force back a hysterical laugh. "I'm not …" She swallowed, and tried again to make her voice work. "I'm not hurt."

He raised his eyebrows, and it was only then that she looked down and saw the blood staining her shirt and trousers, the torn fabric of her jacket, only then that the sharp pain stinging across her body managed to make itself felt.

She blinked for a moment, then took the flask and took a swig of alcohol so strong it burned like fire in the back of her throat. But by the time she'd finished blinking the tears of it out of her eyes, she felt a little more coherent.

"I don't think it's anything serious," she said, her voice hoarse from the combination of shock and the burn of the alcohol. "Just shrapnel."

"Well, get it looked at when we get back to the village, anyways," Rafel grumbled, and turned away, but she saw the way his weathered face had softened a little in relief.

She pulled in a deep breath and leaned back against the wall of the transport again as it lurched and bounced through the narrow cut in the trees.

In the distance, there was another explosion, and she flinched unconsciously, glancing out the scuffed plex at the back of the transport bed.

A massive ball of flames rose for a moment above the trees, then subsided.

The *Dolphin* was gone.

She shook her head. She had other things to be worried about than a broken-down cargo ship.

But … she couldn't help but picture the look on Juska's face.

She'd barely gotten the ship back from Savina, and now this.

She closed her eyes for a moment and sucked in a long breath through her nose. The sharpness of the alcohol had brought her head back from wherever it had been, but now it sat sour in her stomach and made her head spin unpleasantly.

Still, that was probably better than having her head entirely clear right now anyways.

She leaned back against the wall of the transport again, and focused on keeping down the contents of her stomach as the transport jolted and swayed up the path.

By the time they reached the village, the first hint of dawn was already beginning to grey the sky to the east. Savina's head had long since cleared from the alcohol, the dull, stinging pain from the shrapnel cuts throbbing in her body. The transport bounced to a halt and lowered roughly to the ground, and then there were hands helping them out, leading them towards shelter.

She glanced over her shoulder to see someone throw a blanket over the face of the woman whose foot had been blown off—she'd died en route, it appeared.

Again, Savina had to swallow down vomit.

When at last she and the rest of the survivors had their injuries seen to, been bandaged and dosed with painkillers that would hopefully be both more effective and less dizzying than the flask of alcohol Rafel had provided in the transport, they gathered in the village hall, the flickering artificial lights in their sconces casting a strange, wavering orange glow.

"Well, we have the weapons, and we have people who have expertise and strategies that the Joias military won't have seen yet," said Joska. Her face was grim, and Savina had seen how sick she'd looked as she'd watched their battered company stumbling from the transport. "And it cost us to get them here. So we'd best talk about how to use them to best effect."

One of the rebel leaders nodded. "We'll send out Xema to figure out where the army is gathering. In the meantime, let's work on making the weapons portable. We'll need to be able to move if we don't want the military to blow us into a crater. But if we can do that?" He shrugged. "We know these mountains better than they do. With weapons that can do what you tell me these can? I think we can work with that."

Another of the rebels shook her head, her face grim. "Cavaco's taken over the government. A coup. He's going to want all of his forces free to put down any potential resistance in the cities. I'm guessing he's going to come after us first, try to crush us so completely that he only needs to leave a handful of soldiers to keep the peace."

"Cavaco's taken the government?" Joska sounded sick. The woman who'd spoken nodded grimly.

Savina was too exhausted for the despair to register.

At last, the man who'd first spoken said, "If you're right, we're going to have to—"

There was a commotion at the entrance, and then a young woman, her hair disheveled, her face streaked with dirt, stumbled inside. "The soldiers are on their way here," she gasped. "They'll be here in minutes!"

For a moment, everyone stared at each other.

"Which direction did they come from?" snapped Rafel.

The woman gestured, and Rafel gave a quick nod, turning back to the others. "They're not the same soldiers who were after the *Dolphin*, then," he said brusquely. "You must have been right about Cavaco's strategy. I doubt we're the only village who will wake up to a military raid this morning. But we have one advantage, which is they won't have any idea that we have alien technology." He smiled grimly. "So let's give these soldiers a lesson, shall we?"

When they'd finished their hurried conference, Savina pushed herself painfully to her feet. Nicolau was in front of her when she straightened, his face creased with concern and streaked with tears. "Vina," he whispered, wrapping her in a hug. "I'm sorry, I just got done on the weapons. I'm so glad you're alright—" His voice choked off into silent sobs, and he tightened his arms around her until she almost couldn't breathe.

She patted his shoulder awkwardly. "I'm fine," she managed, although every part of her still hurt, and she still felt a little like she might vomit. "Come on, we've got to get going. We don't have much time."

"Vina, listen. You're hurt. You can stay behind this time." His voice was still choked.

She shoved him away, and finally he released his hold on her. "Listen to me, baby brother," she said through her teeth. "I'm the one who protects you. And if you're going to be out there, I'm damn well going out there as well." She gave him a tight smile. "Besides, I'll bet there's not a single person in this entire village who has as much experience killing people as I do. I should play to my strengths."

She slipped out the door before he could respond, but there was a tight knot in her stomach, the leftover fear from the previous night jangling through her body.

Damn Cavaco to hell.

She'd send him there herself, if she had to.

They spread out through the village, positioning the yibo weaponry, half-way assembled, at the entrance. Savina ended up beside Rafel, with the group on the guns. He acknowledged her with a curt nod, and then turned back to watching the dirt street ahead of them.

The sky had gone a rosy pink in the time it had taken them to prepare. The sound of birds chirping and singing, the crowing of a rooster behind one of the houses, the crisp, sweet smell of morning dew on evergreens hung in the air, giving the whole scene a surreal air.

And in the distance, the sharp tread of soldiers' boots.

Savina drew in a quick, steadying breath.

She'd fought so hard, back in the yibo system, to protect the humans, keep them alive. And here they were, back home in a system full of humans, and she was still fighting for her life.

There was something bitter in the irony of the thought.

She pasted on a bright smile.

These humans, she wouldn't hesitate one moment to hunt. After all, that's where she'd learned her skills—here, in this system, killing humans just like the soldiers marching towards her now.

The soldiers reached the outskirts of the village a few minutes later, and stopped at a sharp command from their captain on the outskirts.

The two men on the yibo heavy weaponry, both from Labarinto, moved their hands towards the controls, but Savina shook her head. "Not yet," she whispered.

The military captain was issuing commands in a low tone, gesturing to emphasize his words. Savina couldn't hear what they were saying, but she could guess. Go into the houses, bring everyone out. Don't kill anyone unless you have to.

Even here in the Rim Mountains, the soldiers would probably rebel against the mass slaughter of unarmed families.

The captain gave a curt nod, and the soldiers moved out, splitting up and starting into the houses.

The men behind her twitched, and Savina shook her head again. "Not yet." She glanced at Rafel. "What will they do when they see the houses are empty?"

He gave her a tight smile. "They'll assume we've heard them coming, and are hiding. The only place large enough to shelter that many people is the town hall, so that's where they'll go."

She nodded.

He was right. There were quiet exclamations from the soldiers as more and more of them came out of the homes empty-handed. They regrouped on the edge of town, and the captain gave another curt command.

Lowering their weapons, the soldiers started cautiously forward.

Savina waited until they'd almost reached where she and Rafel were hiding, marching in close formation. Then she turned to the men behind her, smiling beatifically.

"Now," she whispered.

The weapon fired, then fired again, then fired a third time.

Savina had known what it would do—she'd seen it in action in their desperate skirmishes against the yibo. But even so, when the smoke and debris finally cleared, she had to blink a few times before she could take in the scene.

Out of at least a hundred soldiers, there was almost nothing left that was recognizable as human, only a limb or hand or other body part flung casually atop a roof or over a windowsill. The air was thick with a haze of blood and ... other things that Savina didn't really want to consider too closely.

From behind her, she heard a retching sound, as one of the gunners lost his breakfast. Rafel was steadying himself against the wall, a sick look on his face.

"Well," said Savina at last, into the silence. "I think this weapon might get Cavaco to change his strategy after all."

They held a hurried conference in the town hall after the worst of the mess was cleaned up, and the few soldiers who'd survived had been tied up and confined to the wine cellar under the building.

"There will be protests in the cities," said Ignasi grimly. "It doesn't matter how frightened people are, they aren't going to let Cavaco simply take the government like that. If we can keep the soldiers up in the Rim Mountains tied down, it may mean Cavaco can't force the Belt cities into total capitulation."

Joska nodded. There was a bleak look on her face, and a pallor to her skin that told Savina exactly how much their adventure that morning had affected her. "I think that may be our best option," she said quietly. "We've got to give the people in do Sol a chance, because we can't take down Cavaco from here."

"But we can damn well make him work for it," said Esti, another of the rebels.

They spent the rest of the day feverishly preparing the guns to make them transportable. Rumours kept trickling in—villages taken in the early morning hours, their inhabitants, shivering in their nightclothes, carted off to a military camp in the mountains.

By the afternoon, rumours of the location of the camp were trickling in as well.

And by nightfall, they were ready to move.

The battle outside the military camp was bloody and short. The soldiers hadn't been expecting the rebels, and they certainly hadn't been expecting their weapons.

Joska had insisted they keep the deaths to a minimum wherever possible. Even so, the ground around the military camp was slippery with blood by the time Ignasi cut the lock on the gates, and they led the shivering, terrified villagers out to safety.

"We'll hole up in our camp in the woods above Pine Creek," said Ignasi quietly when the last of the villagers had been brought out. "The soldiers haven't found it yet. We can take the weapons there for now, and plan our next move."

Savina nodded, almost too tired to speak. She'd hardly had a moment to sit down since the night before, and her head was spinning with weariness. Nicolau had come to stand beside her, his face sick and deathly pale, his clothing spattered with blood, and Ines stood next to him. They were holding onto each other as if for dear life, and there was a glassy, horrified look to Ines' face that told Savina that the girl was barely holding herself together.

"Let's go, then," Savina said. "Esti, you and your people get these villagers somewhere safe, then rejoin us. Bring anyone who wants to fight back with you. The rest of you, come with me."

The others nodded, and started off to prepare the guns.

It was well past sunrise when they finally reached the rebel's camp. There were far more people than there were of the narrow camp cots, but Savina hardly cared. She fell onto the thin blanket laid out on the hard dirt floor of one of the tents, and was asleep before she remembered her head touching the ground.

By the time she woke the next morning, Joska and Rafel were already gathered with the rebel leaders in the centre of camp, talking quietly. Joska moved over to make room for Savina as she came up. Her expression had regained a touch of its usual dry humour. "I'm glad to see you awake."

"That makes one of us," Savina muttered, dropping to the ground beside them. Her whole body ached, and her head throbbed with the heavy, sluggish remnants of sleep, the residual exhaustion from the day and the night and the day before. "What are you all talking about?"

Joska sighed. "Yesterday will have dealt Cavaco a blow. But next time, he'll have time to prepare, and we'll lose the element of surprise. We'll have to be more strategic in the future."

"We've taken down an army of raiders. We can damn well take down the Joias System soldiers." Savina was almost surprised at the controlled fury in her own voice. She turned to Rafel. "How long has it been since the Joias military has fought in a real war? I mean, something other than massacring helpless unarmed villagers at Swan River?" She saw the quick flash of pain in his face at the memory, but she hardly cared.

"Almost a century, I think," he said at last.

Savina turned to the others, showing her teeth in a bright smile. "We're going to show those bastards what a real war looks like. We're going to show them what it feels like to see their friends die in front of them. We're going to make them remember the smell of blood and the colour of their own guts and the way people scream when they lose a limb or an eye. And then we'll let Cavaco try to convince them to go die for him in a yibo war."

19

Aran

Aran couldn't remember exactly how long he and Istvay had been working. His head was fuzzy with exhaustion, and he knew he'd half-carried Istvay back to bed at one point, but he didn't actually remember when Istvay had rejoined him.

Either way, they were both hunched over the table, and Aran's back ached from being in the same position for so long, and his head ached from strain and lack of sleep, and honestly, it was only Istvay's hand on his arm, warm and comforting, their grip stronger than it had been in a long while, that gave him the strength of will to keep going.

Ani had gone off to sleep under the blankets on Istvay's cot at some point, and when he glanced over at her, he could see the tips of a couple tentacles poking out from the lump under the blanket, flickering odd colours as she dreamed.

He couldn't help but smile just a little at the sight, despite everything.

He'd been worried that Ani would be upset about not being near her babies, and she probably was, but she certainly seemed at least a little relieved to be able to sleep without being pounced on by seventeen rapidly growing hatchlings whenever she lay down.

"Aran!"

He jerked his head up at the excitement in Istvay's tone. They were staring down at their notes, and he knew that look on their face.

"Aran, I think I see what we were doing, back before …" they cast a quick glance at him and trailed off, squeezing his arm.

He leaned into the touch and sucked in a long, steadying breath.

Istvay was alive. Istvay was cured, and once they got everything else figured out, he could finally let that sink in. But he knew, deep down, that he'd probably feel that exact same jolt of frantic panic every time he thought about all the events that had led them both here for a very, very long time yet.

"You've figured it out?" he asked, once he was in control of his voice again. "Pishti, you got it?"

Istvay shook their head, their face still creased in concentration. "Not yet, but I think I know what theory I was using when I figured it out. So I just need to follow the data, and I think we'll have it." They turned to look at him, repressed excitement in their face, a brightness in their eyes that he hadn't seen there for far too long. The dark hollows under their eyes were still there, but he was pretty sure they were already fading, just a little, the colour back in their cheeks, the gaunt, cadaverous look less prominent than it had been. He had to bite the inside of his cheek hard to keep himself from a desperate sob of relief every time he looked at them.

He cleared his throat. "I knew you could do it. Let's get this figured out so we can keep the raiders from razing do Sol to the ground, and then—"

"And then," said Istvay firmly, "you are going to lie down and get some sleep, for hell's sake. You look worse than I did, I think."

Aran managed a grin, and the two of them bent over the documents again.

There was a sharp pounding on the door, and Aran glanced up, frowning. Istvay was frowning as well. "What the hell—" they began.

"Open up!" It was a voice Aran didn't recognize, but from the tone of it, it certainly wasn't one of the students or faculty. "Open up, by government order."

Aran frowned at Istvay. "Government order?" he mouthed. Istvay shook their head, their mouth pinched into a tight line.

"General Cavaco has temporarily taken over the government to ensure the safety of the citizens," the voice continued. "We're under orders to secure the university and its buildings to ensure the peaceful transfer of power. We have word that there may be a rogue scientist here, and we have a warrant for his arrest for murder and high treason."

Something cold started in Aran's stomach.

"Cavaco's taken the government?" Istvay whispered. "Was this something that happened while I was out, and you forgot to tell me?"

"No," Aran said slowly. "No, I'm pretty sure when we brought you in here, Alba was going to talk to the Council, and ..." He paused, the cold knot in his stomach growing larger.

"A coup," said Istvay grimly. "He's taken over." They shook their head, glancing at the raiders, who'd been waiting, surprisingly patiently, in the corner, although part of that could have been Dessi's admirable commitment to exacting harsh verbal retribution when either of the others raised their voices above a whisper.

He must look awful, Aran thought in the back of his head, if Dessi was being this careful with him.

"We know you're damn well in there, Aran, you and Istvay. If Istvay's not dead yet."

Aran jerked his head up at the voice, this time far too familiar.

Istvay caught his eye. "Emeric?" they mouthed. "How the hell is Emeric here? What does he want?"

"I don't know," he whispered back.

There was the same horror in Istvay's expression that Aran felt on his, although in Istvay's case it was overlaid with a question that, if Aran was interpreting it correctly, went something along the lines of, how much energy would it take to punch Emeric in the throat.

"Aran! I know you have some way of controlling these raiders. I know you've allied yourself with them. And you're not damn well getting away with it. You can come out and work with Cavaco to deal with this, or I have orders to drag you out."

Istvay, eyes narrowed, pushed back their chair, swayed, and caught themself on the table. Aran jumped to his feet to steady them, and had to catch himself as well. Istvay turned to him with a look that was half concern, half amusement. "We're going to renegotiate who takes care of who in this relationship at some point," they whispered.

"Aran! If you don't open up, I'm going to tell the soldiers to start shooting."

Krevai had crossed the room to their table. "What's happening, humans?" he asked, his voice an exaggerated whisper.

Istvay sighed. "It's … complicated. The important point is, if those soldiers or that idiot Emeric get in here, we'll probably all end up dead."

Aran almost groaned at the way Krevai's eyes lit up. "Ah. There are humans who want to attack my crew, are there?" he said, not even trying to whisper now. "Dessi, come now, you can't possibly fault me for—"

"No killing!" Aran snapped. "You promised. Istvay and I are holding up our end of the bargain, you'd damn well better hold to yours!"

"Although if you killed Emeric on accident, I wouldn't complain," Istvay muttered under their breath.

"Aran," said Dessi, stepping between them. "I'm sure once Krevai explains to them that we need you and you aren't available to be killed right now, they'll decide to go find someone else to kill." She must have caught the look on Aran's face. "And I'll go with him to make sure things don't get out of hand," she added.

He slumped a little in relief, and Istvay caught his arm to keep him from falling over.

The soldiers were pounding at the outer door now. "Open up! This is your last chance, and then we shoot the door down."

"Zondra, you stay behind to protect the humans," said Dessi briskly. "Krevai, come on."

Krevai's grin was far too delighted for Aran's liking, but Dessi shot him a long-suffering look over her shoulder and mouthed, "I'll take care of this, don't worry."

Then they were out of the room, and the inner door clicked shut behind them, their footsteps fading down the hallway.

The pounding at the outer door stopped abruptly, and Aran waited, hardly breathing, straining his ears for either a shot, or the sound of Captain Krevai ripping out someone's heart—a sound with which he was, unfortunately, far too familiar.

When neither came, and he could hear Krevai's bellowing tones, cut, occasionally, with Dessi's curt, sharp ones, he closed his eyes and dropped heavily back into his seat, brushing a hand across his face.

He was getting too old for this, honestly.

Istvay sat back down as well, and after a moment, pulled the paper back towards the two of them. "Alright," they began. "Now, what we need to do is—"

If it wasn't for Ani, Aran might not have seen it at all. But her soft, bubbling hiss from the bed made him glance up.

Zondra had stood from where she'd been sitting in the corner, playing with her long butcher knife. There was an odd, unsettling smile on her face that was far, far too familiar, and she was stalking towards them, moving with the silence only a raider could.

A moment later, and she'd have been on top of them, and he wouldn't have noticed until her knife had sliced his head from his neck.

In the back of his brain, something stirred, sluggish and oily, and subsided as a sharp shock from Aran's bracelet jolted up his arm. He cursed and jumped to his feet as Istvay did the same.

"Dammit," he snapped through his teeth, shoving Istvay behind him. "I'm already infected, and you're damn well not going to be, not now, not when we don't have any damn materials to make you a bracelet. Stay back, get me the acid wash, I've been doing this for days now. And damn well keep Ani from killing anyone, Sharda will start a war over that and you know it."

Istvay hesitated, then, to Aran's bone-melting relief, did as he asked, moving back to the cot where Ani's hissing had increased in volume as she slithered out from her nest.

"Stop," Aran said, stepping between the raider and Istvay. "Listen to me. Ani will kill that raider if you use her body to hurt me, you know that. I don't know how intelligent you are, but that can't be your plan. If you try to kill me, Ani will kill Zondra, and Istvay is going to go absolutely postal. No one wants that. Just stay back."

"You and your Istvay are trying to kill me," the thing hissed in Zondra's voice. She was stalking closer now, moving around as if trying to find a way past him. "Your Istvay almost has the cure, don't they? And then they'll kill us."

"If you hadn't bloody infected the entire fleet of raiders, maybe that wouldn't have been a problem in the first place," Istvay muttered, shoving something into Aran's hand. "Here, here's the—"

Zondra lunged, sliding around Aran's left side and diving for Istvay, knife drawn. Aran leapt in front of her, shoving her off-balance with both hands, and she rolled and came up facing him, knife still in her hand.

"Aran!" Istvay shouted, and he could hear Ani hissing.

"Keep Ani back, dammit," he gasped, rolling out of the way of the knife as it came down close enough to slice through the sleeve of his jacket, leaving a thin trail of blood in its wake. "Just …"

He yanked the stopper from the bottle Istvay had handed him, rolling out of the way of another knife strike that would have taken his leg off at the knee. Zondra leapt past him, and he grabbed desperately at her, catching her elbow and knocking her off balance again. As she staggered, he pulled himself upright against her body weight, and dumped the entire contents of the bottle across her wrist.

The acid hissed and steamed, and she shrieked, a high-pitched, agonized sound, as it ate into her flesh.

And then she stepped back, her shriek cutting off into a bitten-back hiss of pain, and then a curse, her voice once more the acerbic, antagonistic tones he'd become used to.

Istvay must have released Ani, because a moment later she was enveloping him, and he had to shove her off so he could sit up. "Hey, sweetheart, easy there, I'm fine," he whispered, stroking her. "You're such a good, brave girl, listening to Pishti. You did such a good job, do you want a treat?"

She perked up a little at the word 'treat,' and he rummaged around in his pocket and pulled out a half-eaten bag of crisps.

She slipped a delicate tentacle into the bag and pulled one out, then proceeded to devour it with gusto, crumbs spraying everywhere.

In the background, he could still hear Zondra cursing, and he glanced quickly over his shoulder, then sighed. If Istvay wasn't being quite as efficient in their search for the neutralizing solution as they might have been, Aran supposed he couldn't exactly blame them. At last, though, Istvay stalked towards the cursing raider and shoved the bottle into her hands. "Here," they snapped. "Rinse with that, it'll stop the burning. And for hell's sake, keep an eye on your bracelet next time." Then they turned to Aran, crouching beside him. "Are you—"

Aran rolled to his feet, still breathing heavily. "I'm fine," he said. "I'm alright, thanks, Pishti."

"You're bleeding," said Istvay, frowning down at his arm.

"Aran! What's happened?" Krevai burst back into the room, Dessi on his heels. "Don't worry, the soldiers were very happy to leave you alone once I'd explained the situation, although that scientist friend of yours was less excited about it. I suggested he come in, as we were all quite hungry in here, and then he changed his mind. But we heard shouting ..." He saw the blood, and his expression went dark. "Did any of the soldiers make it in here? Because I'm very hungry, and—"

"No, no," said Aran hastily. "It was just ... it was Zondra. Her bracelet failed, but everything's under control now, so it's fine."

Krevai was glowering between Aran and Zondra, but at last he sighed and ran his hand over his hair. "Well, I suppose I can't leave you alone with any of my raiders then, except for Dessi and me, considering we and the Istvay are the only ones we know are not infected at this point," he muttered.

Istvay put their arm around Aran's shoulder and squeezed, and Aran sagged against them. "Go on," they whispered. "Go clean up, I'll get back to work. We should have something by the end of the day, I think."

Aran nodded wearily, and stumbled into the small bathroom.

He splashed his face with cold water in a probably futile attempt to wake himself up—if a raider attacking him hadn't done it, cold water wouldn't likely be much better—and then turned the water to warm and shoved his sleeve back to examine the wound.

It was hardly more than a scratch, and it had already almost stopped bleeding.

He cupped his other hand under the warm water to rinse it off.

In the back of his mind, he heard a small, metallic *ting.* He frowned, glancing around to see what had made the sound.

And then his heart almost stopped in his chest.

On the floor at his feet lay a thin strip of metal, glinting in the artificial light, a clean cut across the centre of it, where it had been sheared by the raider's knife.

His bracelet.

Damn it to hell.

He could feel his heart rate rising.

It would be alright. They didn't have materials, but between them, he and Istvay could do … something.

He went to open his mouth to call them.

But he couldn't. He couldn't move his muscles at all, couldn't open his mouth, couldn't force his tongue to form words.

The warm water trickled over his hand and ran down the drain, the sound of it loud in the silence.

A revoltingly familiar sensation was spreading over his brain, oily and suffocating and choking, and he was trying, frantically, to fight back panic, because that was how they got you, that was how they took full control of your body …

But this thing had already been in his mind. He could feel it settling into place like a poisonous fog.

Aran, the voice in his head whispered. *Missed you.*

20

Alba

Alba sat at the small, battered kitchen table, Feliu and Yosip across from her. Behind them, a worn-looking woman who must be around Alba's own age was wiping down the counters, the slow way she was moving an indication that she was probably listening in.

Still, Yosip trusted her, and Alba had come far enough not to doubt his instincts.

"So, what exactly can we do to stop this?" Feliu's voice was sharp with strain and weariness. "From the sound of it, Cavaco has already seized control of the main strategic points, and taken the government headquarters. It appears he's also taken the Sao Martim University and any other possible hot-spots of resistance. I'm not sure what the three of us can do anymore." His voice cracked on the words, despair winding through his tone.

Alba pulled in a deep breath. "It seems hopeless, I understand that," she said. "But if you remember, Cavaco's strategy relies on me being dead. The moment word of my survival gets out, it will strike him a significant blow. The coup was peaceful, not because of overwhelming force, I think—he can't possibly have enough soldiers to hold down the entire city of do Sol, let alone the Belt cities and the Rim Mountain villages. The coup was peaceful because the people half-way believe him about the alien threat. They're not going to dare make a stand against the army if there's a greater threat from outside. But if they realize that he's been lying to them this whole time—that he's been plotting against the democratic government, sending people to make backroom bargains with hostile powers to preserve his own position? That the real threat of an alien invasion is a direct result of his own actions and those of his people? I don't think he has enough soldiers to hold down the riots that would break out."

"What are you suggesting, Madam?" Feliu's tone was still sharp, with worry now. "Cavaco is certainly aware of the risk you pose. The moment he hears you're free, he'll spare no pains to find you and kill you."

Alba sighed. "I understand that. Therefore, I suggest that we attempt to make contact with people who are in position to spread word of my survival, and the intelligence we've gathered on Cavaco's actions since his soldiers mutinied on the diplomatic ship. And then I suggest that we find a way to disseminate that information broadly enough that it will be too late to silence it. If enough people know, it may be that he won't dare try to kill us. Or it may be that he will, but in either case ..." She shrugged, forcing her voice steady. "We've cheated death enough times in the past few months. If we can stop the coup and topple Cavaco, I hardly think we can complain if it finally takes its due."

It was odd—the sentence would have been bravado if she'd said it months ago.

Now ... Well, now she found she actually meant it.

They were quiet for a few moments. Feliu's pink face had gone pale, and Yosip looked grave, but she could see in their expressions that they realized the same thing she had. If they wanted a chance at saving the entirety of the Joias System, this may be their only option.

"Very well," said Feliu at last, grudgingly. "I suppose I can look up the contacts I have with the other clerks. They're much more likely to be unmonitored than the politicians, and I doubt we can risk trying to get through to any of the councillors right now."

"Thank you, Feliu," she said quietly, catching his eye.

He looked away quickly. "Don't thank me, Madam, not until we find out if this is going to work," he muttered.

He blinked to activate his wavelink, and she could see his eyes flick back and forth as he searched through the information on his retinal screen.

She glanced down at her hand on the worn wooden table, the veins standing out against the skin, the bones of her fingers stark and visible. It was trembling, and she wasn't sure if it was the accumulated strain and exhaustion, or if it was fear.

Feliu was right—Cavaco would hunt her down, the moment he understood what she was trying to do. He was a merciless enemy, and he wouldn't stop until she and these two men with her—men who had become, perhaps, the closest friends she'd ever allowed herself to have—were dead.

A hand was laid over hers, and she looked up in surprise.

Yosip smiled at her, and squeezed her hand. "Alba," he whispered. "We'll get through this. We've survived a mutiny, a ship's breakup, raiders and yibo trying to kill us, assassination attempts—we'll get through this." He paused. "And if we don't—as you say. At least we'll have done something worth dying for."

His hand on hers was warm, his voice quiet and comforting, and there was still that good-natured twinkle in his eyes that hadn't left since she'd first met him on the diplomatic ship.

She contemplated, for a moment, asking him how he did it—how he could possibly still be hopeful, after everything they'd seen and done.

But she thought, perhaps, that she already knew.

It wasn't, for Yosip, about what was happening around them. It was the fact that he firmly, unshakably believed that people themselves were inherently good. Good enough that no matter how bad things got or how hopeless it seemed, they'd keep trying. That they'd not give up. That they'd keep pushing and working and loving and trying until they righted things somehow, and that even someone like Cavaco or Kachik or Mattin wasn't enough to stop that much goodness. That no one was.

She smiled back at him, and he gave her a small wink, squeezing her hand again briefly before letting it go. And it was odd how much the gesture steadied her.

"I've got it, Madam," said Feliu at last, turning back to the table. "I'll show you my list." He glanced around for a holodisk, and the woman at the sink, who'd been washing dishes, turned, wiping her hands on her skirt. "You need something to copy onto?" she said. "Just a moment …"

She left the room, and returned a moment later with a handful of holodisks. Feliu took one and opened it, blinking a command through to his wavelink, and the information populated on the blank screen he'd pulled up over the disk.

Alba scanned the list quickly.

It was … better than she'd hoped, honestly. Feliu had an extensive list of clerks, for councillors from all three committees.

At last, she tapped a half-dozen names. "Let's start with these," she said. "The councillors they're clerking for all have ample contacts in the news packets, and these two both deal with the general government broadcasts, so they'll have contacts there, even if Cavaco has shut things down. Between them, I suspect they have the know-how to potentially get word out across the entire planet."

Feliu nodded. "Let's hope my information is still current," he muttered.

The first three wavelink lines they tried had been changed.

On their fourth try, however, someone answered, his voice coming through the open line to all three of them around the table. "Feliu?" they asked in frank disbelief. "We were told you'd died!"

"I'm sure that's what Cavaco wished had happened," Feliu said grimly. "We don't have much time. Do you have a way to get through to Councillor Stefanu?"

There was a long pause on the other end of the line. When the clerk spoke again, their voice was weary. "Did you not hear?"

"Hear what?" Feliu's voice sharpened. "What's happened?"

There was another long moment of silence. At last the clerk said. "Hold on, I'll send you the recording through."

There was a moment, and then Feliu pulled up another holodisk and blinked the incoming transmission through.

Alba frowned at the fuzzy image as it slowly sharpened, trying to make sense of the pictures.

Then she sucked in a sharp gasp.

It was a dozen councillors, lined against a flat cement wall. They were bound and blindfolded, and on the other side of them was a company of soldiers. Their commanders were talking in low voices to a figure she recognized, suddenly, as Cavaco.

One of the commanders turned and barked out an order. The soldiers snapped to attention, and one of them stepped forward, checking the bindings on the councillors.

It was only then that Alba saw the bands strapped to their chests.

Her heart stuttered in dread.

The soldier stepped back, and the commander shouted another command.

One of the soldiers turned to a small control panel and punched in a sequence.

The councillors stiffened, as if hit by an invisible force, and collapsed slowly to the ground.

Alba sucked in a gasp of horror as her mind finally comprehended what had happened.

The soldiers had come forward, and were bending over the fallen councillors. One of them looked up and nodded at the commander, and then the video blurred and stopped.

For a few moments, there was complete silence around the table.

"Cavaco is executing everyone who he thinks will pose a future threat," the clerk said into the silence. "These were the most vocal in standing up against his coup. He broadcast this to the other councillors as a warning. I'm afraid that even if what you're saying is true, there won't be many who will dare help you."

Again, there was a long silence.

Alba felt sick to her stomach.

She'd recognized most of the people in that line—Jonatan, from the judicial committee. Benadita, who'd taken up Alba's position after she'd been presumed dead. Catia, one of the few she'd actually been able to count on to stand up to Ander when he wanted to roll over and show his belly to Cavaco.

Dead.

It was hard to let the reality of it sink in.

And yet … it was easier than it would have been, months ago.

Alba had the experience, now, to understand the inherent violence of politics and political disagreements, violence that she'd always been shielded from before, when she sat in the chambers arguing over protocol.

For the councillors she'd worked with, here in do Sol, councillors who'd never seen what she'd seen over the past few months, never felt the visceral, helpless despair of being entirely powerless and voiceless, wholly dependent on the goodwill of others for your very survival—they'd be in shock.

The clerk was probably right. There wouldn't be many who'd be willing to stick their neck out under these circumstances.

"Well," said Feliu at last. His voice was hollow and haunted. "I suppose …"

Alba gestured to him, and, after a moment's hesitation, he opened up the line so the rest of them could speak through it, as well as listen.

"Clerk Ganiz," Alba said sharply. "This is Chief Justice Alba Espina. Cavaco has attempted, more than once, to have me murdered, but I'm still here. And I do not intend to let the General take over the system unopposed. We will get word out about Cavaco's betrayal, and we will let the rest of the planet and the rest of the system know what he's done and why. Your choice is either to help us, or to stand out of our way. Because on this matter, I do not intend to give in."

"Madam Chief Justice?" The clerk's voice had risen an octave, high and almost hysterical. "Is that really you? If Cavaco finds out …"

"He'll kill me, I know. As I said, he's tried before." Her voice was grim. "But if you believe he won't kill you if you sit quietly and don't speak up, you're fooling yourself. You'll die either way. I'm offering you, and the rest of the councillors and clerks and officers willing to take a stand, a chance to make your death mean something. I suffer under no illusion that Cavaco will not kill me the moment he gets the chance. However, as long as I am able to get my message out before I die, it may be enough to save the Joias System."

The clerk was silent for a few moments. At last, they said, "Even if I agreed on the wisdom of that action, Madam, it would be pointless unless we were certain you'd be able to pass on your message without Cavaco shutting down the broadcast or killing you before you're able to speak, and we cannot possibly have that certainty."

"Of course it's not a certainty!" Alba snapped. "But as things stand, it seems to me to be our only chance. Unless you'd prefer for all of us to simply roll over and let Cavaco drag us into a war we have no chance of surviving."

There was a long, long moment of silence. At last, the clerk said, their voice cautious, "Madam. Have you heard what's happening in the Rim Mountains?"

Alba frowned, glancing at Feliu and Yosip. "I've heard rumours of a rebellion. But knowing Cavaco's politics, that's hardly surprising."

"Cavaco is cracking down on rumours, but he can't keep them from spreading. And rumours have it the rebels are using alien technology to fight."

Alba raised her eyebrows. "Alien technology?" Her mind was spinning.

Alien weapons. As far as she'd heard, which was admittedly not much, Cavaco's army hadn't taken the *Dolphin* before it reached Colorida. And the *Dolphin*, she was well aware, had been fitted out with a great deal of technology that had not originated in the Joias System.

It wasn't proof. But she suddenly had a strong suspicion that there was a certain Rim Mountain assassin and cargo-ship captain among the rebels.

"Do you know anything else about this?" she asked after a moment.

"No. But it's possible that, if you could convince them to coordinate efforts with you, they could distract the military and give you the opportunity to broadcast your message."

Alba nodded slowly. Yosip had already stepped to one side, pulling out his yibo communicator. "I'll call the yibo captain to find out what's happening," he mouthed to her, and she gave a brief nod.

"It's possible," Alba said, turning back to the open wavelink line. "It's possible we could coordinate our efforts, if they're willing. But that won't do us any good unless there are enough councillors who will to take the risk of helping us. We will need at least enough councillors to allow us access to the infrastructure we need, and to be in position to take back control of the government should this succeed. Otherwise, there is no point to what we are doing."

The clerk was quiet again. At last, they said, "I'll talk to Stefanu and see if he's willing to help. Between us, we may be able to find some others."

It was a risk. There was always the risk that whoever Ganiz talked to would be frightened enough that they would turn Alba and the others over to Cavaco in order to keep from dying themselves. But Cavaco must already know she'd escaped. And the councillors and clerks wouldn't know their location, just the fact they were alive. Lines could be bugged and traced, she knew that, but at this point, it was a risk they were going to have to take.

"Thank you," said Alba. "I will await your answer. If Stefanu agrees to help, you may contact Feliu, and we will speak further."

When the wavelink line clicked off, the three of them stared at each other around the table.

"The yibo captain confirmed that there were a number of the human refugees, led by our friend Reka Soler, that broke out of the ship a short time ago," Yosip said at last, his face unaccountably grave.

"Surely that's good news," said Alba, trying to push back the fear in her voice. "If that's the case, it certainly bolsters our hope that the rebels will be willing to work with us."

Yosip managed a small smile. "It is good news. However ... the yibo captain is not happy with the current state of affairs. The Joias military technology interferes with ship-to-ship communication, but it hasn't affected the technology they use to communicate through the portal. I was able to convince him to give us a few more days before he called back through the portal for military backup, and thank the Mystery, he doesn't have the weapons capability on the ship to be tempted to start a fight with the soldiers without backup. But even assuming he doesn't change his timeline—which I'm not certain is a safe assumption to make, given the current conditions—we don't have much time to solve this."

"And now we know exactly the lengths to which Cavaco is willing to go to ensure we don't succeed," added Feliu grimly.

21

Savina

The next few days were a blur—battles, retreats, more battles, every day a new village to save, a new village that Cavaco's soldiers attacked. The faces of terrified villagers, adults and children alike, sobbing or screaming. Blood, so much blood that she began to wonder, irrationally, if the whole world would turn to blood—the rivers, the mountain ponds, the lakes, the rain, the morning dew. The days were spent fighting or running, the evenings pouring over maps, whispered conferences with the spies they sent out.

Every time one of them came back, something about the stealthiness in their movements, the silent way they walked, sent something thin and sharp through Savina's chest.

She ignored it.

It was easy enough to ignore, when she hardly had time to breathe in a full breath.

Joska had been right—the Joias soldiers were ready for them now. There were no more armies marching into villages—if they attacked, it was at night, or after setting up a distraction elsewhere, and the rebels would arrive only in time to see the smoking ashes. The soldiers hadn't found them yet, but it was only a matter of time —more than once, the rebels caught an army spy lurking far too close to the outskirts of their camp.

Savina would take the spies they'd caught out of the camp herself and shoot them. They couldn't live to take news back, and she wasn't going to let Joska give an order that would make her sick.

They hadn't heard anything from Reka. Whether it was because she was dead, or because she'd betrayed them, or because she'd simply decided to leave them to their fate, Savina didn't know.

They'd finally readjusted the camp to the number of its occupants, although those numbers were growing daily, as more and more villagers found their way into the mountains. There were even a few who Savina recognized, from their covered hair and dark clothing, as faithful Old Believers. There had been one or two fights that had broken out in camp when the Old Believers first began trickling in to join them, but Joska had made it very clear that anyone who took issue with sharing a tent with an Old Believer had no place in their camp, and soon any overt hostility dissipated.

There was hardly room for hostility between themselves anyways, with Cavaco's soldiers crawling through the mountains like ants.

On the fourth night, Savina crawled into her small, private tent, zipping the flaps shut. She lit the oil lamp, then sat there for a moment, staring at the dancing shadows on the walls, too weary to undress and lie down on her blanket, even though her entire body was aching for sleep.

The camp had finally quieted, the only sound the chirp of insects outside, and the quiet brush of wind through the trees. From inside the camp she could hear the faint crackle of the fire, soft footsteps as people came and went from the food line, but it was quiet and distant, and the smell of woodsmoke blended with the cool freshness of the evening air.

Home. Or as close to home as she'd been in a very, very long time.

Sometimes it would hit her—that she was back here, in the Rim Mountains, maybe a few hours' transport ride from where she'd grown up—and the thought would lodge in her chest like a stone. Like something that didn't belong to her, and she didn't know what to do with, and she didn't know how to get rid of.

There was a faint rustle outside her tent door, and she looked up quickly, her heart pounding, before she relaxed again.

Likely one of the deer mice that liked to try their luck in the tents when the occupants were sleeping, in search of a few crumbs they could carry off.

The noise came again, and this time Savina frowned.

It was soft. But from the sound of it, whatever made it was much larger than a deer mouse.

She stood quietly and crept towards the door of her tent, heart pounding.

It was possible Cavaco had sent people who were more than spies. They'd never quite been able to be certain of every person in the camp, not with all the Rim Mountain villagers and Old Believers pouring in. It was always possible that Cavaco had sent someone here to kill her. And if they'd come for her, she wouldn't be the only one they'd come for.

For a moment, she was struck with the sick, lightheaded vision of Nicolau and Ines, throats cut, blood soaking through their blankets and into the ground, Joska, a knife plunged through her heart, and she almost stopped breathing.

She was at the tent flaps. She palmed a throwing knife in one hand, and with the other, she reached out carefully and jerked back the flap.

For a moment, in the darkness, she didn't see the figure.

And then she did.

She grabbed for the front of the woman's jacket as she swayed and shoved her to her knees. Something in the back of Savina's mind had recognized her—her silhouette, the way she moved, the ineffable sense of her—before Savina had even started moving, but it wasn't until she had the tip of her knife to the woman's throat, pushing her head backwards and dimpling the soft skin under her chin, that her mind realized what the rest of her already knew.

Reka made no move to resist, just knelt where Savina had shoved her. Her head was pushed back at an unnatural angle, the cords of her neck straining as the knife bit into her flesh, but she didn't make a sound.

"What the hell are you doing here?" Savina hissed. The words felt thick and tight in her throat. "How dare you come back here? What are you doing?"

"Savina." Reka's voice was strained, almost inaudible.

Savina pressed the knife harder, until blood welled up and dripped down the blade onto her hand. "Don't you dare."

"Savina." The word slurred a little in Reka's mouth, and it was only then that Savina noticed the way Reka sagged against her hand, the way her body, usually taut and controlled, drooped, her eyes half-closed. "I'm not ... I came to warn you. Couldn't get word through my wavelink, and my communicator's broken. Cavaco's sending ... he's sending soldiers after you, his whole army." She pulled in a wavering breath that turned into a hiss of pain. "You've got to be ready, they'll be here in less than three days' time. He's bringing ... he's bringing them in by transport." Her voice was fading, slurring with pain or exhaustion, Savina wasn't sure which, until it was almost unintelligible. "Had to warn you," Reka whispered.

And then she slumped against Savina's hand, and Savina jerked the knife away just in time to avoid slicing through her throat as she tumbled into the dirt and lay still.

Savina stared at her for a long moment, her heart pounding.

Her hands were shaking, her whole body weak and unsteady, something that was a mix of hurt and anger and sick worry mingling together in a choking sensation that made Savina's muscles weak.

At last, she knelt beside the body, rolling Reka over.

She'd been shot. That wasn't a surprise—Savina had seen Reka come out of a ship crash that should have killed both of them, and then trek for kilometres through a trackless forest, all but carrying Savina along with her. It would have to have been something serious for Reka to pass out.

She remembered the look in Reka's eyes. *I can't just let them kill you,* she'd said. The tight worry in her face, the hopeless despair in her expression.

She cut off the thought quickly.

Reka deserved to die. After everything she'd done, Reka deserved to die, and Savina wouldn't even feel bad about it. She'd trusted Reka, and Reka had stabbed her in the back, walked away and left her to do all of this alone, not because of something Savina had done, but because of who she was. Because of what she couldn't change, even though she hated it with every part of her being.

Reka deserved to bleed out on the ground.

But somehow, she found herself lifting the woman, as gently as she could—Reka was taller than she was, and even though she was slender, every bit of her was solid muscle—and half-dragging her into the shelter of the tent and over to the bedroll.

She pulled back Reka's jacket and inspected the wound. The

blood had dried and crusted, the wound caked with dirt and bits of leaves, and she could tell by the swollen, puffy flesh around it that infection had already set in.

She closed her eyes and cursed quietly.

Damn Reka to hell. Savina had dreamed so many times about watching Reka bleed out in front of her.

But her hands were shaking as she peeled the cloth gently away from the wound.

She'd never been good at treating injuries. She'd spent her whole life building up her skills so that when she killed, she was never the one who was injured, and she always made sure to keep Beni well out of harm's way.

But that had been before they'd gone through the portal. Since then, even she had learned basic first aid.

Reka moaned as Savina worked, her eyes fluttering open a moment, but they were glassy and unseeing.

"Shhh," whispered Savina through a lump in her throat. "Shhh, it's alright. Lie back."

And finally, Reka did.

At last, when she'd done all she could, Savina drew in a deep breath and stood.

Her hands were still shaking, and every part of her felt weak and wrung out, but the wound was clean and sprayed with disinfectant and bandaged, and she'd managed to get Reka to swallow a painkiller and something to take down the fever.

Reka lay limp on the ground, covered by Savina's blanket. Her face was drawn in exhaustion and pain, her hair tangled and splayed out on the pillow, and Savina was reminded, suddenly and unexpectedly, of the first time she'd seen Reka, in a remote space port months ago.

And then the memories of everything that had happened since then. The times Reka had tried to kill her. The times she'd saved her.

Savina turned away sharply, before the memories could drown her, and ducked out of the tent.

It took only a few minutes to wake Joska and the others, and soon they were gathered around the fire, their faces tight with concern.

"If this Reka found us, then …" one of the rebel commanders began.

Joska shook her head, a small, wry smile on her face. "I don't think you know Reka Soler. The fact that she found us means nothing—I've never seen anyone else do what she can do." She paused. "The question we need to ask is, is her information accurate?"

They all turned to look at Savina.

Savina closed her eyes. "I don't know," she said, her voice coming out tired and flat. "I don't know if she's telling the truth or not. But it's Reka, and I've never known Reka to tell a lie."

At last, Ignasi nodded. "If you can vouch for this …" he said, turning to Joska.

Joska's mouth was pinched, but she gave a curt nod. "Savina's right. I may have my differences with Reka, but I've never known her to lie."

The small group around the fire looked at each other for a moment. Esti, another of the rebel commanders, sighed. "We'll send out some of our people to gather information. We need to verify what Cavaco's doing. But in the meantime, we should treat it as though it's true."

Joska stood and laid a hand on Savina's shoulder, drawing her away from the group around the fire. "Where is she?" she asked quietly. "Are you alright?"

Savina shook off Joska's hand and turned away. "I'm fine," she said bitterly. "She was hurt, so she didn't have the chance to betray me or try to kill me before she passed out."

Joska didn't speak for a moment, but Savina could hear the soft sound of her breathing in the quiet of the mountain night, feel the steadying presence of her.

"Savina," she said at last.

"I said, I'm fine!" Savina snapped, whirling on Joska.

There were tears in her eyes, she realized belatedly, and she gritted her teeth and tried to bite back the sob that wanted to choke her. She swallowed hard, and managed to regain control of her voice. "She's in my tent. She was hurt, but I bandaged her up as best I could."

"Do you want me to come take a look?" asked Joska quietly.

Savina could feel every muscle in her body tense. But at last, she nodded wordlessly.

Joska followed Savina to the tent, and checked Reka over quickly. "I'm not a medical expert, but out in space, you learn to treat your own wounds quickly enough, or you die over it," said Joska wryly, standing and brushing off her knees. "I think you've done everything that can be done for her, with the equipment we have here." She paused. "Do you want to try to move her?"

Savina pulled in a long breath, not meeting Joska's eyes. "No," she said at last. "She'll be fine here until she wakes up. I can still use my knives. She won't be able to kill me, even if she decides to try."

Joska gave her a long, searching glance. "Call me if you need anything, Savina," she said at last. "Even just to talk."

Savina gave a curt nod, still not looking at Joska. She wasn't sure that if she did, and saw the sympathy written in the woman's face, she wouldn't simply break down and start crying.

When Joska left at last, Savina paced back and forth a few times across the tent. She was clenching and unclenching her hands, and blinking hard to hold back tears.

This wasn't fair. None of this was fair, she hated Reka, she hated her.

Reka moaned and stirred again in her sleep, muttering something incoherent.

Savina pulled in a long breath, and crossed over to kneel beside the bedroll. Reka's eyes were moving restlessly under her eyelids, and her hair was stuck to her forehead and cheeks with sweat. Her hands grasped at nothing under the covers, her face troubled and cut with pain.

Savina closed her eyes for a moment.

At last, she reached down, smoothing Reka's forehead. "Shhh," she whispered. Reka's skin under her hands was hot with fever. "Shhh, it's alright. I'm right here."

"Savina?" Reka's voice was a weak whisper, thick with delirium, and her hands clutched at the blanket.

"Shhh, yes, it's me," said Savina. Her voice was oddly shaky. She put her free hand down, and Reka clutched at it like it was a lifeline.

"Savina," she muttered. "You have to tell Savina ..."

Savina stroked Reka's hair and held her hand, and slowly, slowly her restlessness subsided. Savina was blinking back the tears blurring her vision, but at last she couldn't anymore, and they dripped onto the blanket, leaving small, wet stains.

"Damn you to hell, Reka," she whispered. "Damn you to hell, I should have slit your throat and be done with it."

But she stayed there until Reka was asleep, until her grip on Savina's hand had softened enough that Savina could pull her hand free without waking her.

Savina slept on the ground that night, and woke cold and stiff.

"Savina?"

She jerked upright, swearing, and glanced quickly around the tent. Then she drooped in relief.

It was Reka. She was awake, eyes open, and no longer as glassy with fever as they had been. She was clearly in pain, but she was Reka, and so the only way Savina knew was the small lines that tightened around the corners of her mouth, the almost imperceptible creases under her eyes.

"You're awake," she said flatly, standing. "I told the others what you told me. You'd better damn well hope it was the truth."

"It was the truth," said Reka.

"Well?" Savina snapped. "What do you want? I'm busy."

Reka was watching her, her forehead creased in that familiar look of puzzlement that Savina had seen so often over the past few weeks. "Why?" she asked at last.

Savina closed her eyes. "Why didn't I slit your throat when you showed up here? I should have." She wanted her words to come out sharp, but she was too tired to pretend.

"I thought you would." Reka's voice was quiet. "You're not Joska. You don't weigh lives. You could have taken my information, and then killed me, and you're good enough that you could have made sure no one else would have known. You have every right to hate me. So ... why?"

Savina had been asking herself the same damn question since the night before, when she'd pulled back the tent flaps and recognized who was standing outside.

"I don't know," she said at last, dully, turning away. "I don't know. Maybe I couldn't. Maybe I'm stupid. Maybe I'm still in love with you, even after what you did to me. Is that what you wanted? Does that make you happy?"

Reka didn't answer.

When Savina finally turned back, Reka had dropped her head back onto the pillow. Her eyes were closed, but her jaw was clenched tightly enough that Savina could see the muscles standing out.

Her stomach twisted a little. "Reka?" she asked.

"I wanted you to kill me," said Reka at last, not opening her eyes. "I wanted you to be the kind of person who'd do that, because I wanted what I did to be justified." Her voice was quiet, but so sick with self-loathing it almost hurt to hear. "And you didn't. Savina, the assassin. Savina, the Old Believer. Savina, who I always believed had no conscience and no morality and no sense of right or wrong. And you won't do what I would have done."

There was a long moment of silence. Savina watched Reka, something sick and heavy twisting in her stomach.

"You didn't kill me when you had the chance, either," she said at last, drawing in a shaky breath. "I guess you're just as stupid as I am."

Reka's eyes had fluttered open again, and she was watching Savina with that same dark intensity as always, the thing that twisted Savina's stomach and left her mouth dry.

"Perhaps I am," she said at last, her voice a whisper. "Perhaps you're right."

She reached up, as if to brush her hand across Savina's face. She hesitated, then let her hand fall. "I'm sorry," she said, the words almost inaudible. "I'm sorry for thinking you'd do that. You were always better than I gave you credit for." She broke off, her face tight with pain.

"Reka?" Savina's chest tightened. "Lie still, I can get Joska—"

"No," Reka gasped. "Don't ... don't get Joska." She visibly forced herself to relax. "Don't get Joska, I'll be alright." She closed her eyes and laid back, collecting herself. Her forehead was shiny with sweat, her breathing harsh and laboured. When she opened her eyes again, there was something in her expression that Savina couldn't read. "I'm sorry," she said at last. "I'm sorry for what I said. I'm sorry for leaving you to do this alone."

"Sorry doesn't change it, though, does it?" Savina couldn't find the energy to be angry, although she probably would be later. "Sorry doesn't bring back the people who died, who might have lived if you hadn't been so worried about your damn pride. Sorry doesn't change the fact you'll abandon me the moment that who I am might damage your reputation. You always say you want to do what's right? You'd damn well better decide that that is."

Reka was silent for a moment. "It … wasn't my reputation," she said at last, quietly. "That was never what this was about. I … grew up being told certain things, and I believed them. And I made them part of who I was. When I lost my family, that was all I had left—my ideas about the world and what it meant and what was important." She closed her eyes. "And it turns out even that was wrong. I didn't actually have anything at all." She paused. "You're right. I didn't come to help here, because I didn't want to work with Old Believers, and I knew that with you and Joska in charge, you wouldn't turn them away. I stayed in the city to gather information instead, and tried to convince myself that was enough. And … and the more I talked to Cavaco's soldiers, the more I realized that they believed the same thing about Old Believers as I did. The people who were willing to kill defenceless villagers in their beds if it meant more power for them in the future believed the exact same things I did." There was something in her voice, something dull and broken, and Savina wanted to reach out and stroke her hair, comfort her like she'd comforted Savina so many times.

But whatever they'd had, back then, Reka had broken it.

She hadn't killed Reka when she'd had the chance, because she couldn't bring herself to.

But they couldn't go back. They could never go back.

"I'll get you something that should help with the pain and the fever," she said instead, turning away.

By the time Savina arrived at the campfire, it was clear that Joska and the other rebel commanders had been there for hours.

"Savina." Joska's face was cut with exhaustion, but she managed a small smile at Savina's approach. "It looks like there's a new variable. I just received a call from our Chief Justice."

Savina blinked at the woman blankly for a few moments before the words she'd said made sense.

Then she swore.

"She told me that she believes our only chance is for her to somehow get word out that she's still alive, and that Cavaco's story about hostile aliens was false. She believes that if the population of do Sol realizes that Cavaco's actions are, rather than protecting the system, leading it into an unwinnable war, it's possible that will be enough to motivate them to revolt."

Savina blew out a short breath and dropped down beside the fire. "And what do you think?" she asked.

Joska shook her head. "I don't know." The weariness in her voice was so thick that for a moment, Savina felt a brief spike of panic.

She shoved it down. None of them had time to rest right now, and it wasn't looking like they would anytime soon.

"It's better than any other option we have." Ignasi sounded almost as weary as Joska. He sighed. "Combined with what your friend the government agent told us, it may be our only option. We won't last against Cavaco's entire army." He gestured to the holomap that was pulled up on a disc propped haphazardly on a camp stool. "If he sends his whole army up here, we can't meet him. But if we didn't try to meet him, just left enough people here to lure his forces farther into the mountains, and in the meantime we sent our people around and took back do Sol, even temporarily …"

Savina leaned forward, her heart beating faster in excitement, despite herself. "We couldn't hold it long."

"No," said Joska. "We couldn't. But we could likely hold it long enough to give the Chief Justice a chance to speak. With luck, that will be enough."

"And if it's not?" Savina snapped.

Joska smiled wearily. "Well, it doesn't seem to me that it will make much difference whether we die in the city or the mountains, in the end."

The rest of the day felt endless. Savina and Joska and the others stayed around the campfire arguing, talking through strategy, and pouring over maps until well after dark. But Savina's mind kept wandering back to her tent, to the cot where Reka lay sleeping.

At last, late that night, she finally rose with the others and made her slow way towards her tent.

She almost didn't want to go inside. She didn't want to see Reka again, because seeing her cut Savina like a knife. Just like every time she saw Reka—her stupid loyalty and bravery and goodness—and realized that Reka could be loyal to other people, but never to her. And she couldn't hate her for it, no matter how much she tried.

The tent was dark when she slipped inside, and she lit the small oil lamp.

It was only then that she realized that the bedroll was empty.

She sucked in a quick breath and crossed over to it. The blankets were folded back neatly, the pillow back in its place. And on top of it, a note.

Savina, it said. *I don't want to be a danger to your camp. I'd only meant to pass on the message, but I had miscalculated how badly I was hurt. You gave me time to recover. I'm returning the favour by leaving before I can pose a danger to you. And ... I'm sorry.*

Savina read through the note again, a knot rising in her throat. She had to fight back the irrational urge to run out after the woman, drag her back.

It would be no use—Reka wouldn't be found unless she wanted to be, and Savina had more important things to worry about.

Damn Reka to hell.

22

Aran couldn't breathe. His entire body was frozen, completely under the control of something not himself, but it wasn't the charak that was stopping his breath.

It was the ice-cold terror trickling down his limbs and up his chest, numb and lightheaded and dizzying.

He fought back desperately against the panic, but he could feel it pulling at him, tugging at him like a riptide, trying to suck him in and swallow him whole.

He couldn't even close his eyes, put his head in his hands, pull in a long breath. He couldn't even do that, because the creature was controlling every voluntary movement in his body.

And outside …

Istvay was waiting outside.

Istvay, who was finally, finally going to recover. Istvay, who was stronger than he'd seen them in months, even as weak as that was.

Istvay, who he might just kill.

Please. He managed to push the thought through his brain, and he felt the charak's grip on his mind stir in response. *Please, don't hurt them, you can do whatever you want to me, just …*

The creature didn't even deign to respond. He could feel its cold indifference as it pulled his hand from under the warm water and shut off the tap.

In the small corner of his mind where he was still in control, he forced back the waves of panic, lapping higher and higher, forced himself to view the situation analytically.

Of course it wasn't going to listen to his pleas. It wasn't a monster, it was simply a predator, and this was how it hunted.

Really, it was a fascinating adaptation, for a small, physically weak creature—have your prey hunt other prey for you. And it had allowed the thing to survive hunting raiders, who were, perhaps, the most dangerous predators in their system.

Well, now that Ani and her babies were back in Joias, he amended.

In other circumstances, he'd actually be enthralled by this. But the cold hard facts of the matter were, right now the person he'd been madly in love with his entire life was waiting for him outside this door. And a horde of maddened raiders was about to hunt their way through the Joias System, starting right here in do Sol, which would probably spark off a war that would destroy the system itself as he knew it. So scientific curiosity was going to have to take a back seat for the moment.

But now that he'd got his damn panic under control again, started thinking through the problem logically instead of the screaming horror of the possibility of hurting Istvay shutting off any rational thought …

He couldn't smile. He couldn't control his mouth enough to do that. And he clamped down on any feeling of satisfaction, hard enough that even this creature wouldn't be able to sense it.

This was a predator. A fascinating, unique, and absolutely deadly predator, yes, but Aran had spent his entire life dealing with predators.

For the first time in a long time, this was something he actually knew how to do.

The creature turned Aran's body towards the washroom door, and he could feel his lips turning up into a sheepish smile, like he'd probably have done himself if he had to confront Istvay after being hurt, no matter how minor the injury. His eyes were focused on the door handle, but from the corner of his eye, he caught a glimpse of what he was pretty sure he'd seen on his way in—a long, jagged spike of wood from the broken door, sticking out like a spearpoint.

Even though he had no control over his muscles, his body was jittery with adrenalin. Still, the charak would be used to that—they used their victims' panic as a tool, of course they'd be used to a system flooded with adrenalin. There shouldn't be anything there to cause suspicion.

He just had to time this exactly right …

The creature put his hand on the door handle and turned it smoothly, stepping up to it to swing it outward—and Aran shoved as hard as he could with his mind, in the way he'd learned to do the last time the thing had taken over his body.

He stumbled forward, his foot slipping on the small puddle of water on the ground from where he'd been cleaning the blood off earlier, and a lightning bolt of pain jolted up his body as the long spike of wood jammed into his thigh.

Tears of agony welled in his eyes, and he could hear his own involuntary grunt of pain, then feel his body brace as the creature went to pull it off the spike.

Wait! He shoved the thought through his brain.

The charak paused a moment, hissing in displeasure, and the grip on Aran's mind tightened.

It was irritated, annoyed that he'd done this to himself—but not afraid.

Not yet.

Now he allowed his grim satisfaction to trickle through, and he could tell when the creature felt it—he could feel its slight unease.

He allowed himself to picture exactly what would happen next.

The charak would pull off the spike. But he'd timed this precisely. The wood had gone in just beside his femoral artery, close enough that one wrong move would puncture it.

And then he'd bleed out on the floor within about two minutes.

Again he could feel that smothering hiss of displeasure, the horrible feeling of suffocating while you could still breathe. Last time, it had been enough to send his consciousness shrinking back into the tiny space it still controlled.

This time, though, he was ready for it.

What are you doing? The creature hissed at last. *Do you think I won't kill you?*

Again, Aran allowed the hint of bleak satisfaction to filter through his mind. "You might kill me," he thought, "but I'll tell you exactly what will happen next. Istvay will come running in here, the moment they realize there's something wrong. They'll see me bleeding out on the floor, and they'll see the bracelet lying on the floor behind me. I've got them the cure for what was making them sick last time you were in my head. And last time you were in my head, they scared the hell out of you, because you saw, right here inside my head where I couldn't lie to you, that they'd do exactly what they said they'd do."

He let himself picture the scene as he talked—he wasn't

completely sure whether this thing communicated in words or thoughts, and he figured it was best to be absolutely certain it got the message. "They'll see this, and they'll know what you did. Right now, they're working on something that will kick you out of my head, and out of the raiders' heads. They aren't working on something that will kill you, because they know I'd hate that. I don't like killing things, not if I can help it, and especially not if they're just following their instincts, trying to survive." He paused a moment. "But I make an exception when the choice is, kill something that's just trying to survive, or let it kill Istvay. If those are my choices, I'll pick Istvay, every single time. You were going to hurt them. And maybe I can't kill you, but believe me—the moment Istvay pulls this door open, they will find a way to kill every single charak, not just on Krevai's ship, but in the entire yibo system. Do you understand me?"

There was a sudden flood of emotion through his head—a frantic panic, combined with an overwhelming sense of affronted outrage.

Wasn't me! He could sense the indignation through the words. *You did this!*

"How are you going to explain that to Istvay?" Aran knew he probably shouldn't let the smugness filter through his thoughts, but he couldn't really help it. "Do you think they're going to stand here and listen to you try to talk to them through my dead mouth?"

He felt a jolt of memories not his own, the sight of Istvay through his eyes but someone else's intelligence as Istvay grabbed his wrist with a gloved hand and leaned forward, threatening horrific things in a soft, reasonable tone that sent shivers through both Aran and the thing in his head. Although probably for different reasons.

"Yeah, that Istvay," he thought grimly. "And believe me, if you think they were angry then …"

He felt the thing's quick spike of panic.

What do you want? The voice in his head was accompanied by a thick fear, a question in his brain.

"I want my body back. I want my mind back. I want you to get the hell out and leave me alone and never hurt anyone I care about ever again," he thought flatly.

The thing shuddered in his mind, and he saw a picture of … something. Something translucent and all but transparent, mostly shapeless. It was difficult to see, but the emotions and memories from the thing in his head gave it shape. He could make out, now, the long "foot," like a slug's, but lined with tiny hooks that would allow it to grip whatever surface it crawled on, a circular mouthpart lined with rows and rows of tiny teeth—perfectly designed to suction up rotting flesh, but not nearly enough to protect itself.

Despite everything, he watched the scene in his head with utter fascination. "You're beautiful," he thought, his mind broadcasting admiration despite himself. "You're absolutely beautiful, look at you!"

The picture sharpened, and he could sense the thing's hunger now, its fear, and he couldn't help the quick wash of sympathy.

Need to eat, the thing whispered in his head. *Hungry. Starving.*

"Look," he began. "I can … listen, I'm sure I can find you something …"

Go home, the thing whispered. For a moment, a picture flashed across his vision—the dark void of space, lit with the distant glow of planets and stars, and he felt a tug of longing, not his own, strong enough to pull tears from his eyes.

Hungry, the voice in his head whispered again. *Eat, go home.* Then he felt a sharp stab of anger and fear, and an image of Istvay superimposed itself over the picture of the vast, achingly beautiful scene. He was pretty sure Istvay didn't look quite so terrifying in real life, but then, after seeing how they'd reacted last time the charak took over Aran's body, he couldn't exactly blame it for exaggerating.

Kill us, it hissed.

"No, they're not going to kill you. I mean, unless you decide to not let me go, then they probably will. They just want to jar you loose from me and the raiders."

Kill us, it said stubbornly. *Hungry. Starve. Never go home.*

He almost frowned, and then realized his expression wasn't under his control either and gave it up. "You're worried that if you can't take over us or the raiders, you'll starve and you won't be able to go home," he repeated in his head.

Yes. Never go home. Starve. He could feel the mix of fear and anger in its thoughts again, and a sharp hiss of hate as it pictured Istvay.

Tentatively, he pictured himself walking towards the translucent creature, holding out a sack of rotting meat.

The thing hissed in displeasure, clamping down hard on his mind, and he felt a burst of mistrust, saw himself yanking out a pistol and shooting the thing.

"I'd never—" he began, then gave it up.

You couldn't talk a wild creature into trusting you like that—either they trusted you in their own time, or they chose not to, and honestly, he couldn't blame them either way.

He sighed internally. "Alright then, what's your solution?" He thought the question, and waited.

Now that he wasn't using every bit of his brainpower to communicate with the charak, he could feel the hot pain of the wood spike through his leg.

He was pretty sure that, if the charak agreed to let him go, he could figure out a way to get it out without severing his artery, but he wasn't completely sure.

It had been the best option he'd been able to think of at the time, but … he was suddenly, painfully aware it might not have been a *good* option.

At last he felt a tug on his consciousness, and he jerked his attention from the sharp, fiery pain in his leg and back to the thing in his head.

Now, he could feel a hint of sulkiness through the anger and panic.

He saw a picture of himself pulling off the spike and walking through the door. He saw Istvay standing to come over, and heard himself shout, "Not hurt! Charak didn't hurt me. I did this. Leave them alone."

He sighed internally. "That's not going to work. They're going to know you took my mind back as soon as I was off the spike, and Ani will too. You can't solve it that way."

There was a sudden, vicious picture in his mind of Ani being shot with a few dozen weapons.

He countered with a picture of the weapons fire fading, and Ani sitting there smugly, blinking up at him. "That's not going to work either."

There was another long pause. Then, at last, the creature thought sulkily, *Bargain?*

"What do you want to bargain for?" he thought back cautiously.

There was another long moment of sulky silence. *Let you go. Don't hurt Istvay. Eat raiders, keep one alive, take us home. We leave.*

"No," he thought firmly. "The raiders are my friends, and even if they weren't, how do I know you don't just decide to kill your way across the Joias System the moment you can?"

There was another long pause.

"Listen," he thought. "I know you're scared. I don't blame you.

But I'm scared too, and so are the raiders. What about this? You give me my body back, but you can stay in my head, like you did when I had the bracelet on. Istvay is going to finish the program that will kick you out, but they're going to do it anyways—we promised the raiders we would. But if you'll get out of my head, and you'll get out of the raiders' heads, they won't need to use it. We can talk to the raiders. They can take you into deep space and let you out to hunt somewhere else, and then they'll use the program to make sure none of you try to stay on when you shouldn't."

There was a rush of dissatisfaction.

"I know it's not perfect, OK?" he snapped through his thoughts. "I'm doing the best I can. And your alternative is that Istvay comes bursting through that door in about thirty seconds, and then there's no deal left for either of us."

There was another long, long pause.

"Aran?" Istvay's voice floated in through the door. "Are you alright in there?"

Aran did the mental equivalent of raising his eyebrows.

"I'm fine!" the charak called back with his voice, the tone impressively carefree, but he knew that no matter how good the charak was, Istvay would hear the hint of pain in it.

From outside, there was the scrape of a chair being pushed back.

A spike of panic flooded through his brain, but it wasn't his panic this time.

Fine! the thing hissed. *But I am in your head until the raiders take us back to our home. And if they don't, I kill you!*

"Aran?" Istvay's voice was almost outside the door.

"You'll have to get out of the raiders' heads too," Aran thought firmly.

Can't! the thing wailed. *Not me! Family! Can't talk to them while I'm in your head.*

He had a sudden picture of a heap of the slimy, translucent creatures, squirming over each other, and a quick flash of protectiveness.

"Oh, they're beautiful," he thought in an awed whisper. "I don't blame you for wanting to keep them safe."

"Aran, listen, if you don't answer me right this second, I'm going to break the door down." Istvay's tone was cut from steel.

"Alright, then the moment we're back on the ship, you talk them into getting out of the raiders, or we use the thing on them," he thought.

Yes! the charak squealed in panic, and then he felt the pressure in his brain release. He gasped in relief and almost staggered backward, and stopped himself just in time to avoid being a very dead body in a pool of blood.

"Pishti, wait," he gasped as he heard Istvay's hand on the handle. "It's … listen, it's fine, I'm just … Just give me a second, okay?"

"Aran? What happened?" He could hear the sharp tinge of worry in Istvay's voice.

"It's … nothing too bad, just give me a sec," he managed. "And, um, you might ask Dessi if she happens to have access to artificial blood for a transfusion? I probably won't need it, but—"

"Aran! What the hell is going on?"

"Just …" He reached down, holding his leg steady against the spike of wood. Blood had already soaked through his trousers, but it hadn't hit the artery, not yet. "I've … listen, I had a bit of a problem with a charak, but it's … I mean, I'm pretty sure we've worked something out, so it's fine."

"Aran—" Istvay was now making no effort to hide the absolute panic in their voice.

"Alright," Aran thought grimly, "Istvay knows you're here now. If you try to take me over once this is out, even for one second, they will not hesitate to hunt you down. Do you understand me?"

There was a wordless, panicked flood of agreement.

"Good." He paused. "Now, just let me …"

There was another wordless flood of panic that seemed to be attempting to convey a sentiment along the lines of, *Be careful, damn you.*

"I'm trying," he muttered.

"Aran!"

He sucked in a quick breath, closed his eyes, and, holding the door steady with one hand, jerked his leg back and off the spike of wood. He couldn't quite muffle a hiss of pain, and he stumbled backward, shoving his palm against the rapidly spreading patch of blood on his leg.

"Aran, I need you to answer me, please." Istvay sounded desperate.

Aran forced himself to look down at his leg, despite the lightheadedness from the pain and shock, and for a moment he felt himself starting to panic at the sheer amount of blood … but when he drew his hand back gingerly, it welled up around the wound, but it wasn't spurting the way it would have if he'd nicked the artery.

He half-fell back against the sink, gasping in relief. "Pishti, it's fine, you can come in now," he managed, and the door burst open and Istvay stepped through. Their face was completely bloodless, their jaw set as if they were trying to fight back absolute panic.

They stopped dead when they saw him, and he realized how he must look: slumped against the sink, blood soaking through his trousers and dripping onto the floor and liberally coating his hands and sleeves and probably smeared across his face where he'd brushed his hair back without thinking.

And then their face went dark with fury, and he realized, suddenly, that the charak might not have been exaggerating all that much.

"Aran, don't move, I'm going to get Dessi, and we're going to get you bandaged up. And then I'll deal with the charaks."

There was a sharp blip of panic from the depths of his mind.

"Pishti, no wait," he managed, shoving himself back as they stepped forward to help him up. "I'm alright, I'm fine, just don't touch me without gloves for now."

It wasn't that he necessarily expected the charak to go back on their bargain the moment it saw the opportunity to infect Istvay. He just wasn't sure it wouldn't.

"Aran ..." Istvay sounded like they were about to either pass out, or burn the entire system down with fire.

He sucked in a quick breath, wincing at the pain even that movement shot through his leg. "Listen. Pishti. I'm fine, but ..."

"You're not damn well fine! You look like you're bleeding out!"

"I'm not bleeding out, I checked, okay? Just ... just put on some gloves and help me sit down, and I'll explain everything, I promise."

By the time he was finally seated and Istvay had handed him a painkiller and cleaned and bandaged the wound, with Dessi looking on and commenting tartly on how close Aran had come to puncturing the artery and actually bleeding out on the floor—he'd shot her an irritated glare at that, and she seemed to finally catch on, because she stopped talking about how long it would have taken before Aran's blood pressure had gone so low that she wouldn't have been able to do anything to save him before Istvay actually fainted from terror—he'd managed to bring his shaky muscles back under control.

Istvay and the raiders listened in silence to his explanation, and from the look on Istvay's face, they very much wanted an excuse to kill all the charaks, not only in the yibo system, but in any system that they might have spread to. But at last, when he'd finished, they nodded shortly. "So there's still one of those things in your head," they said. Their voice was flat, and at the sound of it, there was another frantic blip of terror deep in Aran's brain.

"Yes," he said. "It's still in there. But like I said, we have a deal. It promised it won't take me over again, as long as we promise to not use the cure as soon as we find it, but give the charaks a chance to get back home first. And we should probably send some food back with them as well, that will probably give them more incentive not to go looking for a raider ship to infect for at least a little while." He paused. "Pishti, you really should have seen them. They're absolutely fascinating creatures, they have this mouthpart that ..."

"Aran ..."

"Sorry," he muttered guiltily. He paused a moment. "Anyways, that's the bargain. It can't communicate with the charaks who've taken over the raiders, because they're different charaks—there must be a whole nest of them on Krevai's ship, which is actually ..." He cleared his throat. "Which means we're going to have to get back there. And unless we have the cure finalized, I get the feeling that they may not agree with what their friend in my head has worked out. So I think that's the first thing we have to focus on. You should all wear protective gear around me just to be safe, but as long as it hasn't taken over my head, I don't think it can affect you."

Istvay nodded again, and he could see the self-control it was taking them not to either grab him in an embrace, or start off to hunt down the charaks singlehandedly.

He blew out a shaky breath.

Honestly, he wouldn't have minded Istvay grabbing him in an

embrace right now.

The pain from his leg throbbed through his entire body, and he felt sick and shaky with it, and he must have lost a good bit of blood even without puncturing an artery, because he was lightheaded and dizzy in a way that was completely distinct from the lightheaded panic of earlier.

"Well, I guess we'd better get finished up, then," said Istvay, with a sickly attempt at a smile.

Aran tried to push himself to his feet, then cursed and grabbed the back of the chair to keep from falling over. Istvay grabbed for him, still gloved. "No, stay there! Don't move, I'll … I'll bring the table over to you."

Aran leaned back and closed his eyes for a moment, too exhausted and lightheaded to protest, and a moment later, he heard the sound of table-legs scraping across the smooth floor of the lab.

When he opened his eyes, Krevai was helping Istvay position the table in front of him, and Dessi was pulling over a chair for Istvay.

Krevai paused for a moment beside Aran, fixedly avoiding looking at him. At last, the raider captain cleared his throat. "That was … quick thinking, human," he said gruffly.

Then he turned away and stalked back across the lab to rejoin Zondra in the corner.

"Alright," said Istvay grimly, pulling up their chair and scooting it close to Aran. They pulled the notes around in front of them and pulled up the scanner readouts with a flick of their wrist. "Let's figure this out once and for all, and finally get that damned nuisance out of your head."

Aran ignored the flicker of annoyance from deep in his mind, and leaned forward. Even after all the excitement, he found he was having a hard time keeping his eyes open. "Yeah," he mumbled, rubbing his hands over his eyes. "Let's get this finished."

He wasn't sure how long they'd been working, but at some point he realized the light from outside had faded, and the numbers were blurring in front of his eyes.

And then he jerked up with a start, and realized he was in a cot, and for a moment he felt an absurd spike of panic, because he didn't know where he was, and he didn't know where Istvay was …

"You're awake."

It was Istvay's voice, and he felt his entire body relax at the familiar sound.

"Are you still in control of your body?"

He frowned, blinking up at his friend, and then the irritated grumble in the back of his mind reminded him. "Yeah," he croaked. "Yeah, it's me." He glanced around. "Ani?" he called.

She perked up from where she'd been lying at the foot of his bed, and swarmed up to him, enveloping his face affectionately until he had to shove her off. "Hey, sweetheart, I missed you too, but I can't get you a treat unless I can breathe, okay?"

The sharp worry in Istvay's face had faded a little at Ani's clear endorsement, and they pushed themself to their feet. "I'll go get something for her, you probably aren't going to feel up to walking for a little while," they grumbled. "Considering you decided to impale yourself on a doorframe yesterday on purpose."

Aran lay back for a moment, rubbing his eyes and trying to regain his bearings.

When Istvay returned, they were carrying a treat for Ani in one hand, and a steaming mug in the other. Aran pushed himself up into a sitting position, and once Ani was happily devouring the energy bar, Istvay handed the mug to Aran. "Instant coffee, sorry. That's the best they had in the lab cupboards. But I figured it had been a few weeks since we'd had even that much, so ..." they shrugged.

Aran held the mug to his nose and breathed in the rich fragrance, then grinned up at Istvay. "Have I ever told you how much I love you?"

Istvay chuckled reluctantly. "Over a cup of coffee? I should have thought of that sooner."

Aran closed his eyes and brought the mug to his lips, savouring the earthy, bitter flavour on his tongue. Istvay had made it just the way he liked it, hot enough to warm him but not hot enough to burn his mouth, and the thought made an ache of fondness squeeze his chest until he wasn't completely sure he could breathe through it.

When he opened his eyes again, Istvay was watching him, a soft look in their eyes.

He cleared his throat. "Um. Thank you." He paused a moment. "So, what happened after I fell asleep?"

Istvay sighed and ran a hand across their face. "Krevai gloved up and carried you to bed, and a few hours later Dessi told me if I didn't go to bed, she'd hit me over the head and carry me there too. So you didn't actually miss much." They paused and glanced over at him, and he could see the hint of excitement in their face. "But we're almost there. I just have to finish running the calculations, but I'm pretty sure this is the solution I figured out back on the raider ship. There are some tricky equations, but with both of us coming at it with fresh eyes, I think we'll have it done in a couple hours."

By the time Aran had maneuvered himself to the edge of the bed and gingerly lowered his legs over the edge, wincing in pain at every movement, he was no longer in any state to protest when Krevai stomped over and offered, gruffly, to carry him to the table.

Once he was settled, Dessi came over to inspect his injury, muttering something about a breeding ground for tetanus, and Istvay grumbled something back about, surely she'd spent enough time around Aran to know that if he hadn't been vaccinated for tetanus and rabies and every other damn thing you could be vaccinated for, he wouldn't have survived his damn childhood, then made him swallow some antibiotics and painkillers. They were glowering around the room with a look on their face that made the thing in Aran's head mutter in fear.

"It's fine, they're just like this," he thought, then amended, "I mean, whenever I get hurt they're like this. But it happens a lot."

The charak managed to convey a sense of skeptical incredulity so strong that he felt himself thinking something shamefaced along the lines of, "it's not on purpose," to which the charak responded by shoving a picture into the front of his mind of the spike of wood impaling his leg.

He winced at the memory. "It's not exactly like you gave me much choice," he grumbled in his head.

The charak gave off a distinct air of offence.

"Aran?"

He looked up to find Istvay watching him in concern. "Sorry," he muttered. "I was just …"

Istvay closed their eyes. "You were trying to, what, communicate with the charak?" They sighed. "You know what, never mind. I don't think I actually want to know. Come on, the sooner we get this done and get that thing out of your head, the sooner I can kiss you, and I don't know how much longer I'm going to last without that at this point."

Istvay was right about their work—they'd revised the theory while Aran slept, and now it was just a matter of going through the endless list of data and plugging it into the equations they'd worked out.

At last he raised his head to see Istvay watching him. They were grinning, and he grinned back. "I think we've got it!" he whispered.

Dessi, across the room, perked up. "Humans? You found something?"

Istvay stood, pushing back their chair. They were grinning broadly. "We've got it. Let's get back to the ship, and I'll show you how to …"

There was a noise from the door behind them, and Aran cocked his head as Ani's posture stiffened. Istvay turned at his movement, their face instantly filled with concern. "Aran? Is something wrong? What—"

Then the back door, which shouldn't have connected to anything except the emergency stairway, was shoved open, and a horrified-looking woman staggered through.

Istvay had spun, but swayed on their feet at the sudden movement. Without thinking, Aran tried to push himself to his feet to steady them, but he collapsed back into his chair, hissing in pain and blinking against the blackness crowding his vision.

The woman stumbled up against the table, and Aran saw, suddenly, why she was staggering.

There was a man behind her, twisting her arm painfully up behind her back, a pulse-pistol shoved up under her ribcage.

A man who was instantly, horribly familiar.

"Emeric?" Aran managed, his mind gone completely blank.

Emeric grinned and let go of the woman. She stumbled, knocked off-balance, and as Istvay reached forward instinctively to steady her, Emeric grabbed them by the back of the jacket and swung the butt of his pistol against their temple.

23

Alba

Alba glanced around her in the small, dark basement where she, Yosip, and Feliu were currently crouched, and tried to hide her unease.

There were twenty-seven councillors who'd agreed to help.

Out of the three-hundred-odd on the Council, that was hardly a glowing victory. But it was something. And it would have to be enough.

Now there was nothing left but to finish coordinations with the rebel forces.

"If you're ready, Madam, I'll put through the call," said Feliu.

She nodded without speaking, and he pulled up a holoscreen from the disk and expanded it, so that all present could see.

An image appeared on the screen—a young woman with auburn hair, still showing traces of the black dye she'd been wearing when Alba had first met her, wide, innocent green eyes, and an open, friendly face. She'd lost weight in her months in the yibo system, her comfortable curves not quite so prominent, her round face more drawn and gaunt than it had been. But it wasn't that that struck Alba, seeing the girl again after so long.

It was something about her expression. Something in her posture and bearing.

When Alba had known her, Savina had been hardly more than an opportunist—trying to save her siblings, and kill Alba, and possibly find some way to make the disaster of the broken-up diplomatic ship into something she could gain from.

Since then, Savina had risked her life, over and over and over, to save people she'd never met and didn't know. To keep the system from devolving into war, to keep the humans in the yibo system from being slaughtered. She'd faced enemy fire, from humans and yibo both, faced down raiders. There was a quiet, grim confidence to her now, a weight of responsibility that Alba would never have believed possible months before.

"Alba." Savina's voice was sharp, and bore its usual cutting tone. Alba almost smiled.

Not everything had changed, then.

"Savina. I'm glad to see you." Alba was almost surprised at the sincerity of the words.

Savina narrowed her eyes in badly disguised disgust. "Listen, Chief Justice. We are not friends."

"Perhaps not," said Alba. "But we are allies, I think."

Savina snorted, then sighed. "Fine." She paused. "I don't know the situation in do Sol. But we've received word that Cavaco is sending his entire army up into the Rim Mountains. If our information is correct, they'll be arriving in less than two days. I think he wants to crush us, once and for all, so he can bring the rest of his troops in the mountains home. If he succeeds, I don't think it'll be possible to recover from that. But ... this could be our chance.

If we can find a way to keep his troops occupied here, and in the meantime bring the bulk of the rebel forces down and take the city gates—"

Alba glanced around at the others in the room.

"It's possible," Yosip said. "If the rebel forces can hold back the army long enough for you to get word out, and if the councillors we spoke to are still willing, and if the citizens of do Sol rise up, as we hope, in large enough numbers to overwhelm the troops left in the city—we may have a chance to retake the government." He shook his head. "It depends on a large number of 'if's, I know. We'd have to work quickly, and we'd have to hope that your message has the intended effect. But I think it may be our best chance." He looked over at Feliu.

Feliu sighed, and Alba could hear the worry in his tone. "The assassin is right—we don't exactly have time to wait for something better. If Cavaco brings his entire force back into the city, we'll be waiting months before we find another opportunity like this one, and we don't have months. Once the yibo captain sends word back through the portal, we lose the option of a diplomatic resolution. And to be perfectly honest, if Cavaco is still in power, I can't disagree with the yibos' assessment as to risk—there will be a war, whether they want one or not."

Alba sighed and nodded, turning back to the screen.

Joska stood beside Savina now. The captain's weathered face was even more weary than usual, dark circles under her eyes, but she managed a tired smile at Alba. "Chief Justice," she said. "It's good to see you alive."

"I could say the same," said Alba. She paused. "Savina's told me your plans. She said you'd bring the bulk of your people down to the city while Cavaco's troops were occupied in the mountains?"

Joska nodded. "I think that's the only way we stay alive. But if the city doesn't rise up to help us, I don't think we'll stand much of a chance."

"We'll do our best," said Alba. "As with every time we've worked together in the past few months, I cannot promise results. But I will do everything in my power for you."

Joska nodded brusquely. "I suppose that's all any of us can do. Best of luck to you, Chief Justice." There was a note of genuine respect in Joska's tone that took Alba aback. If she remembered correctly, Joska hadn't been overly respectful the last time the two of them had spoken.

She cleared her throat. "Thank you. Best of luck to you and Savina as well."

The line clicked off.

"Well," said Alba at last, pushing herself to her feet. "If they're going to be here in less than forty-eight hours, I suppose we'd best get prepared."

It was well into the night by the time they'd finished their preparations. Feliu, she could tell, was less than happy with the risk. But he couldn't think of a better alternative, so he contented himself with irritated muttering.

Alba lay awake for a long time that night, staring at the heavy wood of the ceiling beams in her small bedroom.

This was it, then. This was where it would end, all of it—the moment she'd feared and anticipated since before the portal opened. Despite everything that had come in-between, at its heart, this was the same conflict she'd started when she walked into the Council Chambers months previous and proposed her fateful motion.

Either Cavaco won, and began the first in a series of endless wars with yibo, and raiders and whatever other sapient creatures the yibos' portals could open onto—or Alba won, and the military lost its hold on power, and they tried diplomacy and democracy, in all its messy, untidy, uneasy, hopeful imperfection.

She almost laughed.

So much had happened, so much time had passed, and here she was, back where she'd started.

She wasn't the person she had been, though. For better or worse, her time in the yibo system had changed her in ways that were irrevocable.

Only time would tell if those changes meant she was more or less able to do what needed to be done. She, herself, still wasn't sure.

When she finally drifted off, it was to restless sleep and troubled dreams.

She woke in a panic, and jerked upright, looking around frantically for a moment before she realized what had woken her.

There was a loud pounding on the door, and raised voices.

She frowned, listening.

And then someone screamed, and it took Alba a moment to recognize the voice of the woman who'd taken them in. There was the fizz of pulse-blasts, and the sound of something heavy hitting the floor.

Cold panic clutched around her chest.

She pushed herself up, heart pounding. There had to be a place to hide, something. If she could get out, perhaps she could do something for the others.

"Alba Espina. We know you're in there!" The voice at the door was loud and harsh. "Open up, by order of the government."

There was a small window. She was on the second floor, but it was still possible she could find a way to climb through, get herself down.

"Open the door, Alba, or we shoot your accomplices."

"Madam, don't—" Feliu's voice was thin with horror. There was the sound of a fist striking flesh, and Feliu's grunt of pain.

Her feet stopped of their own accord.

"Open the door."

She drew in a long breath.

She could taste the bitter tang of despair in the back of her throat, but she swallowed it down. "Please give me a moment," she called out. "I'm not as young as I was."

She tried to blink through her wavelink to Savina, but as she'd expected, the soldiers must have been carrying a communication blocker. Maybe her yibo communicator—

She closed her eyes, her stomach sinking with despair.

She'd left it in the main room the previous night, after their conversation with the rebels.

She had no way to alert anyone to what had happened.

Slowly, she crossed to the door, and slowly, she pulled it open.

Feliu and Yosip were outside. There was a bruise rising on the side of Feliu's face, but he was standing. Yosip, though, was slumped over, his face grey with pain, and blood soaked through his shirt in an ever-growing red stain.

Her heart lurched in panic at the sight, the breath catching in her throat.

But there was nothing she could do.

Savina was still coming. She couldn't warn her, couldn't do anything to help her. All she could do was hope that somehow, the rebels would be able to take the gates, secure the city without her help.

There was still a possibility. There was still hope, for the rebels, at least.

She doubted, very much, that there was still hope for any of the three of them here.

She didn't fight as the soldiers clamped cuffs over her wrists, or as they shoved her forward.

"You chose wisely, Alba" the military captain said, her voice cold. "Now." She beckoned with a jerk of her head. "Bring the others along as well, lock them up. Cavaco will want to see the former Chief Justice immediately."

24

Savina

Savina glanced behind her at the small band of grim-faced villagers, dirt smeared on their faces and clothing to break up their outline. In the dark shadows of the trees outside of the city walls of do Sol, they were difficult to make out, even in the faint glow from the moon.

The sight reminded her, far too viscerally, of back in the yibo system, preparing to take the city of Chrr, where everything had ended in such a spectacular, horrifying disaster.

And once again, she felt Reka's absence like a broken tooth, the pain sharp and bright and impossible to ignore.

She gritted her teeth, and tried to ignore it anyways. "Come on," she said shortly. "Move out."

They started forward, slipping out from the brush and trees in the regulation green space around do Sol.

It was night, and clouds covered the half-moon, its light dim and wavering. The ground was rough and pitted, and Savina stumbled more than once as she and her soldiers made their way over the open ground.

There were soldiers standing guard at the gates, and soldiers on all the main roads, just as they'd expected. This would only work if they could get inside quickly, and there were people ready to take back the government infrastructure taken earlier by Cavaco. They needed to be in possession of the main strategic points in city by the time Alba gave her speech, or there was no chance any of this would work.

"Savina?" Joska's voice came through her earpiece. "We're in position."

They'd spread out to take the four main city gates at once—the moment the soldiers realized there was a threat, they'd do everything in their power to lock the city down.

"We're in position as well." Rafel's voice was gruff and worried.

"Ready." Nicolau's voice was tight with strain, and Savina couldn't bite back a curse.

Damn it to hell, Nicolau had been much easier to deal with as a concept than he was as a person.

She took a deep breath, and glanced over her shoulder. "Are you all ready?" she whispered.

The three rebel captains standing behind her nodded.

"Alright," Savina said quietly into her wavelink. "Move out."

The captains gestured behind them, and the camouflaged group started forward at a quick jog.

This was going to come down to timing. They needed to take out the guards, take the gates, and take the city as quickly as possible if they wanted any chance to avoid a bloodbath.

Rafel's saboteurs had managed to take out the sensors on the city walls, but even so, the soldiers standing guard spotted them when they were halfway across the distance.

"Who goes there?" one of them shouted, pulling his rifle from his shoulder. "Stop, who—"

One of the Rim Mountain villagers slung their weapon around, and the soldier at the gate dissolved into ash at a shot from the yibo gun.

"Go!" Savina shouted. "Go, now!"

It was too late for secrecy.

The ragged band of them broke into a full run, coming up and around Savina. She waved them past and ran after them, gasping and cursing.

Damn running to hell.

The guerrillas had already overrun the gate guards, melting them with the few yibo weapons they'd portioned out among themselves, or using the old-fashioned methods of rocks or sticks to knock back helmets before dispatching the soldiers with a pulse-pistol shot.

"Go!" Savina shouted as she came up behind them. A Joias soldier turned on her, then stopped abruptly, swaying, as one of her throwing knives found its mark in a gap in his armour.

She shoved him as he went by, yanking the blade from his shoulder as he fell, and then jammed the bloody blade upwards under another guard's helmet and into the soft spot behind her ear. The guard collapsed, and Savina turned, ducking as a pulse-shot from one of the soldier's guns rippled across where her head had been. She came up smiling, and threw the bloody knife with deadly accuracy.

Around her, people were screaming and cursing, shots firing. The guards must have got out the word, because already reinforcements were flooding out of the city entrance.

"Get inside!" Savina snapped over the wavelink. "Don't worry about killing them, get inside. We've got to get to a defensible position."

Already she could see, from the corner of her eyes, several of the guerillas lying bloody and still on the ground.

Too many. They didn't have the numbers to lose.

"Inside!" she shouted again. "Get inside! The rest of us will hold them for as long as we can!"

She caught a glimpse of one of the rebel captains, who'd managed to break an opening. She was gesturing franticly, shouting commands that Savina couldn't hear over the noise. But she could see the guerrillas turning towards the woman, running for the gap.

There was a shot, and the captain screamed and fell, but the Rim Mountain soldiers were already piling through the gap she'd opened into the city.

Something hit Savina hard, knocking her forward, and she stumbled, off-balance, before the pain registered. She turned, yanking out her yibo gun despite the blazing pain in her side, and fired. The soldier who'd shot her dissolved, and then she felt her knees give way under her. She hit the ground hard, and forced herself up, forced herself to roll into a sitting position despite the way the world was spinning around her.

She raised her shaking hand and fired, and fired, and fired again.

A Rim Mountain villager had seen her, and was running towards her, his face grim. He got to her, grabbing her roughly under the arms and hauling her to her feet, and she shot twice more, killing two more Joias soldiers who'd started towards them.

"Come on, let's get you inside," the man who'd grabbed her hissed. "We've got at least half—"

His words choked off, and he staggered. Savina barely managed to catch herself as he sank to the ground, and when she looked over, where his head had been, there was only a bloody mass.

She had to look away quickly.

No time for this, no time to think or feel. They had to get through the gate.

She staggered, and caught her balance as a Joias soldier grabbed for her. She shoved her knife up as hard as she could under his armpit, and he screamed and let go of her.

Pain shot down her entire body, and she bit back a scream of her own as her muscles pulled, trying to keep her upright.

Pain was radiating from the site of the shot, washing in hot waves up and down her body.

But the rebels were in, most of them, at least, and …

And then she realized something that the back of her mind had been trying to tell her for a while.

The soldiers outside the gates hadn't been fighting to stop them. She could see that now, in the strategy they'd used.

They'd only been trying to delay.

The thought formed something heavy and sick in her stomach.

She blinked to activate her wavelink. "Fall back!" she shouted. "Fall back, everyone!"

But it was too late. Even with the pain casting shimmering waves over her consciousness, she could hear the low-pitched growl of the approaching military transports.

Someone grabbed her and dragged her to her feet, but she was too lightheaded to resist. A gun was shoved up against her head, and then someone shouted, "She's one of the ringleaders! Keep her alive, Cavaco will want to interrogate her."

She tried to grab for a knife, but her muscles were no longer under her control. All she could do was slump against her captor and try to keep from passing out.

Hazily, she could see the transports land, see the hatches spring open and soldiers running across the open space towards them.

"Savina—" She could hear the dread in Joska's voice over the wavelink. "Cavaco's soldiers …"

"I know," she managed.

"We're trapped." It was Rafel this time, and his voice was tight with fear. "We're not going to be able to get out, not without a rescue."

"Well, I suppose that makes all of us." Joska's voice still carried that grim humour. "Savina?"

But she couldn't answer. Her tongue was thick and heavy in her mouth, and the entire world had dissolved into nothing but a hot, never-ending pain.

And then, finally, it dissolved into blackness.

25

Over the holoscreen in the council chambers, Cavaco had looked much the same as he had before she left. But now, seeing him up close, Alba could see the changes—the deepening of the lines on his face, the strain cutting through his expression, his jawline, once tight and firm, now puffy from stress and lack of sleep.

She couldn't hold back a small, grim twinge of satisfaction, despite the desperateness of the situation.

The soldiers shoved her into a seat, and she felt an unreasonable surge of gratitude for the fact that she was sitting in a chair, and not one of those damnable yibo stools.

"Alba," said Cavaco. He was examining her, his eyes sharp and hostile, but she refused to drop her gaze.

"Cavaco. I see you have no more respect for decency now than you ever did before."

He gave a small smile. "And I see you're as sharp-tongued as ever. I should have been surprised when I found out you hadn't been killed in the alien system, but then I know you. Death itself would shrink from your sharp tongue."

She didn't deign to answer.

Her heart was pounding, sharp and quick, and she wasn't sure if it was for her own danger, or from the memory of the way Yosip had slumped to the ground when his captor's released him in the small cell, the memory of the bruise sharp and clear against Feliu's temple, or whether it was the thought of the rebels outside the city gates, rebels she was no longer in any position to help.

He must have read some of her thoughts in her eyes, because his smile broadened just a little. "Your little rag-tag army, I'm afraid, is no longer a threat. With enough persuasion, the people they'd left in the Rim Mountains were more than happy to inform my soldiers of their plans. My soldiers returned to the city post-haste. I presume that by now, all the leaders of their little villager rebellion have been taken or killed."

Alba closed her eyes against the sick feeling in her stomach.

For a few moments, the two of them sat in silence. At last Cavaco sighed. "Alba. I admit, I didn't believe your story of aliens who wished for peace. But after an extensive briefing with Mattin, I have come to the conclusion that perhaps you were right—perhaps we do not, at this moment, have the strength necessary to fight an alien war. This has been brought home to me by the rebellion in the Rim Mountains. While it may be possible to survive a yibo attack if we were to concentrate our forces, it is not possible when my forces are divided and scattered. And I know enough about history to know that guerrilla wars tend to be long and bloody. So." He leaned forward, resting his elbows on his knees. "I have a proposition for you, Alba."

She frowned at him, startled out of her despair.

"I think that, at least in the matter of the alien war, you and I have interests that align—the survival of our system as a whole. So here is what I propose: I will release you and your friends. You will speak with the other councillors, and you will inform them that our best option is to work together to deal with the alien threat. We will open a council meeting, and you will be given a position of authority—not, perhaps, a full one-third of the government head, as you had before, but enough that your voice will hold sway. You will agree to give my temporary military government legitimacy to deal with this crisis. And in return, I will agree to a peaceful hand-over of power when the crisis is past, with certain agreed-upon conditions."

Alba stared at him for a moment. Her mind was spinning, parsing through Cavaco's words to tease out the reasoning behind them.

"If I were to agree to this," she said at last, slowly, "I can understand how my assistance would bring legitimacy to your illegal coup. However, this would hardly solve your problems. If we are indeed to be at war with the yibo, then ...."

She stopped abruptly.

Cavaco smiled. "I believe you've discovered the answer to your own question, Alba," he said. "I will need your agreement to put down the rebellion in the Rim Mountains, and I must be able to do it as I see fit. Alone, I hardly think I can do that without risk of the people rising up. But your name has always carried legitimacy. The people view you, rightly or wrongly, as a person of integrity. And if you were to throw your support behind putting down the rebellion in the Rim Mountains as the only way to survive this upcoming alien war—I think it would grant me the support I need."

"Whatever sway my name holds here, I hardly think I'm popular in the Rim Mountains," Alba said sharply. "I very much doubt that even if I put my support behind your proposition, I could convince them to lay down their arms." Even as she spoke, she could picture

Joska's face, stubborn and censorious, picture the betrayed anger in Savina's expression.

Cavaco smiled again. "You wouldn't need to. If the people in the Belt see you offer terms to the rebels, and the rebels refuse to accept them—I believe I would have all the moral authority I need to defeat them."

He leaned forward again. "Alba. You are a politician. You understand, as well as I do, that the good of the few must bow before the good of the many." He sighed, and for the first time Alba heard the weariness behind it. "You have been an exceptionally worthy opponent. Perhaps more worthy than I would have liked. Believe me that I do not relish the prospect of working together with you any more than I'm sure you relish working with me. But I'm willing to put aside my pride in order to salvage the Joias System. Surely you can bring yourself to do the same."

Alba watched him for a moment. "So," she said at last. She was almost impressed at how even she managed to keep her tone. "You would like me to sell out the people in the Rim Mountains, in exchange for you being willing to give up a fraction of the power you've illegitimately stolen, while you fight your war. Do I understand you correctly?"

Cavaco smiled a little. "I am asking, Alba, that you put aside your pride, and you sacrifice a few backwards villagers to save the Joias System. I am offering you a way that we can come to terms with minimal bloodshed. And I think that you are enough of a politician to understand that this is the best possible outcome. The only outcome, in fact, that does not leave hundreds of thousands dead."

For a long moment, Alba was silent.

She could hear, in her memory, Ines's voice, low and hurt and angry. *I wish you'd thought of that eleven years ago.* She could hear Istvay, the weariness and pain behind the anger in their expression. *Did you ever think to ask us? Even once? Or were we so far below your notice that there was no need?*

This should, she knew, have been a difficult decision. She should be agonizing over what to do—because Cavaco was objectively correct. Despite the disgust she felt for the man, his grasp of the politics of the matter was sound. This would allow him to back down from his position without loss of face, and it could possibly even allow her to open negotiations with the yibo before the yibo captain called through the portal for military backup and made war all but inevitable. Possibly send the yibo and raider ships back and close the portal permanently.

But it wasn't. It was hardly a decision at all.

"No," she said, meeting Cavaco's eyes. "I am sorry, Eniko. But the people in the Rim Mountains are as much a part of this system as you and I. And I am not willing to put my voice behind a bargain that sells them out."

Her voice was steady, without even the hint of hesitation. Because the hesitation she might have had, once, had been stripped from her in the yibo system. It had been stripped from her, in a way that would never come back, the moment she let herself see the people behind the faceless mass she'd dreamed up back when she thought she knew better. It had been stripped from her when she'd been forced to come face to face, over and over and over again, with her failures, with her shortsightedness and misunderstandings. With the fact that she knew next to nothing about the people she'd purported to represent all this time.

With the fact that, even then, they hadn't given up fighting for each other, and the realization that, in the end, perhaps the only thing she brought to her position that anyone else could not was the ability to let their voices be heard through her.

Cavaco was staring at her. "Alba," he said at last. "I hadn't thought you, of all people, would choose to sacrifice the entire Joias system to your pique. What, would you like me to beg your forgiveness?"

Alba almost laughed. "This has nothing to do with my feelings. I am simply not willing to sacrifice the interests of people without political power to appease the egos of those with it. I'm sorry, but this is not an issue I am prepared to compromise on."

"So that's your final answer," Cavaco said at last. His voice was still pleasant, but she could see the dark anger behind his expression.

"That is my final answer." Her voice was still, somehow, calm. "I will fight for them until the last breath leaves my body."

Cavaco's brows lowered. "Very well," he said at last. "Then I suppose, Alba, we'd best make sure that is not a long period of time."

26

Savina

Savina woke to a thick, throbbing, mind-numbing pain.

For a few moments she just lay there, letting the pain wash through her and trying to find the rest of her consciousness.

She was lying on something cold and hard. Her wrists were cuffed together, and so were her ankles.

She groaned, and tried to move, and the effort shot hot pain up through her body, leaving her gasping and dizzy.

She slumped back, trying to collect her thoughts.

Her memories were a fog of pain and noise, and it took her a few moments before the jumbled images arranged themselves into some semblance of order.

The battle. They'd been outside the walls, and the rebels had finally broken through. She'd been trying to hold off the soldiers.

She'd been shot.

And …

She sucked in a quick breath.

The Joias soldiers from the Rim Mountains. Cavaco's soldiers had come back.

The frantic calls in from Joska and Rafel, the cries for help.

She squeezed her eyes shut and forced herself to breathe.

They'd been betrayed. Somehow, they'd been betrayed. And, unless things had changed after she'd passed out …

"Looks like our little cultist is awake." The voice outside her cell was harsh and unfamiliar.

She blinked her eyes open to two soldiers peering in through the bars of what must be a cell. The man who'd spoken smiled, a cold, sneering smile. "Are you comfortable, cultist? Cold? I could bring some boiling water, I hear you people love that sort of thing."

The words sent Savina's mind back to the vids she'd seen as a child, the scenes that had imprinted themselves across her brain, hot and visceral, like a fresh wound.

One of the soldiers spat. "You killed good soldiers outside the city. Just wait until Cavaco gets done with you—he'll make you wish you'd never been born. He'll make you beg for what happened in the Cleansing. You people like being martyrs, don't you?"

The soldiers turned away, laughing, and Savina closed her eyes and sank back on the floor.

She felt sick, and she wasn't sure whether it was the pain or the despair that set the nausea roiling in her stomach.

They'd failed. They'd failed, and she'd been captured, and she had no idea what had happened to the others—Joska, Rafel, her siblings.

She blinked in a reflexive effort to activate her wavelink, call them, find out what had happened, but even that movement set her head spinning, and they'd deactivated her wavelink.

She wanted to cry. But she was too exhausted and in too much pain even for that, so she just lay on the hard floor of her cell, and let the pain wash over her in waves.

She'd failed. After everything, she'd failed.

And then, abruptly, a memory flashed into her head—herself, as a child, watching the vids from the Cleansing. Her great-grandmother's face as she watched her children die.

You people like being martyrs, don't you?

Savina pulled in a long breath, and gritted her teeth.

Cavaco was going to kill her. That was obvious. And he'd probably want to do it in front of everyone, to show them exactly what awaited them if they didn't give in.

But then, that was exactly what the Orthodox Church had done during the Cleansing. And almost a hundred years later, those same vids were shown, over and over again, to the descendants of the people they'd tortured.

Savina may hate the compound, her family, everything they'd done and everything they'd taught her—but if they'd taught her one thing, it was that you couldn't kill off belief. You couldn't kill off faith. What was it the Head Order always said? The fires of the Cleansing only purified the belief of the faithful. And he'd been right. Her mother had believed enough to sacrifice her own child.

She managed a small, tight smile, despite the pain.

She still didn't know who the soldiers had killed and who they'd left alive. It probably didn't matter, honestly—she had no hope whatsoever of saving anyone, not from here.

But she knew damn well how to be a martyr. She'd had it drilled into her from her earliest memories. And if Cavaco killed her—at the very least, she could make sure her death would start a fire that would burn him alive.

27

Aran

Aran jumped to his feet with a shout of wordless panic, and Ani stiffened on his shoulder, ready to launch herself at Emeric. But Emeric had already caught Istvay as they staggered, and he shoved the muzzle of the pistol hard under their chin. "Control your damn pet, Aran, or I'll blow Istvay's brains out," he snapped.

Aran grabbed frantically for Ani as she tensed, then grabbed for the table with his free hand as the pain from his leg hit, setting the world swaying.

Ani hissed and tried to wriggle from his grasp, and he held her against his chest. "Ani, no," he gasped. "Please, Ani, just ... please listen to me!"

There must have been something in his voice, because she stopped struggling, although her posture was still tense. He leaned against the table, gasping in pain.

Istvay was standing very still. Their posture was as tense as Ani's, their head shoved back, the cords in their neck visible, but their eyes were fixed on Aran. He knew, suddenly, that they were standing still because they were perfectly aware that if they tried to struggle, he wouldn't be able to help himself from stepping in, and they didn't want to see him hurt. That was all. For all Istvay's talk of saving the system, in the end, both of them must have known all along—both of them would do anything to keep the other from being hurt.

And he knew, abruptly, that he was as much Istvay's entire world as they were his. Everything they'd done to disguise it, when they'd believed they'd die from the defect long before Aran did and had spent their life trying to prepare him to live without them—that had all been a front. Now that he was looking, he could see in their eyes the exact same thing he felt any time there was a chance that they would get hurt—it didn't matter what had happened or why, whether it was his fault or not, they would do anything it took— anything at all—to stop it.

He felt something tighten in his chest, and he couldn't tell if it was helpless gratitude or panic.

"Sit down before you fall down," Emeric snapped, jerking his chin at Aran.

Aran sank into his chair, and Istvay's posture visibly relaxed. Aran blinked a few times, trying to bring the world back into focus, and then turned back to Emeric.

The raiders were frozen, across the room. They'd clearly understood that one move on their part would lead to Istvay's death.

"What the hell do you want?" Aran could scarcely recognize his own voice.

Emeric smiled, but the expression was laced with pure hatred. "You and Istvay are coming back with me. You're going to hand the cure for the defect over to Cavaco. And whatever it is you were working on for the raiders, you're going to give that to Cavaco too."

"I … I don't—Emeric, you don't know what you're doing! The

thing we've been working on for the raiders is the only way to stop them rampaging through do Sol and killing everyone inside!"

Emeric was still smiling, that vicious, bitter smile that Aran remembered so well from the last time Aran had seen him, inside the makeshift prison in Chrr. "I don't know the details you've worked out with these murderers, Aran, and quite frankly, I don't care. These raiders need your cure? Fine. They'll get it if they cooperate with Cavaco. Cavaco needs an alien war. The threat of a handful of crazed raiders will make sure he gets it, and the raiders won't do more damage than we can stand, because we'll be holding your research hostage."

"No, Emeric, you don't understand! It's not—"

"Shut up!" Emeric snapped. He twisted the gun against Istvay's throat, and Istvay hissed in pain.

"Emeric—" He glanced around frantically. Maybe, if he found a way to pass what he and Istvay had discovered through to Dessi, she'd be able to figure out the rest on her own. It would be a chance, at least.

Emeric caught the direction of his glance. "Don't even think about it. You say one single word to those raiders and Istvay dies, and so do you." He snatched up the scribbled-on scraps of paper from the table and shoved them into his pocket. "You." Emeric gestured at Dessi. "Call your raider crew. Tell them they're taking orders from me now."

"I—" Dessi glanced back and forth between Aran and Istvay.

"Now, or these two die!" Emeric snapped.

"Please," Aran whispered.

Dessi looked at him in indecision. At last she sighed and tapped something through her communicator.

They could all hear it buzz. Landru's voice answered, but this wasn't the Landru Aran knew.

"Captain Krevai. The crew and I are going out to hunt. Don't worry, we've almost taken care of the locks. We'll be sure to come find you."

The line went dead.

For a few moments, there was utter silence.

Aran closed his eyes in despair.

It wasn't fair. This wasn't bloody fair! Every last damn thing he'd done in the last … hell, he couldn't even remember how long—stopping the war, working himself to exhaustion to fix the charak infestation for the raiders, damn well impaling himself on a doorframe to keep the charak from killing his friends—all to save people who couldn't bloody well care less about him or Istvay. Krevai wasn't speaking to him, Dessi was furious with him, Emeric, who was one of the people in the damn yibo city who was almost certain to have been killed if the raiders weren't stopped, was threatening him, and the charaks, who, he was pretty sure, every damn person in this system or any other, except for him, would be perfectly happy to wipe out into extinction, had decided to make it so he didn't even have the chance to bloody well kiss Istvay one more time before they all died.

For a moment, he was so angry he was lightheaded with it.

Maybe Istvay had been right, this whole time. Maybe all these people he'd worked himself ragged to save, over and over and over, didn't deserve his help.

But at this point … well, at this point, it hardly mattered.

Istvay was right. He was stupid.

Istvay wouldn't have put it like that, of course. They would have said something about how he was too damn kind and too damn moral for his own good, something that wouldn't have made him feel like there was a splinter jabbed through his lungs every time he breathed. They'd always tried to protect him from the consequences of his own actions.

But Istvay couldn't say anything right now, because there was a gun shoved up against their throat, and it was his bloody fault.

The thick weight of despair draped over him was so heavy he wasn't sure he could have moved if he'd tried.

Vila Nova do Sol would be destroyed, and a war would break out that would rage across the entire Joias System until there was nothing left of it, and it was his own damn fault, because just like Istvay said, he couldn't bear to treat other people the way they'd always treated him. Even if they damn well deserved it.

He slumped, and from the corner of his eye, he caught the triumph in Emeric's smile at the sight.

He was too exhausted to care.

And then he felt something else: a small flicker, right at the edges of his consciousness.

A small, questioning feeling.

Not use this on us? the thing thought at him.

His thoughts were so bitter he wasn't sure he could form them into words. But then, he didn't know enough about charaks to know if it mattered.

"I won't. But probably someone will, sometime. Who knows, you might manage to kill your way across the system for a little while before then," he thought bitterly.

There was a pause, a moment of silence inside his head.

And then, a small, tentative picture.

A picture of himself, reaching out and touching Emeric's bare skin.

For a moment, he sat where he was, too stunned to move.

You won't kill us, the thought bubbled up again, a mix of suspicion and tentative trust.

Aran closed his eyes, trying to keep the smile from spreading across his face, that wondrous bubble of joy that always rose in his chest the moment a wild creature trusted him enough to, however cautiously, come creeping out of its den towards him, wary trust in its eyes.

He straightened. "Emeric," he began, and he had to fight to keep the wonder and sheer, absurd happiness out of his tone.

He reached out, putting a hand on Emeric's wrist.

He felt something surge forward, shoving his consciousness back into its tiny prison from the last time he'd been taken over by the charak, and he had to fight back the hideous, thought-stopping panic.

Emeric glanced at him in irritation, twitching his hand out of the way. "Aran—" he began, his tone sneering.

And then he stiffened, his eyes rolling back into his head. The pistol tumbled from his grip, and he fell backwards, landing on the ground like a felled tree.

Aran winced internally as Emeric's head bounced against the floor.

And then Emeric lay still.

Istvay gasped, grabbing the table to steady themself.

And then they stopped dead.

"What the hell ..." they began, staring at Emeric.

"Aran, what happened?" Dessi asked at the same time.

The charak slithered back to whatever part of his mind it stayed when it wasn't in control, and Aran pulled in a deep breath, almost too dizzy with relief to speak. Then he turned to Istvay, and grinned. "I guess the charaks didn't like the idea of Emeric being in charge any more than we did."

Krevai looked between Aran and the motionless Emeric.

And then he threw back his head and laughed until he was wheezing, bending over and bracing himself on his knees, tears of laughter in his eyes.

"Aran!" he boomed when he'd recovered himself sufficiently to speak. "My little human. Who would have thought …" he broke off, chuckling and wiping tears of laughter from his eyes. "Dessi, our little human will truly never cease to surprise me," he said, turning to her and shaking his head. "I suppose we picked well after all when we invited him to join our crew."

Aran stared, too shocked, for a moment, to speak.

He felt Istvay's hand on his shoulder over his jacket, warm and comforting, and he leaned back against them, closing his eyes.

He still couldn't touch them, not without protection. He still didn't quite trust the charak enough for that.

But …

He sucked in another deep breath, and sent a thought of gratitude towards the thing in his head. Then he pushed himself gingerly to his feet, bracing himself against the pain and bearing his full weight on his uninjured leg. "Alright then," he said, looking around. "I guess we should get back to the ship before Landru manages to break through the locks."

28

Savina

"Please!" Savina's voice wavered, small and pitiful. "Please, I'll do anything."

Cavaco towered over her where she knelt on the ground, curled around the pain in her side.

She had to bite back a small, grim smile.

She was very, very good at pitiful.

"You think I'd let you live if you promise to call your soldiers off?" His tone was sneering, but she could hear the hint of pleasure in it— a powerful man watching his opponent cower in front of him, weak and pathetic. Defeated.

Cavaco may be the most powerful man in the system at the moment. He may be the man who held the fate of every person in the Joias System in his palms.

But Savina had dealt with men like him, more times than she cared to count. And they were all dead. Every last one of them—too full of their own importance, their own brilliance, their own genius, to worry about the pitiful, sobbing, pathetic little Rim Mountain girl in front of them, because her admiration, or her wide-eyed astonishment, or her cowed terror, were owed them as their due. They'd never once questioned that perhaps she might not feel the same frank admiration for them as they felt for themselves. They believed her lies, because they believed the lies themselves.

"Please," she whimpered. "Just please stop hurting me. Don't kill me. Please. I'll do whatever you want, I'll say whatever you want me to."

He watched her through narrowed eyes. She widened her own eyes pathetically—a kicked puppy, whimpering and licking at the boot that kicked it.

At last he snorted. "Very brave when you have an army at your back, aren't you, Savina Moya? You used to be an assassin, killing people when they weren't expecting it and didn't know you were coming. And now you've learned that it's different when the people you try to kill are ready for you."

She blinked, letting tears well in her eyes and drip down her cheeks.

"I have an old friend of yours here, Savina. And I've heard all sorts of things about you. About the lengths you're willing to go to save your own life."

This time, Savina did look up, not trying to hide her shock, and glanced quickly around the room.

Her heart was pounding.

She could play this game out to the end. She wasn't afraid, anymore, of dying. Or at least, she was horribly, viscerally afraid, but she'd managed to resign herself to it anyways.

She wasn't entirely sure she'd be able to hold onto her conviction if she was faced with Juska, or Beni, or Nicolau, bruised and bloodied and beaten.

A door opened from behind Cavaco, and a figure stepped out.

Savina's heart almost stopped.

Even after everything, the sight of Reka sent something jolting through her, something visceral and impossible to ignore, a mix of fondness and love and longing and aching pain.

Reka was wearing the uniform of a government agent, clean and neat, her half-shave a dark shadow against her dark skin, her hair hanging smooth and neat down to her shoulders. She must have still been injured, but she somehow managed to avoid giving any sign of it.

She didn't look in Savina's direction, just kept her gaze on the wall behind her.

"My friend, Reka Soler," Cavaco said, his smile turning cruel.

Savina realized, with a start, that she must have let the emotions through into her expression. She still was—she was staring at Reka as if she'd seen the ghost of a loved one, someone cherished and treasured and now turned into something horrifying and deadly.

"She came to me from the Rim Mountains, shortly after some of the people there had turned over your plans. I had hoped she'd have the conviction to do so herself, but she did not. However, once she realized the way the battle would end, she realized what I believe you are realizing as well, Savina—that there is only one way to ensure that our system is not destroyed by these yibos. There is only one way to prevent the worst-case outcome. I tried to talk the former Chief Justice into this, but she was too stubborn to understand what Reka understands—that we will have to put aside our differences and work together for the good of the system. In this case, that means your little rebel force must give in. There is no other option. When she heard you'd been captured, Reka Soler was the one who told me your pressure points. But it appears I won't have to use them after all."

Savina blinked up at Reka.

She felt as if she were going into shock.

But she shouldn't. She'd always known Reka had a different morality than her own.

For a moment, her mind flashed back to their conversation in the tent.

"You always say you want to do what's right? You'd damn well better decide that that is."

And Reka had. After everything, she had—she'd decided that turning on Savina, and Joska, and Nicolau and Beni and Rafel and Ines and everyone else in the Rim Mountains, was worth it if it meant saving the system.

Reka had always been the one who was willing to sacrifice anything it took for what she believed was right. And suddenly, Savina almost laughed, even through the sick, heart-stopping pain.

In the end, perhaps she and Reka were more alike than she'd ever wanted to believe. Because here they both were, willing to sacrifice everything for what they believed was right.

For Reka, that meant working with Cavaco to take down the rebellion, in order to protect the Joias System. And for Savina—well, for Savina, it was becoming a holy martyr, dying in what would probably be a horrifying way, to protect the people she loved.

She was under no illusion that, if her plan worked, it wouldn't restart the guerrilla war, and perhaps weaken the system to the point the yibos could kill them all.

But Reka was right—she'd let the system burn to protect the people she cared about. Once, it had only been Beni and Nicolau. Then it was Joska and Rafel, and then, for a small, beautiful, painful moment, it had included Reka, as well. And then it had been

Nicolau's adoptive parents and his aunt, her village, the other villages who'd let them in and sent people to them with weapons and food.

Now it was the Rim Mountains, and the compounds, and every last person who didn't want to live under Cavaco's yoke.

"Soler," said Cavaco, turning to Reka. Reka glanced over at him, her face expressionless.

"Tell the guards to take our friend Savina out to the public courtyard in front of the council building. Have the broadcasting set up, so that they'll be able to see her across the city, and into the Rim Mountains as well. Our little assassin has become quite the symbol of resistance. I'd like her to become the symbol of how important it is that we stop this fighting and unite in this unprecedented emergency."

"General," said Reka, nodding in acknowledgement. Then she turned, still not looking at Savina, and strode out the door.

Savina's eyes followed her without her conscious thought. The familiar movement of Reka's body, the familiar shape of her, shoved a knife deep into Savina's chest, the pain of it leaving her breathless. By the time she'd managed to pull herself back under control, Cavaco was watching her with satisfaction. "Alright, Savina," he said. "I'll give you this chance. Make your speech convincing enough, and I won't kill you. Perhaps we'll even find a place for you in our councils, representing the Rim Mountains."

"Thank you," Savina gasped.

She didn't have to fake the shocked numbness in her voice. The sight of Reka had done that all on its own.

Savina was thrown back in her cell to wait, although this time they provided a doctor to look at her injury. There must have been a doctor that had come earlier, as well, while she was unconscious—Savina realized that in a sick, lightheaded way when the doctor Cavaco sent pulled up Savina's tunic and she saw the bandage over the wound, soaked through with blood.

She almost passed out as the doctor checked and re-bandaged the injury, despite the strong painkillers. They were enough to make her head spin and her tongue feel too thick in her mouth, but she was grateful for them nonetheless.

When the doctor was finished, she left, and Savina leaned back against the cold walls of the cell and closed her eyes as the room spun around her, and let the odd detachment brought by the painkillers lull her into a restless, pain-filled slumber.

The sound of keys in the lock woke her, and she glanced around, disoriented, as two soldiers stepped into the cell.

One of them knelt to unlock her leg cuffs, and the other lifted her carefully to her feet. She had to bite back a curse at the shocking pain the movement brought, but he must have felt her stiffen—at least, he paused a moment to let her collect herself before he started them forward.

The painkillers had mostly worn off. On the one hand, that was probably a good thing—it would be easier for Savina to come up with the words she needed if her head didn't feel stuffed with wool. On the other, it meant she had to focus every bit of concentration into placing her feet on the ground as she walked, so that she wouldn't pass out at the jolt of pain that accompanied each step.

Cavaco needed her alive. But she knew from experience that you could live through a great deal of pain.

In the small corner of her mind that was able to focus on anything other than the pain, she took note of her surroundings, the elegant stone walls of the corridor she was being led down.

This must be the council building, then. She'd never been in the council building. And now, here she was. An assassin, turned rebel leader, about to turn martyr.

Her guards led her, stumbling, through the massive lobby. The heavy doors were pulled open in front of her, and she was pushed through them and out into the sunlight.

She blinked at the sudden, disorienting brightness and lost her footing, stumbling on the steps. One of her escorts grabbed her arm and yanked her upright, and she gasped at the sudden shock of pain, blackness flickering in front of her vision. By the time she recovered her senses, she was on solid ground, and being pulled towards a large podium at the base of the steps.

A crowd was gathered in the courtyard, and she scanned the faces frantically. Surely some of the rebels had survived, surely she'd see at least someone … she let out a breath of relief.

At least one or two of the faces in the crowd, she recognized.

She wasn't naive enough to think that Cavaco would broadcast her killing. But if there were people here she knew, people she could trust—well, they'd do everything in their power to see to it that the vids were spread. And maybe one day parents would show her death to their children on the vids.

She closed her eyes for a moment, feeling sick to her stomach.

No child should see that. No child should ever be forced to see that.

But that was the point, after all—she couldn't stop this on her own. She wasn't strong enough. Her life, perhaps, hadn't meant anything important. But her death would be stronger than anything else she could have done.

And then Savina caught sight of a familiar face in the crowd, and her heart stuttered.

Joska.

Joska's face was deathly pale, and she wore a sick, horrified expression that made Savina feel nauseous and a little lightheaded.

Because Joska clearly understood what Cavaco did not.

Cavaco had read Savina's file. He thought he knew her. And honestly, perhaps a few months ago he'd have been correct. But Joska had always seen something in Savina that even Savina hadn't seen in herself. Joska had always believed that Savina was better than she was. And somehow—somehow, she'd started to become that person. That tiny spark of compassion and self-sacrifice that Joska had found and cared for and nurtured had flamed up until Savina wasn't sure there was anything left of her old self underneath it.

She wasn't sure, any longer, that she cared.

She carefully avoided Joska's eyes. She didn't want any sort of suspicion falling on the captain, and she knew Joska wouldn't stare blankly through her, like Reka had. She wouldn't be able to. She'd never been able to hide who she was, or what she believed in, and she'd never tried. Joska was the one with the sort of stubborn morality that lent itself to martyrdom. She'd have done better at this than Savina would.

But that didn't matter.

She'd given Savina something, over the course of the past few months—she'd bound it to Savina's very soul, in the same way the vids of the martyrdoms had been bound to her soul. But this hadn't been through tears and nightmares and trauma—it had been through simple, unquestioning kindness. Compassion. Care. Love. The kind of love Savina hadn't believed really existed. The kind of love that saw all of your flaws and imperfections and ugliness and sickness, and simply ... loved you anyways, because it believed that you were someone worth loving.

Savina still wasn't sure if it was a blessing or a curse. Even now, she wasn't sure if she was glad of it, or if she wanted to curse Joska's name. Without it, she wouldn't be standing here. Without it, all the things that Reka feared about her would be true. She wouldn't, ever, be willing to die for her convictions.

But then, maybe it wasn't her convictions she was dying for, after all. Maybe it was as simple as it had always been—she was willing to die, because there were people out there that she loved, and those people wouldn't accept their freedom if it was bought at the price of something unconscionable.

So she was paying the price they would accept.

She stepped forward to the podium, clenching her teeth against the pain, and let her eyes scan the crowd one last time.

She didn't see her siblings, or Rafel. But that didn't mean they weren't there. And if they were still alive, Joska would find a way to protect them, if she possibly could.

Savina had lived her entire life never trusting anyone. Not even trusting Beni, really, because she'd never believed that Beni could take care of themself. But this, she didn't even have to stop to consider. She simply knew that Joska would look after her siblings, just like she'd always tried to look after Savina, as much as she could. As much as Savina would let her.

Savina took a deep breath. "Citizens of Joias," she said, letting her words come loud and clear. "I have spoken with General Cavaco. And I have a message for those of you who wish to rebel against his new government."

She paused a moment. From the corner of her eye, she was still watching Joska, and from Joska's expression Savina knew she understood what was coming next.

Joska had always believed the best about her, despite all evidence to the contrary.

There was pain in the captain's weathered face, and something else, as well—something that was similar to affection, and similar to love, and similar to hurt, but not really any of those things.

Something she'd seen on the face of Nicolau's adoptive mother, when she'd come out of her house in the autumn twilight and seen him standing there. Something she'd always, somewhere in the depths of herself, wished to see on her own mother's face.

"Savina," Joska mouthed, even though she couldn't possibly tell that Savina had seen her. "I'm so proud of you."

A haze of tears was forming in Savina's eyes, but she blinked it back.

"My message to you is this," she said, keeping her words as firm as she could, even though her voice wanted to tremble. She leaned forward over the podium. "Cavaco is a liar. Don't ever stop fighting. He can send his soldiers to kill us, but he can never, ever kill what we're fighting for. We will not betray our mountains, we will not betray the people we love. We will not let them shoot us down like they did at Swan River. Cavaco may kill me here, where I stand, but my blood will never stop calling out to you to keep fighting. To keep …"

Hands were dragging her away, and fighting them would mean blacking out, so she raised her voice. "Cavaco only wins if we stop fighting!" she called over the noise of the crowd. "He can never win unless we give up!"

She could hear the sound of shouts, scuffles, the noise of soldiers stepping forward. On the wall to one side, a scuffle had broken out.

And from the corner of her mind, the corner that had been waiting for it, she heard the hiss of a rifle. There was an impact that sent an explosion of pain through her body, and distantly, she felt herself falling.

And then there was nothing.

<h1 style="text-align:center">29</h1>

Alba closed her eyes as the screen in front of her broadcasted the sight of the Rim Mountain assassin being dragged up to the podium.

Even now, the sight of the girl's face brought back the visceral fear of a knife at her throat, Savina's voice, cold with hate, hissing threats in her ear. But she couldn't help the sick pang of pity at the girl's pale, drawn face, the way she stumbled, as if barely able to stay on her feet. Her face was gaunt, her wide eyes with bruise-like circles under them.

She wasn't wearing her usual innocent smile. There was a look to her face that Alba hadn't seen there before—a determination, and under it, a sort of peace that was quiet and certain and almost radiant.

And Alba knew, suddenly and unequivocally, that this confession wasn't going to go the way Cavaco wanted it to.

The nausea in her stomach grew, and she wondered, for a moment, when she'd actually started to care what happened to this girl.

She'd always known Savina was dangerous. She'd always known that if and when they got back to the Joias System, Savina would have to be dealt with somehow. Because she couldn't ever be trusted. She was dangerous, and she killed without mercy and without remorse, and she couldn't be allowed to rejoin society. In the end, this was probably the best ending for her, after all—death in a glorious cause, where her name would be remembered and her bravery praised for years to come.

But Alba closed her eyes as Savina approached the podium. Because no matter what the logical part of her mind told her—she couldn't bear to watch what would happen next.

Savina began to speak, voice ringing out clearly over the broadcast, and Alba forced her eyes open, forced herself to find Cavaco in the crowd. And she watched his face.

Beside her, she could hear murmuring from the other councillors who'd been locked into the room with her—surprise, shock, admiration. But she wasn't paying attention to that.

She was watching Cavaco. Because she had to know if this had taken him by surprise as well.

She saw a flicker of something across his features—fury. Rage. And under it …

Shock.

He hadn't been expecting this. Whatever he knew about Savina, whatever he'd been told, he hadn't been expecting this.

She closed her eyes in relief.

Savina's voice cut off, and Alba looked up in time to see the girl being pulled from the podium. Her mouth was still moving, but the sound had been cut. She was shouting, but Alba couldn't tell what she was saying.

She could guess, though, by the restless movements of the crowd, the way scuffles had broken out among the soldiers. She could tell by the way the soldiers grabbed at Savina, pulling her backwards.

She saw the ripple of a pulse-rifle shot, distorting the air. She saw Savina's body jerk, and then fall limply to the ground. And then the camera cut, and Alba and the other councillors were left alone in the darkened room.

There was a moment of total silence.

"What just happened?" asked one of the councillors at last. "What the hell was that?"

"That girl just sealed her own fate," said another, their voice quiet. "She'd best hope that shot killed her. If it didn't, Cavaco will torture her to death, I have no doubt of it."

The door slammed open, and Cavaco strode in, flanked by his guards. The lights flickered on as he stepped inside, leaving Alba and the others blinking in the sudden brightness.

"Councillors," Cavaco snapped. There was a tone in his voice that left no uncertainty as to his mood. "You have a choice—you may lend your voices to calm the people outside, or I will shoot you, one by one. After the display out there, I hope you understand that I will not hesitate. Because the only other option is to watch our system burn, and I will sacrifice every one of you before I see that happen." He turned to Ander, who was sitting near the front of the group. "So, what is it, President?"

There was hesitation on Ander's face.

Alba sucked in a breath.

She could have told herself that, after everything that happened, she wasn't afraid of physical violence anymore. But it wasn't true. The thing about physical violence, the thing about pain that others inflicted on you, whether intentional or on accident, was that it was easy enough to tell yourself you'd be brave in the face of it if you hadn't experienced it. It was easy enough to talk about bravery, and about holding up to torture and pain, if there was no chance that you'd ever have to face that scenario.

When she was still Madam Chief Justice of the Joias System, Alba would likely have considered herself to be courageous. She would likely have assumed, without really thinking about it, that given the opportunity, her convictions would carry her through any pain or threats or torture.

But that had been before. That had been before she'd lain on the floor of her room, bruises around her throat, blood soaking through her nightdress, gasping for breath, the pistol she'd used to save her own life lying on the floor beside her. That had been before she'd been thrown in prison, and been told that she'd be executed in the morning, and realized how fragile her own life really was. That was before she'd fled through the jungle, pain shooting up her entire body from a broken kneecap, dulling her mind and singing through her body, before she'd passed out from pain, and woken, and had to pull her mind back to the present without so much as a rest because they were still fighting for their very survival. That had been before she'd understood what fear did to your body and your brain—before she'd felt what it was like for your muscles to freeze and your thoughts to stop, to re-live in horrible, minute detail every sensation of the most terrifying thing that had ever happened to you, exactly as if you were living through it again.

She knew, now, what pain meant. She knew, in a sick, marrow-deep way, the feeling of the knowledge that your life depended entirely on the good-will of someone else, and that the moment they deemed you not useful, you would die, and there was nothing at all you could do to prevent it.

And she couldn't say, anymore, that she wasn't afraid. She was more terrified than the version of her who'd lived her life out in do Sol could ever possibly have imagined, and even now she could feel the beginnings of that cold, mind-numbing panic lapping at the back of her brain, feel the trembling in her muscles, the memory of her attacker's blood, hot and sticky, cooling against her skin.

But then … well, it had never been about not being afraid.

She'd seen the look in Savina's face. The girl had been afraid. She'd been terrified.

But she'd had something that was worth pushing through the fear for.

And so, in the end, did Alba.

There were people she wouldn't abandon, even if they'd never know. Because she would know. She'd know that, in the end, she hadn't sacrificed them for political expediency.

And maybe that was enough.

"Councillors," she said, half-standing from her chair. "Please, listen to me. We didn't take the oath of our office to uphold the rights of the people of Colorida as long as it wasn't an inconvenience. We have lived with the privilege of our office. And if now we're asked to pay the price of it … perhaps it's a price we owe."

One of the soldiers crossed over to her and backhanded her hard across the face.

Even though she'd been half-expecting it, the sharp, shocking pain of it took her aback, and she staggered. Someone grabbed her arms, pulled her wrists up behind her back, and she could feel her muscles and tendons screaming in protest, the hot, sharp tears of pain that sprang to her eyes.

"Ander," she said, speaking through the iron taste of blood. "You were elected to stand for the people of Joias. You cannot accept the benefits of that position, and then sell the people out when it requires a sacrifice. That's why they chose you to stand for them—because they trusted you to make that sacrifice. You swore to protect them. That is the oath you took."

They were all looking at her now, and she could see the indecision on their faces.

The soldier standing beside Alba backhanded her again, hard enough to leave her seeing stars. The pain of it was searing, and for a moment she couldn't breathe through it.

When she could focus again, she found Ander and fixed him with her gaze. "Cavaco's plan will sacrifice the Rim Mountains. He'll start a war with aliens that we cannot win." Her words came out without their usual crisp clarity, slurred and indistinct through what must be a split lip. The pain of speaking ached through her body, but then … she'd been willing to die for a handful of desperate refugees in the yibo system. How could she possibly do less here?

"If any of you agree with him—if you do as he asks and lend your legitimacy to this—you will have failed every person who put you in office. You will go down in history, whatever history is left after the destruction that will follow, as the people who stood by and allowed this to happen." She drew in a quick, painful breath. "I don't want to die." Her voice was low, but she raised her head. "I don't want to die. But I will, if my choice is that or betray the people who trusted me. And if a Rim Mountain assassin can die for what she believes, I hardly see how any one of us can do less."

There was a long moment of silence. Alba could hear the breath hissing through Cavaco's teeth, and she didn't have to look at him to picture the expression on his face.

He'd always hated it when she'd been able to best him in the Council meetings.

And this was so much more than a Council meeting.

But in this case, at least, she found she hardly cared. She was watching Ander's face.

It was cut with indecision, and his eyes flicked back and forth between her and Cavaco.

And then he drew in a deep breath, as if bracing himself. For one moment, she wasn't sure if he was bracing himself to disappoint her, or to disappoint Cavaco.

"General," he said, turning to Cavaco. "I am sorry. But in this, I think I am forced to agree with Madam Chief Justice."

Cavaco gestured to a soldier behind him. There was the pulse of a shot, and Ander crumpled to the floor.

30

Aran

By the time Aran, Istvay, and the raiders stumbled out of the laboratory, down the lift, and into the main halls of the research building, the building was utter chaos. Aran leaned heavily against Istvay at the door of the lift, gasping at the pain in his leg, and stared out at the confusing mass of students and university staff shouting and yelling, soldiers shoving people away, fistfights breaking out.

"You bastards shot that girl!" one of the students was yelling. "Her blood is drying on that podium, and you think we won't fight back?"

A soldier grabbed the student, hitting him hard enough that he staggered, and then three other students grabbed for the soldier, dragging her down in a flurry of blows.

Dessi, who'd come to stand beside them, looked as grim as Istvay did.

"Aran," Istvay said after a moment. "Stay with Dessi. I'm going to find us a transport."

Aran gritted his teeth against the shooting pain in his leg. "You're not going to make it through there without getting shot at. At least take Krevai or something."

Istvay gave him a skeptical look, and he sighed. "I know, Krevai might start a war. But he's damn well going to start a war if you get shot, and I'm not even going to try to stop him at that point."

"Istvay! Shall Zondra and I get us a transport?" Krevai strode up to stand beside them. There was blood smeared across his face, and he wiped it away delicately.

Aran and Istvay exchanged glances. "You know what, on second thought, having Krevai and Zondra with me is probably the best option, under the circumstances," Istvay muttered. They turned to the raiders. "Come on, let's go before Aran damn well passes out."

Krevai cast a quick, concerned look at Aran, and his grin turned a little more menacing. "You're right, of course. Let's go."

The three of them strode off across the wide atrium of the building, the crowd parting around them like water parting around oil.

Aran and Dessi exchanged glances. "Well," said Dessi. "On the bright side, from the way your Istvay looked, I think it'll be Krevai and Zondra holding them back."

Aran managed a weak smile in return.

The pain in his leg was shooting all the way up and down his body in harsh, hot jolts that left him breathless.

Just get back to the ship, that was the important part. Get back to the ship, and keep the raiders and the charaks from turning do Sol into their personal hunting grounds. The rest he could worry about later.

Across the room, he saw one of the soldiers turn, pulling their rifle into position as Istvay and the raiders strode past.

"Istvay!" he shouted.

Istvay turned, a look of sudden alarm on their face.

And then Zondra had leapt at the soldier, moving so quickly and silently Aran hardly noticed her until she'd ripped the man's head from his body. She held up the gruesome trophy, blood still spurting from it, and then flung it away, grinning sharply.

The room went very silent.

And then a dozen other panicked soldiers raised their weapons, and people screamed and flung themselves out of the way.

"Ani," Aran snapped. "Protect Istvay."

Ani needed no further urging. She'd been tense since they'd all stepped out of the lift, and now she leapt from his shoulder, soaring across the room.

"She's a damn land-devil, and your weapons aren't going to hurt her, and she doesn't like it when people shoot at my friends," Aran shouted as loudly as he could over the chaos.

One soldier got off a shot, which impacted against Zondra's body armour. She turned, smiling so that her elongated canines were clearly visible against her ice-white skin.

The rest of the soldiers fled in panic.

Ani took down two of them before they made it out the door, and then, at Aran's sharp command, she sidled back across the room, sulkiness emanating from her, and pulled herself back up to his shoulder.

The room had emptied with startling rapidity.

"Come on!" Istvay snapped, and they and the two raiders sprinted out the door.

"We'd better follow," said Aran grimly. Dessi nodded, her face tight with worry, and he leaned heavily against her as they hobbled across the room, the floor slick in places with blood, empty now except for the bodies of the three dead soldiers, which, thank the Holy Mystery, Krevai and Zondra had been too busy to carry along as a snack.

By the time they'd reached the door, there was a transport waiting outside. It was barely big enough for the five of them—well, six of them, although Ani was exceptionally talented at fitting herself into small spaces—but Dessi helped Aran inside, then climbed in after him.

"Are you alright?" Istvay snapped through the transport comm.

Aran nodded weakly. "Yeah," he muttered. His head was spinning, and his leg felt as if it had been clamped in a vise which was slowly and inexorably tightening. "I'm good, let's go."

The streets outside were chaos. Whatever had happened to stir it up, there were knots of civilians, armed with nothing but bricks and rocks, struggling with armed soldiers, fights spilling out across the streets and into the alleys.

In chaos like this, the raiders would cut through the crowds like a hot knife through butter, and there would be nothing whatsoever to stop them.

Aran squeezed his eyes shut, praying hopelessly that they'd be in time.

Istvay's knuckles were white on the controls, and Aran could see, whenever he cracked his eyes open, the pallor of their face and the set to their jaw.

They'd been given the cure only days previous, and since then they'd been either frantically working on a solution for the charaks, or caught in the middle of some sort of fight. Aran wasn't sure, looking at them, that they wouldn't simply pass out the moment things calmed down enough to let them.

To be honest, he wasn't sure that he wouldn't pass out the moment things calmed down enough to let him.

When he felt the transport slowing, he opened his eyes and forced back the nausea rising in his throat at the pain in his leg, bracing himself to stand.

And then he glanced out the plex window, and felt like his heart might stop in horror.

They were at the docking bay where they'd left the raider ship. And he could see, from under the door, a red trickle of something that looked a hell of a lot like blood, and there was the loud, methodical pounding against the inside of the door of something utterly determined to get out.

"How long will it take you to convince your damn friends to get out of the raiders' heads?" Aran thought at the charak.

There was an answering spark of sulky irritation in the back of his brain. *I don't know. Need to get on the ship first.*

"Well, it's looking like that might be a little complicated at this point," he thought grimly. "From the looks of things, I'll be able to give you maybe thirty seconds once we're on to figure it out, otherwise, Istvay and I are using the other solution. Because I think we just ran out of time for negotiation."

The charak gave a small blip of protest, and then a grumbled assent.

"You're damn lucky we have to get on the ship to hook into the power before we can use our solution," he responded.

"Aran?" He looked up, startled, to see Istvay in front of him. Their face was pale enough that he almost jumped to his feet, in case they fell over, but the first hint of movement, and the accompanying stab of pain, told him that if he tried it, they'd both fall over.

"I'm good, let's go," he mumbled, bracing himself. He sucked in a quick breath, held it, and pushed himself up on his good leg. Istvay slung Aran's arm over their shoulder and caught him around the waist with a gloved hand, like they'd done so many times before on expeditions when one of them was injured and they both needed to get out as quickly as possible before something ate, disemboweled, or sat on them, and Aran felt himself relaxing at the familiarity of the gesture.

This, at least, he knew how to do.

Krevai and Zondra were standing at the exit to the transport, dark looks on their faces. "Aran," said Krevai, when he and Istvay appeared. "Zondra and I will hold back the rest of the crew. Leave the Ani with us, we may need her. You and your Istvay get onto the ship, Dessi will go with you. But do whatever you're going to do quickly—I'm not sure Sharda will agree to peace if I'm killed here, even if it is the charaks' fault." He grinned, a sharp, anticipatory grin. "Istvay, take care of our Aran. He's my crew, and I don't intend to lose one of my crew. And God help us all."

Aran stared at Krevai for a moment, not quite sure he'd heard right.

Dessi appeared beside them and gave them a quick nod. Istvay hit the controls. The hatch swung open, and a moment later Krevai and Zondra were on the ground and sprinting towards the hangar bay doors.

"Ani, go with Krevai," said Aran, pulling her down from his shoulder.

She gave him a mournful glance, and then launched herself from his arms, catching Krevai's shoulder with the tip of a tentacle and swinging herself up as he reached the bay doors. Krevai and Zondra had already drawn their long butchers' knives, and Zondra sliced through the exterior lock with one swing.

She staggered back, slipping on blood as something inside sprang at her, and then Krevai had yanked the ferocious raider off her and slammed him into the wall. Ani launched herself into the fray, and

Aran shouted, "Ani! Guard! Don't kill, Ani!" even though he wasn't at all sure that she'd hear him, or pay any attention if she did.

Istvay jerked his chin towards the opening, and Aran nodded, and the three of them lowered themselves from the transport and started forward. Aran was leaning most of his weight on Istvay and Dessi strode in front of them to clear a path, a short metal bar clutched in her hands. Aran knew exactly how much she hated violence, but when they reached the door and a raider stepped into their path, teeth barred, she only hesitated an instant before she swung her makeshift weapon, connecting hard with the raider's temple. Their attacker staggered, and Dessi shoved her to one side, grabbed Istvay by their free arm, and dragged them and Aran through the door after her.

Another raider jumped at them as they stepped through the doors, and Dessi staggered back, caught off-balance. In a moment, her attacker had their teeth at her throat.

And then the raider collapsed, and Aran glanced over to see Istvay, a pulse-pistol in their hand and a grim look on their face. "Don't say a damn word, Aran," they muttered. "I don't like killing them any more than you do, but it's not like they're giving us much choice."

"I wasn't going to say anything," Aran muttered back, but he felt a little like he wanted to throw up as Dessi shoved the dead raider off her and scrambled to her feet. Blood was smeared across her clothing, and her face was paler than usual, but she just gestured them forward.

By this time, most of the infected raiders had joined in the fight against Krevai and Zondra, struggling to get past them and out the door. Aran shot a quick glance over his shoulder as they ran in a limping sprint across the open floor of the hangar bay towards the raider ship.

Krevai and Zondra had shoved the door mostly closed, and jammed it so the raiders inside the bay couldn't all attack at once, and Ani was with them, and even the infected raiders seemed wary of her.

But they wouldn't hold out forever.

Hell, he wasn't sure if they'd hold out long enough for he and Istvay and Dessi to reach the ship.

And then they were there, and Dessi and Istvay were pulling him up the mangled ramp, likely smashed by the infected raiders trying to get out.

"Where do you need to go?" Dessi snapped. She sounded almost as sick as Aran felt.

"You take Istvay to the ship's controls," Aran mumbled. He could hardly get the words out around the shooting, red-hot pain in his leg. "They can set things up to broadcast the pulse of electricity through the raiders' communicators, but hopefully we won't need it. I'm going to go find the charaks."

Neither Dessi nor Istvay looked happy with this arrangement, but at last Istvay nodded. "Come on, Dessi, let's go." They turned to Aran, placing their hand on his shoulder. He could see in their face the self-control it was taking them not to pull him into a kiss. "Aran, tell that idiot thing in your head it has until I get the specs set into the ship's machines, then all bargains are off."

Aran nodded.

And then Istvay and Dessi were sprinting up the corridors towards the cockpit.

"Aran!" Krevai's voice came over his communicator, ragged with pain and exhaustion. "I'm sorry. They've broken out past us. Zondra and I are going to go after them, but … I'm afraid there's not much

I'll be able to do."

Aran steadied himself against the corridor walls, his breath coming shallow and too quick, vomit rising in his throat, but he forced himself to move forward, despite the way the pain made his head spin.

"You heard Istvay," he thought grimly at the charak. "You'd damn well better get me to where you need me to go so you can talk to your friends, or it's not going to matter one damn bit what you say or do."

There was a moment of hesitation from the thing in his head.

And then a picture flashed in his mind of a small dark cupboard in what looked like the ship's supplies storage.

"Alright, let's go," he muttered. "And pray to the holy damn Mystery that we get there in time."

31

Alba

The sudden shouting through the amplifiers in the room jolted them all out of their shock.

"General!" someone was shouting. "There are aliens attacking from one of the docking bays in the middle of the city! We're shooting at them, but they have some sort of body armour we've never seen before, and there's nothing we can do."

An image flashed onto the screen.

Alba's entire body froze, her mind jerking away from Ander's limp body on the council room floor. She was back, suddenly, in that horrific moment a few days previous and a hundred light-years away, watching the holorecording of the raiders rampaging through a defenceless yibo village.

Except this wasn't a yibo village, and she wasn't watching something that had happened already. This was happening right now.

There were shocked, sick gasps from the councillors around her as one of the raiders casually disembowelled a soldier, the sound of the

314

man's entrails landing on the pavement almost hidden by the raider's low laugh. The raider bent, pulling open the man's ribcage as if it was made of twigs and yanking out the bloody heart. She ripped it in two with her sharp fangs, then grinned at the soldier who was holding the recording device and stepped towards him.

"General—" the man began, his voice wavering.

The image cut off.

Alba could hear, behind her, the sound of someone vomiting.

She wanted to vomit herself. But instead, she steadied herself against the back of the chair and blinked her wavelink through to Aran's line. "Aran!" she snapped. "What the hell is going on?"

For a moment there was no response.

"Alba, what is this?" The councillor's voice was sick with horror. "I thought you said the aliens wanted peace. That doesn't look like peace to me."

"Aran!"

There was a crackling through her earpiece. And then Aran's voice, weak and distant. "I'm sorry. The raiders are infected, that's all this is. Istvay and I figured out how to stop it. We're working on it, but it's going to take a couple of seconds. I think …"

His voice cut off again.

"Alba …" the councillor's voice was pleading, terrified.

Another video had come up, from a different soldier, Alba assumed, and the shaky picture was showing things Alba wasn't sure she actually wanted to look at.

"It's not their fault," she said in a low voice. "They've been infected by something that's taken over their minds. Aran Romeu has been working on a cure for it for some time now, and he assures me he's found it. We just have to give him time to implement it."

"How much time does he think we have to spare?" The man's

voice was harsh with desperation.

"Give him a minute." Alba was speaking through her teeth. "I've seen him work, and he wouldn't tell us to wait unless he's almost there. If we send in soldiers to attack, I guarantee we'll only be sending them to their deaths."

There was another long moment of silence. Alba wasn't sure she could bring herself to look at the screen in front of them.

And then she heard a gasp of relief, and she forced herself to look up.

The raiders had stopped in the middle of the streets, their blood-soaked knives and claws dripping red blood onto the ground, the looks on their faces ones of confusion.

They looked at each other, and then one of them, a tall, broad-shouldered female that Alba recognized, vaguely, as Krevai's second-in-command, called something to the others.

The raiders dropped the human soldiers they were holding, and turned, loping after her down the streets back towards the docking bay.

Alba closed her eyes and sagged with relief, her grip on the back of the chair the only thing holding her upright.

And then her brain began to process what Cavaco was hissing through the amplifiers.

"I don't care what they've done, this must end." His voice was sharp and furious, and halfway frantic. "Kill every damn civilian or rebel who gets in your way. Open up a perimeter around the docking bay, and bring in the ships. We're going to bomb it into a crater in the ground, and then I will instruct you to open fire on every civilian who doesn't immediately follow orders. Do you understand? You saw the threat these aliens pose. We have no alternative."

"No!" Alba snapped, terror giving her voice strength. "You can't bomb that docking bay! The raider captain there is their war captain. He's the only thing holding the rest of the raiders back from a full-scale attack. And there are currently seventeen land-devil pups in that ship, and Aran Romeu is in there. You cannot do this!"

Cavaco spun on her. "Alba," he hissed. "Have you lost your mind?" His face was sharp with a desperation and a fear she'd never seen there before, under the vicious fury in his expression. "We don't have a choice. You saw what those things are capable of. You think that telling me there are land-devils there will change my mind? Those things are as vicious as your alien raiders! We have to kill them!"

"And how much luck, do you think, you'll have in killing them if you bomb the hangar bay into the ground?" She snapped back. "We've tried that before, do you remember? We've tried several times back on their own planet. And there wasn't a single thing we could do."

The other councillors were silent, watching the exchange.

"You've let yourself go soft," Cavaco hissed. "You genuinely want me and everyone else to believe that you advocate for peace because you want it. But I know what this really is. You've always been too afraid to do what needs to be done. You're too concerned with your image to make the difficult choices. And believe me, we are at the point where difficult choices have to be made. My soldiers are lying on the streets with their hearts torn from their chests, and you want me to sue for peace? There is a docking bay full of vicious aliens, and creatures that could wipe out the entire city of do Sol, and you want me to hold back?"

Alba noticed, in the back of her mind, the small green light on the amplifier screens that told her that the amplifiers were still on.

Her head ached, and her face throbbed where the soldier had hit her, her legs so weak she wasn't sure they'd hold her up. But she forced herself to straighten, and made her painful way across the floor to where Cavaco stood.

To where, if the Holy Mystery granted her mercy, the amplifiers would pick up her voice.

"It's not me who's afraid," she said, making her words ring out clear and strong, despite the way her voice wanted to tremble. "It's not me who's making decisions based on fear. Yes, I am very aware that the raiders could wipe out our city, if they so chose. The reason they attacked is because their minds were taken over by a creature none of us knows anything about. I have no doubt that these creatures, too, are a danger. And we all know how dangerous land-devils are. I am not unaware of the risks. But unlike you, Cavaco, I understand something else—we can't eliminate every risk. We can't kill everything that wants to hurt us, because we simply do not have the strength to do so. Every time we react in fear, we put ourselves in a position that's ever more precarious.

"We tried that with the land-devils—we bombed their planet how many times? And there has never, not once, been a moment when we were not in danger for our lives from them, no matter how much we tried to destroy them. In fact, to my knowledge, there has only been one recorded instance where a human has managed to interact with a land-devil and not lose their life for it. And that happens to be when our friend Aran Romeu adopted an infant land-devil and befriended it.

"As far as the raiders, in the yibo system, they're the things mothers tell their children stories about to frighten them. The yibos have lived with the danger of raiders for centuries, and every city and every settlement is protected with a force-field to keep the raiders away. And yet, I saw with my own eyes how quickly and easily the raiders could cut through those force-fields if they so chose. They went through a yibo city, a city that had been specifically built to repel them, like boiling water through a sheet of ice. And do you know what stopped that war? It wasn't superior technology, or superior firepower. It was that assassin you had shot. She managed to get the upper hand against a crew of them for just a moment, and rather than destroy them, she asked to negotiate. And it was, again, our friend Aran Romeu, who'd befriended them enough that when he asked them to negotiate with Savina, they did so.

"The things that have infected the raiders, and controlled their minds—it appears that this is a danger that the raiders have fought against for as long as they've been a space-faring species. They've never won. But our friend Aran seems to have found a way to protect the raiders against them. No one else, to my knowledge, other than perhaps Aran's friend, Istvay, knows how to do this. These raiders frighten you. I can hardly blame you—after seeing what they can do, I'm not sure anyone in their right mind wouldn't be frightened by them. But what you are proposing to do—bomb their ship into a crater—will not work."

She turned, so that her voice would carry clearly through the amplifiers. "I understand being afraid. But Cavaco, if these soldiers follow your orders, they will be killing perhaps the only person in this system or any other who has found a way to work with these creatures—raiders, land-devils, and charaks. And if they do that—if they follow your orders and kill Aran and Istvay and the only raider captain willing to work for peace—they will have destroyed the last chance we have to escape a war the likes of which you've never imagined. You've seen what these raiders can do. I can tell you what the yibo war force did to our sister colony, Labarinto, when they came through. And I am telling you now, if you do this, you will doom our system to the same fate."

Cavaco stepped towards her, suddenly seeming to realize that their words were all being broadcast across the city. "Commanders, I order you to bring in the ships to bomb the docking bay," he snapped. "Do so, or so help me, you'll hang for treason."

"No!" Alba snapped at the same time. "Drop your weapons and surrender, now, or you'll doom yourselves and everyone you love. I beg of you, do not let fear make this decision for you!"

Cavaco grabbed for her, and she stumbled backwards, her weak knee giving out.

His fingers tightened around her throat, and her mind went blank in panic. She could feel the remembered bruises, feel her breath coming harsh in her chest, feel the familiar tightening panic shutting off her thoughts. She couldn't move to defend herself. She couldn't move her hands to grasp at his wrists, couldn't push herself backward, because every muscle in her body was frozen. Distantly, she was aware of shouting, of voices raised and running footsteps, but she couldn't breathe, and she couldn't think, and her brain couldn't make sense of anything she was hearing.

And then the pressure on her throat loosened. She collapsed to the ground, choking and gasping.

"Madam Chief Justice! Are you alright? Madam, please, answer me."

She could make out the voices, distantly, but she couldn't bring herself to answer.

She felt hands lifting her, laying her out on the floor, fingers pressed to the side of her throat, feeling for a pulse. "She's alive," someone was saying, their voice sharp and businesslike. "Call in a medic, I think she's going into shock. But she's alive, at least."

Gradually, the world came back into focus.

She was lying on the ground, and there were faces bending over her—most of them unfamiliar, but she recognized a few of the other councillors in their midst.

The others bending over her, though—

She gasped, and tried to sit up before someone pushed her gently back. Someone wearing the uniform of a military general.

"No," she gasped. "Don't touch me …"

"Madam." One of the soldiers laid a soothing hand on her shoulder. "No one here is going to hurt you. I apologize for the actions of General Cavaco, but we've taken him somewhere to calm down."

She closed her eyes for a moment, trying to push back the trembling panic enough to let the words make sense.

And then she did, and she blinked her eyes back open again, scanning the room. "What happened?" She rasped. "The docking bay—"

The general smiled. "Madam. You were very convincing, it appears. The soldiers outside lay down their weapons, at our orders. In the end, I believe that you were correct."

And Alba slumped back against the floor and let her eyes fall closed, too weak with relief to speak at all.

32

Aran

"Hello there, beautiful," Aran whispered, kneeling beside the cupboard. His entire body felt light with a mixture of relief and wonder. "Look at you! You're spectacular."

He could feel a grudging acknowledgement in the back of his head as he watched the wriggling, translucent creatures squirming blindly over each other.

"You did it," he thought. "You saved them. Thank you."

There was a wave of something that might have been gratitude, or might have just been its own sort of relief.

For a few moments, Aran crouched where he was. His leg still ached, but the pain was a distant sort of thing compared to the overwhelming happiness.

He reached out a hand carefully. "May I?" he thought. "I won't if you'd rather not."

There was a hint of hesitation, and then a cautious affirmation.

Aran stretched out his hand, hardly breathing.

The things stilled a moment. And then one of them turned its blank eyes towards him, and he watched in utter fascination as it wriggled closer. Its sucking mouthpart was a round hole filled with rows of minuscule teeth, and he could see its digestive system through its translucent skin. It moved like a slug or an amoeba, its body stretching and lengthening, then compressing, and he guessed that at full length, it would reach from the ground to a little past his waist. "I'll bet you're able to expand quite a bit when you're feeding, can't you?" he whispered. He held his hand very still as the creature approached.

"Is this you?" he thought.

The thing in his mind gave a little blip of affirmation.

"Hello there," he thought softly. "It's good to finally meet you."

The thing touched his hand, and he felt a quick jolt through his body. "That's how you infect people, isn't it?" he thought. "One of these days I'd love to study the mechanics of how you do this—take over someone's thought process. That's an incredibly sophisticated mechanism, I've never seen anything quite like it."

The thing in his head felt a little smug.

"Thank you," he whispered, the words choking a little in his throat. "Thank you for letting me see your family. They're beautiful."

The thing gave another little burst of ... something. Aran wasn't sure if it was pride, or gratitude, or happiness.

Miss you, Aran, it whispered in his mind. *Take us home safe?*

"Yes," he thought back, "I'll get them to take you home safe. I'll talk to Dessi, she's a scientist too, she'll make sure Krevai does what he promised. And I won't tell the raiders where you are. You'll be safe here until they let you out, and as long as you leave when they give you a chance to, they won't have to use Istvay's device."

The thing hissed softly in agreement.

And then there was a small, odd, slithering sensation in Aran's brain that, despite everything, shot a sharp spike of panic through him before he was able to get himself under control.

And then …

The thing in his mind was gone.

He blinked, reaching back internally to see if there was anything left.

There wasn't. For a moment, he couldn't decide if the ache that washed over him was relief, or regret.

"Thank you," he whispered again.

The translucent thing nudged his fingers, and again there was that small shock at the contact. But nothing slithered into his mind, no other presence appeared in his thoughts, and the thing turned and crawled back to the mound of squirming creatures.

Aran pushed himself to his feet at last. The movement shot pain up his leg sharply enough that he had to catch himself against the wall. When the world had steadied around him, he limped over to one of the supplies freezers, and pulled out a large chunk of frozen meat. He carried it over to the cupboard and tossed it inside. "You'll have to do something about the smell if you're going to let it rot, otherwise they'll find you," he whispered.

One of the translucent creatures raised its head in acknowledgement.

"Of course," he whispered, smiling to himself. "You probably have something to deal with that already, don't you, if you're able to hide your own scent?"

He watched them for a moment longer, a fond smile on his face. And then, at last, he closed the cupboard and limped back the way he'd come.

He'd only made it a few steps when he heard pounding footsteps, and he braced himself, tensing unconsciously.

Istvay rounded the corner, and stopped dead when they saw him, relief washing over their face. "Aran," they whispered. "You're alright."

"I'm alright," he said, but there were sudden tears choking in his throat. "It's gone, Pishti. And …"

Istvay reached him a moment later, grabbing him in a bearhug that left him breathless. "Aran," they whispered, and then they were kissing him, and he leaned into them and kissed them back desperately.

When Istvay pulled back at last, there were tears running down Aran's cheeks and dripping onto his shirt, and Istvay's eyes were hazy with tears as well. "Aran," they whispered again. "Oh hell, Aran, I've missed you so much …" Then they had him in an embrace again, and he sagged against them.

"The raiders are all alright as well," they said, when at last they let go of him enough to look at him. "They've all got their minds back, and we even tried taking off the bracelet from Landru—she was fine. Still, I think we'd probably better put new bracelets on everyone until they can get up into deep space to let the charaks out. Landru wasn't particularly happy with your compromise with the charaks— she'd just as soon kill them and eat them, apparently they are edible, although with the raiders I'm not sure I trust their taste—but I told her that she was either going to agree, or I wasn't going to train her on how our solution works, and Krevai actually backed me up." They grinned a little. "But anyways, we'd best get you as far away from them as we can before the raiders come find us. I grabbed some scent blocker on my way down here, I'll spread it around so the crew can't track where you've been. I assume you were in there getting to know them?"

Aran nodded, his throat too tight with a mixture of affection and gratitude to say anything at all, but Istvay didn't seem to expect him to. They grinned at him again, stepping away. "Point me in the right direction, I'll spread the scent blocker."

It only took them a few minutes, following Aran's directions. When they'd finished, they came back over to him with a fond smile. "Come on, let's get you somewhere you can sit down."

By the time the two of them reached their cabin on the ship, Aran was having to concentrate very hard to stay on his feet and push back the blackness encroaching on his vision. Istvay paused in front of the door, took one look at him, and swore under their breath. "Alright, we're getting you into bed, and I'm going to get you some painkillers from our supplies, and then I'm going to take a look at your leg, and the raiders are not going to bother us until I'm done," they muttered, unlocking the door. "Dessi," they called over their shoulder, "Tell Krevai and Zondra that they don't get to talk to Aran until I'm done bandaging him up. And before you ask, no, I'm not going to wait for you to take any measurements, you can do that later." They helped Aran inside, and closed the door firmly after him, and Aran sagged with relief.

He'd actually forgotten what it felt like to have someone there to say those things for him, when he wasn't sure he had the energy to say them himself.

Istvay helped him to the cot, ducking under Ani's trailing webs, and he sank down onto it.

Istvay swayed a little on their feet as they let go of him, and had to grab the cot frame for support, but they shook their head at Aran's panicked expression. "I'm fine," they muttered. "Just a little light-headed after all that." They sighed. "Honestly, I think I could sleep for a month and still be tired. But it looks like for once in our damn lives, that might actually be an option soon." They grinned. "But you'll be happy to hear that I called in about Emeric, since I guessed he'd be waking up right about now. It sounds like he's going to have a nice long time in prison to think about what he's done before Alba has time to deal with him."

Aran nodded, still not quite able to speak. Despite the pain, despite everything, he was smiling so wide that his face hurt with it.

Istvay busied themself around the cabin, grabbing painkillers and a glass of water and their emergency medical supplies, and Aran closed his eyes, trying to steady himself. The tip of a tentacle touched his elbow, and he opened his eyes to see Ani's bulbous face peering into his with concern.

He chuckled and held out his arm, and she climbed halfway up, squeezing his bicep affectionately. He rubbed her head, and her eyes closed to half-slits of contentment.

At last, when Istvay came back and began spreading out their medical equipment, Ani gave a reluctant little grumble and slithered down, settling onto the cot beside him.

"Hey sweetheart," Aran whispered. "Thank you for the help out there. We couldn't have done it without you."

She peered up at him for a moment, and then, at last, she turned and made the small, chirruping call that he'd come to learn was the signal for her hatchlings.

The tiny creatures tumbled down from the webbing and appeared out of the cabinets, and he smiled to himself as they slithered and scrambled over to their mother.

Even still, he could hardly believe the luck of it—that he was able, not only to observe the first recorded instance of land-devil parthenogenesis, but to watch the growth of the infant land-devils hatched from the parthenogenesis, and contrast their development against what little he knew of normal land-devil development.

Already, their maturity for their age was noticeable—he couldn't pinpoint with complete accuracy when they'd actually hatched, but they were far more independent than Ani had been at several months older, and they were behaving more like year-old land-devils than infants, even if they hadn't already proven that they were perfectly capable of fending for themselves.

He wasn't sure he'd tell the raiders that just yet, considering how they'd reacted to the mere presence of the infants on their ship, but the implications of it were enough to make him giddy with fascinated delight.

"Aran. Swallow this, then you can go back to daydreaming about your pets." Istvay's voice was wry and full of affection, and Aran blinked up at them, still smiling almost too wide for his face.

They smiled back, then leaned in to kiss him gently. "I don't know if I've ever mentioned how damn much I love you," they whispered, drawing back, then tipped the tablets into his palm and handed him the water.

Aran swallowed the painkillers down, and Istvay took the glass away to set on their work table as Aran turned back to Ani.

This next part would hurt, and it would probably be a lot easier on both him and Istvay if he could distract himself.

"Hey sweetheart," he said, reaching out to stroke Ani again as Istvay pulled out a medical knife and sliced through his blood-soaked trousers. "Can I see your babies? Would that be alright?"

She gave him a sharp, suspicious glance, and then, half-reluctantly, she drew back a little to let him see the squirming mass of infant land-devils.

"They're beautiful, Ani," he whispered. "You did such a good job." He counted them quickly, smiling to himself.

And then, abruptly, he stopped.

"Aran?" asked Istvay instantly, concern in their voice. "Did I hurt you? What's wrong?"

"Istvay," he said slowly. "Can you come here for a second?"

Istvay put down the bloodied medical supplies on a sterile sheet of gauze and rose, glancing at him in concern. They followed his gaze down to the pile of squirming land-devils.

"What's happened with …"

And then Istvay fell silent, and Aran saw on their face that they'd seen it, too.

"Twelve," they said, and there was something like dread in their voice. "Twelve babies. What the hell happened to the other five?"

"I mean … they could have gotten out at any time," began Aran.

Istvay sighed, shaking their head. "When's the last time you counted them?"

Aran frowned. "I … think it was around the time Ani started building her nest. When they were in the cupboard, it was pretty easy, but once she started nesting …"

Istvay closed their eyes for a moment. "So," they said at last. "At least twenty-four standard hours before we left the yibo system." They tipped their head back a little, without opening their eyes. "Look, Aran, I hate to say this, but I think we'd better call Krevai in."

When Krevai appeared a few minutes later, accompanied by Landru and about a dozen of the crew, he was in a jovial mood.

"Aran!" He managed to make his whisper sound much more like a bellow than should rightly be possible. "You did it! I truly did not believe something like that was possible." He paused. "I'd ask you where the charaks are, but I've known you long enough to know you'd let me rip your heart out and eat it right here in the cabin before you'd tell me." He chuckled. "You are truly a worthy crew member of mine, human or no."

Aran managed a weak smile.

On the one hand, it was an almost inexpressible relief that Krevai didn't seem angry with him anymore. He hadn't realized, really, how much of a relief until he'd had the hope, for the first time, that the captain might forgive him. And then it had felt like the weight that had been crushing his chest had been lifted, and he could breathe freely again for the first time in days.

On the other hand, with what he had to tell the captain … he wasn't entirely sure how long Krevai's good mood would last.

By the time he'd finished explaining, Krevai's face had darkened with something close to panic.

"You'd damn well better not tell Sharda about this," he muttered. "She'll kill you both and eat you. I'll tell her myself. And in the meantime," he turned to Istvay. "Do you think you can get me a line through to your Alba?" He grinned a little, despite everything. "That's a human I could get along with, I think. I heard stories from the crew that had her on their ship—turned to them and ordered them around like she was born to it. I can't help but admire a human like that."

Istvay sighed. "Give me a minute, I'm pretty sure I can get her to answer."

By the time Istvay had managed to open a line through to the Chief Justice, Krevai had already pulled the yibo captain on the line and explained the situation.

Aran hadn't been able to catch everything, but from the stunned yibo curses filtering through the line, helpfully translated by his wavelink, he could guess at the man's reaction.

"Yes?" Alba answered at last, Istvay's palmscreen broadcasting her voice through to the room. She sounded exhausted, and her voice was weak and raspy, but there was that familiar ring of command to it that Aran had become accustomed to. "What do you need, Istvay? I had hoped to call you soon anyways, it appears we'll have things to discuss with the raiders."

"Yes, well I'm guessing the raiders are going to have something to discuss with you as well," said Istvay grimly. "We seem to have run into a bit of a problem."

"Alba," said Krevai, once Istvay had explained the situation. "I'm afraid I'm going to have to take the Aran and the Istvay back through the portal immediately, and keep them there after the portal closes. We can't risk the possibility that there are land-devils in our system, without the one person who knows how to deal with them."

"Yes, well I'm afraid I can't let you do that," Alba snapped, some of the usual fire returning to her tone. "As I'm certain you're aware, it is just as likely that the land-devils escaped in our system as in yours. And as you say, Aran is the only person in history, to my knowledge, who's managed to tame one of them."

Krevai's face was darkening in anger. "I'm sure on this the yibos and I are in full agreement." There was a growl to his voice. "You came through our portal. You brought these dangerous animals through. You are fully responsible to us for any harm that might come from them."

"You were the ones, if I recall correctly, who took down the portal and trapped us there," Alba responded tartly. "The land-devils were on your ship, so if anyone could have ensured against their escape, it would have been your crew. I have no intention of putting my own system at risk because of your actions. Aran has fulfilled his end of the bargain. I suggest—"

"You can suggest all you'd like, human." Krevai's voice was

dangerous. "If this comes to a war—"

Aran drew in a deep breath and blew it out. "Quiet!" he snapped, as loud as he could into Istvay's palmscreen.

For a moment, everyone fell silent in surprise.

"Please," he said. "Just … please let me talk."

There was a long, long pause. Krevai was glaring at him, but hell, at this point he was more than used to that. At last, though, the captain nodded grudgingly. "Fine. Our Aran wants to say something."

"Very well." Alba didn't seem any more enthused about the prospect than Krevai did. But on the bright side, Aran thought desperately, neither of them could possibly feel less comfortable about it than he did.

He closed his eyes for a moment. He felt Istvay's hand on his shoulder, and he leaned into it, bracing himself. "Listen," he said at last, without opening his eyes. "There may or may not be land-devils loose in one or both of our systems. The raiders are going to bring the charaks back to their system, but we have no guarantee that one of them won't escape here. You can threaten each other, and Krevai can bring his raiders through and try to hunt through this system, and you, Alba, can send out all of Cavaco's military and try to bomb them to death. But I'll tell you something right now—if either of you do any of those things, you will damn well do it without me and Istvay. We're not your damn property, or your pets—" he opened his eyes long enough to glower at Krevai, who gave him a look of wide-eyed innocence, "or anything else. We're happy to help you, just like we've been happy to help you since the start of this whole thing. But we do it on our own damn terms. And if there's anyone in either of your systems who wants to try to force either of us …" he paused a moment. "Well, you'd just better hope you can get past Ani, is all."

There was a long moment of silence, from the wavelink and from inside the cabin.

"Very well, Aran." Alba's voice was still cold, but there was a hint of humour to it that was almost shocking in its unexpectedness. "What, exactly, do you propose as your terms?"

He glanced back at Istvay, who gave him a small, encouraging nod. His pulse was pounding, and he had to force the words out, because this—talking to groups of people, everyone listening to him—was very close to his worst nightmare.

"I've spent my whole damn life working with things that could kill me if they wanted to," he said at last. His voice was shaking. But this was important. "I work with things that could kill me every damn day. And do you know why they don't?"

In the background, he heard Dessi mutter something about how she suspected that none of them could possibly accept that someone could truly be stupid enough to voluntarily get himself in the situations he did, so it was probably mostly disbelief. He ignored her. "They don't kill me, because I respect them. I don't threaten them, I don't try to hurt them or force them to do anything, I just damn well respect their space. And you know what? Most things, if you're willing to respect them, are more than happy to respect you back. I don't know very much about politics, or about how you negotiate peace. But if I had to guess, I'd guess it was pretty close to the same thing, when it comes down to it."

"What are you saying, Aran?" There was still the hint of a threat in Krevai's voice.

"I'm saying," said Aran, turning on him, "that you're just damn well going to have to figure out how to get along. Because from where I'm sitting, that looks like your only option."

There was another long, long pause.

"Well," said Alba at last. There was an odd note to her voice, and he wasn't sure if it was amusement, or admiration, or irritation, and he quite frankly didn't have the energy to try to figure it out. "I suppose, then, that we'll have to come up with some sort of a peace treaty between the three groups of us. Because as Aran says—I'm not sure what our other options are going to be. I can't let you take him back through the portal, and you can't close the portal and leave him on this side. And if the portal is going to stay open, we'll have to deal with terms and conditions."

Krevai grunted. "Sharda will be absolutely furious," he grumbled.

Aran caught Istvay's smug look, and grinned a little.

"Serves her damn well right," they whispered.

The yibo captain gave a long sigh. "I suppose, if that's our only option, I'll send word back through the portal to ask for a diplomat to be sent through," he said at last, grudgingly. "I had hoped to be done with humans forever after this."

"The feeling, I assure you, was mutual," said Alba tartly. "However, this would likely have been our best option regardless—if our people were left with this level of mistrust, war would have broken out at some point, either from your system, if the Nativist faction once again gained power and decided to reopen a portal, or from ours, if someone like Cavaco were able to whip our people into a frenzy about the dangers waiting for us just a portal away. You destroyed the Labarinto system, because they were not expecting you and knew nothing about you. But we do. And all of us understand that, between raiders and land-devils and charaks, there's not a one of us who could kill everyone else without risking mutual destruction. Therefore, as much as I would love to be able to guarantee peace, I believe that, as Aran said, mutual understanding and mutual commitments are our most likely path to that."

Aran tapped off his wavelink as the others spoke, closing his eyes and pressing his fingers to his temples to try to shove back the growing headache.

Istvay's hand tightened on his shoulder, and he sighed and opened his eyes. They were smiling at him, their expression soft, and when they leaned in to kiss him, he kissed them back.

Then Istvay winked at him, and unbuttoned the top button of his shirt.

He frowned at them, glancing around at the crowded cabin.

And then, a moment later, he heard Dessi hiss, "The humans want to do sex! Everyone get out, we don't want to stress them. They have very strong customs around doing sex, we can't disturb them."

He glanced back at Istvay, whose eyes were sparkling with mischief. They unbuttoned another of Aran's shirt buttons, and behind them, Dessi started shoeing people out of the room.

The last thing Aran heard, before the door shut behind the raiders, was Dessi saying in a loud whisper, "Honestly, Krevai, keeping the portal open will advance our research by leaps and bounds, we can study the humans in their natural habitat and everything. I'm with our Aran on this one."

And then the door closed, leaving him and Istvay, finally, alone. Or, as alone as they could be, in a cabin with thirteen land-devils. And for the first time in what seemed like forever, Aran could feel himself finally, finally relax.

33

There was a small, muted *beep* ... *beep* ... *beep* on the edges of Savina's hearing, tugging at her consciousness in an insistent, irritating way.

She wanted to move, to swat it away, but she couldn't make her muscles obey her.

The irritation tugged at her more insistently now, and she could hear other things, too—voices, whispering words her brain didn't seem to want to interpret.

After a while, the muted rise and fall of voices began to form itself into words, and Savina let them wash over her, because she didn't have the energy to do anything else.

"... possible that she'll be in a coma for some time. The shot didn't hit anything vital, but she was already badly wounded. I'm not sure ..."

"... don't care! She's my sister—"

And suddenly, the groggy, drowsy part of her brain that had been watching the words drift by snapped to attention as she recognized the voice.

It took almost more effort than she was capable of to open her eyes, but the sudden rush of panicked adrenaline helped to bring the world back into blurry focus.

She blinked a few times, even that small motion shooting pain through her body.

There was light, bright lights, and she must be in a room somewhere, but she didn't recognize it at all.

"I'll stay with her, I promise." The new voice, too, was recognizable, calm and reassuring, but cracked with weariness.

"Nicolau?" Savina managed to croak at last. "Joska?"

The voices stopped, and for a moment, there was complete silence.

And then Nicolau gasped, "Vina!" in a choked voice, and a moment later she was blinking at his face hovering over her bed.

"Nicolau," she managed again, trying to blink him back into focus.

"Shhh, Savina." She felt a hand on her shoulder, warm and reassuring, and when she turned her head, just a little, she could make out Joska, who'd come to stand beside Nicolau. "It's good to see you back. How are you feeling?"

Joska's voice held the same dry, affectionate tones she'd become so used to over the course of the last few months, and she wasn't sure why, suddenly, it made her want to break down and cry.

She blinked a few more times, trying to push back the tears. When she was able to see again, a doctor stood beside Nicolau and Joska. "Easy there," the woman whispered, bending down over her cot. "Give me a minute to check your vitals, and then I can get you sitting up a little, if you'd like."

Savina nodded, and by the time the doctor had finished her

checks and raised the bed so she was able to look around the room, Savina had managed to bring herself mostly under control.

Nicolau and Joska were sitting in hospital chairs pulled up next to her bed, and the bright room around her, walls and ceilings painted with cheerful murals of flowers and birds, was a hospital recovery room.

"Savina. How are you feeling? We weren't sure when you were going to wake up." Joska's voice held an edge of tears to it as well. Savina pulled in a deep breath, and for the first time since she'd heard Nicolau's voice and come fully awake, she took stock.

She hurt. Her head throbbed, and her throat was sore, and her body ached with the feeling of having sat in one position for far too long. Pain beat like a heartbeat through her side, and there was another, smaller pain throbbing in her shoulder.

But there was something in the back of her head that told her that she should, by rights, have been feeling much, much worse …

She gasped as the memories began to trickle back in—outside the city, her forces running for the gates. The shocking realization that they'd been betrayed, the shot that had left her staggering.

Falling.

Prison. Cavaco. Her decision to be a martyr.

"What happened?" Her voice came out choked with panic. "What happened? Where am I, what—"

"Shhhh." Joska leaned forward, laying her hand on Savina's uninjured shoulder. "Shhh, it's alright. Everything's alright." She paused, as if gathering her thoughts. "When the soldiers came back from the mountains, some of us were already inside the city gates. There wasn't much we could do against that much firepower, so I instructed the rebels under me to blend in as much as they could, and hide in the crowds. It was the only way I could think of to keep them safe." She paused, and Savina could see the pain heavy in her eyes. "Most of them got taken. Several of them were killed. But there were still a few who'd managed to get inside and blend in, and since we didn't have uniforms, it wasn't easy to find us and drag us back out. I heard that you'd been shot, possibly captured, but at that point, all we had to work with was rumours."

She managed a small smile. "Your brother here was determined to storm the capital and bring you out, but he'd been injured, and even if he hadn't, he couldn't have done anything, since we had no real information."

Savina glanced over at her brother. For the first time, she noticed how pale his face was, the wan, gaunt look to his cheeks, the way his body hunched forward a little, as if in pain.

"Nicolau?" she snapped, her voice coming out harsh with fear. "Nicolau, what happened to you?"

He managed a smile in her direction. "I'm … I'm alright. See? I'm already out of bed, and I walked here by myself, which the doctor said shouldn't have been possible."

Savina's frantic gaze caught on Joska. "Joska—"

Joska gave a small, soft chuckle. "He's alright. He was shot getting into the city, and to be honest, I wasn't completely sure he'd pull through. But he's doing much better now, and he's expected to make a full recovery."

Savina closed her eyes and sagged back against her pillow in relief. "And Beni?" She whispered after a moment. "Ines? Rafel?"

Joska smiled again. "All alive. All injured, but all alive, which is more of a miracle than I'd possibly hoped for."

Savina felt her entire body drooping in relief, and for a moment, they were all silent.

At last Joska cleared her throat and continued. "As I was saying, we didn't know what had happened to you, until Cavaco announced that he had one of the rebel leaders who was going to come speak to the public. I think he was hoping that would calm things down—he didn't have the popular support to keep the city under tight control, and although he'd been sending out raids to try to flush out the rebels, after the weeks of his forces being pinned down in the mountains, he simply didn't have the soldiers or the infrastructure to do so efficiently. I think he was hoping that the fact that he'd caught you and you were willing to speak would be enough to bring down the temperature so that he could get the city back under control."

She paused a moment. "Of course," she added wryly, "I knew you well enough to know that if you'd agreed to something Cavaco suggested, he wouldn't be getting the result that he thought he would." Joska paused again, and Savina realized, with a small shock, that she was brushing away tears. "I can't tell you exactly what I expected when I came out to the square and saw you standing there, but what you did ..." she paused again, shaking her head. "That was courage, Savina. Thank you." She stopped talking for a moment.

Nicolau cleared his throat. "I thought you were the one who was always telling me not to be all stupid and self-sacrificing. And then you go and be a martyr?" He was trying to sound gruff, but his voice, choked with emotion, sounded far too boyish, and Savina found herself smiling.

"After that?" Joska shrugged. "We watched you get dragged away, and we watched you get shot. And then the streets erupted. The rebels and the soldiers were fighting, and riots were springing up everywhere, and the army couldn't bring things back under control without starting to simply fire on civilians indiscriminately. And then the raiders began wreaking havoc, and the entire city was panicking."

Savina felt the blood drain from her face. "The raiders?"

Joska gave a rueful nod that did little to hide the horror on her face. "They didn't make it far, and there were surprisingly few casualties, all things considered. But ..." she trailed off for a moment.

Savina didn't have to imagine—she could still see, in bright, horrific detail, painted across the inside of her brain, what a raider attack looked like.

"At any rate," Joska continued at last, "the raiders stopped their attack eventually, due to our friends Aran and Istvay, I believe. And then Cavaco gave orders to fire on the hangar bay that contained the raiders and the scientists, and all the land-devils."

For a moment, Savina froze at the horror of imagining it.

Joska chuckled softly. "The soldiers were already on edge at the possibility of shooting down civilians—a lot of the soldiers' families live in do Sol, so this was personal to them. And when the Chief Justice somehow got out word of what would happen if they followed these new orders—that seems to have been the final straw. The troops laid down their weapons en mass and surrendered both the government and Cavaco back to the Council."

There were a few more moments' silence, as Savina took in what had happened.

"So why am I alive?" she asked at last, her voice still hoarse. "You said I was shot. Why am I still here?"

Joska paused, her face creasing in a familiar expression of concern. "I'm ... not completely sure," she said at last. "Apparently Cavaco had people in position to take you down should you say something you were not meant to. But ... I heard rumours that every person Cavaco had put in position to shoot you down was killed, and that the only reason you were shot at all is that one of them managed to get off a shot before they died."

Savina frowned. "Who killed them? Was it one of the rebels?"

Joska shook her head slowly. "Not as far as I know. As I said, Cavaco kept your whereabouts, and the fact that you were alive, completely secret. Nicolau and Rafel and I had been searching for any clue of what had happened to you, and we came up with nothing. We assume it must have been someone in the government. Because that's the other thing—you were shot, and then someone on the walls took down the two guards holding you, and then dragged you away. They were masked, and no one knows who it was, but I received word a few hours later that you were at the hospital here. I came as soon as I could."

Savina leaned back against the pillows again and closed her eyes.

Someone inside the government. Someone who'd known what was going to happen. Who'd guessed what Savina would do, and who'd decided to risk their life to help her do it, and not only that— to keep her alive afterwards.

A picture of Reka Soler flashed in her memory, the way Savina had last seen her—striding out of Cavaco's council room, tall and elegant and impassive, not meeting Savina's eyes.

It was possible.

She might never actually know. Chances were, if Reka had done that, she'd been captured or killed shortly afterwards.

She almost laughed, just a little.

Reka had always been looking for a glorious way to die. And she'd finally found it.

And then she found there were tears in her eyes, and leaking down her face, and she couldn't seem to blink them back.

Reka had finally found her glorious way to die, and it hadn't been saving the system after all.

It had been saving Savina.

"Savina? Savina, what's wrong?" Joska leaned forward quickly, her voice tight with concern.

Savina gave a watery smile. "Nothing," she managed at last. "Nothing's wrong. I just … I think I know what may have happened."

Joska raised an eyebrow, waiting, and Savina drew in a long, steadying breath. "I saw Reka, before Cavaco hauled me out to address the square," she said. "He said she'd come back and told him that she'd finally found something that was worth dying for. He assumed that it was keeping the system safe from the yibos and raiders, and so did I. But …"

They were quiet again. Joska reached out and took Savina's hand in a comforting gesture.

"Well," she said after a moment. "I suppose Reka grew up a little too."

"You haven't …" Savina couldn't keep the wretched hope from her voice.

Joska shook her head. "I'm sorry, Savina. I haven't heard from her. If she is still alive, she hasn't tried to let any of us know."

Savina managed a small smile, and for a while longer, they sat in silence.

At last, Joska glanced up, and her face went suddenly worried. "Alright, you," she said, standing quickly and turning to Nicolau. "Let's get you back to bed, I think you've been up for long enough."

Savina glanced at her brother, and sucked in a quick breath. His face was so pale she was certain he was about to pass out on the floor in front of them.

"I'm alright," he muttered, but he allowed Joska to help him to his feet. He turned to Savina, and a quick, genuine smile flickered over his face, despite the obvious pain. "I'm glad you're alright, Vina," he said. "I was … I was so worried about you." His voice choked a little. And then he swayed on his feet, and Savina cursed.

"Joska! Get my idiot baby brother back to his room, we can talk later."

Joska had already caught Nicolau's arm, supporting him. "Easy there," she murmured, and they started towards the door, but she cast a quick, affectionate glance at Savina over her shoulder as they went out. And Savina leaned back on her cot and closed her eyes against the bittersweet lump in her throat that wanted to rise up and choke her.

It was almost three weeks before she was finally released from the hospital. Nicolau had only been released a few days earlier, but he'd taken to haunting her bedside, along with Joska and Beni and even Rafel. Ines accompanied Nicolau most days, and Nicolau's adoptive parents had come up to visit her a few times as well. Even Ignasi and Esti had stopped by to see how she was doing. Her parents didn't come, but then, she hadn't expected them to. She doubted they even knew what had happened.

One day, two weeks into her stay, Alba Espina was brought up to her room. Guards came in first, clearing out everyone else and standing watch at the doors and windows, and then the diminutive woman herself stepped into the room.

She looked exhausted, and much older than Savina remembered, her steps halting and slow. One of the guards leapt forward to pull out a chair for her, and she sank weakly into it.

Savina's heart was pounding in a quick, uncomfortable rhythm, her throat dry.

It had been a long, long time since she'd seen the Judge of

Heresies in person. And now, here she was, sitting at Savina's bedside. Just like Savina had crouched at her bedside, weeks ago and lightyears away, and shoved a knife against her throat.

"Savina," the woman said at last. Her voice was tired, but it still held a touch of arrogance. "I'm glad to see you're recovering."

"What do you want?" Savina snapped. She was trying to push back the mindless panic, but she could already feel it rolling over her in waves.

Alba looked momentarily shocked, and Savina scowled at her.

If she'd been expecting Savina to kneel and kiss her feet like everyone else in this system did, then she hadn't learned a damn thing from their time in the yibo system.

"Nothing," Alba said at last, and Savina realized, suddenly, that her shock wasn't from Savina's tone, but from her question. "I didn't want anything at all. You've already given much more than I could have asked. I simply wanted to come in person to thank you."

There was a long, long moment of silence. Savina stared at her, and Alba met her gaze, unflinching.

"What about the warrant you put out on me?" Savina asked at last.

Alba drew in a long breath, a rueful expression on her face. "As you are currently a folk hero and one step away from a holy martyr, I hardly see that there's anything I could do," she said at last. She paused, leaning in. "Savina," she said quietly. "You have saved more lives than any of us can count. You kept the people from the diplomatic ship alive and helped them escape Kachik. You saved the humans from yibo and raider aggression, and here, you kept people's hope alive when it seemed that all was lost. I cannot tell you in words the gratitude you have earned from me, and from all of us." She paused again.

"I know about your past actions. While normally, I believe, the response to your heroism would be to offer you public accolades, I don't think that's possible at the moment. We live in a system governed by laws, and you've broken most of them, and I do not currently see a way to honour someone whose former career was assassinating some of the wealthiest and most influential businesspeople and politicians in the Joias System. But I can offer you this—I will use my influence to wipe your slate clean. You'll be able to start over, with nothing on your record. I have considered this at length, and I believe that is the best I can do for you. But that much, at least, I will do. And after that—" She shrugged. "I will only be able to protect you so far. If you choose to go back to your former profession, I will not be able to avoid issuing a warrant, although you can believe me that it will pain me to do so. But now, in repayment for your service, I can offer you a second chance."

For a moment, Savina stared at her.

There was something twisting in her stomach, an odd mix of resentment and guilt and gratitude.

A clean slate. A second chance. She'd never honestly thought that was possible.

It wouldn't be a clean slate, not really. Alba's pardon couldn't bring back the people she'd killed, or bring justice to their families. They, at least, wouldn't forget Savina's crimes.

She was intelligent enough to know that what Alba was offering was likely the limit of her ability to offer, and to know what it must have cost the woman to do so—subvert the justice she'd spent her whole life upholding, in gratitude to a Rim Mountain assassin who had never shown any sign of reforming her ways. Knowing she had no guarantee that Savina wouldn't kill more people with her newfound clean record—and doing it anyways.

And Savina still couldn't help how much she hated the woman.

At last, she just nodded stiffly. "Thank you."

To her shock, Alba actually smiled, just a little. "No. Thank you, Savina. Truly. You've done more good than I think you realize."

At last, Savina was cleared to leave the hospital.

She spent the morning wandering around the hospital room, trying out her legs. She still felt weak and sick, and lost, somehow, in a way she hadn't before. The world had changed, and she'd changed, and she wasn't sure what that meant anymore.

And she hadn't realized, until they'd told her she was going to be released, that she didn't really have anywhere to go.

The compound was the only home she'd ever had, really, and she wasn't sure she could face it right then.

She wasn't sure she wanted to.

Perhaps she'd stay in a rooming house for a while, that might be the best option.

But while the hospital staff was gathering up Savina's things, Joska appeared at the door. Her face was still drawn and haggard, but she was wearing her familiar dry smile. And Savina hadn't realized, until just then, how relief would wash over her at the sight so strong it almost made her knees buckle.

"Savina," Joska said, glancing around her at the room. "I don't want to impose, if you have other places you want to be. But I thought if you didn't, you might want someone to pick you up."

Savina was still blinking at her, trying to push back the thick knot of emotion.

"I would tell you you were welcome to stay with me while you decide what to do next, but to be quite honest, my home was the *Dolphin*, and it looks like none of us will be going back there. But

Nicolau's parents were asking if you'd like to come stay with them for a bit, before you moved on. They told me they'd been wanting time to get to know you a little more, and they were hoping you'd come." She chuckled. "Nicolau looked like a puppy who'd just been given a bone when they said that, so I hope that for his sake, at least, you'll come. They've cleared out a bedroom, and they told me you're welcome to stay for as long as you'd like."

Savina was still staring at her.

There was an odd feeling opening in her chest, and it hurt in ways Savina wasn't sure she even understood.

"Rafel and I will be there too, for a little," Joska continued. There was something far too perceptive in her gaze. "They've offered us a place while I find someone who will let me take out a new ship on credit." she shrugged. "I'll likely have to sign on as crew to another cargo ship at first, until I can get together enough funds for a downpayment. But I've done that before. And considering what we just came out of, it might be nice not having to worry about making the next payment for a while."

Savina closed her eyes. Even so, she could see Joska's worn face in her memory, the small, dry smile that twitched at the corners of her mouth when she was amused. The way the woman had so effortlessly outwitted her the first time they'd met. The stupid, stubborn morality of her.

"I'm sorry about the *Dolphin*," she said at last, opening her eyes and praying her voice wouldn't tremble.

Joska spread her hands in a small shrug. "If it wasn't this, it would have been something else. No point in feeling sorry for myself over it."

She'd worked her whole life for things, Rafel had said, and every time they had been snatched away at the last moment. And somehow, even now, she didn't sound bitter, or angry. Just sad, and a little tired.

"Yes," said Savina at last, softly. "Yes, you can tell Nicolau's parents that … I'd like that."

Joska helped her to the lobby downstairs, where Beni and Rafel were waiting.

"Vina?" Beni asked, standing quickly as she and Joska entered the room, even though Savina knew her footsteps would sound the same as anyone else's.

"Hey, Beni," she managed, and then her sibling stepped forward and pulled her into an embrace, and it took her a moment to realize they were crying.

Nicolau's parents' cottage was homey and welcoming, but far too small for all the people it was currently sheltering. And the first night, at dinner, as they sat around the table, the warm, comfortable smell of stew and freshly-baked sourdough bread filling the air and the laughter and conversations floating out on the breeze, Savina felt like her chest was being crushed, inexorably, a millimetre at a time, with each taste of the homemade food, each smile, each kind look tightening the vise a little more.

This was the home she'd never had. This was the childhood she and Beni had bought for Nicolau, but had never experienced themselves. And maybe for Beni, having it now was enough.

But every time Savina closed her eyes, she could picture the choking, suffocating dread of the compound, how badly she'd wanted to get out. How she'd known she never could. She could picture the adults stepping into the abandoned farmer's cabin, feel the smooth wood of the door against her fingers and hear the *snick* of the bolt as she fixed it into place. She could hear the roaring *whoosh* of flame as she lit the kindling and stepped back, feel the mix of horror and terror and sick satisfaction that choked in her lungs like smoke as she listened to the screams from inside, the death-screams of the people who would have hunted Nicolau down.

That had been her childhood. That had been her life. And seeing now what it could have been instead hurt, almost more than living through it in the first place.

Nicolau found her outside after dinner, and came to stand beside her. He paused a moment, as if unsure what to do, and then put a tentative arm around her shoulder.

She could have shrugged it off, but she didn't, and after a moment, he relaxed.

"Vina?" he said at last. "Vina, I'm glad you're here. I … I don't know if I ever told you this, but I always wanted a big sister. I used to make believe I had one, when I was a kid. I called her Rosie." He laughed a little, a small, choked sound. "And now I have two siblings. That whole time I was growing up and making believe, I had two siblings looking out for me."

She managed a small smile. "Apparently it took two of us. I never knew how much trouble you were until we met you on that ship."

They were quiet for a little while. At last, he said, "Vina? What are you going to do next?"

She sighed.

That was the question. She could stay here for as long as she wanted, she knew that. She'd seen it in Edite's face.

But there was something she had to do first.

"I … I suppose I should probably go back to the compound," she said at last. "To tell them goodbye."

They were quiet for a few moments, but she could feel the tension in the arm he'd slung over her shoulder.

"Vina?" he said again. There was something quiet and vulnerable in his voice.

"Yes?"

"Vina, I ..." He was looking down, his expression shadowed in the soft dark of the evening. "I'd like to ... to meet them. My birth parents. If ... if you don't mind me coming with you." He looked up quickly. "I don't mean ... look, Beni's told me enough to know that ..." He drew in a long breath. "I guess ... I guess I'd just like to see where I came from. Where you grew up. I'd ... I'd like to know that about myself. About you and Beni."

Savina squeezed her eyes closed against the hot sting of tears, even though she couldn't have told anyone why she was crying.

"If not, it's alright," he added hastily. "I'm not ... Vina, please don't cry, I'm sorry ..."

She cleared her throat. "No," she said at last. "No, it's alright. I don't think they can possibly be a danger to you anymore, not after everything that's happened. Or to me or Beni. They can't hurt us anymore."

He was still watching her, and there was an understanding in his face that she hadn't expected.

"We can hire a transport to take us up there tomorrow," she said at last. "It'll probably take all day, but as long as you don't mind ..."

"Yeah," said Nicolau softly. "Yeah, I don't mind." But she could feel the way his arm trembled on her shoulder.

Savina was right. By the time they'd hired a transport, wrangled a price, and then traveled the long, bumpy ride over narrow dirt tracks, it was well past midday. Joska, Beni, and even Rafel had insisted on coming along, and there was some small part of Savina, the part of her that would never, really, not be afraid, that was glad.

But in the end ...

Well, she was glad that Nicolau had asked.

Because she needed to finally tell her parents. To lay out in front of them what they'd done. To ask them why. To show her mother everything she'd lost, by putting her faith above her own child's life.

Maybe her mother would never actually understand. Savina was old enough to realize her parents might never understand. They'd probably condemn her and Beni and Nicolau as unrepentant sinners who'd go straight to the Void. But at least she'd finally have said it.

Savina asked the driver to put them down a little way from the compound. She didn't like making Rafel walk—he'd never admit it, she knew, but she'd seen how heavily he'd been limping on his prosthetic leg recently. But she couldn't exactly bring them to the gates of the compound, either—she knew well enough how wary the people inside were of the outside world.

They hiked the half hour up the rough dirt path in silence. Beni, walking beside Savina, didn't seem to even need the echolocator in their wavelink, the path so familiar that they and Savina could probably have walked it in their sleep.

As they got closer, though, Beni bumped Savina's shoulder. "Vina?" they whispered. "Do you smell that?"

Savina frowned.

Now that Beni had mentioned it, there was an unfamiliar smell in the air, harsh and unpleasant, like burning rubber.

Joska glanced over, and Savina could see the sudden concern in her expression as well.

Savina closed her eyes for a moment, trying to steady her heart rate. Then she forced herself forward, up through the last small stand of trees until they opened up on the valley between two hills where the compound lay hidden.

For a few moments, she just stood there. She could hear, vaguely,

Beni come up beside her, feel her sibling's hand on her shoulder. She heard Nicolau's soft curse, and Ines's little gasp of horror, saw, from the corner of her eye, the way Joska stiffened as she saw what lay below them.

"Vina?" Beni's voice was soft and frightened. "Vina, what happened?"

Savina closed her eyes and swallowed hard to keep the bile back from her throat. "I don't know," she said at last. Her voice sounded strange and hollow. "I don't know what happened. The compound is … gone."

"This was Joias soldiers." Rafel's voice was grim. "You can see where they came in over that hill. The compound wouldn't have stood a chance."

Feeling like she was walking in a dream, Savina started slowly down the hill towards the charred remnants of the place where she and Beni had grown up.

Rafel was right—as she got closer, it was easy to see what had happened. Some of the larger guns, or maybe ground-disrupters, had taken the walls of the compound down, and then, when the soldiers had finished whatever they'd done here, everything had been set ablaze.

She reached the broken outer walls, and ran her fingers along the black, charred stains on the shattered cement.

They'd been built to protect everyone inside from the outside world. But it had always been, as long as Savina had lived there, protection against the impurities of the outside world, the corruption of the Orthodox religion. It had been a century since Old Believers had been hunted down by the Joias government. But standing here, amid the ruins of what had been her home, Savina realized with a sudden, sick certainty, that no matter how many walls they'd built, no matter how many weapons they'd amassed—it had never mattered. Just like her mother had told her as a child: if the army wanted to kill them, it would, and there was nothing they could do about it. Nothing but hide, and pray.

And it seemed that hadn't been enough.

"What … what happened to all the people inside?" Nicolau's voice was soft, tone muted with horror. "Maybe if we talk to Alba, maybe she can find where they were taken."

Savina glanced around, still not quite sure she'd be able to speak. Not sure what she'd say if she could.

And then she saw Rafel's face, and she felt something sick and cold hardening in her stomach.

He saw her looking, and shook his head slowly. "I'm sorry, Savina." His voice was quiet and sick. "I'm sorry. I saw it in the military myself. They'd have been furious about what was happening in the Rim Mountains with the rebellion. And the Rim Mountain villages aren't the only ones who lay the blame for everything they don't like at the feet of the Old Believers. Bigotry is alive and well in the military, I can tell you that from experience."

"What—Vina, what's he saying?" Nicolau was looking at her, something pleading and horrified in his eyes, and she didn't want to answer, because she didn't want what Rafel was saying to be true.

"Vina?" Beni's voice was quiet and sick. "Vina, I can't see. Please. Tell me what happened."

Savina drew in a long breath and walked over to where Rafel stood.

There was a long trench, dug and filled in, the earth fresh-turned and broken, and she dropped to her knees beside it.

She caught a glimpse of a scrap of fabric in the newly turned earth—something bright and covered with embroidered flowers, the edge of a child's jacket.

"All of them," she whispered. She wasn't sure who she was talking to. "It's all of them, isn't it? Even the children."

When she glanced up at Rafel, she saw the confirmation in his face. "The soldiers wouldn't have let any of them live," he said quietly. "If they killed enough of them, they wouldn't want word to get back. And this compound is so isolated, I doubt they'd have worried about anyone finding out, at least, not soon enough that there would be consequences traced back to whoever gave the order."

Savina closed her eyes.

She thought she might vomit.

She couldn't actually feel anything—this was too big, too much. It was impossible to put a feeling onto something like this.

She'd hated her life in the compound. Ever since she was seven years old, and had risked her own life to save her baby brother, she'd hated it. She'd seen the rot in it, she'd felt how its tendrils wound around her, choking her, suffocating her.

Her mother. Her mother and father, thrown together with everyone else inside a mass grave dug out by the soldiers who'd shot them.

She'd known every one of these people by name.

How many times had she dreamed of taking a match, burning the compound to the ground herself?

The trees around the compound, where she and Beni and the other children had played, had been caught in the fire as well. Some of them were still standing, others had been reduced to charred stumps. The dirt hill where she and Beni had played dolls. The rusty playground and swings in the centre of the compound, still visible as a charred lump of metal.

There was the scrap of a coat caught in the dirt. That meant they'd burned the compound afterwards. Maybe they'd burned it to hide the traces of their crimes. Maybe, in two or three years, no one would have known—they'd come across the burned structures and not even know what had happened. Who'd lived here.

The endless hours in services or prayer, the holovids of her great-grandmother.

No child would be forced to watch those again. No child would, because the people who'd been holding on to her great-grandmother's memory had been killed as brutally and violently as the people in the vids, and for the exact same reason, even a hundred years later.

She wasn't crying. The pain was too deep, too immense for tears. It was too big for anything, too big to comprehend. It was a huge, gaping chasm cut down the middle of her that all the fresh-turned earth in the world couldn't cover.

"Savina? I'm so sorry, Savina." Joska's hand was on her shoulder, Joska's voice, sick with horror, in her ear.

She shook her head slowly.

There wasn't anything Joska could say. There wasn't anything anyone could say.

This had been her home. As much as she'd hated it, this had been the only home she'd ever had. This wasn't some human settlement in the yibo system, some place she'd get up and leave and never have to come back to.

This had been her home. And there was nowhere she could go, in this system or any other, to escape what had happened to it. What Cavaco's soldiers had done.

She could feel something rising under the numbness—something hot and destructive and overwhelming.

Rage.

Because she knew exactly what was going to happen to the soldiers who'd done this: nothing. She knew exactly what consequences Cavaco would suffer. He'd deny that he had anything to do with it, deny that the soldiers were working under his orders. This would be just an unfortunate side effect of a war he'd built, nurtured, and then set loose, all for his personal gain. This ugly trench of dirt that contained the bodies of her family, of all the people she'd known and grown up with, of the child whose jacket had been caught in the dirt as they covered her over—they would mean nothing. Less than nothing. They were Old Believers, after all. No real loss. And Cavaco was an important man in government.

"Can you explain this to Beni?" she whispered. She wasn't sure how she was even speaking. "I don't … I can't …"

"I'll tell Beni and Nicolau," said Joska. There was a note in her voice, something uncharacteristically hard, that Savina wasn't sure she'd ever heard there before. But her tone was sympathetic. "And what are you going to do, Savina?"

"I don't know," said Savina at last. She was still staring at the long trench, the freshly turned dirt. "I … don't know." Something was choking in her throat. "This … this wasn't supposed to happen, Joska! It wasn't supposed to be like this! I … I wanted to tell them they were wrong. I wanted them to hurt. But not … not like this! Damn them. Damn them all, damn them to the Void!" She was shouting by the time she finished.

Joska paused, then crouched beside her in the dirt, let her arm rest on Savina's shoulder, and didn't say anything at all.

34

Alba

Alba sat in her familiar seat in the Council Chambers, looking out over the familiar faces.

There were far more missing than she'd hoped. Even after three weeks, she found her eyes skipping over the empty seats, as if, if she was somehow able to ignore the fact the seats weren't filled, it wouldn't be true—that their previous occupants would have somehow survived everything that had happened.

Not all of them were dead. There were a few councillors who were recovering in the hospital. Some would be back in their old seats eventually.

But there were far too many who'd never come back.

It was an odd feeling, being back in her old place, listening as the Speaker called the meetings to order, while the weight of horror and sorrow and disbelief pressed down across the entire Council Body heavy enough to choke and smother, and no one willing to speak it aloud.

She sighed to herself, and tried to pull her mind back to the topic at hand.

Aran had likely had the right of it, in the end—had the yibos and raiders simply gone back through the portal and closed it behind them, it was unlikely she'd have ever been able to convince the Council to stop preparing for war. Even after everything, there were those who supported Cavaco—if not his methods, then at least his reasoning. And she could hardly blame them—the few minutes the raiders had slaughtered their way down the streets of do Sol had left images that people would never forget.

Better to leave the portal open. Better to keep a dialogue open between the species than let images like that fester in the dark. And if that land-devil's hellish offspring were enough of an impetus to keep everyone peaceful while more stringent measures and countermeasures were ironed out, then she supposed she could be grateful even for that—although quite frankly, the thought of those demon-spawn loose on the system, possibly in do Sol itself, was enough to give her nightmares.

Today, though, there were neither raider nor yibo diplomats present.

Today, they were going to finally deal with the subject that had been hanging over the Council since they reconvened after Cavaco's defeat.

"Honoured Councillors, the prisoner, former general Eniko Cavaco, will be brought in." The Speaker's voice, just like everything over the past few weeks, was both familiar and absurdly unfamiliar, jarring by its very normality.

A rustle spread through the assembled councillors, a quiet murmur of voices, as the door opened and two guards stepped in, General Cavaco between them.

Even in handcuffs, Eniko Cavaco's bearing was the same military straightness that she'd seen every day in the Council Chambers for the last ten years, and his face bore the same arrogant self-assurance it always had. But there was even more grey in his hair than she remembered, his face haggard and exhausted, and she felt a grim spark of satisfaction to see it.

His eyes roamed the crowd, and came to rest, at last, on her.

She narrowed her eyes, meeting his gaze.

"Councillors. Chief Justice Alba Espina has requested her time."

Alba drew in a deep breath and rose. "Councillors," she said, pitching her voice just loud enough to be heard clearly through the amplifiers. "I need not remind you of the crimes of this man. You lived through them yourself. But in order that we are all working with the same information, I would like to present a list of those killed under General Cavaco's watch." She turned and nodded to the Speaker, and the woman tapped her staff on the floor, lighting the holoscreens in front of each councillor's seat up with the briefing Feliu had prepared earlier that week.

For a few moments, she stood in silence, letting the councillors read through the list. She'd provided it earlier, but her words would have more weight to them, she knew, if each councillor was sitting in front of a list of the names of those in their ranks who'd been shot on Cavaco's orders, the numbers of dead soldiers and dead civilians, the cost of what he'd broken.

The seams in Joias society, papered over for so many years, had been torn wide open in the past few weeks, and Alba wasn't sure if something like that could ever be repaired.

"Councillors." It was odd how, even now, those few horrific weeks in the yibo Advisory Chambers were enough to want to put a tremor in her tone, that pleading helplessness that came when you were not in charge of your own fate, when someone else held the lives of you and everyone you cared for in their palms, and your only safety lay in convincing them not to close their fist and crush you.

Here, she wasn't helpless. Here, her voice held weight. And yet, it took an effort of will to make her words come out firm and strong.

"I propose that we prosecute the General, as well as any of the officers below him and any of the members of the Military Committee who agreed with, aided, or abetted him, to the full extent that the law allows for treason. I ask you this, councillors, because I know how often we have swept the crimes of the powerful and well-connected into the corners, rather than dealing with them in the open. I understand the impulse to forgive these crimes, because prosecuting them will expose things about ourselves and our own complicity in this that will not be comfortable. But I believe that this is the only way forward."

"Permission to speak," came another voice.

The Speaker glanced at Alba.

She drew a deep breath, then nodded, conceding her time.

"I would like to remind the Council," the woman stated, standing, "the context in which these crimes that our Chief Justice refers to were committed."

It was a member of the Military Committee.

Of course it was. The Military Committee knew well enough that there were far too many in their ranks who'd either actively assisted Cavaco, or at least turned a blind eye to things they were duty-bound to prevent.

But then, that described so many of the councillors that Alba wasn't certain she could count them all. Perhaps it described herself as well—she, too, had been so certain and comfortable in the Council's protocol and politeness that she hadn't seen the shark lurking beneath the still waters. Or if she had seen it, it had been a problem that was academic and distant, because the shark wouldn't, of course, come for her. They were all far too civilized for that.

"Our Chief Justice has suggested that the General be prosecuted to the full extent of the law for treason. But our Chief Justice was not present when the portal closed, leaving us with no information about what had happened on the other side. She was not present when we feared for our very lives, in desperate need of someone to confront the problem with a firm hand. Perhaps the methods used by Cavaco were not correct. I can agree that there should be censure for the occasions when he took things too far. But I believe that in this whole affair, the General acted out of concern for the citizens of this system. At all times, I believe, he wished to protect us from threats that, as we have seen, were very real indeed."

"Protect our citizens?" Alba snapped, her voice deadly quiet. She saw the Speaker's abortive move to stop her, ask her to please wait until she'd been recognized on the floor, but she was too angry to care. "Which citizens, exactly, do you believe he was protecting, when he sent his soldiers out to massacre Rim Mountain villages? Which citizens was he protecting when he instructed his soldiers to shoot down civilians in do Sol in order to get to the rebels? Which citizens, exactly, was he protecting when his armies raided Old Believer compounds on his orders? Tell me that. Or do you believe the only lives worth protecting are the ones in this room?"

There was silence when Alba finished. At last, an older man from the People's Committee stood—the interim leader of the Committee while they found a replacement for Ander. "Alba." His voice was heavy with condescension. "I understand that you are upset. Cavaco injured you, and I'm certain having suffered physical injuries makes one wish for revenge. However, it's the Joias System we must think of, not our own selves. Tearing open old wounds will hardly bring peace. What's done is done, and we must move past it."

There were murmurs of assent around the room.

Alba wanted to scream. She wanted to shake the man by his throat and ask him how in the hell he thought wounds could heal if this whole Council refused to acknowledge they existed, covered them over and let them fester and rot until they burst, and spilled their putrid hate and resentment over the entire Joias System.

But she could see by the expression on the Speaker's face that, although she may have let Alba get away with interrupting once, she would not do it again.

"Permission to speak," another member of the Military Committee piped up.

The Speaker nodded in his direction.

Alba closed her eyes, for a moment so weary that she simply wanted to sag into her seat, let this discussion take place without her.

She'd known that this would be the outcome. She'd known that no matter how loud she spoke, she'd never convince these people that peace could never come on their terms. That even if it could, peace at the cost of proving certain lives worthless, and certain lives worth so much that they'd never stand accountable for their crimes, was a peace not worth having. They had to present a united front to the yibos and the raiders, and she knew it.

But she couldn't let this go unopposed, even if the outcome was already determined.

She forced herself to stand straight, forced her tired brain back to the words the man was speaking.

From the corner of her mind, she caught a rustle, a small disturbance around the doors of the chambers.

And then the doors slammed open, and every councillor in the room turned as the guard at the door staggered inside, blood streaming from a vicious gash across the side of her neck. Her hands were pressed down on the injury, her face pale.

Someone stepped through the doors behind her, a figure Alba recognized instantly.

The pretty little Rim Mountain girl looked much the same as she had in the holodisc Alba had seen months earlier, when she'd issued the warrant. Her time in the hospital had taken away even more of her natural curves, and there were lines of weariness in her face that hadn't been there before. But she was smiling, showing all her teeth, in a charming, innocent expression that somehow conveyed an unspeakable menace, and there was a hard, cold fury in her face that Alba had never seen there before.

She was holding a pulse pistol in one hand, and something small in the other that Alba couldn't quite make out.

The ceremonial guards had spun at her entrance, raising their weapons, but she snapped, "Stop where you are, or I shoot Alba."

And it wasn't until then that Alba noticed that the pistol was pointed directly at her head.

She almost laughed.

Of course—with Cavaco in chains and the President dead, she was currently the only remaining duly appointed Head of Government. If Savina wanted to make a point, Alba was the one to threaten in order to do so.

"Thank you," said Savina, her smile widening. "I'm so glad you listened to me. I wouldn't have hesitated to shoot Alba—ask her, she knows it. But that wouldn't have been all. I planted explosives around the roof of this chamber, and I'm holding the controller down with my thumb right now. The moment I release the pressure, it comes down on all of us." She laughed, charming and bell-like. "Some of you might survive. But I don't think anyone here wants to take that risk, do you? After all, you're all very important people. Not like the people in the Rim Mountains, whose deaths you can all forgive so easily. Not people like my family, whose compound was burned and who were thrown into a mass grave by soldiers commanded by this very important man." She gestured with the hand holding the controller at Cavaco.

He'd turned to face her, and his eyes were hard. Savina met his gaze, and for a moment, Alba saw something in the girl's glance that terrified her.

It was the look of someone who'd lost everything, and has nothing at all left to lose.

Everyone in the room was frozen in horror.

Alba could feel the cold fear climbing her own spine. But then, she'd grown used to working through fear over the past few weeks.

"Savina," she said, clearing her throat.

Savina turned to look at her, and again, there was that flash of hopeless hate in her eyes. "Don't bother, Alba," she hissed. "I heard what you were discussing. You were all just going to let this monster walk free. Maybe give him a few years in prison, but a nice prison where he has all his needs met. The councillors who helped him weren't going to face any charges at all, were they? Maybe a note on their record, maybe, horror of horrors, a forced retirement to the countryside. Was that it?" She drew in a long breath.

"My family was killed," she said at last, fixing her gaze once more on Alba's face. "They were Old Believers, in a compound in the Rim Mountains. They weren't part of the rebellion, but they were Old Believers, and the soldiers were angry, and who was going to know? Who'd care enough to punish them, even if they did know? My family was executed, along with everyone else in the compound— adults, children, everyone. They were thrown into a mass grave, and the soldiers burned the compound to the ground. Did Cavaco mention that? No? But it wouldn't have mattered if he had, would it?"

"Savina." Alba tried to keep her voice steady and reasonable, despite the horror the girl's words started in her chest, despite the fear clutching her lungs and stopping her from drawing in a full breath. "I didn't know. And I am not sure I can honestly say it would have made a difference to the proceedings today. But it would have to me, and I am truly sorry."

"Sorry doesn't bring them back, though, does it?" There was a desperation under Savina's words, a stark pain that was almost too much to listen to. "Sorry doesn't unbury them from the mass grave. Sorry doesn't bring back the children who your friend here had shot, does it?"

"No," said Alba quietly. "It doesn't." There were quiet murmurs from the seats around her, but Alba ignored them, focusing her attention on Savina. "It doesn't bring them back. There's nothing I can do to bring them back, much as I might wish to. So what do you want, Savina? Why are you here?"

"What do I want?" the girl snarled. "I want every damn person in this room to know how it feels. That's what I want. I want to burn the Joias System to the ground. I want every one of your families to feel what I feel right now. What my siblings feel. What all those people in the Rim Mountains feel, who will wake up tomorrow, just like they did today, just like they will for the rest of their lives, and feel like there was a hole cut out of their chests, because that man standing there in the middle of your damn Council Chambers wanted a little more power. That's what I want." She was breathing heavily, and Alba could see the tears starting in her eyes.

She felt weak, and sick, and so, so tired, and somehow she

couldn't even bring herself to be angry at the girl. "I'm sorry," she said again. "I'm sorry, Savina."

Savina's smile widened, showing her teeth. "Not as sorry as you will be, I promise you. I spent the last however many damn weeks fighting and bleeding for you—for every last one of you, while you were cowering. I grew up hearing from my parents that you all were monsters. I grew up hearing that every one of you deserved to die. And I fought for you anyways. I thought I was fighting for justice. I thought I was fighting for the Joias System, and that once the military was out of power, everything would be alright. I thought my parents were wrong, I thought it was just people like Cavaco who needed to be stopped. But it isn't, is it? It's every damn one of you. It's the entire damn system. And now that you're not in danger anymore, you don't care. You thought I'd be your little rebel martyr when you needed one, and then go sit quietly in the corner while you justified Cavaco and his soldiers destroying everything I care about? Damn you all to the Void. You wanted a martyr? You have one. I will happily die to see you burn. If I have to contact the raiders and tell them to come and hunt their way through this system to bring you to justice, I'll do it."

There was a momentary silence in the chambers.

And then, from the audience chamber, there was a stirring as someone moved.

Savina spun on them, not taking her pistol off Alba, and then Alba saw her sag, just a little.

It was Joska.

The cargo ship captain pushed her seat back deliberately, and stepped over the barrier to cross the room to Savina.

"Stay back, Joska, or I swear to the Mystery I'll kill you," Savina hissed. She wasn't speaking loudly, but in the utter silence, her words were clearly audible. "I'll kill Alba, and then I'll kill you."

"Savina." Joska's voice was low. "If that would make it better for you, go ahead and kill me."

Savina was sobbing now, silent sobs that shook her whole body, but she was still holding the pistol steady.

Joska reached her, and put an arm around her shoulders, and for just a moment Savina sagged into it. And then she straightened with an effort. "Fine, Joska." Her voice was quiet, but it carried easily. "Go ahead, tell me what I'm doing isn't justified. Go ahead and tell me I need to put my gun down and let the political process work this out, let them pass laws that say that all the crimes that Cavaco and the rest of these bastards committed aren't actually crimes after all, because they're not crimes if you're rich and important enough. Tell me I need to stand by and watch while they punish the people you and I were fighting alongside to save this whole damn planet, because they weren't polite enough to the soldiers who were trying to kill them, they didn't lodge a respectful protest and then let themselves get shot. Tell me to watch as they keep on passing laws against speaking Mountain Dialect, or turn a blind eye to the kind of hate towards Old Believers that let a whole company of soldiers agree to execute children and throw them into a mass grave. Tell me that, Joska. Tell me that with a straight face, and I'll put down my gun right here and let them take me away."

There was a long moment of silence. And then, at last, Joska spoke, so quietly that Alba had to strain to hear. "No, Savina. I won't tell you any of those things. You deserved better than this. We all did."

Savina blinked at the captain in shock for a few moments. "You … you aren't going to say anything about me killing people?" she said at last.

Joska smiled, a small, weary smile. "You already know how I feel about that. I'll tell you that revenge isn't enough, it can't be enough, and it won't make this better. But you deserve justice. You deserve that the people here, and the soldiers, and every other person who was complicit, be held to account. And whatever you decide to do— if the guards want to stop you, they'll have to kill me first to get to you."

Alba wasn't sure she was any less shocked than Savina looked, honestly.

At long, long last, Savina nodded, not taking her eyes from Joska. "You were always a better person than I was," she said quietly. She closed her eyes for a moment, and in that moment Alba saw, for the first time, the bone-deep weariness in the girl's posture. "So tell me, Joska—what should I do? If you don't want me to kill them, what should I do?"

Joska shook her head. "I'm just a cargo-ship captain. I don't know."

For another long moment, there was silence. And then, at last, Savina turned back to Alba.

There were tear-streaks on her face, but her expression was set and determined, and it reminded Alba, suddenly, of how the girl had looked when she'd stood in the courtyard of the council building, ready to die for a revolution that would go on without her.

"There's nothing you or anyone else can do that will give back what you took away from me," she said, her voice cutting through the silence, cold and hard and dispassionate. "But Joska is right—I'm not you. I won't betray the trust of the people I care about just because it's easier than the alternative. This isn't just about Cavaco. It's not even just about you. It's this whole damn system. But you are the ones in power right now. So this is what you will give me: Cavaco will pay for what he did, and every damn one of you who helped him will pay too. Not a special court with special accommodations because they have money and power, the same punishment you'd give out if they were poor, or homeless, or spoke Mountain Dialect. And the rebel soldiers who fought to keep you safe—you won't punish them for that. You'll treat them the same as the enlisted soldiers. And you will damn well appoint rebel commanders to help oversee your committees, to make sure it happens. I'm tired of living in a system where someone can make laws that will never affect them, without the input of anyone who'd be affected. And I want your Mystery-dammed Orthodox religion out of my damn government. I don't want the Head of Government to be one of the two pillars of your damn church. I want ... I want justice." Her voice grew quiet as she finished, and Alba could hear the tears under it.

The councillors were looking at each other in panic, and none of them dared move.

"I believe," said Alba at last, "that your requests are reasonable. This is not the way I would hope politics would be conducted in the future, but—" she held up a hand to forestall Savina's protest, "I understand how you could have believed this was your only option to be heard." She paused a moment. "Perhaps," she added, almost to herself, "it was your only option."

She turned to the rest of the council, deliberately taking her gaze from Savina, even though the hair on the back of her neck rose at the threat. "Councillors. While Savina's method was far from conventional, I believe that she has made points that are difficult to refute, considering our history as a nation."

She noticed, from the corner of her eye, words flashing across the holoscreen. *We aren't able to get to the roof to disarm the explosives without alerting the assassin, and we don't dare do that, as she may release the controller. We tried to contact Aran Romeu, as his land-devil would likely be able to take the assassin down from a distance without her noticing, but he refused to answer his wavelink. His assistant, however, did answer, and used language which I will not repeat, but the essence is that I believe we are on our own.*

Alba had to bite back a grim smile.

In fairness, they deserved it.

"I propose, councillors, that we make the commitments that Savina has asked for. I propose we bring in rebel commanders and people from the Rim Mountains, and give them voices in any justice we deal out. Because these things are best dealt with in public, in the light. We've all seen the fallout from the Swan River massacre a decade ago. That was swept into the corner, because no one wanted to hold those in positions of power to account, myself among them, and it has continued to fester a decade later. Perhaps once, we could convince ourselves that this was the right course of action, that there are people who are so important that they must not be held to account because it would destabilize our system. But we can no longer afford to do that. I believe what will truly destabilize our system is our insistence on continuing a course of action that we already know will be ineffective, because we are too afraid to face our own sins."

There were a few moments of stunned silence.

And then, at last, scattered nods among the councillors.

They were afraid. Maybe they'd actually heard what the girl said, heard the pain and desperation behind her words and understood it, finally, or maybe they were only agreeing because Savina was holding a weapon that could kill them. But they were nodding, and for now, that was enough.

Another message flashed across the holoscreen. *We may have found a solution, Madam. There's someone who worked with Cavaco who is willing to try to take the assassin down before she's able to hurt anyone.*

From the corner of her eye, she caught the hint of movement from the opened door—someone moving so quietly that even Savina seemed not to have heard them. They were dressed in a soldier's uniform, but she couldn't make out their face under their helmet.

She felt herself freeze unconsciously—if Savina suspected, for even one moment, that someone was coming in behind her, there was no way she wouldn't simply kill Alba, if not take down the whole building. And she couldn't respond to the holo-message without betraying what she'd seen.

But somehow, the thought of what would happen when the soldier reached the girl made her sick to her stomach.

Cavaco had seen as well. Alba saw it in his face when he turned to look at Savina, saw it in the narrowing of his eyes and the small hint of satisfaction on his face. "And who are you to be asking for justice?" he said scornfully, the first time he'd spoken since he'd arrived. "You? A Rim Mountain assassin? An Old Believer cultist, who grew up in a compound? What do you know about our laws? Don't you think they condemn you?"

"Of course they condemn me." Savina's tone was just as thick with scorn as Cavaco's. "Your laws condemn me for murder. But you've killed thousands more than I have. Why would I respect laws that would punish me more harshly than you?"

"You see?" said Cavaco, turning a little so the other councillors could see his face.

Behind Savina, the figure had moved incrementally closer, until they were close enough, almost, to touch the Rim Mountain girl. Close enough, likely, to grab the controller from Savina's dead fingers after they shot her, and hold the button down to keep it from going off.

Alba had to bite back the irrational urge to shout a warning to the girl, even though it would certainly mean her own death.

"You see how this girl thinks? She believes there should be no order in our system. She believes that people like her should be able to run rough-shod over our laws and our traditions. She believes that she is above the law, and should dictate who the law applies to."

The figure behind Savina had pulled out their weapon, in a smooth, silent motion.

Cavaco turned back to Savina, a glint of triumph in his eyes.

The weapon fired.

Cavaco's body teetered for a moment, then fell forward. Half his head was gone, blood and brains sprayed across the decorative wood panel behind him.

Savina half-spun as the figure pulled off her helmet, shaking out shoulder-length black hair. Her face was bruised, as if she'd been badly beaten, and Alba could see the pain in the way she stood and moved. But her half-shave was clean and neat, her strong, sharp features as elegant and dangerous as ever.

Savina's mouth had gone into an "O" of surprise.

"No," said Reka Soler into the silence. "Savina doesn't want to destroy the order of the system. She just doesn't think it should be controlled by people like you."

"Reka?" Savina's words were hoarse with disbelief.

Reka smiled at her. "Savina." Her voice was low. "I'm so sorry."

"I …" Savina was still staring at the woman, and for the first time, her pistol wavered.

One of the other guards stepped forward, but stopped as Reka's pistol swung towards them. "Don't move," she said, her voice even and deadly.

Savina pulled in a long shaky breath.

"Savina. You go. I'll take the explosive, and I'll give you a twenty-minute start. That's probably all I can promise before someone gets around behind me, but I will give you that." She paused. "I'm sorry. They were looking for someone to kill you, and I thought it best to end that line of inquiry as soon as possible. And after everything I've heard here ..." she shrugged. "I thought it best not to trust the councillors to decide Cavaco's fate."

Savina looked up at her, and there was something in her gaze, something curious and a little soft. "You're always looking for a glorious way to die, Reka Soler."

"You're not dying for this, Savina. I won't let you. I've let you get hurt enough times in the past, and I won't do it again." Reka's voice was low, but there was a sharp intensity to it. "You told me I had to decide what was right, and where I stand. And ..." She gestured around her. "I've decided."

There was a long moment where no one moved.

At last, Joska sighed. "Savina," she said. "Give the pistol to me. I haven't killed anyone recently, so I'm not sure how they could arrest me for this." There was a tone in her voice that said she was perfectly aware how they could arrest her for this, but was determined not to show it. "I'll hold the controller, and you two can leave. And I'm not Reka, but I'll give you twenty minutes if I possibly can."

Savina and Reka exchanged glances.

Then Reka turned and caught Alba's eyes. Her gaze was sharp enough that Alba had to stop herself from taking a step back.

"Alba," the government agent said. "You've agreed to Savina's terms. You've agreed to reform the government, and bring the people who were in charge of this coup to justice. And the rest of you," she let her eyes slide over the Council Chambers, "you've agreed to this as well. I suggest you follow through on your promises. Because Savina isn't the only person who's angry about all this. And the people in the Rim Mountains have learned what it feels like to stand up for themselves against an army. And furthermore," she added, smiling just a little, the expression knife-sharp, "if after all you decide to take the cowards way out, and let your important friends buy their way out of justice, I promise you that there is no security you can hire that will ever let you feel completely safe. Because there is no security you can hire who will be better at their job than I am."

She turned back to Alba. "Joska will go free. She will not be implicated in any part of this, because all she has done is try to keep there from being bloodshed. And I believe, Madam Chief Justice, that if you look through your records, you will discover that the Joias System Government owes this woman a cargo ship, to replace the one she lost in your service."

Alba blinked at the government agent for a moment.

And then, despite the sharp bite of fear in her chest, she found she had to hold back the smile that wanted to form on her face.

"I believe I shall," she murmured.

Reka studied her for a long moment. "Good," she said at last. "I hope, Madam Chief Justice, that I am correct in my trust in you."

She turned to Savina and whispered something, and Savina nodded.

There was a brief moment where Savina transferred the controller to the cargo ship captain, and the councillors held their collective breath. And then it was done, and Joska stood in the middle of the chambers—worn, tired, with lines of exhaustion and sorrow on her face and a twinge of wry humour at the corners of her mouth—an entirely unexpected political terrorist. Savina turned and flashed that innocent smile at the Council that set an instinctive terror in Alba's chest. "If you touch so much as a hair on Joska's head, I will rain down horror on you like you have never seen, I promise you," she said, in that breathy, innocent voice.

Then Reka turned to her, slipping an arm around her shoulder in a gesture that was unmistakably tender, and the two women stepped back through the doors.

Immediately, the guards started for the floor where Joska stood, weapons at the ready, but Alba raised a hand. "Enough," she snapped. "We gave our word, and I suggest we abide by it." She paused. "And when the twenty minutes are up—I believe we will have some proposals to discuss."

35

Savina

"I'm going to miss you, Vina." Nicolau's words were muffled, and he kept wiping his sleeve over his eyes. Ines stood close to him, her arm wrapped tightly around his waist, and even though her head barely came up to his chin, he seemed to be pulling strength from her.

Savina sighed internally, then stepped up to him and pulled him into a hug. He clung to her, and his sniffles turned into sobs, his face buried in her shoulder, and she could feel his shoulders shaking.

"I love you, baby brother," she whispered, when at last he let her go. She found she had to turn to wipe her own eyes as well.

They were gathered in front of the small cottage where Nicolau's adoptive parents lived: Savina and Reka, Joska, Rafel, Nicolau, Ines, and Beni.

"I'm going to miss you too," said Beni quietly, when Nicolau stepped back, still wiping his eyes.

Savina tried to smile at her sibling, despite the sharp ache in her chest. "Yeah," she whispered. "But … I'm glad you found a place for yourself. You'll be a better cargo ship's crew than I ever would have.

You never really liked killing people, did you?"

Beni managed a small smile. "I've already got Rafel hooked on my audio romances."

Rafel scowled, and Savina managed a small, choked laugh.

"Well, I guess things won't be the same without you," Rafel grumbled. "Probably a lot less dangerous, and a lot calmer, but …"

She sighed and shook her head. "Don't try to fool me, Rafel. You always hated me, and the feeling's mutual."

He gave a small snort, but she saw the gleam of tears in his eyes.

Joska stepped forwards at last, and put a hand on Savina's shoulder. There was no hiding the tears that glittered in the captain's eyes, but she smiled, that small, wry smile that had somehow become the most comforting thing in the world.

"How's your new ship treating you?" Savina asked. "I know it's not the *Dolphin*, but …"

Joska smiled again. "I've named her the *Zephyr.* I think she'll be a good little ship. Your Chief Justice pulled some strings, I think—she's permit-ed in every port in the system, I checked, and all the permits are pre-paid for life. So who knows? I may actually build up a little capital in time to retire one day." She paused. "Unless I run into another ship hijacker, of course. You never know what life will throw at you."

Savina closed her eyes, fighting back the thick lump of emotion trying to choke off her breath. Then she stepped forward and put her arms awkwardly around the woman.

For a moment, Joska stiffened in surprise. Then she pulled Savina into an embrace, and there was something about the steady warmth of her that felt like a soothing balm on the sharp, aching thing in Savina's chest. "Look at you, Savina," she whispered. "I'm so proud of you. I'm proud to call myself your friend."

And for a while, Savina cried silently into Joska's shoulder, and Joska rubbed her back and let her cry.

When she finally stepped back, Joska gave her a small smile. "So. You and Reka are leaving." She shook her head, her smile fading. "I'm sorry you couldn't come back home."

Savina managed a smile of her own. "It's alright. I don't … I don't know that I ever really had a home. Besides, you know me—I wouldn't have lasted a month without finding some law to break, or slitting someone's throat. It's better this way. I think after my last little stunt, even Alba wouldn't be able to pardon me."

Joska shook her head, but her expression was fond. "I'm still sorry. You deserved better than this." She paused. "All the rebel commanders asked me to pass on their regards. You're a folk hero, you know. They're already writing songs about you. If you ever wanted to come back, there'd be no shortage of people willing to offer you shelter."

Savina looked around at the small gathering of people, standing in the warm dark of the autumn evening.

The only reason she could even stand here, she knew well enough, was that Alba had managed to tie up the warrant on her head in bureaucratic red tape—a final farewell, perhaps, or a final thank you. Savina wasn't sure which, and she wasn't sure she wanted to know. But it wouldn't last forever. Even Alba could only delay the searching hand of justice for so long.

But … She glanced behind her to where Reka stood, strong and stoic and patient.

Reka could probably delay that searching hand forever, if she put her mind to it. She'd always been one of the most talented of the government agents, and Savina could understand why.

Reka caught Savina looking and smiled. There was something

warm and soft in her expression that Savina had only ever seen directed at her, and she found herself smiling back. And despite the sharp, empty ache in her chest—despite the pain and the horror and the fear, despite the pictures that would probably always haunt her nightmares—a soft, sweet happiness washed over her, for just a moment.

She was, for the first time in her life, surrounded by people who loved her. Not people who needed her, or were depending on her, or saw her as a figurehead or a mascot—people who loved her.

She hadn't actually known how that would feel.

"It's alright, Joska," she said again, turning back. "Reka's found us a ship, and I doubt anyone Alba sends after us will be able to find us if Reka doesn't want us to be found. We're going to be alright."

Joska nodded, and for a moment, no one spoke.

Edite poked her head out of the cottage door and called, "Savina! I know you're leaving, but if you're ever back on Colorida, there will always be stew on the stove and fresh sheets on the spare bed."

Savina smiled at her, and didn't bother to remind her that she was a wanted criminal.

The woman knew that. And she'd made the offer anyways.

"Don't you dare forget to call, Vina," Nicolau said, stepping forward for one more hug. "Ines and I are thinking about heading back to the Rim Mountains, maybe starting a farm close to her family. But our wavelinks will still work."

Savina smiled and nodded, and finally, finally, she turned back to Reka.

"Are you ready?" Reka whispered. Like always, when her eyes caught Savina's, they stripped away everything she'd been trying to hide.

But she wasn't trying to hide anything, not anymore. Not here.

Not now.

She didn't need to.

She nodded, and Reka bent and kissed her hair. "Let's go then, my love."

And Savina kissed her back before they turned and started down the darkening cobblestone streets towards the spaceport.

Alba

The orange light of the setting sun glowed off the clean whitewashed walls of the Old Quarter of do Sol. Alba sat back in her chair and watched it, letting her tight muscles relax. The light breeze brought the rich scent of the autumn flowers drifting across the wall, and she breathed in deeply, a quiet happiness settling over her.

"It's beautiful, isn't it?"

She glanced over to where Yosip sat, across the small stone table from her. His chair was pushed back as well, his expression distant as he looked out over the streets.

"I didn't expect to be back here, to be honest," he continued, finally.

Alba cleared her throat. "Nor did I."

They were quiet for a few minutes, watching the sun rays floating between the tall, old-stone buildings turn from orange to pink to red. The garden lights in the courtyard flickered on behind them, the soft chirp of insects starting in the tall bushes.

"So. How did things go in the Council today?" Yosip turned to her, and there was something about the familiar, friendly twinkle in his eye that made Alba return his smile.

"Well, we were informed this morning that at least two infant land-devils have started colonizing one of the smaller moons in the yibo system, which has made both the yibo and the raiders highly motivated to come to an agreement that will be acceptable to all parties. So that has been helpful, at the least. Feliu insisted on staying late to finish up the latest draft of the agreements. He is entirely in his element—I think neither the yibo nor the raiders had any idea of the depth of background research our diplomats would be armed with, thanks to him."

Yosip smiled, and she smiled back, then sighed. "As far as matters in our own system—it's been more difficult than I had hoped, but I think we will, ultimately, be able to figure out a way to accomplish the majority of the promises we made to Savina. There was a not insubstantial portion of the Council that wanted to ignore them, saying that the promises were made under duress, but ..." she shrugged. "I simply refused to back down. And the advantage to being the only remaining properly selected Head of Government is that my word here carries much more weight than it did back in the yibo Advisory Chambers."

Yosip chuckled, a soft, warm sound. "I'm glad you were able to bring them around."

Alba sighed, turning her gaze back to the darkening streets. "In honesty, her points were all good ones. I wish I could say that if she'd brought things through the proper channels, she'd have been heard, but I think you and I both know that's not the case. The Council was all but ready to let Cavaco go off to a quiet retirement, and no matter how hard I worked to convince them otherwise, there would have been no appetite for a substantial punishment for any of the war crimes committed in the Rim Mountains. It would have been the Swan River massacre all over again, but a hundred times the scale. And she was probably right about the treatment the rebel commanders would have received, too." She shook her head. "I honestly believed, for most of my life, that our system was just. That anyone who wanted a voice could have one, if they were patient and behaved themselves properly."

For a few moments, Yosip didn't speak. At last he turned to her, his usual friendly sincerity written across his features. "Not everyone is willing to hear that lesson when they're given it, Alba. I'm glad you did." He paused. "You know, I was told by more than one person, when Feliu approached me to be your diplomatic aide, that you were harsh, inflexible, arrogant, and far too convinced of your own importance to listen to counsel."

Alba stared at him for a moment, then she huffed out a small, surprised laugh. "Well, I suppose you were not misinformed."

He leaned forward over the table, laying his hand over hers. She could feel the warmth of it, the calluses and wrinkles more suited to a Rim Mountain farmer than a diplomatic aide. "No, Alba. They weren't correct at all, it turns out. And I'm glad of it." He smiled, that habitual twinkle sparkling in his eyes, and she found she was smiling back.

"I'm being sincere," he said quietly. "It was an honour working with you."

"And with you." She found there was something caught in her throat as she said the words, and her eyes were blurring a little with tears.

He leaned back in his seat again, and so did she.

"And what will you do now?" she asked. "I believe you have the standing now to ask whatever you wish of the government, based on everything you've done over the past few months."

Yosip was still staring out at the streets, the distant look back in his eyes. "I don't know, to be perfectly honest with you." He smiled, just a little. "Perhaps I'll go back to the Rim Mountains for a little. It's lovely there in the autumn, I seem to recall."

"And after that?"

He turned to her again, still with that small half-smile that was just a little sad. "After that? I'm not sure."

Alba cleared her throat. "If you wanted to spend more time here in do Sol—I know you have more than enough friends wherever you go. But … I should be glad to see more of you."

He glanced at her, raising his eyebrows. "As an aide, you mean?"

She smiled. "No. As a friend."

His smile in return was warm and genuine. "As a friend? I think I would like that very much."

Aran

"Hey! Wake up, sleepyhead. Were you planning on staying in bed all morning?"

Aran blinked and rolled over, then closed his eyes and smiled at the rich, comforting aroma of freshly brewed coffee. "Pishti?" he mumbled.

The blanket was pulled back, letting in, for just a moment, a shock of cold air from outside, and then the much more welcome sensation of Istvay settling in beside him. "Mmmm," they whispered. "It's warm in here. No wonder you're not up yet." They leaned in to kiss him, and he kissed them back, and for a moment, there was nothing in the world except Istvay, right here, next to him.

"Yes," he mumbled between kisses. "I think I might just stay in bed all morning, now that you mention it." He flipped Istvay onto the thin mattress, pinning them, although it wasn't nearly as easy as it had been weeks before. They laughed, reaching up to tangle their hands in his hair, and for a moment he was so overwhelmed by happiness that there wasn't room for it in his body.

And then Istvay yelped and swore, wriggling out of the blanket. "Dammit," they muttered, fishing in their pocket and pulling out a very offended-looking land-devil hatchling. "What the hell is wrong with you, you little demon-spawn?"

The hatchling blinked up at them with its wide, innocent eyes, and despite the interruption, Aran couldn't hold back a grin. "I think he likes you, Pishti."

"He's stung me enough damn times," Istvay muttered.

The tiny thing had wrapped its tentacles around Istvay's hand and was resisting any attempts to dislodge it, although, Aran noticed, Istvay didn't really seem to be trying very hard.

"Alright," they said at last, scooping it up deftly and cupping it against their chest. "Will you leave me alone for five minutes if I let you sit on my supplies pouch?"

The tiny creature's body perked up, its colour going a delicate, curious blue.

"Well, I guess I'm up for the day whether I want to be or not," Istvay grumbled. "Coffee?"

Aran smiled as he rolled out from under the blankets and pulled them haphazardly back up. Ani dropped down from the roof of the tent, landing on his shoulders, and cast a suspicious glance in Istvay's direction. The clear contentment of her hatchling seemed to reassure her, though, because she settled onto her usual perch with a soft, questioning chirrup, pushing her bulbous head under his chin for attention.

Aran chuckled as Istvay shoved a mug of fresh coffee into his hands. "Let me wake up a minute, Ani, and then I'll go get you a snack."

She grumbled, but settled in to wait.

When he ducked out of the tent after Istvay, they already had a fire going and the two camp chairs pulled up beside it, the smell of woodsmoke in the fresh chill of the late autumn morning a perfect accompaniment to the strong, earthy taste of the coffee. Aran ignored the chair Istvay had pulled up for him and nudged their chair back, sliding in behind them and resting his chin on their shoulder. He slid his free hand around their waist. "So, Pishti," he whispered in their ear. "It looks like you've been adopted. That little one hasn't left you alone for weeks. Have you named him yet?"

"I thought I was supposed to be the one doing the adopting," Istvay grumbled, clearly trying to sound irritated, and failing badly.

Aran kissed the hollow behind their ear, and smiled as they shivered and relaxed against him.

They gave a heavy sigh. "And yes, I've named him. I thought since we already had one named Total Annihilation, I'd go with Complete Destruction."

Aran blinked for a moment, then his smile widened, a soft, warm smile that felt at home on his face these days. "You named him after Dessi!"

"I named him after Dessi," they said, tone rueful.

Aran laughed and reached down to where the small creature was perched. It hissed at him and backed away, then, as he held his hand still, it crept closer and wrapped a tentative tentacle around his finger. "She'll be so happy, next time she comes out."

"*If* she comes out, with how busy she is studying that 'fascinating allistic neurotype' in humans." Istvay gave a rueful laugh. "I'm still not sure exactly what you told her, but now every damn raider in this system or the yibo one thinks allistic people are charming, if a little strange, and very rare, and is completely convinced that loud noises or touching people without their consent might actually kill them."

Aran shook his head. "I ... I didn't—I just answered her questions, and I think she sort of ... extrapolated from there."

Istvay sighed again, and pushed away a little so they could turn and look at him. "Speaking of that—did you get the message about them wanting us to come back to do Sol for the events when the raider delegation arrives back to continue the talks? And I'm pretty sure they were planning on awarding you another Medal for Scientific Advancement for the cure for the defect."

Aran nodded.

"And?" Istvay's tone was grim, and a little sympathetic.

Aran drew in a breath. "I, um ... I told them I'd be happy to record a speech for them to play if they wanted, and Krevai and Dessi know where we are if there's anything they want to talk to me specifically about. They didn't exactly like it, but I didn't exactly give them a choice. And I think everyone's afraid of offending me right now, so ..." He shrugged. "I may as well get them used to it, I guess." He paused. "And as far as the medal, I told them they could go choke themselves on it. It was at least as much your discovery as it was mine, so it would be in your name or no one's at all, and furthermore, the last damn medal they gave me had better be revised to have your name on it too, or I'd be giving it back. So I'm pretty sure you're going to be hearing from them soon."

Istvay pulled back a little more, staring at him. Then they chuckled, shaking their head, and the look in their eyes was so fond and so soft that Aran almost had to blink back tears.

"I'm not sure if I've told you this lately," they said, "but I love you, you know."

Aran grinned and looped his arms around their waist, pulling them in closer. "Do you?" he whispered, nuzzling his face into the corner of their neck.

Istvay rolled their eyes, and then shivered again as Aran kissed down their neck. "Dammit, you're going to make me spill my coffee," they grumbled, but he could tell they were smiling.

Aran bent and placed his own cup of half-finished coffee on a patch of mostly flat earth, then took the cup from Istvay's hand and placed it beside his own. "Dessi?" he whispered, holding out his hand to the tiny creature. When it climbed onto his fingers, he placed it down on the ground as well, far enough from the hot coffee that it shouldn't be in any danger. Then he lifted Ani from his shoulder and placed her gently beside her offspring. "Watch your baby for a minute, sweetheart," he whispered. "Pishti and I are going to be busy."

When he straightened, Istvay had half-stood. They turned so they were straddling his lap, facing him, their brown eyes sparkling with mischief, and Aran's breath caught at the sight. He blinked up at them, momentarily unable to formulate a thought.

They chuckled softly. "I thought we were going to be busy," they said, sliding their fingers into his hair and leaning in for a kiss. Aran kissed them back, tightening his arms around their waist. And he hadn't realized happiness could be like this, filling you up and spilling over and covering everything until the entire world and everything in it was beautiful.

36

Epilogue

"Don't move, or I'll blow your damn brains out."

Joska froze, her hands stilling on the *Zephyr's* controls at the voice from behind her.

She heard the door to the ship's small, tidy cockpit slide open, the harsh click of mag boots on the floor, and from the corner of her eye, she could see figures pushing inside.

"I'm sorry, Captain, I—" Rafel grunted, as if he'd been shoved.

"Shut up!" the newcomer snapped.

Joska held herself back from spinning around, and drew in a long breath. "We're not going to try anything." She kept her tone calm, her posture still frozen. "I don't want anyone to get hurt."

"Good. You're smarter than you look. Take your hands off the controls and turn around slowly."

Joska did as she was instructed.

The four figures who'd crowded into her cockpit, armed to the teeth, were clearly pirates. Rafel was standing to one side of them, swearing softly, his arms raised.

She closed her eyes for a moment and breathed a quick sigh of relief. At least they didn't seem to have found Beni.

"What do you want?" She managed to keep her tone steady, still, despite her pounding heart.

The man who appeared to be the leader sneered. "We heard that you were carrying cargo that was worth a hell of a lot of money. We thought we'd come see for ourselves, maybe take some of it off your hands."

"I don't know where you heard that. I'm just a cargo ship captain, and I'm doing a routine run. You can look through my cargo manifesto if—"

The man stepped closer to her, shoving his face into hers. "Shut up," he hissed. "You think I'm stupid? We know exactly what you're carrying, because we ran into a little friend of yours recently, and she was more than happy to tell us everything we wanted to know." He glanced over his shoulder and gave a jerk of his head. A moment later, two other pirates shoved their prisoner into the crowded cockpit—a pretty young woman, with an open, innocent face, brown skin, and auburn hair. Her eyes were wide and terrified, and she was whimpering a little.

Joska felt her shoulders relax. "Savina," she said, her tone wry. "I'm glad to see you here safe. And where's Reka?"

"I'm so sorry, Captain!" Her voice was a pitiful little whisper. "They have her, too. I didn't mean to tell them, honest, I just—"

"Shut your mouth," one of the pirates snarled, bringing his gun around and shoving it under the girl's throat.

"Don't kill them," snapped Joska, taking an unconscious half-step forward.

The pirate looked up at her with a cruel grin. "You don't want me to kill them? Well, that will depend on—"

"I wasn't talking to you," said Joska through her teeth, keeping her eyes fixed on Savina.

The pirate looked between Joska and Savina, a hint of confusion beginning on his face.

From the corner of her eye, Joska saw a figure detach itself from the shadows, moving as silent as a ghost.

"Savina—" she said, keeping her voice as stern as possible.

Savina gave her a small wink.

From the back of the cockpit, a pirate screamed.

At least, Joska thought wryly, Reka cleaned up her messes. If she remembered correctly, Savina had never been too concerned about scrubbing blood off of things, but the government agent was fastidious. When she was done, and the unconscious bodies of the pirates dragged back onto their ship, you could hardly have told there'd been a disturbance at all.

Savina was watching, with her wide, innocent eyes and a helpless air that Reka seemed both to expect, and not to mind, and Joska smiled a little.

Perhaps those two were a better fit than she'd ever imagined. Savina, at least, seemed happy. And although Joska still wasn't an expert at interpreting Reka's expressions, there was a softness about her that hadn't been there before, and something tender in the glances she kept throwing Savina's way.

"Well, Savina," Joska said at last, standing and coming over to the girl. "It's good to see you again. Although we could have just arranged to go for coffee on a spaceport somewhere."

Savina blinked up at her. "I don't know why we keep getting caught by pirates, but I'm so glad that they always bring us here before we manage to get away."

Joska found the corner of her mouth was twitching in amusement. "Hmmm," she said. "Is that what's happened?" She paused. "Honestly, Savina, when I said I thought I'd be able to make enough for retirement, I meant hauling cargo."

Savina's eyes widened even further. "I know! It's not my fault that you keep getting all those silly little rewards for the pirates' capture. But I guess since they just keep coming to attack you, and since you're the one who brings them in, the port authorities can't really do anything else, can they?"

This time, Joska did chuckle, shaking her head fondly. "Well, Savina. This is the third pirate ship this month. I hope you're able to find a place where no pirates will hunt you down and take you captive for a little while—that must be exhausting work."

"Oh, I hope so too!" Savina's voice was breathy, and much too sincere. Then, at last, the wide-eyed innocence of her expression dropped, and she smiled up at Joska, a genuine smile this time. "Rafel?" she said, turning to him. "How's the captain doing financially? Honestly? I know what a bleeding heart she is—probably gives half the money she makes away to people who don't deserve it."

Rafel glanced at Joska with affection, then snorted and turned back to Savina. "With how busy you've kept her 'capturing pirates,' she hasn't had a damn chance to." His tone was irritated, but Joska could hear the hint of fondness under it.

Shaking her head, she reached out a hand and helped the young former assassin to her feet. "How are you and Reka?" she asked quietly. "Are you alright? Any problems with the warrant the government issued?"

"No problems with that." Reka had come to stand behind Savina. Her hand rested lightly on the small of Savina's back, and her voice held its usual laconic amusement. "At least, none that Savina and I can't deal with." She gave a small huff of laughter. "I don't think Alba is sending her best, to be honest."

Joska found herself smiling a little as well. "Don't ever tell her you figured that out." She paused. "Savina? Did you get a chance to talk to Beni? I know they miss you."

Savina's smile widened, unconscious and genuine in a way she'd never smiled when Joska had first met her. "Beni was helping us reel the pirates in. We had a nice long time to catch up."

Joska chuckled again, ruefully. "So now I'm dealing with insubordination in my crew, too." She shook her head, and squeezed Savina's shoulder. "Take care of yourself. And I wasn't joking about the coffee. I'm making a drop on Rochesa in two days' time." She cast Savina a wry glance. "Assuming no more pirate incidents. Meet me there? I'd like to catch up."

Savina glanced at Reka, and an unspoken communication passed between them.

Then she turned back to Joska. "Alright," she said, her tone a little more muted. "Alright, we'll meet you there. I've … missed you."

"And I've missed you, too, believe it or not," said Joska, squeezing the girl's shoulder again affectionately.

"We need to get going if we're going to haul that pirate ship back," Reka said in a low voice. "Beni tagged it with the *Zephyr's* codes?"

Savina nodded.

Reka leaned down and kissed her hair. "Then let's go, my love," she whispered.

And then the two of them were gone, leaving Joska and Rafel looking after them.

And Joska found she was smiling, watching them.

Thank you for reading!
I hope you enjoyed the series, and thank you for coming on this journey with me. I couldn't have done it without readers like you!

You might also enjoy The Ungovernable series, also by R.M. Olson.

A mouthy ex-smuggler pilot, a grumpy demolitions expert, a tech genius and a hacker. They're pulling a job on the most dangerous weapons dealer in the System. They're stealing tech that could change the course of history. And every one of them has something to hide.
What could possibly go wrong?
"Spectacular and thrilling! Olson's debut novel is filled with compelling characters and endless excitement." -SD Simper, author of the Fallen Gods series

You can order book one, Zero Day Threat, on Amazon.

www.ingramcontent.com/pod-product-compliance
Lightning Source LLC
Chambersburg PA
CBHW031831310726
48972CB00005B/1244